Muddy Waters

And The Man in the Chimney

by B.J. Vaughn

WHITMORE PUBLISHING CO.
PITTSBURGH, PENNSYLVANIA 15222

ISBN: 978-0-87426-079-3
eISBN: 978-0-87426-250-6

Printed in the United States of America

First Printing

For more information or to order additional books, please contact:
Whitmore Publishing Co.
701 Smithfield Street
Pittsburgh, Pennsylvania 15222
U.S.A.
1-866-451-1966
www.whitmorebooks.com

Foreword

This book is the result of a persistent dream of my youth, when night after night I found myself on the field of battle looking for a Civil War soldier. I would find him huddled on a deserted battlefield in a hole by a chimney. When I completed my first book, I sat thinking of what to write next and this novel came to me. From the first page to the last, the story emerged so easily that I could not but wonder. The Sequel, *Blue Waters*, picks up the story with Penny's wedding and continuing through the equally difficult period of Reconstruction. Maybe in some ways the time following the war was even more difficult, as a defeated people faced an implacable North determined to punish its sister States. Hardships of every kind faced southerners, both black and white. A new South emerged where Penny and Ryan, along with their friends and neighbors, would work to make it one that would offer peace and prosperity to their children.

Many of the characters peripheral to the story are actual citizens of Kinston, Lenoir County, and New Berne during this period; however, the main characters, Penny, Ryan, Rye-Rye, John and Sarah Bartlett, Brett Bartlett, Fitz and Cora Kennedy, Martha and Isabel Madison, Daniel Kennedy, Marcus, Moses, Mammy, Lucinda, Jeremiah, Caroline Framingham, Lizzy, and Hattie, are all fictitious and do not resemble and are not based on any actual denizens of the area.

Except for those cited above, all other Union and Confederate soldiers mentioned in the text actually served in the conflict. The people of Woodington, Deep Run, Kinston, and New Bern (spelled "Berne" at the time) not listed above lived during this period in the locations described. Today many of their descendants live on land that has been in their families for hundreds of years. Fountain and Alcy Blizzard and Nalphus and Sarah Johnson were my great-

great-grandparents. Perry, Josea, Joseph, and Blaney Blizzard all served in the Civil War. Perry is buried in a mass grave at Fort Harrison, Virginia, killed during the Battle of Cold Harbor. Josea lies in Hollywood Cemetery in Richmond, Virginia.

I owe a great debt of gratitude to my grandfather, Lonnie Denny Blizzard, who took me to the attic in his house. (As a child I was too afraid to go alone, convinced that the darkened places beyond the framed-in walls held ghosts.) He patiently showed me the trunks filled with treasures from the past, explained them to me, and taught me an appreciation for history and my own heritage. When I began the book, I went online to research the Battle of Southwest Creek. One cannot imagine my amazement when my uncle's name, Dr. Lonnie H. Blizzard, popped up as the author of a definitive article on the First Battle of Kinston. I had not realized his expertise on this particular battle. In fact, he was instrumental in the creation of a collection of artifacts at Lenoir County Community College, where he served as president for many years, and the Kinston Visitors Center, which houses numerous artifacts of the family that he loaned for display. He loaned me two non-published booklets compiled by a leading family of Woodington and Lenoir County, the Rouses, in which the names of related families and interesting anecdotes have been preserved.

My gratitude is immense for the encouragement, advice, and suggestions offered me by my best patron and critic, Helen Johnson Brumbaugh, of both my visual and literary art. It's good to know she is in my corner to give me praise or a swift kick when called for. My husband, Giorgos A. Sgouros, showed me patience and tolerance as he suffered lonely hours while I worked. I thank my daughter, Joanna Elizabeth Meredith, for her unstinting love and support. Also vital to this effort was Elliott Fisher, my friend and computer guru, and Robert Lewis Waldrum, who helped me with formatting the book. A very special thank you goes to Alice Osborn, gifted poet and teacher of creative writing, who edited this novel for me. Her energy level puts the Ever-Ready battery to shame.

Joanne Gwaltney Ashton, friend and former president of the New Bern Historical Society, loaned me numerous materials and directed me to the New Bern Library, where staff member Victor Jones provided valuable insight and resources. My thanks also go to Dr. Brantley Briley, President, and George "Bud" Vick, Jr., Vice President of Administration Services, Lenoir Community College, Kinston, NC, for the tour and courtesy they extended in my early research.

Chapter 1

The cannon barrage had gone from earth-shaking, heart-pounding repercussions to a soft rolling in the distance. The thunder-making armies of the rebelling South and the opposing North were like two beasts stalking, mauling, and clawing one another and then skulking off to lick their wounds until they could attack again. The battered homes and lives of the local people were but peripheral damage, just a byproduct of the conflict.

Penelope Bartlett Kennedy's limbs were stiff from crouching in the depression of a reeking crater dug into the edge of the thick piney woods that grew along the bank of the creek and she shook. Whether it was bitter chill of the December night, the residue of terror, the knowledge that the stench in the icy earth beneath her bespoke of death, or fear of discovery by the scavengers, she couldn't have said. Her horse had broken free of the branch where she had looped her reins and ambled over to nuzzle her shoulder as if urging her to leave, but she knew she should stay where she was until the scavengers, just so many human buzzards, had finished picking over the dead and left the field of carnage. Even so, Penny, as she had been called since the baby fuzz of her infancy had been replaced by coppery golden auburn hair, didn't know if she could abide one more moment of that hell. But she could not leave. Somehow she had to find him.

Had it not been for that need, she would be safely nestled by the fireside in her home that lay alongside Southwest Creek drinking a cup of sassafras tea. Her favorite English tea was now but a memory of a world before the ravages of war and deprivations brought about by the blockade of North Carolina's coastal ports. With so few to work their fertile dark loam, there were scant crops to sprout, grow, and ripen under a benign sun, and of course, no market access had there been. It had been a long time since she had money for

1

luxuries. And it had been a long time since her husband, Daniel, had warmed their big plantation bed under the split-shingle roof.

It had been three years since she had been the belle of the winter ball of 1859, where he asked for her hand in marriage, a formality as both the Bartlett and Kennedy families had long expected this merger of land and fortunes. Grandchildren had been expected, too, but to date she'd had no luck in fulfilling that and with her husband missing, chances were slim that it would happen anytime soon. Even if he had been at home, she thought wryly, the likelihood of that occurring now was about as likely as gold pieces falling from the sky. She couldn't forgive him and with a daily reminder of her anger, she couldn't forget.

She must have slept because the sun was just beginning to peep over the horizon of the brown-stubbled and frost-rimed field. The field, now covered with bodies among the withered stalks of corn, was ringed on two sides by woods with the creek forming a third margin. All lay quiet except for the chirping birds that wintered in the branches above her head. Again the horse nudged her and whickered softly in her ear. "Time to go," the horse seemed to be saying. Slowly she stood.

As the blood flowed back into her stiff extremities, the prickles began. Creeping warily from hiding, Penny surveyed the land in front of her. It was littered with the dead and the detritus of war but none of the scavengers, who had fanned out on either side of the moving army, lurked on the site of the battle for Kinston. The Union forces were even now making their way to Goldsborough, intent on destroying the railroad bridge over the Neuse River, a vital supply line to the Confederate army in Virginia. The armies had moved on to new arenas of conflict, leaving her alone in the morning cold. She was hungry and tired, but the vision still beckoned. She was compelled to oblige it.

It wasn't the first time that Penny had experienced that strange sensation of a living dream unwinding before her eyes. She had not been sleeping, for the battle raging the previous day just over the forest behind her house had left her unnerved and jittery from the adrenalin of fear. And then some power beyond her control had urged her to leave her fireside and come to this battle site. In the dream she had seen him, wounded and huddled by the chimney of a burned-out house. And he was calling her to come. She couldn't see his face, didn't know if he were family, friend, or some stranger. She only knew she had to rise from the enveloping warmth of the feather mattress she had warmed with coals from the fireplace and go forth into the night to find him.

She had come to this field behind the Wallers' home, now but a burned-out shell barely discernable through the privet hedge and pecan trees that encircled it like a moat. The chimneystack still loomed, soot streaked but intact, just as she had seen it in her dream vision. Was the man who had called to her waiting for her there? Leading the horse, Penny made her way across the rough ridges of old plow rows. She paused by the outhouse, effectively re-moved from the line of vision of the house by the hedge and untouched by the fire. She listened but heard nothing except the low moaning of a rising wind.

"Stay here, Polly. Be a good old horse and don't make a bunch of noise. You hear now?" Fondly she patted the graying muzzle. Poor old Polly, the only horse she had left.

Nervously, Penny extracted the Butterfield revolver she had loaded and tucked into the pocket of her coat before leaving her house. It was her father's and he had taught her to use it when Daniel had joined General James Mar-tin's troops, now stationed in Virginia. She was alone on the big plantation except for those few Negro servants who had remained. More like family than servants, she was mostly grateful for their company, but at times the extra mouths to feed and bodies to comfort and protect were almost more burden than blessing. Yet she could not turn them out. Although she had freed them when given the plantation by her father, she felt a responsibility for them all. Across the South, others like them had remained: the old, the children, and the timid, who feared the unknown perils of chasing after the Union army and freedom, or the ire of those who owned them. Penny's fa-ther had reared her to be strong and she had never flinched in the face of duty before. She could not now when she might well have wanted to, a lone woman, barely out of her teens, with all of the men in both Daniel's and her families now gone, either dead or fighting, and her mother frail and fright-ened of this new and chaotic world. Griping the revolver's hilt, she made her way through the opening in the privet and cautiously crept toward the cin-dered ruins.

The crunching of the scattered and charred timbers beneath the soles of her sturdy shoes sounded as loud as the Chinese fireworks display her father and mother had taken her to Wilmington to see the year of her sixteenth birthday. She paused among the ruins and listened. There, just above the rustling of the wind in the bare branches that previously provided shade for this once grand home, she heard it—a soft moan, not wind but human, someone in pain. And it came from the sheltering column of the ruined chimney. Penny cautiously ad-vanced toward the source of the sound. Rounding the back of the chimney to the hearthside, she tugged a piece of fallen roofing tin to one side. Under it she could see two boot-encased legs and blue pants with a stripe along the outside.

An enemy soldier lay huddled there partially within the shelter of the fire-place, not conscious but not unconscious either. He called out when he heard her approach. So this was the man who had summoned her in the night, a man who was not only a stranger, but a threat to all she had held dear and loved. She wanted to turn on her heel and leave him to die in a land that did not want him, but she could not. Crouching, she grasped him by the shoulder and pulled him over. His head was bloodied from a forceful blow, a bullet had pierced his right shoulder, but otherwise he seemed uninjured.

"Can you move? I need to get you out of the cold and attend to you or you'll die." *Do I really care?* she asked herself. She looked at him, seeking dispassion and some permission to leave him there. It didn't come.

"Help me," he croaked through lips parched with thirst. "Please, help me."

Penny shook him to alertness and watched as he tried to rise but fell back from the throbbing pain that shot through his temples. "You have to help me. I cannot lift you. I'll get my horse and come back for you, but you'll need to get into the saddle. I'll help you, but you must help, too."

"Go for the horse. I'll try," he managed to say before slumping back against the still-warm bricks, exhausted from the effort it had taken to arouse himself.

Urging old Polly forward, Penny guided her to the fallen man. "Give me your left arm. I'm going to help you to stand and then I'll try to get you into the saddle. Use your good arm to pull yourself up and I'll push. Can you do that?"

Again he responded, "I'll try."

After several attempts that resulted in the Union soldier only sinking back to his knees beside the horse, Penny managed to hoist him into the saddle.

"You're going to have to hang on. It's a pretty long ride and we've got to go through some swampy land and thick woods to get there." The woods and swamps had kept her safe from the Yankees, but it wouldn't be easy trying to get back through them. Clucking to the horse without waiting for a response, she led him into the sheltering woods and onward to her home.

It was a long and difficult process to get through the thick undergrowth, avoid the swampy areas, and keep the man in the saddle, where he sat slumped over, barely conscious. Repeatedly she stopped to clear brush from their path. Fearing detection from either friend or foe, she took the deepest and most difficult path through the woods. She knew that it would prolong the journey but she had no other choice. Occasionally she heard him moan in pain, but he did not fall from the horse. It was late morning before she walked past the corncrib and into her own backyard.

"Moses, please get out here and help me. I've rescued myself a damned Yankee man." She snorted to herself, *And just what am I supposed to do now?*

"Yas'um, Miz Penny," Moses said as he pulled the man from the saddle and into his arms. "Where'd ya want me to put 'im?"

"Put him in the back bedroom upstairs and get a fire going in the fireplace. Also, have Mammy Rena fetch me some hot water and clean lint. She'll need to tear an old sheet into bandages and I'll need a sharp knife, a needle, and some thread. Hurry."

Penny went to the pantry and found whiskey and the healing herbs that her Grandmother Lou had grown in her garden or had taught her to find in the woods around their home: balm for fever and Betany tea, which she kept brewed for her mother's megrims. Lou Bartlett had shown the young Penny how to gather, dry, and prepare them, and how to use them to treat the myriad of maladies that afflicted both owners and slaves alike. Granny Lou had been the local granny woman, called for in times of sickness and need. At her death the previous spring, Penny had taken her place in the community attending childbirth, sickness, and wounds for her neighbors, since any doctor was some six miles away in Kinston and generally came only for the most seriously ill or injured. Leaving the pantry, she paused to grab a candle and a striking flint so she could sterilize the knife she would use to probe the wound for a bullet. If there was one in his shoulder, she knew it would have to come out or the man would die of infection.

Climbing the polished oak stairs that curved gracefully to the second-floor landing, Penny turned left and walked to the end of the Palladian-windowed corridor and entered the last bedroom. Moses had place the wounded man on the bed and removed his boots, shirt, and jacket. Now he leaned over the lit fat lightwood kindling on the hearth, where he was busily adding logs. Soon the uncomfortable chill would be gone from the room. It helped that the morning sun was pouring radiant warmth through the window beside the bed and illuminating her patient.

She paused to study him. He was taller than she had realized, slim but broad of shoulders. His dark hair was matted in dried blood at his right temple and his cheeks were covered with the stubble of a two-day-old beard. Feeling her eyes on him, he opened his own. She gazed into blue the color of the summer sky. His finely molded mouth was tight with suppressed pain. Although the worse for wear, he was a remarkably handsome man in the prime of his years, somewhere between his late twenties and early thirties. Judging by the quality of his uniform, he was a man of means and an officer.

"I'm going to give you a bit of whiskey to dull the pain. I've got to get the bullet out of your shoulder and clean your wound because you're already fevered. I don't think you've suffered anything serious, but with that head injury you're not going to be up and about for several days. When I get you on your feet, you must leave here. Do you understand what I'm saying?"

"Yes, I do. And thanks for helping me. I fear I was quite overlooked by my departing comrades." He managed a sardonic smile. A puzzled look crossed his face. "How did you know to find me?"

"You told me," she remarked cryptically.

He looked at her quizzically but was prevented from questioning her by the creak of the opening door.

Mammy Rena, Moses's wife, lumbered into the room with the items Penny had requested and walked up to the bedside. "What you done found yo'sef, chile? This sho look like a Yankee man to me."

"He is, Mammy. We're going to heal him and get him gone before some more Yankees come looking for him."

"That we is, we sho is!"

"Hold him up so I can get some liquor in him and then I'm going after that bullet."

"You got a name, Yankee boy?" Mama inquired as she pulled him up.

"Ryan, Ryan Madison," he sputtered as Penny poured a healthy dose of whiskey between his cracked lips.

"Soon as I get the bullet out, I'll give you some water. I know you're thirsty. Then you'll need to rest so you can heal. I'll clean your head, too, but there isn't much I can do for that except to give you an herbal tea to help with the headache. Now be still while I get that bullet." Turning, she continued. "Moses, Mammy. Ya'll hold him for me, please."

"It's not necessary. I won't move," Ryan announced with grim determination.

Her reply was a skeptical. "As you wish."

Penny bent to her task and except for a suppressed groan of pain when she poured whiskey into the raw wound and probed for the bullet, Ryan lay rigidly still. As she probed, she could see the dark shine of metal gleaming wetly in the blood-welling depths. Fortunately the bullet had not splintered the bone nor pierced any major vessels.

"Ah, I've got it," Penny exclaimed triumphantly. "Now we'll get it cleaned, stitched, and bandaged up. The stitching will hurt, too. Are you okay, Mr. Madison?"

Through gritted teeth, he managed to say, "I'm fine, thanks."

Noting the sweat beading his forehead, she laughed. "I'm sure you've been finer than you are now."

"That I'll not dispute." He smiled weakly and closed his eyes.

Penny finished cleaning the wound, stitched and packed it with boiled lint, and then wrapped clean linen strips around his shoulder to hold the lint in place. She knew the lint would absorb any bleeding and protect the tender wound. Next she gently sponged Ryan's head wound, relieved to see that except for a large lump that indicated a probable concussion, it didn't seem too serious.

Tucking the Jacob's Ladder-patterned quilt snuggly around him, Penny turned and said, "Mammy, give him water a little at the time, and sit with him for a while, please. I'm going to wash up and try to get a couple of hours of sleep. If you need me, call."

"Yas'um, Miz Penny. You do that, chile. He gonna be fine now." Mammy sat in the chair beside the bed that Penny had vacated and began her vigil.

The sun was sinking in the western sky, casting the trees beyond her window into dark shapes against the reddening glow. Penny sat up, momentarily dazed. Then remembering why she had been sleeping away the afternoon, she climbed from her bed and turned down the corridor to her patient's room. She found Ryan peacefully slumbering and Mammy gone, probably to the kitchen to prepare the evening meal. Noting his trousers on the peg by the door and a basin of soapy water, she knew Mammy had cleaned him up. Mammy hated a dirty body on her clean sheets. She felt his forehead but found only a slight elevation of temperature, reassuring her that the bullet had been removed in time. His eyes blinked open.

"I thought I'd dreamed you, Miss...ah, Miss?"

"I'm Penelope Kennedy, Penny to my family and friends. You may call me Mrs. Kennedy." She didn't smile when she said it. "How did you manage to get yourself curled up in the chimney of the Wallers' burned-out house?"

"I was knocked from my horse by a bullet as we were leaving the battle-field and struck my head on a stone or something when I fell. Then when I came to, it was cold and except for the dead, I found myself quite alone. I vaguely remember crawling to the chimney and finding it warm, deciding to rest there until I could go on. I think I must have fallen asleep. Then near morning, I came to again in great pain. That's when you found me."

"Drink some more of this tea. It'll help with your headache. Judging by the lump on your head, it must be a mean one."

"It reassures me I'm alive. At one point, I didn't expect to be."

"If you had not found that chimney and the sheet of tin to give you some protection from the cold, you might not be."

"I suspect I owe at least equal thanks to you for finding me and bringing me here." Pausing, he added, "I realize that my current allegiances don't make me a particularly welcome guest." He smiled apologetically, hoping to illicit something beyond a remote frown from the beautiful woman standing by his bed.

"Well, that can't be helped at the moment, now can it? I don't have an extra horse for you, but I'm sure you'll be on your feet in a day or so and you can walk to wherever it is that you were supposed to go." She didn't add "and good riddance," but she thought it. "I'll send Mammy up with some supper for you. It won't be much." She reminded herself, Thanks to your Yankee block-aders, no such luxuries as sugar, coffee, and tea can reach us, and if they do, the prices are prohibitive. "If my house were on the road, I'd have been robbed blind like my neighbors. At least we still have something."

"My apologies, Mrs. Kennedy. Unfortunately that is a byproduct of this war that your hot-headed cousins in South Carolina brought upon you."

"They may have begun it, but we're in it, too, and proudly." She wheeled on her heel and stalked from the room. Here was her enemy resting on a feath-ered bed in a warm room, when she could only hope that her own men were huddled around campfires on some battlefield. Better that than dead, wounded, or a prisoner, she thought.

Her father, John Bartlett, had left her mother, Sarah, alone on their neigh-boring plantation, Pineview, and joined the Confederate forces camped out at the Becton farm near Wyse Forks. That had been three days ago, and she had heard nothing since. Early in the war, her brother, Brett, and Daniel had joined the army stationed in New Berne under General Branch. She had heard noth-ing from Brett for weeks. Her husband's last letter had come from Richmond three months past, telling her that he was in the hospital from a Minié ball that had pierced his thigh. Her father-in-law, the parsimonious and feisty Fitz Kennedy, had ridden off with her father. Mr. Kennedy, well into his fifties and suffering from lumbago, had gladly left his empty house, Belle Terre, in the care of his overseer, Oscar, and a neighbor. His wife, Cora, had died the previous spring from the same influenza that killed her Granny, and he found the loneliness oppressive. Penny suspected if he survived the Yankee bullets, it would be an adventure he would enjoy and if they killed him, he might well consider it a fair bargain. Unless her father arrived home shortly, she would have to collect her mother and bring her home, where she could at least keep her fed and tended. How she would have loved to be eighteen again with no husband, no worries, and no war, the doted-on daughter of an indulgent father.

With the bang of the door behind her retreating back, Ryan ruefully admitted to himself that he could not fault her for her hostility. He knew people in the countryside had suffered deprivations brought on by the circumstances of war and, of course, exacerbated by the killings and confiscations of the enemy army and its attendant scavengers. Not only the Yankees, but the Confederates as well, used scavengers to "requisition" supplies from local farms.

But he wanted this woman to like him. Something about her golden eyes and lithe form awakened a hunger in him that he'd never before known. It made no sense to him in his current condition and the barrier of opposite politics between them that he should feel this deep soul-level connection. He had to leave and she would be just someone in his memory who'd helped him survive to lead another group of men into battle to kill her friends, neighbors, and family. Her cold, self-contained anger made their friendship more than unlikely. And yet she had come for him and saved him. What had brought this woman from her home in the middle of the night to find him? She had not told him, but he would ask again.

In the kitchen Penny sat alone at the table, picking absentmindedly at the supper of cornbread, roasted pork, cabbage slaw, and the peas that Mammy Rena had dried during late summer. She wasn't hungry, though she should have been, as she had eaten nothing all day. Her mind was simply too preoccupied with all of the problems that she must deal with in the coming days to be concerned with food. Mammy came into the kitchen and looked at the barely touched meal on her plate. Penny knew she would begin scolding and not wanting to deal with the coming diatribe on her eating habits; she turned to the older woman.

"Mammy Rena, your dinner is really good and I'm sorry I can't eat more of it. I'm just too tired and worried to eat. If you'll save it for me, I'll try again later. Right now, I'm afraid we're going to have to see if we can make some broth for Mr. Madison. I think supper is too heavy for him until we see how he does. Do we have any meat that we can use?"

"I thought of dat, Miz Penny. I got me a chicken I just plucked. I gwine stick it in de pot and make some broth right now. You just sit der and drink some of dat chicory coffee while I work."

"Thank you. I think I will."

Penny watched her making the broth and again thanked her lucky stars that Mammy and Moses had stayed with her. Their daughter, Lucinda, and her infant, Jeremiah, who was much too light to have been fathered by one of the field hands, had stayed as well when the others ran off. Even though she resented Lucinda for suspicions she could not prove concerning Jeremiah's paternity, she had never voiced them.

Lucinda worked in the house normally but because both she and the five-month-old baby were unwell, Penny had told her not to worry about her chores. She knew sixty-year-old Mammy was weary from trying to do both cooking and cleaning for them all, as well as relieve Lucinda when the crying baby became too much. Moses stayed busy tending the livestock that they kept hidden in the woods, where poachers and scavengers were less likely to find them. He hauled firewood and did the heavy work that the women couldn't manage. Penny regretted that running back and forth to her mother, checking on her father-in-law's house, and attending the sick children of the Smiths down the road had left her little time to ease their burdens. Mammy had been like another mother to her and it saddened her to see the woman growing older and prone to suffering from the complaints of age. The added work only exacerbated her aches and pains.

"Does Lucinda need any more of the Yarrow tea for her cold?"

"Naw. Thank you, ma'am. She doing better dis evenin'. Je'miah, too. Don' you be a worr'in' none. You sho got a nuff on yo' plate wid out worr'in' about dem."

Penny noticed that Mammy always looked uncomfortable when she mentioned Lucinda and the baby, confirming what she feared but hesitated to name. Penny reminded her, "You know those of us here come first, but I am glad to know they're doing better."

Mammy knew that it was true. They did come first to Penny and that knowledge hurt her all the more, as she knew the pain Penny felt as a result of the actions of her daughter and Penny's husband. Mama was torn between her love for this woman who had been so good to her and love and pity for the daughter that so chaffed at her station in life.

They continued to chat companionably while the stock simmered. When it was done, Penny dished up a bowl of the chicken stock, arranged some fresh bread on a plate, and poured a pitcher of cold spring water. She added a heavy crystal goblet of herbal tea to the silver tray her grandmother had given her at her marriage.

Slowly she climbed the stairs to where the sick man lay, noting as she did that the stairs had little rolls of dust curled against the risers. Mentally she made note of another item to add to the list of things that needed doing. Get them done she would. She vowed this war would not turn her into a slattern, would not remove the graciousness from her life, and would not reduce her to a whining shadow of her former self.

Pausing to catch her reflection in the mirror above the George III chest at the top of the steps, she could not help but chuckle. With her hair straggling from its chignon, a faded dress, and eyes circled with fatigue, she might be falling a mite short of the mark she had set. Squaring her shoulders, she pushed the bedroom door open with her hip. In the dim of the darkened room she could barely discern Ryan's face against the snowy pillows she had arranged behind his head. Placing the tray on the table by the bed, she lit the candle she had left there earlier and poked up the glowing embers in the fireplace, adding more wood as she did so.

"Excuse me, Mr. Madison. Are you awake?"

"Hmm. I think so." Slowly and carefully he sat up against the pillows, wincing at the continued throb in his temple and the tenderness of his arm when he tried to use it.

"I have a light dinner for you. If you have no nausea, tomorrow I'll see if you can manage something more substantial. The main thing now is to get liquids into you." She carefully adjusted the bandage on his shoulder; it seemed to have ceased bleeding. "I'll bring you a nightshirt when I finish feeding you your dinner. It'll be cold in here tonight. The temperature is really falling outside. It's a good thing that you're inside, as even that chimney wouldn't be enough to keep you from freezing."

"I think I can manage to feed myself, Mrs. Kennedy, although the prospect of your ministrations is most pleasant." He grinned up at her, pleased when he caught her almost smiling back before she caught herself.

"Nonsense. Your right arm is in a sling and Mammy Rena would kill me if I let you get soup all over her clean sheets. Tomorrow if you're better, I'll let you sit at the table by the window there."

"Then perhaps we can strike a bargain. If you'll permit me to call you Penny and I'm Ryan, then my total cooperation will be all you could wish for." He found himself holding his breath as he awaited her answer.

Penny bit her lower lip and considered him beneath her lashes. He was undoubtedly one of the most attractive and appealing men she had ever met. If he wanted to call her by her given name, where was the harm? "Ryan it is then."

She marveled that she was so calmly ministering to an enemy in her own home. She had known for over a year now that Kinston, while not an important military objective in and of itself, sat astride the route from New Berne, which the Union had held since March of 1862. Fortunate for the South, the important Wilmington and Weldon Railroad Bridge in Goldsborough, twenty-five miles further west, were still in Confederate hands. But she wondered for how long if General Foster had his way. The battle that had ranged over the swamps and fields around Kinston had been but an impediment to their implacable advance. Would Goldsborough prove any more successful in stopping them? She knew the bridge was a crucial link in the supply line running to the Confederate army that she heard was even now facing a major battle at Fredericksburg, Virginia. Her father had told her about the ironclad battleship under construction at White Hall, a spa town on the Neuse near Goldsborough that had been known since Indian times for its seven mineral springs thought to have salutatory value. Surely General Foster would aim for that as well.

Chapter 2

Penny pulled back the heavy velvet drapes drawn over her bedroom window to keep the night's chill out and peered at the new day. Thick frost blanketed the hedges and trees. Like most yards in rural eastern North Carolina, there was no lawn, just smoothly swept sandy ground. She saw a squirrel scamper across the expanse to find refuge in a stately pecan tree. Even though the house, Pleasant Glade, was only three years old, having been built as a wedding gift from her father, the tall trees that surrounded it gave an air of long-time permanency. She loved the simple elegance of her home: the formal Georgian lines, the Palladian windows at both ends of the second-story hall. Four bedroom doors opened off the hall. Hers was the room on the right front and like the one on the opposite side of the hall, it was airy and spacious. The other two bedrooms, while ample and well furnished, were not so grand in scale. That thought brought her back to the moment.

She finished opening the drapes to allow sun into the room. The fire had been newly invigorated by Mammy making the room, while not warm, at least not bone-shaking cold. Crossing to the armoire, she opened the door to find a dress for the day. Suddenly she wanted to be pretty. The drab dresses she had worn like uniforms the last couple of months had no appeal. Pushing past them, she reached for an apple-green dress of a heavy enough velvet to be warm, but trimmed with black edging and heavy lace around the square neckline and around the hem, which gave it a stylish air. No, that is ridiculous, she thought. That was just too darned fancy. Rummaging again she found the perfect one. The dress of pale blue wool as soft as down had red bands around the sleeves and skirt, snowy white collar and under sleeves, and red buttons down the bodice. She donned her petticoats but decided to forego hoops and the confining stays of a corset in the interest of practicality, as was her custom when at home; the dress was enough without overdoing it. After all, she asked herself, whom are you trying to impress? The face that popped in her head like a jack jumping from his box was Ryan, the Union soldier resting in the bedroom down the hall. Momentarily she was annoyed with herself, then she shrugged in denial. She was only twenty-two years old, married to a man who mostly treated her like an adored sister and ignored her, and she was tired of looking frumpy.

Smoothing the dress, she turned to the mirror where she arranged her hair in the simple chignon she preferred, added a comb to keep it neatly in place, and surveyed the results. It was a definite improvement, she thought, and something she needed for herself alone. She knew she was pretty and that she possessed a figure better than most. She'd never been conceited about herself and just accepted the reality of who and what she was with honest modesty. Lifting her chin, she marched to the door, throwing it open, and started down the hall to her patient's room.

He was still sleeping, and just as in her room, heavy damask drapes had been drawn across the windows to keep out drafts. Mammy had kept the fire going in his room during the night, making it comfortably warm without being hot. Penny crossed to the windows to open the drapes and, as she had done at her own window, looked out into the morning.

Ryan lifted his head when the light poured into the room and the first thing he saw was her form silhouetted in the window. Taking the chance to study her without her knowledge, he noted the change of attire and the alluring woman who stood there. "Good morning, Penny. You look really nice today."

"Oh, you're awake." She crossed over to him and leaning down, pressing her cool hand against his brow. "Good, the fever is going down. You still have a huge lump on your head, though. I'll get you some more of the herbal tea and a warm compress for your head. That should help some now that it's turning into a bruise." Noting the admiring light in his eyes, she allowed herself a small smile of satisfaction; it was good to know she was still attractive. "Do you feel like sitting up and having some breakfast?"

"I would love some breakfast. I must be getting better because I'm hungry as a bear. Those aromas coming from the kitchen smell mighty appealing. Bacon?"

"Bacon, biscuits, huckleberry jam, fresh butter, scrambled eggs, and grits, unless I miss my guess. Mammy Rena loves to cook for company."

"If she feeds me like that every meal, I'm going to desert the army and stay here."

He laughed. "Now tell me, please, what exactly are grits?"

"It's kernels of corn that have been ground. It's boiled until it's tender and then seasoned with gravy, butter, or whatever. You can add cheese, too. By itself it's pretty bland but with bacon, ham or sausage, and lots of pepper, I confess, I love it. I guess you could call it southern comfort food."

"I'm hungry enough to try anything."

"I'll bring you some hot tea, too. I'd rather wait on her strong chicory coffee until your headache is better. Unfortunately with the blockade, coffee and tea have to be made from whatever we have growing locally. We're lucky the farm is not on the beaten path or I wouldn't have bacon and butter. One of the armies would have taken it all." She paused. "Before I bring your breakfast, I need to check your shoulder to make sure the stitches are okay and the bleeding is stopped. I'll try not to hurt you but it will be tender."

"Not to worry. It won't be nearly as painful as the process of acquiring this." He snorted and pointed at his shoulder.

Penny opened the top of his nightshirt and pulled it over but still couldn't manage to open it enough to get to his shoulder. "I'm going to take off this sling and your nightshirt. Could you help me by pulling the end of it up?"

Ryan struggled to comply and, using his one arm, managed to lift the hem of it from the bedding while keeping himself modestly covered. He winced when his weight shifted to his injured side. The movement had renewed the throb in his head but not as much as the previous day.

"That's good. Now let's get this over your head so I can get the bandages off and see what's happening under there."

She laid the nightshirt on the bed and again noted the deep broad chest. Ryan obviously had taken care of himself. He was all toned muscle and no fat. The black fur of his chest was just enough to look invitingly soft. Stop it, she told herself. This man is the enemy and in a day or two he will be gone from your life forever. Handsome or ugly are neither of any importance. That scolding did not stop her from feeling a frisson of desire when she touched him that left her momentarily dizzy. She had never felt anything akin to it when her husband had held her; she did not know that such intensity of feeling could exist. The disconcerting series of emotions left her clumsy and furious. He bit his lip with pain when she moved his shoulder abruptly.

Penny bit her lip with distress. "I'm sorry. I'll be more careful."

Penny collected herself and, with a deep breath, continued to unwind the bandage. Underneath, the lint was only a little bloodied. Pulling it aside and gently blotting the wound with a clean cloth dipped in whiskey, she noted that the stitches were holding the flesh well together and there appeared to be little redness or swelling.

"This is doing fine. As soon as we get that headache under control, you can be on your way." Pleased with her work, she smiled. "Now we'll pull the nightshirt back on before you become chilled, and I'll get your breakfast."

She hastened from the room but not without a backward glance. Ryan had known enough women to see the momentary flash of desire in her eyes before she had quickly suppressed it. He smiled to himself, happy that this beautiful and competent woman was attracted to him. He anticipated her return with his breakfast and another chance to engage her in conversation. It was not to be. When the door opened, it was Mammy Rena bringing his breakfast.

"Mawnin', Mistah Ryan. How you feelin' dis mawnin'?"

"I'm fine except for being neigh unto starving to death. I surely hope you plan to save my life with some breakfast."

"Dat I do. I got you plenty of breakfas' here, and iffn it ain't a nuff, I kin git some mo'." Mammy Ryan helped him up against the headboard and placed the bed tray across his legs. "Miz Penny tol' me to he'p you iffn you cain do it fo' yo'sef."

"I believe I can manage. I thought Mrs. Kennedy was going to bring my breakfast, but since she didn't, I could surely use some company. Why don't you have a seat in that chair? No doubt with all of this cooking and your other chores, you could use a rest."

"I sho kin. Dis rheumytism git me when it be col' like dis." Mammy settled herself, grateful for the opportunity to visit.

Ryan wasted no time in getting to work on the breakfast. The bacon, eggs, and biscuit were the first order of business. Warily he eyed the grits, stirred them with his fork, and cautiously took a bite. A thoughtful look crossed his face and he tried another. "You know, I think I could get to like this and I know I could get really accustomed to your cooking. These biscuits are the lightest I ever ate."

Beaming with pleasure, Mammy leaned over. "Do you got a nuff a dat jam? I be happy to git some mo'."

"This is fine, just fine. Now tell me why I have the pleasure of your company and not Mrs. Kennedy's."

"She sho is one purdy woman, ain't she?" Mammy, suspecting his disappointment, grinned at Ryan before continuing. "An a good'un. She works mighty hard takin' care of de sick folk, seein' to dis here farm, and her fambly's, too. Now don' you be gittin no idees now. She been marritt fo three year to Mistah Kennedy. In fack, she and Moses done gwine to her daddy place to check on things, fo' gwine to her husband daddy place to check on it, too. Den she gwine to de Smiff's place cause dey young'uns got de croup. Miz Penny make a dee-coction to fix 'em up. She be a fine woman make no mistake, Mistah Ryan."

"I'm sure she is. I mean no disrespect by my curiosity. I still don't understand why she was out in the cold of the night and happened to stumble across me. But I'm most grateful she did."

"Miz Penny jus know things. I hear say she got de sight. I don know 'bout dat. But dere's folks 'round here think she a conjer woman and dey say be kerful not mess wid 'er 'cause she got de magic. Sometimes she kured peoples dat wus so sick de doctah gabe up. I do know she a good woman, but she got huhsef some sadnesses lack we all do." Mammy clamped her mouth shut, worried that she had revealed too much to this perceptive man.

Ryan could tell by the stiffening of her posture that she had retreated from any further inquiries. Changing the subject, he complimented the breakfast and thanked her for making it for him.

"Happy you like it. Now let me git dese things to de kitchen and I git yo' clo'es and wash dem fo' you so you can leave here clean and go back to yo' soljerin'. You bes' be careful when you do, too, 'cause folk 'round here ain' real happy about y'all traipsin round messin' wid things and shootin' up on folk."

"Why, Mammy, aren't you glad that you're going to be free? You can leave and make a whole new life for yourself."

"Humph. I been free eber since I been give to Miz Penny. She tol' me she don' want no slaves on dis here plantation. It sho did make Mistah Dan'el mad but she stood her groun' stubborn as any ole mule, she sho nuff did. Dis farm from her daddy and mama. She tol' him she wouldn't hab it lessen we all free. She make him pay us a little money fo' de work. Dis my home and my man, Moses. My daughter and gran'chile here, too. I ain' gwine nowhere long as Miz Penny need me. I dun took ker a dat chile her whole life. Ain't gwine nowhere."

"It's a happy person who knows where he belongs and wants to be there." Ryan smiled engagingly at the proud loyal woman.

"Dat's de truf." Standing she took the tray and his clothes and left the room.

Ryan found the chamber pot and relieved himself. Once back on the soft downy mattress, he closed his eyes and waited for the pounding that began whenever he moved about to cease. By the bed was another glass of the tea Penny had given him for headaches. He drank it before sliding under the covers. Staring at the ceiling, he pondered what the black woman had told him before once again drifting into sleep.

When he awakened, the afternoon sun was casting long shadows across the floor. The house was quiet, but in the distance he could hear someone chopping wood. The regular thump of the axe created a steady rhythmic sound. Probably Moses, he thought. An uncomfortable fullness in his bladder compelled him to use the chamber pot. He was relieved to see that someone had emptied it while he slept. The room was getting chilly he realized when he had finished. Walking to the fireplace, he stirred the coals awkwardly before using his one good arm to add more logs to the fire. The effort exhausted him and set up a new pounding in his head. He had just tucked the bedcovers back around him, when the door swung open.

"I see you've renewed the fire. I'm sorry you had to do it yourself, as I suspect the activity just aggravates your headache. I brought you some more of the herbal tea. In a few minutes you won't feel nearly as much pain." Penny crossed to the bed with the outstretched glass. Her fingers touched his ever so lightly when he took the glass. She jerked back as though she had been burned. Looking up she caught his eyes locked on hers.

16

"You are truly a magnificent woman." Ryan continued looking into her eyes for several moments before she looked away.

"Thank you. I, ah, I…." Penny paused, flustered and unsure what to say. She repeated, "Thank you. You're too kind." Taking the empty glass from him and ruing the curiosity she felt, she said, "It can be difficult, but if you would like me to try to get a telegraph to your wife telling her you're injured, I could try."

"My wife?" His mouth twitched with humor. "I regret that to date no one has done me *that* honor. I have only a mother and sister at home to mourn my maladies and hopefully be grateful that I am still among the living. I will write them as soon as I'm up and about. Please don't concern yourself, as I know how difficult the telegraph service is at the moment."

"Oh." She was secretly relieved that there was no wife to claim this man's affection even while acknowledging that she was not free to do so either. "I must confess to curiosity about your home and how you came to be here."

"I'm from Baltimore. It's a city of divided sympathies and I fear my mother and sister were most annoyed with me for taking this course of action. I had not seen them for many months and didn't have the nerve to face them when I enlisted, so I sent a letter. The responses were somewhat less than complimentary in reference to my basic intelligence. When I write that I've been injured they are going to feel quite justified in their assessment, I assure you." He smiled. "You see, since graduation from Harvard, I have lived the last few years in New York, where I accepted a partnership in a law office founded by my uncle. In a moment of decreased sanity, I felt moved to enlist. So you have here a former attorney who is now practicing the more difficult art of war. Specifically I am a colonel in the Union forces with a troop of New York cavalry under my command. I've been stationed at our garrison in New Berne since we took the town. I'm supposed to be out there protecting homes such as yours as the army advances. General John Foster feels that we do not need to make things more difficult for the inhabitants of the area than need be. Not all Union generals feel the same and Foster's own troops, despite orders to the contrary, can be difficult to monitor."

"In a day or two, when your head stops aching every time you move, it should be safe to resume your duties for this saintly general. I'm sure we're all grateful to have a bunch of Yankees taking care of us. Of course, if y'all just went home, we wouldn't have to worry, would we?" But she said it with laughter in her eyes, taking the sting from the sarcastic remark.

He chortled at her spunk.

She moved to the fireplace and poked at the logs, sending a shower of sparks dancing up the chimney. She knew she should leave and help Mammy with the evening chores, but she wanted to be near this man, to feel the magnetism that drew her even when she was away.

All morning, as she had visited her mother and checked on the running of the Bartlett and Kennedy farms in their owners' absence, she had found her thoughts turning to him, picturing him and wanting to be with him. At the same time, she had been fearful and reluctant to return, unsure of her growing emotions. Maybe if Daniel and she had been in *love* rather than *like* when they married, she wouldn't feel this emptiness inside that yearned for a man to find her special. They had grown up like brother and sister, playmates, tormentors, and promised mates almost from birth, but no spark of attraction had ever ignited a passion in their relationship. Perhaps that lack is what had led Daniel to find release in another woman's arms, a darkly forbidden and therefore more exciting passion than the bedding of his wife. She didn't know. She only knew she ached to be the one who caused a man's eyes to light with yearning, passion, and possession. Was the attraction merely because Ryan was openly admiring of her, and he was so very comely to the eye and in proximity, when all of the other men were away getting themselves killed and maimed in a senseless war, or was it something unique to him? She was playing with fire, a fire she could not afford and dared not ignite. Heaving a sigh, she turned to leave. "I'll bring your dinner."

"If it's as good as breakfast, I'm most ready." Again he smiled warmly, locking her eyes with his. He could sense that she was attracted to him and he wanted her to know that he felt that same stirring when he looked at her. He refused to think about the fact that he was a soldier of an army that had invaded her homeland, that he was of necessity leaving as soon as he was able, and that she was a married woman. He only knew that he wanted her and he was accustomed to getting almost any woman he truly wanted. But then seduction for momentary pleasure was one thing. He asked himself if that was his only reason for wanting this woman. Did he want more? Did he dare to want more, or would that lead only to difficulties for them both? He closed his eyes and lay back against the pillow. Dealing with these gnarly questions only increased the pounding in his head.

Penny carried Ryan's dinner, and rather than eating alone at the kitchen table or the even more forbidding one in the dining room, she had added her own dinner as well, along with a bottle of French white wine that she had taken from her husband's extensive wine cellar. Although she had not grown up drinking wine, under Daniel's tutelage she had become an appreciative lover of good wine with her dinner. Why not enjoy someone's company, she thought, after months of dining alone?

Although dinner was a simple one of chicken salad made from the chicken Mammy had killed to make broth, fresh yeast rolls, skillet sautéed sweet potato slices, and a pie made of apples she had dried, she felt like a glass of good wine to go with it. She would not have opened a bottle for just herself.

She carried the heavy tray to the table by the window and pulled up two chairs. "I'll give you a blanket to wrap around you, and you can move over to the table for your dinner."

She handed him the blanket from the back of one of the chairs that she pulled up to the gate-leg table and turned modestly away while he wrapped it around his lower body. After drawing the ball-fringed drapes to keep the chill out, she busied herself arranging dinner on the table.

Ryan wrapped the blanket about himself. Pulling on the slippers resting by the bed that he suspected belonged to her husband, he noted the fit. Ryan was delighted when he saw that she had brought two plates of food and two wine glasses. His progress must have been greater than he imagined. He relished the prospect of further seduction over wine and dinner. His arm hurt and his head pounded but he hungered to explore his passion for her. Besides it might provide distraction from the misery, he mused.

He had found in his romantic affairs that experienced married women and widows were the best for assignations. Virgins were much too protective of their virtue and he was in no hurry to trade his freedom for the temporary possession of that small barrier. His experience with marriage, judging by that of his parents and friends, did not establish any great urge to duplicate the misery.

Taking his seat at the table, he enjoyed the romantic domesticity of the scene: firelight, heavy drapes drawn, a large comfortable bed in the periphery of his vision, a beautiful woman beside him, good wine, and what looked to be a delicious dinner served tête á tête.

"Forgive me for presuming on your company for dinner, but I confess I am quite tired of dining alone. Years of habit prevent Mammy and Moses from joining me and except for a weekly dinner at my parents, my dining has been alone for much of the last year. I trust you will find the wine acceptable. Would you do the honor of pouring?"

"With pleasure, madam. That I can manage with one arm." Noting the vintage of the fine Graves Sauvignon Blanc, he poured a bit in his glass, swirled it, and inhaled the aroma. "Superb selection, just enough oak and an excellent year for Bordeaux, particularly the white ones. You know your wines, Penny." He poured for both of them and then lifted his glass in a toast. "To dinner with the most beautiful woman I know and my recent savior." He smiled at her. "Forgive me that we meet under such unfortunate circumstances. It is not what I would have preferred; however, I refuse to chastise fate for bringing me to you at whatever pain to myself."

"Thank you. Except for the fact you're a damned Yankee, you're not so bad." Penny smiled and sipped her wine, looking at him through her lashes. She was unaware of the seductiveness of the glance.

"You're going to have to stop that or I'll never manage to eat a bite."

"Sorry?"

"You have no idea what an enticing woman you are. After quite some time traveling in the company of dirty and often uncouth men, you catch me starved for a different kind of companionship. And not only have I found it, but the epitome of all that I could have wished for."

Uncomfortable, Penny changed conversational direction. "Do you like the rolls? Mammy actually lets me make them. I've been doing it since I was a child and I love it, love to smell the yeast and work the bread, to knead and shape it."

"They're wonderful." Aware that he was moving too fast for her, he applied himself to the surprisingly good dinner, keeping talk away from the two of them to help her relax. Candlelight, wine, and a crackling fire were his allies. When the pie was nothing but crumbs on the plate, Ryan leaned back and stretched his legs to the fire.

Taking a last sip of the wine, he asked, "How did you develop such excellent taste in fine wine? I must say I haven't run into anything except some homemade wine or cheap whiskey for months now."

"I can't take too much credit. The wine is some that my husband shipped from France when he was on the grand tour following graduation from Princeton University. We have wines from all over Europe—ports, Sherries, cognacs, and brandies, too. He became very interested in them during his year abroad. We were married when he returned and he brought them here to the house my parents built for us. There's even a wine cellar of sorts. Fortunately, it's well hidden and this farm is off the main road or the wine would have been 'requisitioned' by our army or yours long before now."

"My compliments to your husband. He obviously has a cultivated palette for both wine and women."

Penny remarked wryly, "Certainly in wines."

"Not in women?" he probed.

"Our parents expected us to marry from the time we were infants. We never discussed it, really. It was just arranged following his education and grand tour when he was expected to settle down here and help with the running of the farms. I guess I was just part of a package deal arranged by our parents and we went along with it." She didn't realize the unwitting note of bitterness that crept into her voice. She questioned herself for revealing so much to this stranger. But then she knew he would soon be gone and she needed so much to just talk with someone. With her best friend, Ann Herring, ill, the opportunities to confide had been few.

Ryan heard it. Pressing the advantage, he leaned to her and, taking the empty glass she was clutching so fiercely he thought the stem would snap, set it to one side. Looking into her glowing eyes, he slowly drew her to him and tenderly pressed the softest of kisses on her slightly parted lips. He could feel her freeze with panic. To keep her from drawing away, he lightly stroked her hair with his hand, while gently keeping her lips near his. Using his tongue, he teasingly traced the outline of her mouth before letting it slide into her still-parted lips. She gasped with shock but he refused to release her. Again he teased her lips and this time she opened her mouth willingly for him to explore. Suddenly passion seized her and she was responding to him. The kiss deepened and Penny felt herself spiraling out of control, panting, frantic with a hunger so deep she felt it could never be sated. Ryan sensed her need and felt his own rising to equal intensity. Standing he brought her to her feet and began to guide her to the beckoning embrace of the bed.

Suddenly she moaned in despair. "I cannot do this. I cannot."

"Shh." He soothed her, not because he wanted to but because he could not bring himself to hurt her. "It's okay. You don't have to."

Chapter 3

"I'll send Mammy with some more of the tea for your headache," Penny stammered as she slipped from his room. She was shaken and shocked at the depth of her response to this Union soldier, a man she should despise. But then he was just a man and she a woman, so politics are often inconvenient but not a deterrent to the path of the heart. But it was the tenets that formed the foundation of her character that had proven the greater barrier. Her strict breeding and innate sense of honor cautioned her of the error of the actions she would have liked to take behind that bedroom door. Had she succumbed to the passion she felt for this man, she knew she would have felt soiled. The fact that her husband had not honored the bonds of marriage and had insulted her in her own home did not mitigate her own sense of guilt at almost betraying those vows. She swore she would permit neither the weakness of her flesh nor anger at her husband to undo her.

In his now cold and lonely bed, Ryan rued the rash precipitousness of his own actions and feared that he had driven her from him for good. No doubt the morning would find him faced with eviction, he surmised ruefully. From the standpoint of practicality and his obligation to return to duty as expeditiously as possible, a rapid departure should be his goal, but it wasn't. To that end it might be prudent to be more accommodating to his injuries. While all that day he had studiously tried to ignore them, tomorrow would find a far different agenda. He intended to mend the nascent relationship with this woman and for that he needed time. He belatedly realized that the attraction he felt for her was more than just carnal lust, but something deeper that he could not define, that maybe he feared defining. He drank the decoction for his headache and eased himself against the pillows. He knew it would be a restless night as his mind kept cart-wheeling through the memories of the past few days and the route that brought him to this bed, in this house, and with a woman who haunted him when he closed his eyes, lying in an equally lonely bed just down the hall.

He had come to hate the war. It was far from the noble venture he had envisioned when he volunteered at the enlistment center around the corner from his offices. Instead it was intense physical discomfort: filth, vermin, cold, little protection from rain or sleet, mud, poor food, stale clothing, and general misery. It was blood, pain, gore, and scenes of such horror that they colored his dreams with terror. It was inhumanity, the unleashing of the beast in man to perpetrate his cruelty on enemy soldier and often civilian alike. It was the senseless destruction of property that often meant the difference between survival or starvation, the burning of a home that had sheltered generations, the raping of defenseless women, and the soul-scaring of innocent children. As a man who had cherished his sense of honor, he was appalled at the lapses that the exigencies of war had brought him, the brutality that he had been powerless to prevent, the killing that he had done to keep from being killed, and the fear and hatred that he saw in the faces of civilians when his conquering army rode past. He prayed nightly for a quick resolution. But in the face of an implacable and determined foe that fought on despite lacking the resources of his own army, he knew it would not be.

Penny tossed and turned that night as well, relieved when the gray light of dawn illuminated the gap in the drapes announcing the end of her torment. Rousing herself, she drew on her shawl and slippers and quietly crept down the stairs to the kitchen connected to the main house by a covered passage. She regretted that the danger of fires necessitated this architectural arrangement, as a kitchen that was part of the main house would have been far more convenient and not nearly so chilly to get to in the early morning. Going to the pantry that opened off the back of the kitchen, she rummaged for the dried red clover, cherry, and ragwort she needed to make more tea to relieve the croup symptoms of the Smith's children, Marty and Patty; St. John's Wort for Jeremiah's cold; and more headache remedy for the man sleeping upstairs. At the last minute she grabbed a ginger root to compound a strong decoction to take Ann Herring, who was ill with typhoid and living with her mother-in-law since her husband, Stephen, had gone to war. Even though Dr. Charles Woodley or Dr. Lewis Miller had ridden out from Kinston to attend her, now Penny knew they would be too busy treating the wounded and dying to worry about anything or anyone else.

Adding wood to the fireplace, she then turned to the opposite wall and her pride, the modern cast-iron cook stove that Mammy still treated with suspicion. Penny got the fires started to warm the room and make breakfast. She knew Mammy would be in to help as soon as Moses gave her the pail of fresh milk. Soon she had the teas simmering as well as a pot of chicory coffee. Pouring some of the fresh brew, she sat at the scarred oak table, cupping her hands around the warm bowl of the cup. She was sitting there when Mammy arrived a few minutes later.

They exchanged greetings and Penny helped her get the breakfast going before climbing back up the stairs to dress. She opened her armoire to extract the worn drab gray dress that she knew to be the least flattering choice she could make. Tugging it on, she turned to the mirror and hastily arranged her hair. Now to face Ryan.

Determined not to shrink from him, she knocked on his door and when he called out, she entered to find him sitting in bed, his features twisted with pain. He could have told her that the dark circles around his eyes were from lack of sleep, not pain. True enough his shoulder and head were sore and uncomfortable, but not as much as he wanted her to think they were. Forgetting the blush that she knew had spread across her features at the anticipation of facing him, she rushed to his side.

"What's wrong? You look as though you're in a lot of pain." She pressed her hand to his forehead but could detect no increase of fever.

"I guess I'm not doing as well as I had hoped. My head is really throbbing this morning. My shoulder is uncomfortable, too. I hope it's not getting infected. Would you mind checking it for me?"

"Let's get that shirt off and undo the bandages. It looked fine yesterday and you don't appear to be fevered so let's hope it's nothing."

Just to keep the process in motion, Ryan winced and drew back when she lifted the bandage. "Ouch, it really is tender."

Penny looked carefully at the stitches and the color of the wound. It seemed to be mending nicely. Perhaps the increased pain was from the flesh reknitting itself, she thought. Perplexed, she remarked, "Your wound seems to be healing well. I think I'll leave the bandage off so it can get more air. The swelling in your head is only about half what it was, so it's doing better as well. It concerns me, though, that your headache is worse. Perhaps you should lie more quietly today. You'll have your meals in bed. And no more alcohol until that headache is gone."

Damn, Ryan thought, he would have liked to share another bottle of wine with her over a private supper. But maybe he had at least bought time. In what he hoped was the convincingly meek look of a suffering man, he agreed, "I'm afraid that's probably for the best. I really feel pretty under the weather this morning."

"I'll bring you some breakfast. You're not nauseated, are you?"

Hastily, for fear he would be back on broth, he answered, "Oh, no, no. My stomach's fine."

"Well, that's good anyway." For the first time since entering his room, she smiled. "I'll be back soon and I'll bring breakfast and some freshly brewed tea for your headache."

When she left, Ryan congratulated himself on gaining a little more time, although it was with some regret that he anticipated more of that tea. He didn't at all care for the slightly mint taste of it, even though he admitted that it did help his head. What he truly craved for his breakfast was a strong, rich cup of good coffee, not some chicory substitute. But Mammy's cooking was something to relish.

As Penny descended the steps, she heard the sound of shouting from behind the house. Hastening to see what was happening, she dashed into the passageway between the house and kitchen. Emmaline Nunn Williams, daughter-in-law of Nancy Williams, widow of Colonel John Williams, who lived a few miles away, came running into the backyard calling her name.

"Emmaline, over here."

It was obvious she had run most of the way and had been crying. When her heaving stopped long enough she could talk coherently, Penny took her by the shoulders. "Honey, what's wrong?"

"It's the Yankees, Miss Penny. Mama Williams is crying so hard she's just about crazy. They stole everything they could tote off and messed up the house something awful. But worse than all that, they hauled Ann out into the yard, sick as she was with typhus, and made us leave her there all night. It was just too much for Ann. She died this morning." Grasping Penny's hands, she begged, "Please come help us. I don't know what to do."

"Sit down and rest a spell in the kitchen with Mammy Rena. I'll have Moses hitch up the wagon and we'll go see what we can do to help Miss Nancy. We'll fix things somehow." Penny paused. "I'm so sorry about Ann. She was my best friend most of my life. I just can't believe she's gone. I knew she was sick but somehow I hoped she'd make it. In fact, I had planned to take her some herbal tea today. Poor Stephen, he's going to be heartbroken." She remembered both of their wedding days. She had been maid of honor when Ann married Stephen, and Ann had served as matron of honor in her own marriage to Daniel. Feeling tears threatening to spill from her eyes, she shrugged and mentally collected herself.

"Thanks, Penny, we know you cared for her, too. I hate to do it, but I'll have to write Stephen Herring what happened. I've got to write my Eddie, too. He's going to be so mad they killed his sister like this." She shook her head. "Mama Williams made that Yankee general furious because she kept goading him about her 'four sons who are off fighting damned Yankees.' He turned that pack of good-for-nothings loose on us to do their worst, and that they did. They wrecked the house, tore up clothes, stole anything they could carry, and killed the animals and just left them laying about the yard. Just hacked the legs off some of them and left them to die. They even tore up the family Bible for just pure spite. It was so horrible; I thought I'd die. At least they didn't rape us."

"Go on in the kitchen and get warm. There should be some breakfast by now and I have some coffee brewed."

Penny walked to the woods and called Moses. She knew he would be in the hidden pastures and sheds tending to the animals at this time of morning.

When he emerged through the thick undergrowth, she told him what had happened and asked him to load the buggy with some extra food and hitch up old Polly. Moses walked off muttering, "What dis worl' comin' to? Jus' beat all, it sho do."

Penny walked into the kitchen to find Mammy comforting Emmaline with warm food and a gentle hand on her shoulder. "Mammy, I'm going to leave you in charge today. Our guest seems to have had a bad night. Would you take up some breakfast and see to *her*."

Mammy looked up quickly and immediately caught the drift of Penny's thoughts and the emphasis on the sex of their guest.

"I do dat, honey. Now don' you go worr'in' none. I take ker ob eberthin'. Dat Missy upstairs be jus fine."

"Thanks, Mammy Rena. I don't know what I would do without you."

"I don' neither. It's a good thing you ain't got to worry 'bout it none. 'Cause I be here." She patted Emmaline's shoulder while looking over her head into Penny's worried eyes. "Iffn you need anything, send someone for my Moses, you hear?"

"I will, Mammy. Soon as Emmaline and I finish breakfast and the buggy is ready, we're going. I'll be back before night."

"You be kerful on dat road, chile. You know iffn it ain't de Yankees, our own boys be lookin' to git dat hoss and buggy."

"I know and I'm taking my gun. I intend to use it if I must." There was no way anyone was going to take the buggy with its well-sprung leather seats and jaunty cover that Daniel had ordered from the Dibble Brothers Carriage Works in Kinston shortly after their wedding.

"Dat good. But I sho don' wan' my chile out der wid no manfolk's pertection."

Penny hugged the woman who had cared for her since she was in the cradle. "You know I love you, Mammy Rena. I'm going to be fine, so don't worry."

Penny knew that it was imperative to get to her destination with as little exposure as possible. Fortunately woods and swamp protected her thousand-acre farm. On the front side of the farm, a small lane led to the road but unless one was specifically looking for the opening it was easily missed. From the woods at the back, a smaller path with a narrow plank bridge crossed Southwest creek and opened onto British Road, which she needed to take for a short distance in order to reach Lilburn Hill, the Williams' Plantation in the Woodington Church community. The less time she could spend on either Wilmington or British Roads, the happier she would be. British Road roughly paralleled the Neuse River Road running along a ridge of high ground that snaked through the swampy terrain on the south side of the river, making it a major east-west thoroughfare.

The path wound a circuitous route through the pocosin or swamp that formed the bulk of the barricade around her farm before emerging onto the road. It was a longer route but more protected. It was tough going for Polly, as the path had been allowed to grow up with brush, weeds, and encroaching trees. The exit onto the main road was camouflaged by brush and tall grass. When Penny drove through, she climbed down from the two-seater buggy and carefully pulled any bent grass and bushes upright so the entrance was undetectable as a road.

Penny spoke little to the woman beside her on the road to the Williams'. It was just as well, as Emmaline was lost in her own grief. So much death seemed to be swathing its way through the people she had known all of her life. Willis Wooten, who had been the object of her teenage infatuation, had died in February of a bullet wound. Billie Rouse, Martin Holland, and Jeremiah Harper died not long after. With Sam Loftin, Bright and Jessie Harper, Jessie Noble, Jimmy Williams, Johnny Waller, Ann's husband Steven Herring, and both Emmaline's husband and his brothers and Penny's own men folk away in the army, Penny wondered how many more deaths would come to their tight-knit community. Then there was Charlie Holland, who was her husband's best man at their wedding, and Jimmy Rouse, who lived just down the way. With all of the men gone, only women and children and the very old and infirmed were left to cling to the remaining vestiges of life and property in the face of this frightening new world. When Penny thought of her own father fighting with the Tuckahoe Braves, as they called themselves, officially Company D of the 27th Regiment, she wanted to cry as Emmaline was doing, gut-wrenching sobs that seemed to originate in her toes and build to a crescendo before escaping to rend the air with the sound of her agony. She knew later when she had time, she too would mourn her friend Ann but not in the loud wails of Emmaline. Penny's grief was a quieter, more inward thing.

As they approached Wilmington Road, she saw the signs of war glaring at her in every direction. Detritus caused her to detour around obstructions in the road. Cannon and bullets had bedraggled trees along the way, and occasionally the reek of decaying flesh permeated her nostrils. With trepidation she neared the crossing. As a major route from Kinston to the port in Wilmington, the road was far more heavily traveled than the road she was on. Stopping the buggy fifty feet back from the main road, she got out and approached it with wary steps, listening for any traffic. Hearing nothing, she walked into the middle of the road and looked both ways. It was clear as far as she could see in both directions. Quickly she walked back to her horse.

"Okay, Polly. I know you don't care for moving fast, especially with a load behind you, but we're just going to have to do it. Okay, old girl?"

Penny climbed back onto the seat and clucked, slapping Polly's back with the reins. "Come on, girl, move it!"

Emmaline looked up to see they were crossing the Wilmington Road and knew the journey was nearing its end. Now she would have to face anew the devastation and heartbreak that she had so briefly left behind. "Thank God there's no one on the road, Penny. I just couldn't deal with any more soldiers or stragglers."

"Believe me, that's about the last thing I want to see myself," Penny snorted.

Crossing the main road, they continued about a quarter of a mile past Hines Mill on the banks of Southwest Creek and continued to the Williams house. As they neared the house, Penny could see various household furnishings scattered about the yard, along with the bedding where they had dumped the dying Ann. The sight caused her to choke on a sob, which she quickly squelched, knowing as she did that she needed to be strong for the Williamses.

Nancy Williams walked from the front door as she drove up. Penny saw that the narrow windows on either side of the door had been broken. She made a note to check when she got home for glass that she could have Moses install to keep the winter winds from whistling through the wrecked house.

"Miss Nancy, Emmaline told me what happened and I just want to tell you how very sorry I am. Whatever I can do to help, you know I will. Somehow we are all going to make it through this. You just need to hang on and be strong for your boys. They're going to need to know that you're coping here at home, or it will be even harder for them."

"I realize that, Penny. It's just when I walk through my home it just tears me up to see the senseless wreckage. And then poor Ann to just be dumped in the yard to die. What kind of animals treat people that way? It just beats all." She sadly shook her head as she pulled Penny into an embrace. "Will you help me see to Ann? She needs to be laid out. I've washed her and I have her clothes ready. I sent word to the mill to tell the foreman what happened and they're making a coffin for her. I can't get hold of the preacher, so we're just going to have to bury her and have a service later. Maybe when Stephen gets home. I sent word to her family to ask what they want to do."

"That's going to be fine; now you don't go worrying about it. You know I'll help you any way I can. First I have some food in the buggy I need to unload, so you can get something to eat. Emmaline told me they took or destroyed about everything y'all had."

"That they did, the thieving jackasses. I wouldn't give a owl-hoots damn if they all got blown to hell."

Penny and Emmaline took the bags of food and the two chickens in a cage that Moses had loaded in the boot behind the buggy's seat and carried them to the back porch. "Emmaline, you take care of putting this away and if you've got a coop in the woods where the scavengers can't find these chickens, put them in it; otherwise you might want to leave them in the cages until one can be built."

Penny then entered the house, saddened by the destruction that greeted her at every turn. Mrs. Williams had preceded her to the dining room, where Ann's body, wrapped in a blanket, was lying on the badly scarred and gouged table. The two women worked together to dress the body and ready it for the coffin that had been promised by late afternoon. The dress was one provided by neighbors, as soldiers had destroyed all of Ann's. Then they started the process of cleaning and sorting through the debris that littered the house. Finally at three, Penny knew she had to leave in order to get home before dark.

"Do you have someone to dig the grave?" she asked.

"We do. Fortunately a couple of the darky women and their men have stayed on and will help me and there are the men at the mill as well. They're old but capable of getting a grave dug. We're thinking of digging it at the Woodington Meeting House. My poor, poor Ann, she didn't deserve to die this way." Mrs. Williams stretched her back and pushed errant strands of graying hair into the severe bun resting near the crown of her head before hugging Penny goodbye.

"No, she didn't, Miss Nancy. She was one fine, sweet woman," Penny said as embraced. "If you need anything you just let us know, you hear?"

"That I will. You be careful getting home now."

Penny waved goodbye from the buggy and began the trek back, as carefully as the one that she had made to get to Lilburn Hill. It wasn't until almost full dark that she and a weary horse drove into the backyard of her home. Moses met her and, taking the bridle, led the horse first to the barn to stow the buggy and then to the makeshift stable in the woods. She was ready for a supper and her bed but knew she needed to check on Ryan before she could sleep. Mammy called her into the kitchen, when she heard her step onto the passageway. A plate of fried chicken, collards, rice cooked with canned tomatoes, and sweet potato biscuits was waiting for her on the table. Beside the plate Mammy had placed a wine glass and a dusty bottle of red wine, which looked to be the Chianti from Daniel's cellar that Penny had put in the dining room cabinet. She gratefully sank into the chair and ate her dinner, filling Mammy in on the events of the day as she did so.

"So, is Mr. Ryan doing any better tonight?"

"Sho has done some gripin' today, sho nuff." Mammy shook her head. "Jus' don' make no sense to me. I sho thought dat man gittin hissef better. Ain't hurt 'is eatin' none, though."

"Have you given him his dinner?"

"No'am. I wait fo' you. I figer you need to check on'im fust."

"If you'll make a plate for him, a goblet and the rest of this wine, I'll take it up and see what I can do. And thank you, Mammy. It was so nice to come home to a good meal after this day. I confess if it hadn't been for you, I would have just gone to bed hungry. I'm too tired to even think of cooking." She gave Mammy a hug as she took the tray.

Ryan heard her footsteps in the hall and, turning from the fireplace, hastened to get back under the covers, where he pretended to be sleeping. Finding his door ajar and the light from the fire illuminating his recumbent form,

Penny walked to the table and lowered the tray. She walked to the bed and she felt his forehead for fever. Ryan fluttered his lids and slowly sat up.

"Good evening, Ryan. Mammy tells me you've had a difficult day. Are you still hurting?"

"My headache maybe is a little better but this arm is still mighty sore." Ryan noted the weary sadness that etched her features and his heart ached for her. "I'm just so sorry, Penny. Mammy told me what happened. I don't know how to begin to tell you how much I despise the senseless atrocity the Union troops committed against your friends. There is no excuse for making war against helpless women. When I return to camp, I intend to lodge a protest about this. It may not do much good and certainly nothing can bring this woman back to life, but I must do something."

"Thank you. I must admit it was pretty bad, so much senseless destruction and to haul a dying woman into the yard and dump her like so much garbage is just unconscionable. It's a hard thing to see."

"I'm sure it is. Again, I'm sorry."

"Oh well, enough of that." Penny pointed to the tray. "Do you feel like sitting up to take your supper? It really is a good one. I ate some before I came up, along with a good red wine. If your headache is better and you think it will be okay, there's some wine as well, a good Italian red."

"It sounds wonderful. If you'll hand me that robe Mammy brought me, I'll sit at the table. Please join me. I confess it's been a long lonely day and I worried about you on the road."

"Thank you, Ryan. I appreciate that. Do you need any help?"

"No, no. I can manage."

Penny turned to stir up the fire as he donned the robe and joined her at the table. She was happy for the opportunity to just sit and make small talk with this man who was far nicer and more sensitive than she had anticipated. But then she told herself, he was just another human being caught up in a war that neither of them had begun. They talked quietly over the meal and she found herself even more drawn to him than on the previous evening.

"Ryan, I've been thinking. There's no way you can ride from here to join your troops wearing that uniform. You'll be going through country where people will shoot you on sight when they see that blue uniform. I have some clothes of Daniel's I'll give you to wear when you leave and a little money if you don't have any. It's Confederate, but if you spend Yankee money here you could raise some mighty high eyebrows. I don't know if it is enough to buy a horse or not but I can't spare more. I also think you need to go back to New Berne. I don't know where your army is or what has happened so that seems safest. We don't get much news because we're so isolated. I'll go to Mama's tomorrow and see if they have heard anything over there."

"Keep your money, and don't worry. I've been thinking that New Berne's the best option, too, and I would appreciate the clothes. I know in that uniform

I'd just be a target. I realize it would be safer for you if I leave soon and the minute I'm able to walk that distance, I'll go."

"Please, you must stay until you're well. That's a long trip in the best of circumstances and these are far from best." Penny said, "I see you still have the tea for your headache. Do drink some before going back to bed. It will help you sleep." Penny started to rise but was stopped by his hand reaching to hold hers.

"Don't go yet. Just sit with me by the fire."

"If I do, I'll just fall asleep in the chair. But I'll check on you after I take the tray down, if you'd like to get back in bed."

Ryan heaved a sigh, realizing that he had no right to intrude on the worn-out woman who stood before him. Even in the old dress with her hair straggling about her face, he found her beautiful. It struck him that she was also one of the kindest women he had ever met. "Don't worry about me. You just get some rest and I'll see you in the morning."

Chapter 4

When Penny arrived with his breakfast tray, she found Ryan dressed and standing by the window, looking out at gray clouds that threatened the promise of snow. He had already put logs on the fire and it was burning brightly to dispel the gloom outside.

"It's a cold one out there this morning," Penny remarked in greeting.

"It looks it." Ryan turned to her. "I'm going to try staying out of bed today and if possible, I would very much like dinner downstairs with you tonight."

"Of course, if you think you're up to it." Penny lowered the tray to the table. "I want to remove the stitching from your shoulder this morning. Once that's done it should mend even more quickly. Just be careful not to overexert and pull the wound open."

"No danger of that. I don't feel that energetic yet." Ryan laughed.

"After the injuries you had and the loss of blood from the bullet wound, I'm not surprised if you still feel a little weak." Penny smiled. "I'll leave you alone until after breakfast and then I'll come undo those stitches."

Penny went to her room and found the small manicure scissors she would need to remove the stitches. The next stop was the herb pantry, where she found the figwort she would use to make a poultice for the wound afterwards. A pan of hot water, a soft clean cloth, and whiskey for sterilization and to take the edge from pain completed her preparations. She paused in the kitchen to talk with Mammy.

"Mammy Rena, would you ask Moses to ride over to Mama's and check on her for me? I also need him to stop by Mr. Fitz's to see if the overseer is taking good care of things while he's away." Penny smiled apologetically. "I should do it myself, but after yesterday, I just want to stay home today."

"Don' you go an' worry 'bout it. My Moses be glad to go fo' you." Mammy patted her reassuringly on the back. "Sho hope yo' Mama doin' better. Delia say she been a mite poorly fo' some time now."

"It's her heart. It's weak and despite the medicine that Dr. Miller gave her and my own herbs, she just doesn't seem to get much better. I'm worried about her, too. At least Nancy Herring is staying with her while Pa's gone. Even so I surely hope Pa gets back in a day or two. Besides, I don't like the idea of him traipsing around in this weather. He's too old for soldiering. He should be at home keeping Mama cheered up."

"Dat man could make de dead happy. Neber did see nobody could make a body laff like 'im."

"He's a jewel for sure. Mama was one lucky woman when she got him."

"Dat sho nuff so." Mammy noted the things in Penny's hands and commented. "Sho gwine miss dat Ryan. It good to have a man 'round de house agin' eben iffn he a Yankee. He still a fine man and good lookin' one, too."

"Sounds to me like you've been doing some visiting while I was away." Penny grinned at the elderly woman.

"I has fo' sho. He a good'un to talk to and 'sides somebody gots to take ker of 'im when he cain' do fo' hissef."

"I'm sure he appreciates all you've done for him. I know I do. Which reminds me, we need to find some clothes he can wear when he leaves. He can't go walking through the countryside in that blue uniform; otherwise digging out that bullet will have been a waste because someone would for sure put another in him."

"Dats a fack. I git something that look mo' natur'l for 'im. He ain't leavin' today, is he?"

"No, no. He's still too weak. I doubt he could make it to the end of the lane."

That both turned at the sound of the kitchen door swinging in on creaky hinges. Ryan stood there proudly holding the breakfast tray. With Daniel's ill-fitting pajamas and a blanket around his shoulders, it had been a struggle to carry the loaded tray. "I thought it was time I started contributing to my keep. Besides, it will save you the trip upstairs with all that stuff, Penny."

"You give me dat tray, boy. You ain't 'sposed ta be haulin' things 'round yit," Mammy scolded as she fussed about getting a fresh cup of chicory coffee for him.

It was obvious to Penny that she had adopted Ryan like a stray puppy.

"You git nuff breakfas'? I got mo' iffn you hongry."

"I'm fine. Once again, you outdid yourself. That sausage and gravy were superb. I don't think I've ever eaten better food. Mammy, I think I'm going to kidnap you and take you home with me."

Mammy beamed wide enough to split her face and swatted playfully at him. "Don' you go teasin' me now."

"I'm very serious. The only thing that stops me is terror that Penny would shoot me if I tried. One bullet this week is about all I can stand."

Penny smiled and pulled out a chair at the table. "Have a seat and we'll get those stitches out."

She worked quickly and efficiently. Except for an occasional sharp intake of breath, Ryan sat immobile while she worked. Penny mopped up the few beads of blood from the site of the stitches, applied the antiseptic poultice, wrapped the shoulder with a bandage to protect it, and busied herself putting things away. Ryan enjoyed her quick, sure movements and smiled when he caught Mammy observing him with interest as he openly watched her. Penny felt his eyes on her and reveled in the warmth that this knowledge brought.

"Since I'm downstairs and determined to stay out of bed for awhile, is there something I could do to help out? Maybe I could oil that hinge if you gave me some oil. Any other little job that I can do, I'm willing."

"I'll get the oil later. I don't think that will bother your shoulder to do. I also have some books in the parlor if you'd like to read."

"Thanks. I think I would like that. It's been ages since I had time to lose myself in a good book."

"It might be a good idea if Mammy puts some clothes in your room for you to change into first. That uniform wouldn't be too big a success should a neighbor drop by. If that should happen, remember to say you're my cousin and you just stopped by on the way to rejoin your troops from South Carolina. Emmaline told me that they were fighting with our boys." She paused. "Do you think you could try to sound a little more southern?"

"Why ma'am, that won't be any problem at all, ma'am," he announced in an exaggerated drawl that had both Penny and Mammy laughing at him.

"Come on, boy. Let's go git you some reg'lar clo'es," Mammy ordered.

Penny smiled as they walked out with Ryan docilely following in Mammy's wake. She went to the parlor to light a fire in the iron grate so he would at least not freeze to death while he enjoyed a book. She smiled at the shelves on either side of the dark green marble fireplace. They were full of good books since she herself was a reader. Dickens, Melville, Shakespeare, and Emerson stood side by side with Harriett Beecher Stowe's novel. She knew Ryan would have no problem finding something to keep his interest. As for her, too many chores were waiting for her to consider that luxury.

She looked around the room and was pleased with what she saw. Rather than heavy Victorian furniture that was becoming the vogue, the furnishings were a mixture of George IV and Hepplewhite. She fluffed the needlepoint cushions on the rich green damask Adams settee with the urn ornamentation on the back and moved a yellow floral armchair to the sunny window framed by green, cream, and burgundy satin striped drapes with a green fringe border that matched the sofa. The Wedgewood Portland vases and Bayre bronze lion on the Grecian motif mantle were gifts from her grandmother, as was the marble portrait bust of her grandfather that sat on the chest between the front windows. It was a beautiful room with the pale green tone-on-tone wallpaper, butter-colored moldings, and rich Turkish carpet adding a unifying expanse of color.

It really needed dusting, she noted, but it would have to wait for another day. Satisfied that he would be comfortable, Penny returned to the kitchen to resume her chores. She intended to bake bread. She always made bread when she needed to get troubling thoughts from her mind. She knew Mammy would notice, but with all that had occurred in recent weeks, anyone would be bothered. She admitted to herself that part of what troubled her was the fact that Ryan would be leaving and once again the house would be empty at night except for her lone presence.

Mammy returned to the kitchen to inform her that a more appropriately dressed man was happily settled in the parlor. She left the kitchen to gather eggs for the red-velvet cake she wanted to make for dinner. Mammy was putting on a good front for the guest in keeping with the hospitality of former days. She had obviously taken a great liking to him to be going to such trouble. Penny suspected the fare in the days after he left would of necessity be far more austere, as they were rapidly running through dwindling supplies. Even though they had been more fortunate than others who had been visited by army scavengers from both sides who were assigned to requisition foodstuffs from the populace, the funds for buying such staples as sugar and refined flour were limited to Confederate notes as she was quietly hording her gold, silver, and Yankee money. Even with money, flour, sugar, and salt were becoming scarcer and more and more expensive. In addition to the Confederacy tax of ten percent of what she produced, she also tried to send excess vegetables and meat to the Tuckahoe troops in order to do her part to support these men who were her friends and neighbors.

She finished kneading the bread, wrapped it, and set the covered bowl on a chair near the stove, where it would rise up fluffy and light. That done, she went to her office to do her account books. It was increasingly difficult to find the money to pay the servants left on the farm, but her integrity forced her to economize in other areas as long as she could. If the war continued for much longer, she wondered where the money would come from. She knew unless something changed she would be forced to spend the gold, silver, and Yankee dollars. Perhaps they could try to plant some cotton in the spring, she mused. She rejected that idea when she remembered the prospects of getting it to market in England were increasingly risky. What could she grow or create to bring in income? And who had any money to buy? The problem vexed her as she turned it around and around in her mind but could find no solution. But an idea kept tickling the back of her mind; she waited for it to solidify.

Returning to the kitchen, she shaped the dough into loaves and put them into the cast-iron oven. Soon the aroma of baking bread permeated the air, reminding her that she had eaten little at breakfast. Lunch would be sketchy, as she planned a good dinner in the dining room in honor of Ryan's first evening dressed and up.

Gathering a slice of leftover apple pie, a chunk of cheese, and a glass of milk, she carried them to Ryan in the parlor. He had nodded off with the book dropped to the floor by his chair. Penny picked it up and placed the book and food on the piecrust table at his right elbow. She leaned across him to reach the tabletop and Ryan, now awake, took the opportunity to rest his hand at her waist before she could straighten up.

"I like this kind of service, Miss."

Deftly turning her, Penny fell into his lap as his arms encircled her.

"I want to kiss you," Ryan whispered. He didn't wait for a reply but proceeded to do just that.

At first Penny held back, but she was soon as lost in the kiss as he was. "Ryan," she murmured, not sure what she was going to say, except "Stop," or was it..."Please don't stop." Finally she pulled back and smiling stood on shaky legs. "If I don't check my bread it's going to be as black as cinders."

"Check your bread and I'll eat some pie." He winked at her. "Then if you'll come back, I'd like some real dessert."

"If you don't behave, I'm going to be putting more stitches in that shoulder of yours."

"Ouch. Is that a threat?"

"Only if it needs to be." She left the parlor with a song in her heart. It felt so wonderful to have a man like Ryan to tease her and remind her that she was still very much a young and desirable woman.

Both Mammy and Moses were in the kitchen when she walked in. Mammy had already removed her golden loaves of bread from the oven and put in the layers for the cake. A large bundle rested on the slat back chair where Ryan had sat earlier.

Moses pointed to it and said, "Dis here from yo' mama. She say it be too risky to keep in her house and she want you to hide it fo' huh here. It yo' mama's silver."

"Thank you, Moses. Of course I will." Her parent home was on British Road and with both armies marching back and forth, it was too exposed for safety. "Are she and Miss Nancy doing okay?"

"She say dey be fine and you not to worry none 'bout dem. Dat spinster lady take good ker o' yo' mama."

Moses went on to tell her that the Becton's youngest son, Johnny, had ridden over from Vine Swamp to tell them the latest news. His brothers, Frederick and Edward, had stopped by home after the fighting to let their parent know they were uninjured. The brothers told their family that Kinston had taken heavy damage from shelling and Yankee looting. Many people had fled to kin people in the countryside, abandoning their homes to whatever fate was in store. Others had gathered at Cobb Washington's mansion, Vernon Hall, atop the highest point in Kinston, and shortly thereafter were fleeing for their lives in the face of bombardment from gunboats in the river. Although the water was low and had prevented them coming all the way to the town, they still lobbed in enough explosives to do considerable damage to property and nerves. It seems that Foster had also dumped a large contingency of camp followers on the east side of town and left them there. Initially he had allowed them to trail along for what he euphemistically called "morale" purposes.

Kinston, named Kingston prior to the Revolution, had been one of only a handful of towns in the state that could boast of a population of a thousand or more people and it had begun to prosper despite lacking some of the advantages of New Berne. Now it would be hard put to recover anytime soon.

The brothers had been in the fighting around Goldsborough and reported that the Union army under General Foster had managed to destroy the railroad bridge. Even though they had done some harm to the ironclad that was under construction in Whitehall, it had not been severely damaged as the Rebels had held them off. In retaliation, Foster had ordered every building in town burned except for the Whitfield house, which they were using as a hospital, and one other small building. Having suffered heavy losses and a not overly successful raid, Johnny said the Union army was headed back to New Bern.

"Did Johnny mention whether or not he had seen Pa or Mr. Fitz?"

"No'am. He din' say."

The news was bad and not hearing anything of her family made it worse. Penny heaved a heavy sigh and picked up the bundle. She took it to the wine cellar, cleverly concealed behind a hidden door, and there she buried it under one of the casks in the dark back corner. She next looked for wine, this time selecting two bottles of a dry Châteauneuf du Pape for dinner. That done, she climbed back up the stairs.

"Mammy, Ryan and I will be having dinner in the dining room tonight. I hope you don't mind serving it there."

Mammy grinned. "Das fine, chile. It gwine be a good 'un, too. I done soak dat ham and it bakin' right now. I foun' some cress down on the crick bank fo' a salat and I made a swee' tater soufflé and some fiel' peas wid snaps. I took a jar dem canned peaches and we gwine hab a cobbler, too. I 'preciates you set de table fo' me."

"It sounds divine. I'm going to so love that watercress. I have craved something fresh. I'm on my way to the dining room to do the table right now."

Penny walked out humming, happy that she had a nice dinner, good wine, and a handsome man with whom to share her evening. In the dining room she pulled back the heavy velvet drapes of rich cream trimmed with gold cording. The lace under-curtains let in the last rays of a dying sunset. Soon she had a cozy fire going in the grate. Finding the lace tablecloth her mother had given her, she carefully draped the table. Next she took the George III candelabras, inserted fresh tapers, and set them on the table. She opened the bottom drawer of the sideboard and lifted out the chest containing heirloom flatware that had been passed down to her from her great-grandmother and removed what she needed. She then lifted the Sevres plates from the China Cabinet and set places for the two of them. Napkins embroidered with her initials completed the table. I need flowers, she thought, and then remembered the pink Sesanqua Camellias blooming in the side yard. Dashing out she gathered a bouquet, stopping in the kitchen to put water in a vase. Mammy grinned behind her back when she ran out.

"Dat chile happy, I belieb," she said to no one. Mammy was glad because she knew that Penny had suffered in her marriage from a neglectful and unloving husband. She had never liked Daniel and now that her daughter's child was a daily reminder of the man, she liked him less. She blamed Daniel for the pain and trouble he had brought both to her daughter and to the woman she loved like one. Although Lucinda's pride and ambition had made her vulnerable, his unbridled lust for the forbidden had sealed all their fates.

Penny stood back, admiring her efforts. For the first time since Daniel had left, she was going to eat in the dining room with someone. She tried to check her excitement at spending the evening with Ryan but could not forget the kiss in the parlor earlier. She told herself to stop dreaming for something that could never be, but her mind refused to obey. She walked past the parlor on the way to her room to freshen up for dinner and noted that Ryan must have gone up to rest, as his book was lying on an empty chair.

Standing in front of her armoire, she considered what to wear and chose the heavy green velvet with black braid and trim that she had rejected a couple of days before. She knew it was becoming to her copper hair and golden eyes. She felt like a dinner party, she thought, so why not wear her most flattering winter dress? Slipping it on over stays and petticoats, she was reminded that she had not bothered to wear them for months now. It was all she could do to get the stays laced on her own, but she managed. She tugged at her camisole to push it low enough that it would not show above the décolleté neckline of her dress. Next for the dress: Carefully she pulled it over her head and, using her button hook, managed to get all of the buttons careful ensconced in their loops. Leaning over she brushed her hair until it shone and then flipped it back. Carefully she pulled it up into curls on top of her head, pinned each into place, and stood back to check the effect in her mirror. She needed jewelry. Selecting the gold necklace with a diamond and emerald pendant and matching earrings that her father had given her for her eighteenth birthday, Penny carefully put them on. Nervously she bit her lips to redden them. It will have to do, she thought.

Slowly she descended the curving stairs. Ryan was waiting at the bottom. Mammy had obviously been busy, too, as she had provided him with an evening suit to match the formality of her own. *Oh, Mammy,* she said to herself, *you are one devious old woman* when she saw the man waiting for her at the foot of the stairs.

As Ryan watched her descend the stairs, his breath caught in his throat. She was undoubtedly the most beautiful and impressive woman he had ever seen. Suddenly he was nervous. Oh, how badly he wanted her to like him. Then he stopped himself. Would *liking* be enough, he asked? He knew in every fiber of his being that he not only wanted to possess this woman and call her his, but he wanted her in his life for as long as he lived. He thought, as horrible as it was, he could almost shoot her husband on sight just because Daniel could lay claim to what he himself was denied.

"You are the most exquisite woman I have ever known, magnificent in every way." Ryan extended his hand to her to escort her to the dining room.

"Thank you, Ryan. You're most kind."

Clasping the hand that she rested lightly on his arm, he led her to her chair and held it for her to be seated.

Glancing up at him, Penny smiled. "You're pretty handsome yourself, Mr. Madison. And one woman in this house is totally charmed with you."

"Dare I hope you mean you?" Ryan grinned with elation.

"Oh, I was referring to Mammy." She purred flirtatiously.

"Tarnation. That's not quite my goal," Ryan said with tongue-in-cheek.

The candles were lit and Mammy must have been waiting in the butler's pantry because no sooner were they seated than she entered the dining room carrying a large silver tray with the ham, sweet potatoes, peas, and salad. The fresh warm bread and butter were already on the table, along with the opened bottle of wine. The cobbler was sitting on the sideboard. She put the dishes in front of Ryan to serve, glanced at Penny, and beat a hasty retreat.

"I think you've subverted her. She's become your accomplice, I fear."

"I? Surely not." Ryan grinned. "Can I help it if I like her cooking and I tell her so? Plus, while you were gone, she was most welcome company. You are fortunate to have someone like her. You know she loves you like her own?"

"Yes, I do. She's been a part of my life since I was born. I don't know what I would do without Mammy Rena."

"Lucky for you that's not a problem. She wouldn't dream of leaving you. May I?" He lifted the bottle inquiringly.

"Please."

Pouring a glass for them both, he carefully sat the bottle back into its coaster and lifted his glass. "To you. May you always be a part of my life."

Penny knew how remote that possibility was considering the obstacles to that happening; nonetheless, she lifted her own glass and clicked the rim of his. "To better tomorrows."

He lightly touched his glass to hers and continued. "To tomorrows with you. Then they will be better."

Penny looked at her plate in confusion. She lifted her napkin and slowly placed it in her lap, buying time before responding. "I hope you'll enjoy dinner. Mammy has gone to a lot of trouble to make it special for you."

"I think she made it special for us." Ryan lifted his eyebrow in challenge. "You know for some reason, she's on my side."

Refusing to acknowledge the challenge, Penny responded. "Would you serve, please?"

The dinner was as delicious as Penny knew it would be. By the time Ryan had opened the second bottle of wine and served dessert, they had established a comfortable rapport. Ryan was an amusing and interesting raconteur and she had frequently laughed at stories he told. In a way his easy manner and sense of humor were reminiscent of her father. Penny knew she had drunk far too much of the wine and had looked far too often into his mesmerizing blue eyes, but she was contentedly happy.

When he arose from the table and took her hand, she had no power not to follow.

He pulled her to his side and slowly walked with her up the stairs. At the top, he momentarily hesitated and then continued to her bedroom, opened the door, and led her in. Kicking the door behind them, he drew her into his arms.

"I would not have believed it possible after so many years of running from love, but my darling girl, I fear it's found me. I want you, yes, because you're beautiful and desirable, but I want you more because I think I have fallen in love with you. Please let me stay with you tonight."

Penny reached up and lightly touched his lips with her fingertips to silence him, not knowing if he spoke the truth and not caring at that moment. Then she slowly began to undo her buttons. Ryan pushed her hands away and continued until each of the buttons was released, then he slowly lowered the dress from her shoulders. "God, you're so beautiful."

He kissed her then and she responded with all of the repressed passion and love that Daniel had spurned. For this night if no other, she was determined to belong to this man who had upset the pattern of her world and brought her a love she never thought to know.

Holding her from him, he continued the slow removal of her clothes. The light from the fireplace made her coppery hair a glowing halo of fire that drifted down to her waist when he unpinned it. He buried his face in the soft fragrant depths of it and felt that he had touched paradise. Penny groaned low in her throat, firing his passion. Quickly he began to disrobe himself all the while kissing and exploring her lush curves. When they both stood naked in the firelight, he stepped back and drank in her beauty just as she visually explored his taunt body. His arousal was more than apparent, making her suddenly shy. She and Daniel had never stood naked before one another and she was momentarily embarrassed.

Reaching out to cup her breasts, Ryan whispered, "Come to me. Be mine, Penny, all mine."

Penny had never known such transports of passion and longing, the wonder of fulfillment with a man. She knew she should feel guilt, but all she could think of was how very glad she was that this man had come into her life. Later she would deal with realities, she told herself, but tonight he was hers and she his.

Sated after their lovemaking, she turned to him and rested her head on his shoulder. "I didn't know loving could feel this way."

"Somehow, neither did I," Ryan replied and realized he meant it. Holding her against him, he felt his body responding anew. Again he kissed her, slowly exploring and appreciating the enticing curves of her body until he could again enter her and make her his in the timeless rhythm of man and mate.

In pleasurable exhaustion they settled for sleep curled in one another's arms.

Just as she drifted off, Penny murmured so softly that Ryan thought he had imagined it. "I love you. Now, always, no matter what happens."

Lightly he kissed her hair and pulled her to his side. Sleep was slow coming to him. He wanted to seize this moment and make the world stand still, stop the war, and just stay in this woman's arms until he was an old man with years of loving her in his memory. Somehow he knew he also had to find a way to protect her from the army in which he served and the perils that awaited her on every side. Shifting his weight to ease the dull ache in his shoulder, he finally slept as the soft light of the glowing embers cast their dying light against the wall above the bed.

Chapter 5

The light was pouring through the window, telling Penny that she had slept far later than was her wont. The warmth against her back reminded her that she was not alone. The memory of the evening came back to her and she smiled to herself, knowing that it was one she would treasure as long as she lived, even while a part of her felt remorse at breaking a vow of honor.

"Good morning," Ryan murmured against her hair. "Don't even think about getting up yet. I have a strong urge to renew a certain acquaintance."

"If we don't get up soon, Mammy's going to be up here, shaking us out of the sheets."

"No. She won't. Not this morning."

"Why do you say that?" Penny turned to face him.

"Because I told her we would be sleeping late."

Penny's look of chagrin lasted only a moment. "Then maybe we should go back to sleep," she teased.

"Give me a minute or two and we'll see how sleepy you feel."

Sometime later they left the warmth of the bed to hastily don clothing, as the fire had died in the night. Penny knew she needed a bath and Ryan as well, but it would have to wait until she could get a fire going in the fireplace and hot water carried up to the tub that she kept behind a screen in her room. Together they descended the stairs to a quiet house. In the kitchen, Mammy had left fresh biscuits, butter, strawberry preserves, and slices of the baked ham from the night before. Coffee was still warm on the stove.

"I guess Mammy is out tending to chores while I'm lazing away."

"I don't think I would say you've been lazy this morning," Ryan remarked with a smile. "Let's eat some breakfast and then I'll help you with whatever I can do."

After breakfast, Penny found the oil can and Ryan applied himself to the hinges throughout the house. Getting out the large pots in which she heated bathwater, she filled them and set them on the stove. Then she cleaned the dishes from their breakfast and swept the floor. Calling to Ryan, she asked him to come help her when the water was hot enough for a bath. Between the two of them they got the water to her bedroom, pulled the screen in front of the fire where the heat would be reflected back, and poured in the water. She added a fresh bar of the French soap she treasured and placed two large towels over a chair by the fire to warm.

"Why don't you go first?" Penny invited.

"Why not together?"

"That's an interesting idea, but if you'll note the size of this tub, I think you'll agree it isn't very practical." Penny laughed.

"Someday, I'm going to have a big tub," Ryan muttered as he climbed in.

The water felt heavenly. He would have loved to soak but knew if he did, she would have to bathe in cold water. Getting out, he reached for a towel and invited her to claim the tub. Still shy with him, Penny removed the last of her clothes and carefully stepped into the water. When she was finished and dressed, they emptied the water through the window. Penny dried the tub and together they returned the tub and screen to the corner.

He pulled her into his arms and kissed her. Moving away from him, Penny looked out into the front yard at the sound of hooves.

"Oh, no. Someone's coming. Please go to your room and get in bed, and I'll go see who it is. Unless you're a good actor, if any Rebels find you here, you're a dead man and I'm in a heap of trouble."

"Be careful and if you need me call." Ryan patted her bottom as he walked past.

Penny paused at the door, a frisson of foreboding crept down her spine. A vision of something evil intruded at the periphery of her mind, warning her. "I think I'd better take my revolver just in case."

"Do you know how to use it?" Ryan asked skeptically.

"I do," was her grim response.

When she reached the bottom of the stairs, she heard footsteps already walking to the front door. Before the knock could sound, she swung the door open, holding the revolver at her side hidden by the folds of her skirt. The man standing there was huge, just over six feet and perhaps three hundred pounds. Even from where she stood she could smell the reek of him. His hair and beard were bushy and probably full of lice, she thought. He took his felt hat from his head and casually beat it against his leg.

"Could ya spare a mite o' grub and maybe some fodder fo' my hoss, Ma'am?"

She noticed his eyes darting around the foyer and hall.

"I 'spect your menfolk're off ta the war. Kinda remote lack here fer a woman alone, ain't it?

Ignoring his question, she ordered, "Go around the house and wait by the kitchen door. I'll see what we have."

"Thank ye kindly."

Penny threw the bolt on the front door as she watched him walk past the windows towards the back of her house. He had a shifty look about him that immediately put her on guard. Checking the revolver to make doubly sure it was loaded, she walked down the hall and opened the door to the passageway to the kitchen. When she did, he was waiting. Surprising her with an unexpected shove, Penny fell back to the floor, wedging the revolver under her right leg. He was on her before she could free it and take aim. She struggled with him as he used his body weight to hold her and his hands to push at her skirt. Realizing he intended to rape her, she opened her mouth to scream but he immediately clamped his hand over it, almost choking her in the process. If only she hadn't sent Ryan to the room at the end of the hall, she thought as she struggled in rising panic.

The man suddenly released her. Ryan had hit him hard in the jaw, knocking him off Penny and onto the floor. Then a shot rang out and the smell of cordite hung in the air. Penny didn't know who was shot, but she could smell the odor of blood and knew someone was hit. Opening her eyes, she saw that the man whose legs were still sprawled across hers was bleeding from a large hole in his chest.

"Oh, my God, you've killed him," she exclaimed in shock.

"If I haven't, I damned well mean to." Ryan checked for a pulse and, finding none, straightened up. "Are you all right? He didn't hurt you?"

"I'm okay, just shaken." Penny looked down at the body. "I'm going to need you to help me. We have to get him out of here and buried, before Moses or Mammy come looking to see what happened. The fewer people who know about this, the fewer questions and problems later."

Together they wrapped him in an old bedspread and dragged him off the passageway into the yard. Pointing to the woods, Penny helped drag him into the thick underbrush.

"If we can get him down to the creek, we can roll him in. There's enough water running after the rains that it should wash him a ways down."

"We'll try it. With my shoulder like it is, I don't think my shoveling would be as efficient as we would need." Pausing for a moment to think, he continued. "Wait here. I'm going to get his horse and remove anything that might identify him. Then I'll come back and do the same with the body. We can say that the horse must have wandered off from the battle. At least I won't have to walk to New Berne now."

"I'll get his pockets," Penny said as she stooped beside the bloody bundle. Still rattled from her scare, she closed her eyes and took a deep breath before searching the body. It was obvious from the three ladies rings and bracelet she found that he was a thief as well as a rapist. She found his wallet containing only a few Confederate notes but no identification. Shoving the jewelry and wallet back, she decided to leave it all on him. She wanted nothing of his.

Ryan walked up leading the roan. She stood and brushed off her hands as though she would remove the contamination she felt from touching the man and his things.

"With no uniform and no identification it's hard to say where he came from. He's just a good-for-nothing pig who's been roaming the countryside preying on defenseless women. I'm glad you shot him."

"So am I. There was nothing on the horse either. I'm going to toss his reins over a branch in the woods here and I'll come out and 'discover' him later. Can you help me drag this swine again?"

"Let's go. I'm ready to get this over with."

Together they managed to move him to the creek. Looking for a deep pool and finding it just a short walk down, they rolled him off the bank and into the muddy water without waiting to watch him sink into the dark depths. Walking back to the house, Ryan told her that instead of getting in bed as she had instructed, he had grabbed his pistol and silently descended the steps. He felt his anger soar anew when he related how he had rounded the corner just as the man gripped her jaw.

Now he wondered who would protect her when he was gone, for go he must. To stay would make him a deserter to his own army and he would still be an enemy to the other. Neither option would be good for his health. Sadly he took her hand.

"Penny, I wish I could stay with you and keep you safe until this madness is over, but I can't. With this horse, if I'm careful I can get back to my station in a day. It's best if I leave tomorrow." He looked at the hurt in her face and hated himself for causing it. "Please forgive me, dear one. I'll come back to you when I can and I'll try to get letters to you."

"I knew you would leave me from the beginning, so don't apologize. It has to be. Let's forget it for the rest of today and tonight. It will be soon enough to think about it when tomorrow morning comes." Penny smiled tenderly up at him.

Skirting the far side of the house from Mammy's cabin, Ryan and Penny entered through the open back door. Together they scoured any residue of the dead man. "Let's sit in the parlor and pretend we're an old married couple. I don't want to do anything except enjoy what time together remains and forget about the last hour."

"Okay, Ryan. If you'll build the fire, I'll go out back and see where the others are. I'm going to say that I shot the gun off accidentally if they ask. I'm hoping Mammy and Moses were down in the woods on the other side of the farm taking care of the animals. Maybe if they heard something, they won't realize it was from here and won't ask. Their daughter, Lucinda, was taking her baby and going to visit friends on Mr. Fitz's plantation, so she's gone all day."

"Good."

Penny wrapped her shawl tightly about her, wondering if the shaking was from cold or a belated case of the nerves. When she reached the narrow path that led to the animals, she noted tracks that told her they had indeed gone to tend them. Continuing on she found the couple in the makeshift stable, grooming old Polly while the two work mules looked on with interest. Neither one seemed to have noted anything amiss judging by their relaxed conversation when she entered.

"I hope the animals are doing okay. I worry about them down in the swamp like this, but I suppose they're safer here than in the barn," she announced when they looked up at her entrance.

"Dey doing jes fine, Miz Penny. Ain't no need to worrit none. I takin' good ker of 'em," Moses assured her.

"I know you are and thanks, Moses. By the way, Colonel Madison is leaving tomorrow. I wondered, Mammy, if you could make him a packet of food to take along. It's about thirty miles of hard traveling to get to New Berne and he's going to have to be sly about it, so who knows how long it'll take."

"Dat I do, ain't no problem. We sho cain' hab him ride off hongry and nothin' to take wid 'im." Mammy grinned at her. "I hopes he feelin' bettah today."

Repressing an answering grin, Penny responded, "He's not complaining."

Mammy's shoulders shook with silent laughter. "No'am, I don' speck he be."

"Is there anything I can do to help here, Moses?"

"No'am, Miz Penny. I 'bout done." Moses continued brushing old Polly's coat to remove the burrs and tangles as Penny turned to go back to the house and the last hours she would spend with the man she now knew she loved.

She didn't want to think that she might never see Ryan again, but she had to acknowledge that it was a strong possibility. Either she would let that knowledge spoil their last hours together or she would push it to the back of her mind to deal with it after he was gone. Suddenly she stopped under the Spanish moss that draped nearly to her shoulders from a huge oak. The massive tree had stood like a sentinel since long before white men had come to these shores. Oh, my God, she thought. What if I'm pregnant? How could I ever explain it to Daniel or our families? Oh, please, she thought, as badly as I would love to have his child, please don't let it be. The fact that in all of the months with Daniel she had never quickened gave some reassurance.

It was the seventeenth of December. In one week it would be Christmas. And a lonely one at that, she reflected. On a sudden impulse she walked into the tool shed in the backyard and grabbed a hatchet. Even if Christmas was a week away, she was going to celebrate that very night. Walking back to the house, she had noticed a small cedar, thickly branched, and a holly covered with bright red berries. She would chop the branches and carry them to the house to decorate the table and mantle in honor of the season and this last night with Ryan.

When she walked into the back hall, Ryan was standing there with a worried look on his face. With relief he noted the branches in her arms and the excited smile on her face. He knew immediately that she wanted to share Christmas with him. "I wondered why you were away so long. Come into the parlor and we'll put some of those branches on the mantle and maybe in the dining room. I feel like a celebration with the woman I adore."

"Aren't they beautiful?" she enthused. "I decided to do Christmas early. Unless Pa gets back, it will just be my mama, Nancy, and me for dinner that day. I dread the thought...so, tonight's going to be my Christmas."

"Mine, too." He lightly kissed her on the top of her head as she bent to select the branches for the mantle. "Let me help you."

When both the dining room and parlor were redolent with the aroma of cedar and candles were glowing in the sconces and chandeliers, they stood back to admire their efforts.

"It's beautiful, Penny. Thank you for making this last night even more special. Do you think we could rob that cellar for a bottle of champagne, or is that an impossible dream?

"Great idea. I do have champagne. Come down with me and you can select one." Penny took his hand and led him to the hidden door and where she sprung the secreted catch.

Together they carefully descended the stairs. At the bottom, she took the lantern and flint she kept there and made light to guide them to the champagne.

"My word, darling. What a treasure trove this room is," Ryan admired as he looked around. "Let's see what's appropriate for tonight, shall we?"

"You chose."

"This '58 Clicquot should be perfect. Who needs food with you, champagne, a beautifully decorated fireplace, and a warm fire?"

"You may not need dinner, but I do. I'm famished." Penny laughed.

"Then let's make it an early dinner. I want to say a proper goodbye tonight as I must leave by daybreak tomorrow," Ryan remarked as they reached the main level.

"I'd like that." Penny saw no point in false modesty at this point. She wanted this man as much as he wanted her.

Although it was only four in the afternoon, the shadows were already lengthening, reminding them both that their time together was growing ever shorter.

"Give me a minute, and I'll bring something to the table. Do you think you could manage in the dining room? Everything you need for setting the table is either in the sideboard or the china cabinet."

"I'll manage. Don't be long." Ryan pressed a kiss on her upturned lips. "I'm already lonely."

Happily, Penny entered the kitchen and rummaged in the pie safe for leftovers to make a quick dinner. She sliced some cheese and ham, put the leftover sweet potatoes in the oven to warm, and sliced two pieces of red velvet cake. At the last minute she spread some butter on the bread from the day before and toasted it on the hot stovetop. It's simple fare, she thought, *but* it will have to do. Surveying the tray she rued the lack of fresh vegetables and the salad greens she so loved, but in winter they were still months away.

When she entered the dining room, the table was set, candles lit, the fireplace newly poked up, and the champagne opened. Ryan ushered her to the seat at the head of the table and then seated himself beside her.

Pouring the champagne, he lifted his glass in a toast. "Until my return, may you keep safe."

"Until your return, may you keep safe as well," Penny responded. "You'll be in far more danger than I am here. Our visitor today was a fluke. Strangers generally don't see the lane to the house because I've made it a point to make it as unobtrusive as possible."

"Is there anything more you can do to discourage scavengers and trash like that man floating in the creek?"

"I've been thinking about that. I'm going to have Moses and his daughter help me move the split-rail fence around the paddock down to the road. With only old Polly and the mules stabled down in the woods, we don't really need it. I figure if I use the rails I can build a fence along the road across the entrance to the lane. I can always circle around it with the horse or climb over on foot; however, it means I won't be able to use the wagon or buggy and that could be a problem. I can't go to church on horseback because my neighbors would be scandalized. And I won't be able to haul supplies in or produce out."

"You could hide the wagon or the buggy across the road in the woods and cover it with brush. That way, if you need it you can access it. It just means that you have to haul things from the road to the house or vice versa. And don't worry about the neighbors. In wartime no one is immune from changes to the normal way of doing things."

"That's for sure." Penny heaved a heartfelt sigh. "Let's not think about war tonight. I'm already so sick of it."

"I am as well." Ryan steeled himself not to think about the dangers that the coming days, months, and possibly years would bring him; otherwise, he knew he would despair. Deliberately he pushed that to the back of his mind and began to regale her with stories of his boyhood escapades and some of the funny events in camp. She laughed until tears ran when he told her about this old man in Virginia who had come from his house brandishing a sword left from the Mexican War and begun whipping one of Ryan's soldiers on the behind while he was trying to steal apples from the old man's tree. "Poor Joel dropped all of the apples and ran. He wasn't hurt except for his bruises and, of course, his pride. I'm glad it was Joel and not one of the more brutish ones or the old man might not have fared so well." He paused and asked, "Have you been to New Berne, Penny?"

"A couple of times, but it's been a while. I haven't been since y'all captured it and moved in."

"It's a beautiful little town. During the months that I have been there, I have come to like walking the tree-lined streets and admiring the prosperous homes. I love looking out over the water. When I have time, I take a sailboat out and sail up and down the Neuse and Trent rivers that meet there. I was told it was settle by the Swiss, hence the name New Berne, and it was at one time the capital of colonial North Carolina."

"That's right. There was a beautiful capital building for the governor that was the talk of the colonies. Unfortunately, it burned in 1798 and only the foundations and the stable remain. Actually New Berne was originally named Neuse-Berne, and the name eventually evolved to New Berne. The Neuse part of the name for the river, and Berne for the home town of Baron Christoph Van Graffenried, who received the charter in the name of the Swiss Company to found a settlement there. Many descendents of the Palatines, as they were called, live not only in New Berne but all the way to Pollocksville and Trenton, as well as Kinston."

"I'm thinking about buying a piece of land that I have my eye on once the war is over. I don't know what I would do with it, but it's so beautiful I ache with wanting it every time I see it. Obviously I know nothing about farming, but it's just on the edge of town and I can practice law anywhere. I'm just not sure now much business I could expect as a Yankee.

"Eventually the Confederacy will lose," he continued. "It doesn't have the resources to compete against the industrial might of the Union. A defeated people hold even greater animosity against the victors than the victors do against the defeated. It might be a long time before I'm welcome."

"Ryan, I won't lie to you, it will be very difficult. In the South, we trace our roots back and family matters a lot to us. There are families here who've been here since they came over from Europe. And most of us are kin or related in some way, no matter how distant. The first thing people do when they meet someone new is find out who they're kin to, who their grandparents and great-grandparents were. Even a southerner from another area is an outsider as far as they're concerned. For you, the obstacle is even greater. You're not only a northerner but you serve in an army that is occupying our land and at times doing so with brutality and vengeance. People will be slow to forget."

"Yes, I fear that's true. But I intend to wage a careful, personal, low-key campaign to appease when possible, charm if I'm able, and outright make friends with the New Bernians with whom I come in contact. It won't be easy and it'll take time. But people are people the world over, both good ones and bad ones. I'm going to trust that the decent people will react with decency if I treat them with decency, respect, and concern, even knowing that I am their enemy by political divide."

"Ryan, are you so sure we will lose?"

"It's only a matter of time. You simply don't have the resources in the South to sustain this kind of war. You arguably have the best generals to lead your army, but the biggest advantage you have is bold courage and determined cussedness, plus you're fighting on home turf. I would never have believed the tenacity with which your men fight in the face of such overwhelming odds. Also, your boys grew up toting guns and shooting. That puts our mill workers and factory laborers who never touched a gun before at a disadvantage. But they learn really fast when it's their lives on the line. I also think that because your army is essentially a non-professional one, they have a more freewheeling and creative way of thinking, which is a certain advantage for them."

"I would like to think you're wrong about us losing. I hate to think of so much loss of life and property all for nothing." Penny sipped slowly on her champagne, thinking. "In North Carolina we're different from some other southern states. In some ways we are almost two states, as many of the mountain people are pro-Union. There are few slaves there and for that matter less anywhere in our state than some. For instance, South Carolina has far more slaves than we do. We don't have as many large plantations. More often it's small farmers tending their own land, raising their own crops. The right of the sovereign states to determine their own rights and regulations is far more important to the bulk of our populace than slavery. Yes, we do have slave owners who hate to see the loss of the institution. There are those right here in this community who adamantly defend their right to own slaves, my father and father-in-law among them. I'm not one of them. I deplore slavery and all it implies and refuse to have it on my land. That I can control, but I cannot, nor have I the right, to tell my neighbors and kin what to believe and feel. For them it's a matter of economics. They think slave labor is cheaper. Considering the initial cost and the destruction of morale, I disagree. My workers are paid, granted not a lot, but they also have housing and food, and because they are freed men they work harder for me than those on my families' farms. I first got the idea as a teenager when I met Blackledge Harper. He has over a thousand acres near Deep Run and uses only paid labor, no slaves. I figured if he could do it, I could, too. My family and Daniel were both upset with me, but I stood my ground until they gave in."

"I admire your courage in bucking family tradition in that regard. I'm sure it wasn't easy, but then I suspect that would never stop you from doing what you believe to be right." Ryan paused, glancing around the room. "Penny, when I'm gone remove your valuables from the house and hide them somewhere they'll be safer. The door to your cellar is so well hidden no one could find it if he didn't know where to look and how to spring the latch. Do the same thing with a reserve of food, seeds, metal tools that can be melted down for bullets and weapons, and the other things you cannot afford to lose. Of course, that still leaves the danger of fire. That man today may not be the last to find his way here. Next time, there may be no one to help you. I fear for you, darling."

"I'll be more careful. I was foolish today and far less wary than I should have been. I should have trusted my instincts more because I knew he was trouble when I heard the hoof beats. I promise not to let it happen again. If you had not been here, I would have paid a heavy price for my negligence."

"Enough," Ryan said as he pushed back his chair and stood. "Let me help you get these things to the kitchen and then I'm going to go check on my new horse. I've decided to call him Windfall since he came unexpectedly and at an opportune time. Not that his rider was welcome, but the horse, yes. After that, I'd very much like to go upstairs with you."

In the kitchen, Penny busied herself cleaning and stowing the things they had used while Ryan checked on the horse. Mammy had been in, and Penny was pleased to note the tow sack filled with food that she had prepared for Ryan's journey. It was enough for two or three days, even though if luck were with him he might even manage in less time. She wondered if he were recovered enough for the possible rigors he might encounter but decided other than a last check of the wound, she would not challenge his decision to leave so soon. She realized it was for the best, even as she mourned the necessity of it.

Ryan walked in just as she was banking the kitchen fires and wordlessly extended his hand to her. She took it and quietly followed him into the house for another night in his arms, perhaps the last she would ever have. Determined not to think of that, she lifted her chin and welcomed the coming hours with his arms around her, loving her and giving her hope that tomorrow could bring happiness. Somehow, if only she believed, surely God would not leave her to live her life the way she had endured the last three years.

All too soon dawn arrived. Neither of them was sleeping. Not wanting the last of their time together lost to oblivion they had held one another throughout the night, sometimes making love, occasionally talking softly.

Ryan kissed her on the face and sought her lips. "I do love you, you know? In five days, you've changed my life and I'm so glad for it."

"Even if it brings complications? But, yes, I love you, too, even so."

"Divorce is a possibility if it comes to that. Let's just trust in the fate that brought us together to find a way for us to make a future with one another." Ryan held her tightly to him. "I have to go, dear one."

"I refuse to say goodbye."

"No need. I'll be back, so let's copy the French and say 'au revoir'."

"Until we meet again, darling Ryan."

Climbing from the bed, they quickly donned their clothes. Ryan rolled his uniform in a bundle and tied it in an old pillowcase. He would stuff it into the saddlebag on Windfall and hope he wouldn't have to explain it. Together they went to the kitchen, where Mammy had hot biscuits, bacon, fried eggs, grits, and coffee waiting.

Ryan beamed with pleasure when he saw her efforts for him. "Pack your bags, woman. You're coming with me."

"Lawsy, Mistah Ryan. You know my Moses ain' gwine tolerate me runnin' off wid another man. 'Sides I got to stay here an' see Miz Penny don' starve."

"Well, in that case, I'll not kidnap you yet."

"Thank you, Mammy. I appreciate you getting up so early to see him off with a good breakfast. I'm hungry as a bear this morning myself," Penny said around a mouthful of grits.

When Ryan was finished eating, he picked up the tow sack of provisions, walked over to give Mammy a goodbye hug, and then, pulling Penny to him, kissed her tenderly. "Soon, dear one. Soon I'll be back."

"Soon, Ryan." Penny choked back the sob that threatened to escape and bravely smiled as he walked into the early morning light. In a few minutes she heard the horse's hoof beats as he galloped down the lane. It was bad luck to watch him leave, but she had wanted to so badly it was hard to stay in the kitchen.

Turning to Mammy, she smiled brightly. "I've got work to do. I'm going to pack up some things that I don't use when I'm here all alone and then, I'm going to ask Moses and Lucinda to help me build a fence. So, do you think you could take care of the baby the next couple of days, Mammy?"

"We gwine do what we gotta do, Miz Penny." Mammy patted her hand and Penny squeezed hers in return.

"We'll manage somehow. We always do." Penny smiled. Leaving the kitchen, she began organizing for the coming project.

Chapter 6

At the end of the day Lucinda and Moses sank onto the front steps of their cabin, as tired as she was. Every bone in her body ached and her hands were a mass of blisters, but with the others helping, the fence was at last built. Using the old rails gave it a weathered look that belied its recent vintage. The wagon was ensconced in shrubs on the other side of the road and Penny had carefully carried her valuables to the cellar, grateful that the house sat on a knoll that allowed for a dry cellar. She sat at the kitchen table while Mammy rubbed her aching shoulders. The baby lolled at her feet on the pallet Mammy had put down for him.

In her gratitude, she had managed to squelch some of the animosity she felt for Lucinda. She sensed the woman was equally wary of her. For years, theirs had been an uneasy relationship. Lucinda was intelligent, ambitious, and more than a little determined to rise above her current station in life. To that end, as a child she had studied as hard as either Penny or Brett when they did their evening lessons. Sarah Bartlett had encouraged the child to learn and had loaned her own children's books and helped her with troublesome words. Despite John's disapproval, Sarah had quietly and determinedly schooled Lucinda until she had taught her as much as she could. As Lucinda matured into an attractive and openly sensual woman, Penny had watched her turn speculative eyes on the men in the neighborhood. Daniel had been one even before he and Penny had married. Even then she had suspected Daniel of an involvement with Lucinda. Now with his only child born to this woman, Penny struggled with resentment.

"Thank goodness that's finished. I don't think I could move another rail if my life depended on it."

"I sho hope you take some time fo yo'sef now. A body cain' do but so much." Mammy understood her well enough to know that part of the reason she had worked so hard was to push from her mind the loneliness she felt since Ryan's departure three days prior.

"That's for sure. Right now, I'm going to eat some supper and then heat some water for a good soaking bath. I'm too tired to carry the water up, so I think I'll bring the tub down."

"No'am. I gwine take dat water up dem steps fo' you while you eat yo' supper. I fix a fire in de fireplace, too, so you don' freeze to def. Jes watch dis here baby fo' me."

"Thank you, Mammy. I'll do that."

Penny ate her dinner as Mammy bustled about getting water. When she climbed the steps with the last pail of water, Penny picked the baby up from the floor and looked carefully into his light coffee-colored face. Were those features like his, she wondered? Putting Jeremiah down, she patted him on the head. "You can't help where you come from, can you, little man?"

When Mammy returned to the kitchen, Penny bade her a weary good-night and climbed the stairs to her room. The bath looked like heaven waiting there by the fire. Quickly she dropped her soiled clothes on the floor and climbed into the tub. She drowsed there until the cooling water drove her out. Quickly she toweled off and, pulling her gown and robe on, sat in the chair by the fire. Soon she began to nod.

She didn't know how long she slept, but the embers told her it had been at least an hour, maybe longer. For a moment, she could not remember what had awakened her. Then it came back, it was a dream. It seemed to be her father, although the face kept getting lost in the thick fog. The fog that was so much the color of his hair that she thought for a moment he had lost it all. He was calling her, telling her to take care of her mother, that he was on his way back to her. Penny had seen two horses riding behind him with one man slumped in the saddle. She could not tell if he were injured or just tired, nor could she see his face. "Tomorrow I must go to Mama," she whispered to herself, "but for now I'm going to bed."

It was raining when she awoke and the thought of going out into the weather made her want to roll over and stay in the warm bed. Drat it all, she swore. I know I have to get up from here and get going. Weary and still aching from the unaccustomed hard manual labor of the last few days, Penny dressed and went down to breakfast.

Mammy was bending to take hot biscuits from the oven when Penny entered the kitchen. Mammy brought the biscuits to the table as Penny seated herself, and placed them beside the scrambled eggs, butter, and jam that were already on the table.

Penny reached for the pot and poured a cup of the bitter chicory coffee. "Is there any more sugar, Mammy?"

"No'am, I 'fraid not. I git you some honey fo' dat coffee."

"Thanks, Mammy. I'm going to see Mama today and I'll see if I can borrow some sugar from her. If not, maybe someone over there is riding into town and they can pick up some for us."

"It mighty messy out der dis mawnin fo' ridin' 'round de coun'ryside."

"I have to, Mammy. Pa told me to go."

"You done dream agin?"

"I did. It's okay. He's on the way home."

"It do beat all, how you do dat." Mammy shook her head.

"I just wish Pa'd told me to wait until the rain stops." Penny laughed.

When she finished her breakfast and cleaned and stored her dishes, she found an old topcoat of Daniel's and a felt hat. They would at least keep some of the rain off, she hoped. She stuffed the revolver in her pocket and picked up the bottle of Lily of the Valley tea she had made for her mother. The decoction seemed to ease some of her heart symptoms.

Moses had Polly saddled and waiting by the passageway when Penny emerged from the back door.

"Thanks, Moses. You're a dear. And in case I haven't said it before, I just want you to know how much I appreciate you helping me build that fence."

"Miz Penny, don' you worry 'bout it none. I glad to do it. Now you be kerful lak gwine ober to yo Mama's."

"I'll do it, Moses. Expect me back by supper," Penny called as she rode away.

It wasn't a particularly cold day, but because of the damp, by the time she reached her mother's door she was chilled to the bone. Going in the back entry, she called out, "Anybody home?"

Nancy answered from her mother's sunroom in the rear of the house. Windows on three sides made it brighter than the other rooms and her mother loved to lie on the chaise lounge there and read. "We're in here, Penny. Come on back."

Penny walked into the room and closed the door to keep the heat from the roaring fire trapped inside. The cold weather was a terrible vexation for her mother, since her heart condition affected her circulation, making her feel the cold more so than other people. Her mother was indeed in her usual spot, dressed in a flowing dressing gown of softest pink. Nancy, sitting by the fire in a straight back chair, was a total opposite. She didn't sit so much as stand erect while seated. Her spine was as stiff as a ramrod, her features austere to the point of skeletal, and with the drab gray Spartanly plain dress there was nothing that rendered her soft and feminine. Penny noted once again that it was little wonder that the woman had remained a spinster. Fortunately, what she lacked in looks she made up for in just plain goodness. There wasn't a mean or selfish bone in her body. Whenever she was needed you could count on her being there, no questions, no payment asked. Obviously the room was overly warm for her, as her face was beaded with perspiration.

"Hey, Mama, Nancy. Y'all doing okay this morning?"

"Penny, angel, you get yourself over here and give your mama a kiss. I've been so worried about you. It's been days. I just don't know what you've been up to to stay so busy."

Penny bent to kiss her cheek as ordered and turned to Nancy. "Nancy, if there are any angels in this room, it's you. You just don't know how much I appreciate you helping us out while Pa's away."

"Don't mention it, Penny. I'm glad to do it. Besides, I think my parents like getting me out of the house from time to time." Nancy smiled at Penny in high good humor.

"Nancy, why don't you get yourself a breath of fresh air while I visit with Mama. And if you don't mind, ask Delia if she has any extra sugar I could borrow. We're completely out."

"Thanks, I'll go do that right now."

When Nancy left, Penny took her mother's hand and softly said, "Mama, Pa's going to be home soon. He wants you to take care of yourself for him. I brought some medicine to stimulate your heart. I want you to drink it for me. You've not had any more spells, have you?"

"I confess, it's been worse than usual because I've been so worried about John. You know we've heard nothing since he left and with so many injured, killed, or taken prisoner, I'm just about beside myself." Her mother sighed. "Oh, Penny, I'd die if something happened to your father. And I worry all the time about my boy, too. Brett's written us nothing lately."

"I know, Mama. But he's going to be fine and he's coming home, I just feel it. Pa's coming, too, and it won't be long now, so you stop worrying and feel better. You don't want him to be all upset if he gets home and finds you doing poorly, now do you?"

"You know not." Her mother smiled gently. "And you, darling. You look so tired. What have you been doing with yourself?"

"Building a darned fence." She had no intention of divulging the days spent with Ryan. Her mother would never understand.

"What on earth are you doing building a fence?" Sarah asked in shock. "That most certainly is not work for a woman."

"I wanted a little insurance against intruders." Penny had no intention of explaining the most recent motivation for that, either.

"I wish a fence would solve it for us. Sitting so close to the road this way, we had both armies stopping by here on the way to fight. Delia told them the doctor had quarantined me because I'd caught cholera. They couldn't light out of here fast enough. They surely didn't want to come in the house after that, I can tell you. And bless Marcus for getting the livestock hidden and the meat from the smokehouse into the attic when he heard they were coming."

"I know, Mama." Penny had heard the same story on her previous visit and worried that her mother was becoming increasingly repetitive and forgetful.

56

Sarah drank some of the tea that Penny had made. While she continued to sip it, they talked on in companionable fashion. Because of her location on the main road, they got more news than Penny. She told Penny that she had just heard that James and Percy Ann Nunn's son Ben had died in the fall in some hospital in Maryland. The family still had not heard exactly when or where his body was, only that he had died of a wound he received at Sharpsburg. Not all of the news was bad. Sarah and Nalphus Johnson's four-year-old, Madison, and their little daughter Mary Susan were finally over the croup thanks to the herbs that Penny had sent. Nalphus was away serving with Martin in Virginia and had not been heard from either. Calvin and Martha Herring had a healthy new baby, Eveline. That made two children for the Herrings, as they already had a year-old son, Curtis, who had just begun to walk.

Both women turned at the sound of Nancy's shouts and pounding feet as she ran into the room.

"Penny!" she called. "Can you come to the kitchen, please?"

Sarah sighed. "Delia probably burned her hand again. That will make three times this week. I swaney, she has been so distracted lately."

"I'll see to her, Mama. Don't go worrying now." Penny hurried to the door and, closing it behind her, met Nancy in the hall. Penny held her finger to her lips in warning.

Nancy whispered to her, "It's your father. He's in the kitchen and he's hurt. I can't tell how badly, Penny. But he surely needs a doctor."

Alarmed for her father and her mother's probable reaction to the news, Penny ran ahead of Nancy to the kitchen. When she entered she saw her father slumped onto the table and realized from the posture that it was he she had seen slumped in the saddle in her dream. Seated at the table with him were a weary Fitz Kennedy and Nalphus Johnson.

"Glad you're back, Nalphus. Your wife, Sarah, is going to be thrilled to see you." Turning to her father-in-law, she asked, "Is he conscious?"

"Just barely. He's badly hurt. He took a bullet to his lower leg. The medic dug it out but I fear it's become infected, probably from riding through muddy swamp water and creeks. His fever's pretty high, Penny."

"If you men will help me get him on the table, I'll see what can be done. Delia, would you hand me the scissors?"

Her father opened his eyes for a moment and weakly tried to smile at her. She leaned forward to hear what he was trying to say. It sounded like, "Don't tell your mother until you see if you can fix me."

"Shh, Pa. You're going to be fine, I promise. And Mama is doing better, so try not to worry. Just rest and let me get to work on your leg."

Penny quickly cut his pants leg away while Fitz eased off his boots. Without asking, Nalphus fetched a bucket of water and put it on the fire to heat. When the leg was free of the blood, dirty water, and the pus-soaked bandage,

Penny examined the wound. It would have to be opened and the pus drained if he had any chance at all of keeping it.

"Nalphus, let me know when that water starts boiling. Would you find a really sharp knife and hold it over the flame until it's red hot?" She looked up and smiled at him. "By the way, you'll be glad to know Mama told me she heard both of your children have recovered from the croup."

"Thanks, Penny. We appreciate all of your help. Sarah wrote me that you made some treatments for them," he replied as he searched for a sharp knife.

"Nancy, I need some whiskey and clean bandages. Delia, tell her where to find them and then see if you can find some maggots for me. I may need them to clear out any decayed tissue. Also send someone over to my house and have Mammy Rena pack me a couple of days of clothes and the herbs I need for treating fever and a wound. She knows what they are. Oh, and do take send her some sugar if you have any to spare. Fitz, I need you and Nalphus to hold him still when I open the wound."

Delia and Nancy hastened to do her biding. Nancy was back quickly with the whiskey. "Here's the liquor. I figure you need it soonest. I'll go get the bandages now."

"Thanks, Nancy." She lifted her father's head and said, "Pa, if you can drink some of this, you won't feel what I'm about to do quite so much."

Obediently he took some of the whiskey while she held it to his lips. His eyes met hers. "Don't take off my leg, little girl. Please."

"We won't, Pa. You're going to be standing on both of them soon."

Penny could only hope it wasn't a lie. The wound was seriously suppurated and taking the leg might be the only way to save his life. She knew she lacked the skills to do it properly and they would have to fetch Dr. Miller if it came to amputation. One bright note was that she could see no sign of gangrene yet. Penny poured some whiskey over the infected site and gently mopped it as clean as she could.

"Okay, if you could hold him still I would appreciate it."

In order to render him immobile during the surgery, Fitz stationed himself at her father's shoulders while Nalphus secured his legs.

Penny took a deep breath and exhaled slowly. "Hang on now, Pa. It's going to hurt like Hades."

Quickly she sliced into the wound and watched as bloody pus poured from the incision. She allowed the pus to flow until it seemed to stop, then spreading the wound she poured in more of the whiskey. Nancy had quietly entered the kitchen, and Penny spoke softly to her. "Hand me some hot compresses, please. Dip them in the water and wring them out. I want them as hot as you can stand without burning yourself."

"I think your father has passed out, Penny," Nalphus observed.

"It's a blessing. Hopefully I can finish hurting him and get him bandaged before he comes to." Taking the compresses that Nancy handed her, she pressed them over the wound, hoping to both encourage more pus to release itself and to bring healing blood to the area. Satisfied that she had done all she could for the moment, she wrapped the leg, leaving the wound open so it could drain.

"If you men can get him up to his bed I would appreciate it. Nancy, when Delia comes in, if she has the maggots tell her to put them in a dish for me and drape a damp cloth over it to keep them in. Then get a basin of warm water and a clean washcloth. I want her to sponge my father off as best she can and put him in a nightshirt." Penny turned towards the door at the soft knock.

Coming in without waiting for an invitation, Marcus, her father's overseer, handed her the bundle of clothes and herbs that he had fetched from her home. "These are the things you asked for. I just want to say I sure am sorry about your father. If there's anything I can do to help out, just let me know."

"Thank you. You must have really hurried to get back so quickly. I appreciate you bringing me these things." Penny opened the bundle and extracted the dried Elder flowers. Finding a small kettle, she crumbled them in and added boiling water. Allowed to steep and then strained, she would give it to her father to help his system fight the infection. She had also found it useful in reducing fevers. "If you'll wait here, Marcus, when the others get back from carrying my Pa upstairs, we'll see if we can rustle up something for y'all to eat. Nancy, would you take my father this tea? If he's awake try to get him to drink it. Also, please leave a glass and pitcher of water by the bed." That done, Penny declared, "I'm going to go placate my mother. Until Pa is a bit more on the mend, I'm not going to upset her by telling her anything. I'd appreciate it if everyone will avoid mentioning any of this to her."

Nancy nodded. "I suspect that's for the best as frail as she is. I'll put some tea on soon and start putting together some supper as soon I get back from upstairs. Why don't you visit a minute with your mother before checking on your Pa? Delia and I can manage down here."

"You're a dear. Thank you. I won't be long."

When she entered the back hall, Nalphus and Fitz were descending the steps. Quietly she said, "Shh. I don't want Mama to know what's going on just yet. If ya'll go to the kitchen, Nancy will fix you something to eat. Don't leave, though, until I come down because I want to hear what happened."

"It's a hell of a story, let me tell you...excuse me, Penny...heck of a story. I've spent so much time in the company of men I'm going to have to refresh my manners around ladies." Nalphus smiled apologetically.

"Don't worry about it. I like a hell of a story," Penny said with a grin.

Fitz chuckled, shaking his head. Giving her an admiring look, he thought once again that Daniel got himself one prize of a woman when he got her.

Easing open the sunroom door, Penny walked over to her mother's chair. Sarah was breathing softly and evenly. Good, she thought, she needs the rest because I don't have any idea what the next few days may bring her. Taking her mother's book and putting it on the floor by the chair, Penny wrapped a soft blanket over her before adding more logs to the fire. She would have Delia bring her some supper and sit with her for a while.

Sarah and Delia had been together for more than three decades and got on much better than Penny did with the woman. Delia was Mammy Rena's younger sister. Where Mammy was all soft, rounded comfort, Delia was bone and hard angles with a disposition to match. Penny had suffered through enough of her harsh scolding as a child to appreciate just how stern the woman could be. With her mother, however, Delia was as soft and loving as Mammy— gentle and patient and eager to please the woman she adored. For that, Penny could tolerate Delia even as she strained to like her.

Climbing the stairs, she relished the smooth glide of her hand up the polished walnut railing. As much as she loved her new house she missed this one. It had a mellowness about it that her own lacked. Oh well, she decided, some day mine will be old and mellow, too. Pushing open her father's bedroom door, she walked over to the bed where he lay. Delia had beaten her to him. Obviously anticipating the need for a bath, she had just finished pulling on his nightshirt when Penny entered. Not only that, but a fire was blazing in the fireplace. Penny wondered just how long Delia had spent looking for maggots.

Delia looked up as she entered and a bit sheepishly apologized, "I real sorry, Miz Penny, but I jes cain fin' no maggits. I done look 'bout eberwhere I know. I figer I ought to git up here and fix up yo' Pa since I cain fin' none."

"That's fine, Delia. I'll look tomorrow. Hopefully, I won't need them, but if I do, maybe I'll have more luck." Penny thought of the body rotting in the muddy waters of the creek and shuddered. "I'm glad you thought to take care of Pa. You must have read my thoughts." Delia had always had a mind of her own so there was no point in reminding her of her earlier instructions. Over the years, Penny had found that confrontations with the woman only resulted in frustration for her.

Penny bent down to take John Bartlett's hand as Delia tucked in the covers. "Pa, are you awake?"

"I am, but I'm sorry for it. This leg of mine hurts something awful."

"I'm sorry I had to hurt you some more, but if it's to get better, there was no other choice. I've got some tea that I want you to drink. It will help you heal and it's good for your fever, too. Later I'll bring you something to help you sleep if you see you need it. As soon as Nancy finishes dinner she's going to come up and sit with you a bit and I'll be back, too." Penny patted his hand reassuringly. "You rest now. You need it.

"Delia, when you get everything finished up here, come down and have some supper and then if you will, take Mama hers and keep her company while she eats it. I have a tea for her as well to help her sleep."

"Yas'am, I be der dereckly," Delia promised as Penny walked to the door.

"Penny, I'd greatly prefer whiskey to tea, if you don't mind, or maybe a bottle of Daniel's fine wine." Her father gave a ghost of his old smile to her.

"Another time, Pa. You already got your whiskey for tonight."

Penny walked out chuckling. Her father always knew how to bring a smile no matter how grim the circumstances.

Nancy had the meal on the table and Fitz and Nalphus were busy polishing off a big slice of apple pie. Judging by the obviously diminished platters, they had eaten ravenously while she was seeing to her father.

Penny noted the plate Marcus had left on the table and assumed he had left to attend to evening chores. "So how on earth did all this happen and what's been going on since Pa left here?"

"Nalphus, I'll get the story started and then you can take over," Fitz began. "Well, Penny, when your Pa and I rode off we headed on over to the Bectons' place at Wise Forks, where some of our troops were camped out. We figured we might be too old for digging and such, but we're both damned good shots. And before we let those damned Yankees walk all over us, we might as well let them know we're here. At any rate, it appears they got a couple of our scouts and persuaded them to talk. Before we knew what hit us, they had us surrounded. Over a dozen of us were killed as best I could figure and they took eleven of us captive, John and me being two of that bunch. They took our horses, so all we had to depend on were old Pat and Charlie here," Fitz snorted as he slapped his thighs. Penny could see that he relished reliving every moment of the drama.

"Well, sir, they marched us until we were plum tuckered and we kept falling further and further behind. Our guard wasn't much to speak of and didn't figure old codgers like us could be too dangerous. He was getting tired, too, so when he looked away, we took our chance and ducked off the road into the woods. The guard fired after us and that's when one of his bullets got your Pa. Thank the Lord he was too sorry to get down off his horse and come after us. We laid low in the woods the rest of the night and then started walking trying to meet up with some more of our boys. It was mighty slow going with your father limping bad and in fierce pain. Finally we ran into the scattered remnants of our company on Upper Trent Road. They had a medic with them and he dug the bullet out. He didn't have much to work with except a dirty pocketknife since everything he'd been carrying got left over at the Bectons' when he scampered. Our boys were busy trying to get dug in for an attack and it was obvious we weren't going to be much help at that, but we bedded down for a couple of nights with them. I figured if the Yankees attacked we'd just dive in and do some shooting. Well, it soon looked like your Pa was getting worse not better.

"By the last morning there your Pa was in right smart pain so I took him to Zenas Parker's place. His wife, Mary, did her best to clean him up and get him comfortable but it was obvious she didn't know much about treating wounds like that. After a couple of days, I decided I'd better try to get him to a doctor in Kinston and get that wound looked after. So we started trying to walk Wilmington Road into Kinston since the Parkers' horses and mules had all been confiscated. Under the best of circumstances that's a pretty good walk, but considering your Pa's condition it looked neigh on to impossible. John's a determined man, though, and he said he was damned well going to make it, so we kept going. By the time we got to Woodington, we could tell things were in a mess where there'd been a passel of fighting all around. I decided we couldn't go much further without some rest, so we stopped at the Waller farm. They gave us some supper and put us up for the night. By the way, their cousin's place got burned out."

"Yes, I know," Penny said.

"Next morning we set out again and we hadn't gone far, when we heard horses coming. Well, I just about had a heart attack, I can tell you, because we didn't have anything except a pistol the Parkers' had given me and three bullets. That was all they figured they could spare, I reckon. So we crawled back into the bushes and waited. Well, we no sooner got ourselves hidden than the horses stopped and these two Yankee scout fellers started walking into the woods to answer a mighty urgent call of nature. Well, they set about their business serious as could be, never knowing we were there. By the way they were groaning I think they ate something that didn't agree with them. I got them both before they could get their pants up.

"That's how we got us horses. Kinston looked more likely at that point, so we kept on going. The bridge was torn out so we had to swim the horses over Southwest Creek. Kinston was messed up something awful, yes-siree. What the damned bombardment didn't get, the Yankees about finished off when they got into town.

"I couldn't find Dr. Miller or Dr. Woodley, so I went looking for Dr. Smith. That was a pure waste of time. He was determined to take John's leg. After all he'd been through, John was about crazy with pain and aggravation and purely determined he was going to keep his leg. He grabbed my pistol with the one bullet left and told him he'd addressed it in the doctor's name and if the doctor came any closer, he was going to see to it got delivered. At that point Dr. Smith prudently decided he wouldn't be taking on any new patients, so we decided we might as well get on home. We started to saddle up when we saw Nalphus here riding down the street. All right, boy, I've about talked enough so it's your turn with this here story."

Nalphus began, "As Mr. Fitz said, I was riding down the street and saw the two of them and it was obvious even from where I was that Mr. John was in trouble. So I rode up to them and asked if I could help. They told me they were trying to get here. Since I wanted to go home and see Sarah for a couple of days before going back to war and y'all are close by, I told them I'd ride along and help if needed."

Penny interrupted, "Excuse me, Nalphus, but I thought you were in Virginia with General Martin. What are you doing back in Kinston?"

"I am stationed in Virginia. At the same time General Foster was attacking here, we were fighting around Fredericksburg. Fortunately we were luckier than the troops here and manage to win the battle. After losing New Berne to Burnside, it felt mighty good to us to give him a whipping when we got the chance. Afterwards, hearing the railroad bridge in Goldsboro was being attacked, Martin decided to send a courier to Goldsboro to report to General Evans and find out what was going on down here. He picked me. When I got to Goldsboro, our troops were already repairing the bridge. It shouldn't be more than another day or so before it's back in use. Not finding Evans there, I asked them where he was and they told me he was probably holed up with his bottle in Kinston, so I high-tailed it here.

"I came through Whitehall on the way and I can tell you there's not much left. They had themselves one heck of a bonfire, burned some two thousand barrels of turpentine, and set fire to the town. The Union sent a swimmer to torch the gunboat we're building there but our artillery kept him busy enough dodging bullets so he didn't have time to do anything. The gunboat had little damage. I took a look at it and it is for sure a wonder, I can tell you. I can hardly wait to see it firing on the Union boats along the coast. When that happens, it ought to ease things a little with the blockade.

"Well, I got to Kinston after some trouble and reported in to General Evans, who'd taken a room at the St. Charles Hotel. When I found him he was reeling drunk, celebrating losing the battle, I suppose. His officers are purely disgusted, I can tell you. After delivering the letter from General Martin, I have permission to take a three-day leave to see my family. I'll go back to Evans for any papers he's sending Martin, then catch the ShooFly from Kinston to Goldsboro, as the bridge will be open again by then, and from there go on back to Virginia."

"What's the ShooFly, Nalphus?" Nancy asked.

"That's the daytime train between Kinston and Goldsboro. They call the night train the Cannonball. That stretch of railroad is called the Old Mullet Line because it hauls fresh fish from the coast inland. I always get a laugh out of that name."

Penny, having heard no mention of Brett and Daniel, who were serving in the same company, was compelled to learn if he knew anything about them.

"I'm sorry, Penny. I know you're worried and I should have told you right off. Brett was in the fighting at Fredericksburg and he's fine. He sent a letter for y'all that I gave to Mr. John this morning. As for Daniel, last I heard he was still in the hospital in Richmond but doing better and should be back with us soon.

"I thank you for the supper, but I need to get going. I don't have much time at home and as you can imagine, I want to see my family."

"Of course, Nalphus. You go on and thank you for taking your time to help Pa." Penny hugged him as he was leaving. "When you see Brett, tell him we love and miss him. And if Daniel gets back to the company, ask him to write me. I've heard nothing in months. You'd think Phineas Davenport's instruction at Woodington School House, not to mention the year at Lenior Collegiate Institute, would have taught him to write. I'll send letters over to your house before you leave if you'll be good enough to take them for me."

"Be glad to; just send them to me."

Fitz stood and gave Penny a hug. "You and Nancy excuse me; I'm ready to be home and in my own bed. I'll come back over tomorrow and check on your Pa. Goodnight, ladies. Lock up behind me."

Chapter 7

Ryan's trip to New Berne was not quite so quick and easy as he had hoped. With Confederates quietly leaving their posts to go home and check on families that had been in the path of the recent battles around Kinston, the road was crawling with men who would have happily sent him to perdition. Tired of hacking his way through underbrush when he was forced from the road, he decided to leave the road and skirt around the northern edge of Dover Swamp and try to navigate the railroad bed to New Bern. It ran mostly through swamp and woods, so he wouldn't be so exposed.

By that time he had consumed most of a day and with night approaching, he just wanted to pile up some pine branches and make a bed that would give him some protection from the cold. He found a small spring that ran with clean clear water and set about making camp. With his shoulder beginning a serious throbbing, he knew the hacking had not done him any good. Once he finished his makeshift pallet he saw to Windfall, who was proving to be as steady a mount as he could have wished for. He was grateful that Penny had thought to tell him about the oats in the barn that he could get on the way out; otherwise, the horse would have had nothing but some winter grass. With the horse fed, he rummaged in the tow sack until he found the ham biscuits Mama had packed for him. There was also a generous piece of the red velvet cake that Ryan had instantly loved with the first rich moist bite. With his stomach satisfied, he took the blanket from the knapsack and shook it out, praying it wasn't too infested. He regretted he had not thought to get one from Penny, as the idea of vermin on his body made him itch just to think about it.

It was a miserable night. His shoulder ached relentlessly and no matter how he turned, the pine branches managed to find a way to poke him. Thinking about the filthy blanket made him toss it to one side, but it was so cold he ended up hauling it back. But the worst misery was his loneliness for Penny. He cheerfully would have sold his soul at that moment to be holding her in his arms in her warm bed. Somehow he swore he would find a way to see her before too much time elapsed. He promised himself that no matter the problems, she was going to be his some day. Thoughts chased around his head like dogs after a squirrel. Strive as he might, he couldn't see any easy solutions for their dilemma. When he thought of the other man who could claim her as his wife, his heart ached with sadness. When he thought of the man who had tried to rape her, the murderous rage he had felt again coursed through his veins. When he thought of the dangers that she would continue to face as a lone woman, attended by only two old people, their daughter, and her infant, he worried. When dawn began to lighten the woods around him enough he could resume his journey, he was glad to leave his pallet and go.

By mid-morning he reached the railroad bridge and turning east, headed for New Berne. As best he could recall from the headquarters' maps, he had to cross about fifteen miles of swamp. If he were forced to leave the railroad bed, to escape detection or to allow for a train, he would be in treacherously swampy terrain. By a bit after noon he felt he was making good time. Congratulating himself on progress was to prove premature.

Windfall suddenly started limping. Ryan reined him in and jumped from the saddle.

"So what's wrong, fellow? I sure don't won't you to go lame on me." He walked him a couple of steps forward, observing the horse's gait. "Uh-huh, looks like that front hoof is giving you some trouble."

Ryan pulled up the lame hoof to see what was causing the problem. Wedged in the tender part of the hoof was a stone that he must have picked up from the rail bed. Using his knife he pried it out and put the hoof down. Windfall shifted about but still seemed to be favoring that hoof. Ryan's day had just grown longer.

He was hungry, too, so he sat on the edge of the trestle and ate another ham biscuit. With a sigh, Ryan stood up when he had finished his meal and started walking, leading the horse behind him. He trudged on a little, noticing the cardinals that hopped about in the pine trees adding a bright red note to the green and brown winter landscape. Occasionally a blue jay would flit through the branches. Their singing and the chirring of squirrels was the only noise that broke the quiet other than that made by man and horse. Ryan prayed it would stay that way. By the time he emerged from the swamp, the sun was settling low in the sky. He had been forced to stop repeatedly during the hours of walking to rest until he could draw on enough reserved energy to continue. Exhaustion threatened with every step.

He knew he would have to camp yet another night, as he still had about seven miles to go. He hoped by walking and then letting the horse rest overnight, he would be able to ride by morning. He didn't relish the idea of being on foot in the countryside, where he would be more exposed.

Finding a likely spot of woods with a clear stream for water, he again set about making a camp. Instead of trying to hack pine branches, fearing further damage to his shoulder, he started gathering the brown straw-like broom sedge that grew in abundance on the edge of the woods. At least there would be no branch ends to gouge his weary bones and with enough straw he could forego the blanket. He pulled out the blue poncho-like cape that was a part of his winter issue to use for warmth, regretting that he had not thought of it before. He gave Windfall the last of the oats and pulled out the final ham biscuit. Looking longingly at the last piece of cake, he reluctantly left it in the sack since it would be the only food for breakfast the following day. He would have liked to start a fire but feared the odor of smoke carrying on the humid air would be detected by a nearby farmer. In the fading light he glanced anxiously at the lowering clouds, praying the rain would hold off until he could get back to New Berne.

It was a hungry, dirty, and weary man who trudged into headquarters the next day. The clerk at the desk in the outer office looked up when he entered. Ryan had changed into his uniform in a small copse of woods on the edge of town. Had it not been for that, Sgt. Jim Spangler would not have recognized the New York Calvary Colonel, as he had never before seen him with an unshaven face nor smelled the reek of body odor on him.

"Colonel Madison, it's good to see you! We thought you was lost in the action at Southwest Creek. I'm mighty glad to see you made it, sir."

"So am I." Ryan smiled but was too tired for more friendly chatter. "Would you tell General Foster I'm reporting in? Unless there's some pressing urgency to see him now, I'll see him later after I have a chance to bathe and get something to eat."

"Yes, sir. No problem, sir. He ain't here no how. When he comes in, I'll tell him you're back. He'll be happy for sure, as he's flat out missed those poker games with you."

That done, Ryan went looking for his orderly, Bobby Richards, to request bathwater, soap, towels, and something to eat after his bath. As hungry as he was, he could not stand another minute without a bath. He knew the frequency with which he bathed was a joke with his men, who could go weeks without bathing and not regret it.

He had bathed and was toweling dry when Bobby returned to his quarters bearing a tray of steaming food. Ryan wrapped the towel around his hips and inhaled deeply. The aroma of coffee had never smelled so good. Smiling in genuine pleasure, he remarked, "Bobby, right now if you were a woman, I'd be tempted to marry you. That tray is the best-looking thing I've seen in three days." Ryan laughed. "The bath water is a close second."

"I'm so glad to see *you* back, if you were a woman, I'd marry *you*," Bobby replied, laughing. "Regrettably, they assigned me to Colonel Mix when you didn't come back. He's okay, I suppose, but not nearly as good to work for as you are. He tends to be a trifle contentious and overbearing. I think he's jealous of your popularity with the men, judging by some of his comments. I hope I'm there when he hears you're back."

Bobby continued, eyeing Ryan's exposed shoulders. "I see you took a bullet but it looks like it's healing okay."

"I had a good doctor," Ryan offered without explanation.

Smiling with satisfaction when he had eaten his fill, he leaned back in the chair to enjoy the coffee. Bobby had taken the clothes he had worn to be washed and his uniform to be cleaned. He intended to keep the clothes Penny had given him for visits to the Woodington community. Now that he had made the trek, he thought he had a better understanding how to do it more expeditiously. He knew he had to be with Penny whenever he could manage time away. He would take her sugar, tea, coffee, flour, and all of the things that would make it better for her. For the moment, there wasn't much more he could do, except to put out the word that her farm and the neighboring one belonging to her parents were strictly off limits. Whether or not that would be sufficient, he didn't know.

The rain had begun to sound a steady rhythm on the roof by the time he had finished his coffee. With the dark of the day and the rigors of the past weeks, Ryan decided the best use of his afternoon would be rest. His men, the general, the whole damned army, the war, and all else could just wait. He was asleep by the time his head touched the pillow and did not awaken until reveille the following day. He sat up, rested and ready for the day's obligations. Following breakfast, he reported to General Foster.

"Colonel Ryan, I'm glad to have you back and see you're none the worse for wear." Foster raised one eyebrow. "Besides, I need time to win back some of that money you've won from me. Your luck at cards has to break sometime."

Ryan could tell from the tone of his voice that he was in an irascible mood. "Yes, sir. Actually, sir, for awhile I feared it had." Ryan went on to describe the events that had transpired and the reason for his survival. Although given the general's mood he knew he was pressing his luck, he requested that Penny and her parents be granted special dispensations.

Foster considered him for several long moments that had Ryan wishing he had waited. "I'll see to it," he conceded. "Sounds to me like I should order her to report for duty. She might be better than some of the sawbones we have."

Ryan breathed a discreet sigh of relief. "Thank you, sir. I appreciate it."

"Have a seat. I want to hear what you know since I left the area."

"Yes, sir. Unfortunately, I was wounded as I explained and sequestered on a remote farm. After the skirmish at Southwest Creek, I know nothing of the battle or of conditions in Kinston. On that score, I'm sure you're far better informed. Returning, I kept off the main road and for most of the way followed the train tracks through the swamp. I'm sorry I have no better intelligence to report, sir."

"I suppose it can't be helped," Foster grudgingly admitted. "Like I said, we're just glad to have you back."

He went on to reveal to Ryan just how frustrated the whole expedition had been. The loss of men in the face of minimal results was worrisome. To that end he had exaggerated his accomplishments, reporting to Washington that he had destroyed both the bridge south of Goldsboro and also the iron clad at Whitehall by ordering Henry Butler to swim over and set it afire.

He seemed embarrassingly eager to justify his deception, Ryan thought. No doubt the opposition he had encountered had left him shaken and more than a little uncertain as to his next move. His mood was unlikely to improve any time soon, Ryan surmised.

A thoughtful Ryan left the office to muster his own troops. The news had spread before him that he was back. When he entered their midst, the men greeted him with a rousing cheer that left him grateful for their loyal support.

With Christmas only four days away, Ryan's thoughts frequently returned to the memory of the farewell dinner in the pine-bough decorated dining room where he and Penny had celebrated the holiday early. Even though the daylight hours were filled with the duties his post entailed, the nights in his bed left him time to remember her and yearn for her embrace. He plotted a chance to return to her.

The opportunity came from an unexpected source. On the night of the twenty-second, General Foster sent for him. "I need you for a little reconnaissance mission since you seem to know how to move around alone a lot better than some of the others. I want to know the status of the bridge at Woodington, what's happening with that iron clad, the Wilmington-Weldon Railroad Bridge, and any other intelligence that might be useful. I'd like you to leave at dawn tomorrow if you are sufficiently recovered to do so. Feel free to requisition whatever you may need."

"Yes, sir." Ryan saluted him smartly as he departed.

He was hard put to squelch his elation at the prospect of a detour. Even though the clouds still threatened to spit rain and there were the perils of a countryside in which he would be the enemy, he didn't mind. He was up and packed before the sun had risen. When he rode out of camp on Windfall, the tow sack he had carried earlier was now bulging, not only with the food he and his horse would need, but tins of the real coffee and tea Penny adored. On the other side an additional bag held fifteen pounds of flour, ten of sugar, and ten of salt. In his breast pocket was the Christmas gift he had hastened to buy from one of the few jewelers in town that would trade with him. Most were closed except for recognized friends, and Zeke would have been, too, had it not been for a favor Ryan had done him when he took his side in an altercation with a Union soldier. Ryan was also carrying an extra pistol and bullets.

Ryan felt the strong muscles of Windfall stretching in a brisk trot. He suspected the unnamed man rotting in the muddy waters of the swamp had not been the original owner. Windfall's thoroughbred bloodlines made him an expensive animal, more than a drifter like him could afford. He had taken to Ryan immediately. Ryan absentmindedly patted the animal's shoulder as he ducked to miss a branch. He had reached the small copse on the edge of town where he would shed his uniform and don the clothes he previously had used to avoid detection.

"Whoa, boy. Time for me to get out of these duds and into some Rebel camouflage," Ryan said as he pulled on the clothes Penny had given him.

The horse whickered, giving his shoulder a small bump as he redressed. "You know what I'm saying, do you, boy?" Ryan laughed at the horse in high good humor. "You know who we're going to see? The prettiest, most glorious woman in the world, that's who."

Checking the surrounding fields before leaving the safety of the trees, he was relieved to see the stubbled land lay empty but for the tassels of old cornstalks waving gently in the rising wind. The sun was just beginning to light the horizon, making the trees of the woods on his left flank dark against the lighter sky. Until he reached the relative safety of the swamp, he would be wary, not knowing what or whom he might encounter. He had ridden only a couple of miles when he saw a wagon approaching. It looked to be loaded with hay, probably destined for calvary horses in New Berne. Or so he hoped.

As he neared the wagon, he cocked his pistol and held it in his lap, ready if he needed it. The farmer merely nodded when he drew alongside and rode on. The remainder of the journey to the lower edge of Dover Swamp where he would pick up the railroad track proved uneventful. With no mishaps, he found he was making far better time than on the previous journey. He pushed Windfall as hard as he dared, bypassing Kinston along the edge of Gum Swamp and staying to the South of the Neuse River. As he neared Kinston the terrain was so swampy on the southwestern side he was forced to drop lower, eventually emerging near the small hamlet of Sandy Foundation. A haystack in a field just past the community beckoned him. It was hidden from the road and far enough from the weathered and desolate-looking farmhouse that he felt safe. A series of ditches and shrubs between him and the house provided an added degree of security. It seemed a comfortable place to spend the night.

He shoved his bundles under the edge of the stack and pulled down enough hay to make a pallet. After eating a light supper and seeing to Windfall, he wrapped himself in a blanket and was soon sleeping under the twinkling stars as the darkening sky made him invisible to the world beyond.

"Wha' cho doin' thar, boy?" The demand was peremptory and loud enough to jar Ryan from a pleasantly erotic dream. "What?" He shook his head in momentary confusion before remembering where he was. Looking up, he met the glaring eyes of a farmer wielding a pitchfork like he meant to use it.

"Whoa, friend." He hoped he sounded a little southern. "I'm just passing through on the way from my cousin Daniel Kennedy's place over near Woodington. I've got to report back to Colonel Clingman in Goldsborough this morning. After the Yankees moved on he gave me leave to visit some family who were in the middle of the battle for Kinston. I'm real sorry if I've bothered you by being here."

The farmer stood there unsmiling, studying him. Ryan could feel sweat trickling from his armpits as he warily waited for some reaction. Finally the man relaxed and lowered the pitchfork.

"No harm done, I reck'n, jes git a move on. We don' much cotton to strangers 'round here." Ryan couldn't tell if the grim line of the man's lips had relaxed or not when he asked, "I seem ter recollect the Kennedys. They okay over thar?"

"Their place was back from the road enough, that they're all right. Some of the neighbors got real torn up, though."

"Sorry to hear it but it ain't no surprise. Them sorry Yankees messed up a streak all through here. Sons of bitches." He shook his head with disgust.

"That they did," Ryan agreed as he stood up.

Satisfied, the man walked on his way. Ryan wasted no time reloading the horse. Pulling a map from the saddlebag, he established his bearings. He was soon skirting the edge of the forest that rimmed the farm heading west toward Whitehall. By midmorning he had hidden in the edge of the woods to observe the modest repair work needed on the gunboat and was on his way to the cliffs that rose along the edge of the Neuse River just south of the railroad bridge. When he neared the bridge, he again crouched in the woods, observing the rapid repair work. Obviously Foster would not be pleased with what he had to report. That left only the bridge over the creek in Woodington, which he would check on the way to Penny's.

He knew with the shadows growing long on the ground, it would mean another night on the road before he could reach her. Whistling softly for Windfall, he climbed in the saddle to begin the trip east toward Kinston. He thought it might be better to avoid any more haystacks. Awakening with a pitchfork in his chest was not his idea of a good morning. By nightfall, he had reached Strabane, where he left the road to angle off into the woods again. Finding a protected glade tucked into the woods and the ruins of an old cabin, he decided it was as good a place as any to spend the night.

Ryan was glad to leave the saddle. Even though he had spent much time riding in the last few months, rarely had it been for such an extended period. After a light supper, he poked around the cabin ruins but decided the condition was so unsafe and unappealing he would be better off sleeping in the open. There was no broom sedge growing in the forest opening to make his pallet softer. Reluctant to make his shoulder sore again chopping pine boughs, he decided the hard ground would have to do. With the saddle for a pillow, he stretched out to sleep. It was a crisp, clear night with only a soft wind rustling the pines above his head. For a long time he lay unable to sleep. Windfall shuffled about munching some grass before he too seemed to be ready to settle for the night. Ryan watched the stars appearing, naming the constellations he could identify. Finally he fell into a fitful sleep.

Morning dawned, waking Ryan with the chirping of birds in the trees above his head. In the distance a rooster was crowing and another seemed to be answering. He gathered his things and was once more in the saddle. By midmorning he had passed the field with the haystack and was nearing the town of Deep Run. There he would skirt the small community and follow the road to Woodington, where he would check the bridge over Southwest Creek and then make his way by British Road to Penny's plantation.

He'd met a couple of wagons and several men on horseback during the past two days' excursions. Each time he had put his pistol at the ready. Keeping a steady gait, tipping his hat, and looking those he encountered in the eye seemed to give the impression that he belonged. It helped that with the war on, soldiers frequently went on unofficial furloughs to help their families out at home or just to check on them. Thus strangers on the road were not as remarkable as they would have been a couple of years earlier. Occasionally a woman at a clothesline or dipping water from a well would hold up her hand in greeting, or children would tumble from a yard where they were playing to gape at the stranger riding by. His biggest aggravation, other than extended confinement in a saddle, had been the dogs that plagued him whenever he rode by a farm. It seemed to him every household kept a pack of coon dogs that would chase after the horse, yapping at his heels until they gave up the game to plop down in hard-packed dirt yards to wait for something else to plague. Windfall never flinched. He just kept the same steady gait, ignoring any nuisances. Once again, Ryan blessed the horse if not the source of attaining him.

When he neared the creek, he paused to survey the battlefield. It was still littered with broken guns, cooking pots that had been blasted to chards, spent shells, a grease bucket, broken or bent bayonets, shovels with handles broken off, and various other paraphernalia that had been left behind in the melee. The trees told the tale of the ferocity of the battle. Some had been reduced to splintered stumps, others were missing their tops, and the rest were as ragged as tatters on a scarecrow. Their bark stripped trunks were studded with imbedded bullets. He could not help but wonder that anyone could escape such carnage. Men were not the only things killed. Horses and small animals and birds that lived in the blasted trees were also victims and their rotting bodies added to the stench. Some of the trenches that had been dug for embattlements were now mass graves with dirt thrown over the tops of the bodies to keep animals from ravaging the dead. As a boy, Ryan had loved Dante's *Inferno*. Reminded of the three volumes, he now felt as though indeed he was looking at some medieval description of an inferno, the very maw of hell. Shrugging off a sense of despondency, he climbed back on Windfall's strong back and trotted down the road to the creek.

The bridge was still in bad shape, but some support timbers had been shored up and enough planking laid that a horse or man could cross. In time it would again support wagon traffic and, if needed, the machines of war. Ryan jotted notes in the report he was preparing for Foster, ate some hardtack, and allowed his horse to drink from the creek, still roiled from a recent rain and flowing full and brown around the timbers that had fallen from the bridge. Closing his journal, he breathed a sigh of relief. It was Christmas. By nightfall, he would be with her.

Chapter 8

Penny curled up in the bed that had been hers since she out grew the cradle. It was comforting to snuggle under the fluffy covering, filled with down plucked from her mother's flock of geese, and watch the shadows of trees moving on the ceiling. A full moon made the room almost as light as day. She heaved a sigh of relief that after two days of hot compresses and the herbal teas, her father's leg seem to be improving with less puss and redness. His fever had come down as well to a less alarming level. If he continued to improve, the danger of losing his leg would be a thing of the past.

A concerned Fitz had visited each day to keep him company. As she had suspected, the wartime adventure had given him a new zest and lease on life. She had even caught him flirting with Nancy, who seemed totally at a loss as to how to react to the irascible widower.

That afternoon, when it was obvious that her father was fully alert and in less pain, she had gone to her mother and told her that her father had arrived and she had put him in his bed to rest. She helped her mother ascend the steps, taking each one slowly to avoid undue stress on her heart, and watched as she embraced the man with whom she had spent the last twenty-eight years of her life. Her father had pulled her mother onto the bed to lie curled against him with her head on his shoulder, his injured leg safely on the opposite side. Penny had smiled tenderly at her devoted parents before walking softly from the room to give them privacy.

Later she helped her mother back down the steps and to the dining room, where she and Nancy joined her at dinner. Penny noticed that her mother only picked at her plate. Raising her eyebrows in inquiry, she caught Nancy's eye; in response, the older woman lifted her shoulders and nodded. Penny knew that her mother's appetite, while never robust, had now become almost nonexistent. The arms that emerged from her lace-edged dressing gown were thin to the point of emaciation. While she was still an attractive woman, hollowed cheeks and sunken eyes now diminished the beauty to which she had once laid claim. The pale green of the dressing gown only served to exaggerate her pallor. Penny fretted over dinner, mentally running through various herbal concoctions, desperate to find one that would reverse her mother's decline. Even though Dr. Miller had been grim in his prognosis the previous fall, Penny was determined to find him wrong.

She was so lost in thought that she was momentarily startled when Nancy addressed a question to her.

"Penny, is there anything in particular that you would like to do for your parents' darkies for Christmas? Your mother was just telling me that typically they give them new clothing, a little money, and extra food for a celebration in the quarters."

"Oh, Lord, with all that's been happening recently, I completely forgot." Penny thought a moment before continuing. "There's no question of going in to town to buy anything. At the moment with Kinston so messed up, I doubt that would be worth the effort. I don't know how much money Pa has at home to work with, either. I'll ask him about it in the morning. Generally Mama helps sew clothes for all of them, but this year I have no idea how much has been made for anyone. With so many of the hands gone, I don't know what was done in the way of weaving, cobbling, and so forth. The food's not a problem. We'll have Delia get a ham or two and some sausage from the smokehouse; there's dried fruit and vegetables in the pantry and we can dig up some sweet potatoes."

In Eastern North Carolina many farms were largely self-sustaining. Shoes were made on shoe lasts that were carved to the size of each person's foot. In the cobbler's shed bearing her initials were lasts from her childhood that documented her years of youthful growth. There was no differentiation between left or right foot, as the soles were flat and the toes squared off. These were the everyday shoes of the family and the shoes of the slaves. For dressier occasions the family had driven into Kinston to purchase the shoes they needed from Curtis Supply Store.

A room downstairs in both her house and her parents' held a loom for weaving cloth, as well as spinning wheels and wooden carders for removing burrs from cotton, wool, and flax and for pulling the fibers into soft, silken fluff that could be spun. There were patterns, a large table for laying out fabric, stools for working at the wheels, chairs, and needles and scissors. The family purchased fine wool, silks, satins, damask, velvet, and any other fine fabrics. The everyday clothing of the owners was made from the same homespun as the clothes of the slaves. When clothes became worn, they were cut into squares or rectangles for quilts or into strips for rag rugs.

During the spring, summer, and fall growing seasons, every scrap of food not needed for the daily meals was preserved. Peach, apple, pear, plum, walnut, and pecan trees were planted on every farm. In the fall nuts were gathered and stored in bags in the pantry. Before a killing frost, green tomatoes were gathered and placed in the pantry to ripen, extending the fresh tomato season by a few weeks. Vinegar made from their own apples was used to preserve various kinds of pickles. Small green tomatoes and cucumbers would be made into sweet pickles. High-acid fruits and tomatoes were canned in the new sealable jars that Penny and her mother had purchased just before the war began. Prior to that they had been dried and some was still preserved that way. Jams and preserves were prepared and carefully stored in the pantry. Hot red peppers were strung on string and hung in the attic to dry, along with beans and peas that were spread on clean sheets, and herbs that were hung in bunches from the rafters. Pumpkins would be harvested and their seeds carefully saved and parched. Peanuts would be dug, onions, carrots, and turnips pulled, and any other vegetables remaining in the garden harvested before the onset of frosts. In winter collards and cabbage provided the only fresh green vegetables, as they survived all but the coldest of temperatures.

The corncrib would be filled with corn by late October or early November before the advent of the rainy late fall and winter seasons. A corn-sheller operated by a handle would shell the corn for chickens and livestock. Some shelled corn would be put in a barrel with lye and water to soak until it swelled and the husk fell away, thus making hominy, which was eaten by both humans and pigs. Popcorn made in the fireplace was a special winter treat. Potatoes were dug and put in a shed, where they would last until late winter. Sweet potatoes were dug as well and placed in special hills made by lining a slightly elevated area of soil with straw, adding the sweet potatoes, covering with more straw, and then topping it all with a sheet of tin weighed down with bricks. Stored this way, they too would last until late winter.

In the woods, huckleberries and blackberries grew in abundance, requiring only the effort of gathering, and honey trees would be noted and later carefully robbed. A few farmers tended beehives as well. Molasses and corn syrup were made to provide additional sweeteners. Along streams and ditch banks, wild watercress, dandelions, and Jerusalem artichokes were free for the gathering. Grapevines provided fresh grapes in late summer and excess grapes were made into jelly. Even the hulls were made into a sweet preserve, as was the rind of watermelons. Many of the farmers prided themselves on the scuppernong wine they made at the end of each growing season.

Chickens provided both eggs and meat, as did guinea fowl, ducks, and geese. Cows contributed milk, cheese, and butter, and in spring any extra bull calves were slaughtered for meat; however, the main meat came from hogs.

When the weather turned cold in late fall, hogs that had been fattened on roots, grain, and slops would be slaughtered. Penny's father had a large tin-lined vat that she and her brother had used for a swimming pool in summer when they were youngsters; however, at hog-killing time it would be filled with boiling water and the hog carcasses would be immersed to loosen the hairs. Afterwards, the hogs were hung by poles inserted through the leg tendons and scraped to remove any remaining hair. The carcass was then slit from throat to anus and the intestines and other internal organs carefully removed. The intestines, rinsed repeatedly to clean them of any residue, would be used for sausage casings or chitterlings, which were pickled in vinegar and seasoned with salt and pepper. Scrap meat from the body would be used to make sausage. Organ meat could not be saved and would be eaten immediately. The head was boiled and the cooked meat made into pickled souse.

Shoulders, hams, and side meat would be carved away and placed in a wooden, salt-filled vat in the floor of the smoke house to remove moisture and then hung by wire from the rafters, where they would be smoked along with air-dried sausage. Afterwards, the hams and shoulders were rubbed with pepper and wrapped in clean muslin to protect them from the larvae of skippers, then re-hung from the smokehouse rafters. Some sausage, seasoned with sage and crumbled red pepper, would be packed in cans of lard to preserve it. Fat was heated to render the lard and the leavings were placed in a special press to extract any residue of lard. Then the pressed, rendered fat would be placed in pans and dried in the oven to make cracklings. Penny hated the fat part of cracklings but the crisp bits of meat she loved and would pick out for nibbling. Sometimes Mammy would break up the cracklings and mix them into the biscuit batter. Served with molasses, it made a delicious winter breakfast. Lard, which served as a preservative, was also used in making biscuits and for frying. Some of the skin was dried and baked in the oven until crispy. The skin from butchered cows was reserved for making leather. Pigskin was rarely used for that purpose, as shoes made from it tended to stretch and quickly lose their shape.

Winter was the time for eating pork, whereas more chicken was eaten in summer, along with the occasional mess of fish from local streams and ponds. Sometimes when there was enough fish, the big iron wash pots were be placed over an outdoor fire to make fish stew. Bacon was rendered in the bottom, then onions, potatoes, and fish were added in alternating layers. Chopped tomatoes were then stirred in to make a soup-like stew and finally a few pods of red pepper were casually tossed in. It was then left to cook until the potatoes were tender. At that point eggs were cracked onto the top of the bubbling stew to coddle. Served with bread or crackers, it was a rare treat. The baying of hounds, punctuated by shots, announced the prospect of wild game: deer, rabbits, squirrels, possums, wild turkeys, and quail.

Many of the farms along creek banks had their own mills for grinding the rye and wheat grown on fertile acres into flour. Corn was ground into grits and cornmeal. The meal was used to batter fish and to make cornbread, a staple in the diet of both rich and poor.

The farmers themselves or those who had the luxury of trained slaves made many of the various tools and implements necessary for daily living.

Self-reliance had been a necessity during the days of early settlement, and for many it had become an ingrained way of life. Now with the war reducing the opportunity for trade and the lack of exportable crops with the men gone to war, those left behind on farms like theirs could survive as long as the armies left them alone and the tools did not wear out. Salt, refined sugar and flour, notoriously short-lived cotton carders, metal tools, etc., still had to be purchased, but on the whole, they could wrest their needs for a while from the soil and forests around them. The citizens of the South's towns were not so fortunate and suffered far more from the pangs of hunger.

Penny and her servants had worked hard all summer and fall, planting, tending, and preserving the food they would need for the winter. With only the four adults and an infant, they had more than an ample supply of food. She had stayed so busy on her own land that she had not monitored her parents' concerns. Besides, with her father at home, there had been no need. Now she realized how little she could provide Nancy in the way of answers. They would have to call on her father for illumination, since her mother, because of her health, had been removed from the daily running of the house.

Penny and Nancy cleared the table and took the dishes to the kitchen, where Delia would wash them. Her mother retired to her chaise, as it seemed to help her breathing to sleep there. They made sure she was well covered before going up to her father's room to settle him for the night. He had eaten heartily of his supper and Delia had already taken the tray. He was sitting up in bed when they entered.

"I think you must be feeling better, Pa. That's the first good meal you've eaten since you returned."

"I was as hungry as a starved fox in a hen house. I guess that's a good sign." Her father looked up at Penny as she stood by his bed. Quietly he remarked, "Your mother's not been eating much for some time. I'm tough, I'll survive, but I confess I'm deeply concerned for her."

"I am too, Pa." Penny's sigh was an echo of his own. "She was thrilled with Brett's letter. I'm glad he made it sound like a fun adventure. She would be so worried if she knew just how very bad it is."

"You still heard nothing from Daniel, I take it?" He felt that something was wrong in his daughter's marriage and regretted that he and Sarah had so promoted it. Penny had never talked to him about it, but when he had seen Daniel and Penny together following their wedding and until Daniel joined the army, he could see that they did not have the rapport and deep affection that he and his wife shared. It was another burden on his heart.

"No, no letter from Daniel. I sent Nalphus letters to take to both Brett and Daniel. Maybe we'll hear something soon. By the way, since Fitz is alone, I have invited him to join us for Christmas dinner. You always enjoy his company." She paused. "Pa, Nancy asked a good question over dinner. Tomorrow is Christmas Eve and I have no idea what to do for the slaves for their celebration. The food's not a problem. But for the token money, and whether or not there are new shoes and clothes, you'll have to tell me."

"I already asked Marcus to get me some crutches, so I can get up and see to things. I have some money in the safe, and the darkies have kept the weaving and cobbling going. It's not as efficient as when your mother could oversee it, but it's something."

"That's a relief." She turned and smiled at Nancy. "Now Pa, I'm going to show Nancy how to dress and pack your wound so it heals from the inside out because I'm going to need her to take care of you. I'll stay here until Christmas dinner. Then I need to go home and make some Christmas cheer for Mammy Rena and her family. I thought I would ask Marcus to ride over to Pleasant Glade tomorrow and tell Mammy I'll be back by late afternoon on Christmas."

"That's fine, my dear. Nancy is a jewel and we'll manage together very well. You take care of your people. I wouldn't expect anything less."

Afterwards lying in bed and remembering her day, she made a mental note of the things she needed brought from home so she would have gifts for her parents and Nancy. In the fall she had ridden into town and found a beautiful silk and lace dressing gown for her mother with matching shoes, for her father she had a new pipe and felt hat from the Peebles store in Kinston, for Fitz a new cravat and a box of cigars, and for Marcus she had purchased gloves and a hat. Not knowing then that Nancy would be a part of the household, she had nothing for her. Mentally ticking off possibilities that she could scrounge from home, she suddenly thought of the blue and gold embroidered shawl her husband had given her on their last Christmas together. She had never used it and it would be perfect for Nancy. She would have Mammy get the tissue-wrapped scarf from her bedroom drawer when Marcus went tomorrow. That worry resolved, she devised a menu for the Christmas feast to give Delia and made plans for the decorating of the house with fresh greens. So much to do, she thought, as sleep at last claimed her.

Christmas Eve brought her a flurry of activity. Marcus had ridden to Pleasant Glade that morning to fetch the items she requested. She had also asked him to take a hatchet and bring fresh pine, cedar, and holly to decorate the mantles. She would have liked some running cedar, too, her favorite for decorating, but didn't want him to take time to search for the more rare greenery. She had given him instructions for the holiday dinner that she would have at her own home for her and her people.

While Marcus was taking care of that, she and Nancy, under her father's supervision, had made holiday packages of clothing for every man, woman, and child still living at Pineview. Into each she had slipped a Confederate five-dollar bill. When she turned to her father, sitting at his desk with the injured leg propped on a footstool, to ask if he had something for her mother that needed wrapping, he merely smiled and shook his head. From the twinkle in his eye, she knew that he must have taken care of family gifts before he left for battle. That chore done, she knew it was time to deal with Delia. Rather than outright orders, she had found it more effective to make suggestions and then guide, as Delia considered herself the boss of the kitchen and had little patience for any interference.

After an hour of negotiations, Penny had confirmed the dinner menu she planned all along: a roasted goose, cornbread dressing, collards, baked sweet potatoes, beans and tomatoes, stewed apples, yeast rolls, and pecan pie with whipped cream. Rather than ask Delia, she would look along the creek bank for any wild watercress or other tender greens for the salad she craved.

With Nancy assigned to decorating once Marcus returned, Penny took her shawl from the peg by the backdoor and stepped out into the brisk morning. The cold and damp of the last few days was gone, leaving the sky a brilliant wash of clear blue and making the gentle wind mild. She relished getting out of the house and walking in the woods. The time at her parents had left her little time to herself. She realized she had grown accustomed to being alone and she had come to need it. Her footsteps were soon muffled by the pine straw that carpeted the woods. Sunlight dappled the ground where it sifted through the canopy of live oak, cypress, and pine trees. She could hear squirrels chattering in alarm at her invasion and blue jays squawking to claim their territory. She loved the peace of it. Here all was as unchanged as it had been since the beginning of time, just nature, untouched by war or the altering hand of man.

Underfoot, pine straw gave way to green and gray mosses and the earth grew damp. She had reached the creek bank, where knobby cypress knees pushed their way upward. She loved the cypresses; their feathery leaves she found beautiful. The knees or adaptive roots that braced the tree in the swampy land and reached above the water to prevent the tree drowning had a novel charm. Just as she had hoped, she found a lush green bed of fresh cress and happily filled her basket with as much as it would hold. Dressed with vinegar and some salt and pepper, it would be her favorite part of the meal.

As she walked back to the house, she thought of Ryan. She saw his blue eyes in the blue of the sky, felt the warmth of his touch in the sun on her back, and she ached with longing. She would have liked to have a girlfriend with whom she could talk and share the joy of the love she had found but knew it was a secret she could ill afford to divulge. Even if Ann had not died of typhoid, she would never have dared tell even her. She realized that she had no physical reminder of him at all, not a tatter of fabric, no letter, nothing to tell her that he had ever been in her home, in her bed, and yet he was now lodged securely in her heart. She smiled when she remembered her earlier Christmas celebration with him and knew that no matter how dear her parents and the traditional Christmas dinner with them, it was that dinner with Ryan that she held more closely to her heart.

Christmas Eve dinner was a quiet one with only she and Nancy at the table. Her mother and father had taken their meal together in the sunroom. She admired the decorations that Nancy had made for the mantles and dining room table using candles and ribbons to enhance the natural beauty of the greenery. Penny had to admit that Nancy had far more talent for it than she did. Nancy glowed with pleasure when Penny complimented her efforts.

"Thank you. I really enjoy doing things like that. I like to sew and embroider, too. When I was a child I was always drawing things or sewing fancy doll clothes. I guess I regret that I'll probably never have a home of my own to decorate but that doesn't mean I can't enjoy decorating someone else's."

"Umm, I'm not so sure about you never having a home. I notice Mr. Fitz has been paying you a lot of attention the last few days. He's mighty lonely in the big old house over at Belle Terre. I think the war has put some new life into him at least. It's certainly got him acting real frisky with you. And he's not so old that he can't remarry." Penny couldn't resist the good-humored teasing.

Nancy blushed and then laughed. "He's a dear, really. I'm sure he's just being nice. I certainly can't envision him courting me."

"We'll see." Penny could tell she was secretly pleased at the unaccustomed male attention and was happy for her.

Marcus gratefully accepted his gifts the night before and then left to visit distant relatives before returning mid-afternoon. The slaves had all received their Christmas packages and were enjoying their own feast. Christmas dinner for the family was in progress, with Fitz sitting beside a blushing Nancy, her mother and father seated at opposite ends of the Georgian dining table, and Penny facing Fitz. With a toast drunk, and the food served, they chatted companionably, glad that despite the recent ordeals and the ravages of war they were together to celebrate the season in a warm and comfortable home and with ample food.

After dinner, with a roaring fire blazing in the fireplace, they gathered to exchange gifts. Penny gave a surprised Nancy the scarf and beamed when tears of gratitude glinted in the woman's eyes. Her mother and father had bought warm leather gloves for her, as well. For Nancy, the biggest surprise of all came when Fitz handed out his gifts for the ladies: For her mother it was a ruby ring, for Penny a lovely strand of pearls, and a cameo brooch for Nancy, all possessions of his late wife, Cora. Nancy sat with the broach cupped in her hands, her mouth agape.

"Well, what do you think, Miss Nancy?" Fitz asked and then couldn't resist quipping, "I thought about a ring but decided you might like this better."

They all laughed when Nancy gasped, "Oh, no, no. The brooch is fine. I mean it's really wonderful."

John stood up and, with the help of the crutches, hobbled over to Sarah and leaned down to kiss her lips. "For you, wife."

81

Sarah opened the felt bag. Inside was a beautiful set of tortoise shell combs ornamented with gold and diamonds that she had craved, but dared not ask for, due to their expense. "Oh, John, these were far too dear, I know, but I do so love them."

Penny's gift from her parents was a yellow silk ball gown sprigged with embroidered Lilies of the Valley and edged with matching yellow lace around the décolleté neckline, scalloped hem, and the full elbow-length sleeves. The dress and matching shawl were from a dressmaker in Kinston, who had sewn for both Penny and Sarah and knew their sizes.

A delighted Penny ran to her father and mother and kissed their upturned cheeks. "I just love it!"

As soon as the gifts had all been opened and proper expressions of gratitude passed around, Penny stood to leave. "A Happy Christmas to you all. Pa and Mr. Fitz, I am so glad y'all are home again. I don't want you running off like that anymore. We need to keep some men at home to take care of us women. I hate to leave you all, but I need to get home now or Mammy will never forgive me. I'm sure she's been cooking all day. I don't know how I can eat again, but I'm going to have to try."

She left them still talking and laughing. Fitz and John were regaling one another with relived incidents from their adventure, careful not to dwell on the period following her father's injury. Nancy was as animated as she had ever seen her and openly touched to have been so generously included in the celebration. Her mother had even eaten more of the delicious dinner than Penny had expected. In the backyard, Marcus waited with her parents' buggy, Polly tied to the back. Penny was grateful she would not have to ride horseback with her lovely gifts and her portmanteau.

"Marcus, you're a blessing. I really do appreciate the ride home."

"I'm glad to do it. I'm off to visit my cousins, the Cauleys, in Woodington. With both James and John off fighting, they are feeling kind of low. Your Pa gave me a Christmas package to take to the poor house there, too."

"He never misses doing it. With all that's happened, I didn't know if he would remember."

"Penny, I really appreciate the gloves and hat. It means a lot to me that you thought to do that."

"You're welcome, Marcus. Of course I remembered you."

When they pulled into Penny's yard, Moses was waiting to take the horse.

"Mammy say you need to take yo' stuff on up de stairs and leab her 'lone in de kitchen. She say stay outn dat dining room til she call fo' you and you need to dress yo' bes' cause she got a su'prise fo' yo' Christmas."

Penny laughed and thanked Marcus for the ride and winked at him. "That's exactly what I intended to do anyway. I think there are things in my room some people around here are going to be looking for. I suspect I need to get them packaged up or I might not get any dinner."

Chapter 9

The aroma of roasting meat assailed Ryan's nostrils when he rode around the corncrib into the backyard, making his stomach growl with hunger. He tossed the reins over the loop at the back passageway and dashed into the kitchen, hoping to find Penny there. Instead it was Mammy's broad beam as she leaned over the oven that greeted him. He stood there smiling at the array of food she had already placed on the table: pecan pie, apple cobbler, collards, candied sweet potatoes, and a salad of fresh watercress that he knew Penny loved. Finished with basting the goose, Mammy turned expecting to see Moses or Penny.

"Law he'p me. Is dat you, Mistah Ryan, or is you a ghos'?"

"I'm no ghost last time I checked." Ryan grinned at the smiling woman. "Is Penny in the house?"

"Naw, suh. She ober at her mama and papa's. Huh pa got a bullet hol' in his laig and she been nussin' him. She be back ter night dough for Christmas dinnah an' de giftin'. Lawsy me, she gwine be fit ter be tied."

"I tell you what, Mammy. If I don't get myself busy I'm going to be gnawing on this food long before dinner. I'll take my horse to the woods and get him rubbed down and fed. On the way back I can cut some fresh greenery. Why don't I take care of decorating the dining room and setting the table? I think we'll just give Miss Penny a little surprise."

"Dat you do. Dat you sho *do!*" Mammy bowed with emphasis. "Gwine ter be a happy Christmas 'round dis house. Sho is."

Ryan stepped back to the kitchen door and opened it to bring in the bags of food. "I brought some tea, coffee, sugar, flour, and salt. I thought perhaps you could use them. I know Miss Penny's mighty tired of chicory coffee."

"Dats fo' sho. We mighty grateful."

"You put these where she won't see them when she comes in. I'll tell her about it later. We don't want to give away our secret, now do we?"

"Naw, suh!" Mammy shook her head in vigorous denial.

Humming, Ryan left the tantalizing aromas of the kitchen to begin his self-assigned chores. He joyfully anticipated her reaction. Soon he had the horse settled and the fresh greens cut. It was growing chilly again, he thought as he glanced at the dark clouds that were beginning to gather on the western horizon. As unlikely as it was, he would have been happy to see a white Christmas with the earth wrapped in a pristine blanket, making the land serene and beautiful. He thought nothing was quite so comforting as sitting around the hearth while snow fell in big flakes, isolating each home to its own joys.

He returned to the house to decorate the dining room and lay a fire in the fireplace. When he had finished with the table and the decorations, he walked back to the kitchen to tell Mammy he was going to stay there until she told Penny to go to the dining room for her dinner. He found Mammy setting the kitchen table for her own family's celebration in the main house rather than their cabin. Mammy explained to him that it was the custom for them to eat there since with all of the cooking she was doing, it was too much for her to do two separate meals. Besides, she went on to explain, all of the servants were invited to the dining room before the family meal to receive the Christmas gifting. Ryan could tell she was excited at the prospect.

Leaving her to the goose, dressing, and cornbread that she was still minding in the oven, he found the book he had begun days before and settled by the dining room fireplace to wait. Before many minutes had passed, he was asleep. The light tapping of quick footsteps ascending the stairs awakened him and told him that Penny was home. He looked at the room, glowing softly in the firelight, and realized he had never felt so at home. Crossing to the table, he lit the candles. He would have gone to the cellar for a bottle of wine or champagne but respected that without her permission he should not. Soon he would hold her in his arms. The thought made him want to leave the room then and there and climb the stairs after her. It was all he could do to reseat himself by the fire and pick up the book.

He had read perhaps a dozen or so pages when he heard her footsteps descending the stairs, followed by the sound of something deposited outside the dining room door. She was obviously honoring her promise to Mammy.

Wondering why she had been made to promise not to go into the dining room, Penny made her way to the kitchen. Mammy was putting the finishing touches on the dinner and her family had assembled for the much-anticipated Christmas gifting.

Mammy Rena looked up when she entered and smiled. "Eberthing ready, Miz Penny. We kin go on ter de dinin' room now."

Penny noted that Mammy, Moses, Lucinda, and the baby were dressed in their finest clothes and all were smiling broadly. This Christmas evening celebration had long been the highlight of their year. She had worked hard to insure that they would not be disappointed, even though it had strained her budget to guarantee it. Leading them down the hall, she turned the knob and stepped across the threshold. Had she not still been holding the knob when the door swung inward, revealing a smiling Ryan seated by the fire, she thought she might have fallen.

"Ryan! How wonderful. What a glorious surprise! You and Mammy surely did pull a fast one on me." She crossed the room as she talked to throw herself into his outstretched arms. "It is so wonderful to see you."

Ryan hugged her tightly, his eyes closed to shut out everything but the sensation of holding her. He released her and held her at arm's length, just drinking in the sight of her. He had still said nothing. Looking into her amber eyes that had flooded with quick tears, he softly said, "Merry Christmas, Penny."

"And you," she whispered.

Mammy and Moses had taken their place on the left of the sideboard. Lucinda and the baby moved to stand beside them. Penny turned to face them and caught Lucinda's curiously appraising eyes on Ryan. She would leave Mammy to deal with her daughter. Lucinda would not spoil this holiday for her. At that moment, she knew that nothing could.

"Ryan, would you get me the packages from the hall, please?"

He returned to the dining room with the four packages she had placed on the floor on her way to the kitchen. She took each of them and placed them on the sideboard, then turned to face Mammy and her family. The first package she gave was to Jeremiah. Lucinda took it and smiled with pleasure when she saw that it not only contained the expected clothing and money, but Penny had also added a stuffed toy animal. With dignity she said, "On behalf of my child, I thank you."

Ryan instantly noted that Lucinda's diction and grammar were perfect. He thought she was a handsome woman with delicate features and a feline grace. Her slim figure carried her simple clothing with an innate elegance. Mammy had told him that she was descended from kings in Africa; looking at her daughter, he could believe it. Lucinda reached to take the package that Penny offered her. Ryan noted that she avoided any eye contact with Penny and wondered at the reason. Lucindaopened the package to beam with pleasure at the new shoes, clothing, and the money. Penny had also given her a soft woolen scarf that she had purchased in town.

Again Lucinda said, "I thank you."

Penny quietly replied, "You're welcome, Lucinda. I hope you and your son will enjoy your gifts."

"Moses," she continued, "this one is for you."

Moses opened his package to find the clothing and money as expected. Penny had also included a new pipe and the tobacco he so loved. Grinning with pleasure, he thanked her as he caressed the bowl of the briarwood pipe.

Mammy stepped up as Penny extended the final package. "For all your hard work, I thank you and hope you will like this."

Nestled in the package was a beautiful royal blue dress of the softest wool that Penny had asked the dressmaker in Kinston craft for her. Beside it were the shoes, homespun clothing, and money that were customary.

Mammy slowly lifted the dress and held it against her body. "Dis here de nices' dress I eber own. I sho do thank you, Miz Penny."

Penny beamed as she hugged the pleased woman. Laughing at her pleasure, Penny said, "Mammy, you deserve angel wings and golden slippers, but you better not go collect them anytime soon."

Ryan, who had watched the gifting ceremony without comment, spoke. "I think I need to make my own contribution to your holiday celebration." Reaching into his pocket he found four silver dollars. He quietly handed each of them one, laughing when Jeremiah tried to gum his before Lucinda hastily took it. "It's Yankee money but it will buy more than the Confederate script."

"You sho is one fine man, Mistah Ryan. We thank you and we mighty glad you here fo' Christmas." Mammy thanked him for her family, obviously touched by the unexpected largess. Turning to Penny, she said, "If you ready fo' de food, I gwine bring it on in an' den we gwine hab ourn in de kitchen."

"Please. That would be great, and I hope you enjoy yourselves."

As soon as the four had exited the room, Penny hurled herself at Ryan, kissing him with passion. Only the presence of the others had restrained her, as she knew it had Ryan. "Oh my God, Ryan. You have just made this the nicest Christmas ever. Let's go get some champagne and celebrate."

"You go, Penny. Another bottle of the Cliquot would be wonderful." He reluctantly released her.

"I'll be back directly." She left in a whirl of skirts, pleased she had changed into her new yellow silk gown. At the time she had thought it foolish to dress up, as she had fully anticipated having the expected formal dining room dinner in solitude. Now she was so glad she had worn it. She had thought it would lift her spirits at the lonely celebration that she would have skipped, had it not been expected and Mammy's way of gifting her. She had added the emerald necklace and earrings when she saw how lovely they were with the new dress. She suspected her mother and father had the jewelry in mind when they selected the fabric.

When Penny left the room, Ryan took the ring he had bought her and silently dropped it into the champagne goblet he had positioned by her plate. He wanted to see her face at this second surprise of the evening. He hoped that she would find it as lovely as he had. While he waited for Penny, Mammy came in with a tray bearing part of their dinner. Lucinda followed with the rest.

"Mammy, I swear you have outdone yourself. This is a feast fit for kings."

"Thank you, Mistah Ryan. Y'all enjoy it now."

"That we will," Ryan promised as he helped lift the dishes onto the sideboard.

As they left, Penny entered bearing aloft the champagne. "I have it. Now if you'll just open it, we'll have our holiday feast."

"I think I can manage that." Ryan noted her dress and how it complimented her figure and coloring. He was pleased that she was wearing the necklace that he remembered. "That dress is perfect on you, by the way."

They both laughed at the pop of the champagne cork as he expertly opened the bottle.

"Well, Penny. Let's have those goblets and we'll make a toast."

Penny lifted the two goblets to be filled. Pouring a small amount in each, he noted with relief she had retained the one he intended for her. He held his up and she clicked his glass with her own.

"For the man I adore. You've made this day magic."

"And to you." Ryan watched as she lifted her glass to sip. He saw her pause and then squint into the bottom of her glass.

"What's this?"

"Why don't you drink up and then dump it out? I believe you'll be able to tell then." He smiled at the surprise on her face.

Quickly she drank the champagne and then poured the glittering object into her left palm. "Oh, Ryan. It's beautiful." In wonder she lifted the ring to the candlelight, admiring the central emerald surrounded by diamonds. Silently, biting her lower lip, she slipped the ring onto her right hand.

"Oh good, it fits perfectly. I hope you like it, Penny. And I hope when I'm not with you, that ring on your finger will keep you company and you'll know that in my heart, wherever I am, I *am* with you."

Tears of joy spilled from her eyes and glittered on her lashes as she looked up at him. "Ryan, you have no idea how much this means to me. Just today I was thinking that I didn't have anything of yours that I could hold in my hand to reassure me that you are real and not just some wonderful dream. Now, I may miss you, but I have something of you with me always. Thank you so much."

Ryan gathered her into his arms and hugged her as though he would never release her.

Laughing, she said, "Okay, we'd better start on Mammy's dinner, because if we don't eat something she's going to be upset."

"Well, we can't have that. Besides, I'm *ravenous*." With a promise in his eyes, he added, "And for you, too."

Penny's eyes mirrored the promise. Taking her napkin and placing it in her lap, she suddenly looked up in consternation. "Oh, no. I have no gift for you. I didn't know you were coming. Oh, Ryan, please forgive me."

"Foolish woman, don't you know just being with you is the biggest gift in the world?"

They finished their champagne and dinner and ascended the stairs to Penny's room. Ryan collected his things from the guest room, where he had hidden them, and settled by the fire in the chair opposite the one Penny had taken.

"It's so good to be here, dear one. I have missed you more than I thought possible."

"I've missed you, too. Even though I was so busy with my father and organizing Christmas at both their house and mine, I still thought of you constantly and worried whether or not you had made it safely to New Bern."

"How is your father, Penny?" Ryan asked with concern.

"It was touch and go for a day or two, but he's on the mend and will be fine. He may have a permanent limp but it shouldn't be too noticeable. He's just happy not to have lost his leg." Perplexed, she asked, "What brought you back here so soon? I never dreamed that you would return so quickly."

"Neither did I, but when the general told me that he needed me to ascertain the level of sustained damage to the bridges in the area, I didn't refuse the offer." Ryan took her hand and pulled her to her feet. "That's a spectacular dress but I don't think you need it anymore. Shall we?" he asked, pointing to the bed.

Penny looked into the blue eyes that were smiling down at her and began to remove her jewelry. When she reached his ring, she hesitated. "I'm not taking this off, not ever."

"I think it's okay to keep that, but I'm happy to help you with the rest. Turn around, please."

Slowly he unbuttoned the back of her dress and pushed it from her shoulders. Leaning down he trailed kisses across the top of her back. As he continued to undress her, the trail of kisses progressed to each newly bared area of her body. Penny thought she would go mad with longing before he finished removing the last of her clothing. When he began to undress himself, she stopped him with a soft touch of her hand and finished the job for him. Together they walked to the bed and a night lost in one another's arms. They were drowsy with fatigue when dawn began to spread its light into the room.

Rousing himself, Ryan walked to the window and pulled the drapes closed. Quickly he returned to the warm cocoon of the covers. "It's sleeting. It's going to be a nasty day out there."

Penny didn't answer; she was sleeping. Curling his body around hers, he drew her to him. She sighed softly in her sleep. Soon he was sleeping as well, glad that the weather had prevented him leaving and bought another day with her.

It was late when Ryan awakened. Penny had already stirred the embers in the fireplace and placed fresh logs on to burn. Ryan watched her blowing on the coals to make the fire catch. Soon it was blazing, taking some of the chill from the room.

"Come back here, darling. I want to talk to you before I brave the cold."

Smiling, Penny returned to the bed. "Too tired for anything but talk?" she teased.

"Ah, you wanton, insatiable woman, I'm not that tired." And he proceeded to show her just what he meant.

Afterwards nestled together, Ryan began. "Penny, I have thought of us and what to do so often. I cannot live knowing you belong to another man. I love you and you love me. To continue a charade would be an injustice to three people. I know from what you have told me that you and your husband grew up together but were never in love. I don't know what you are holding back about the relationship, but I can't help feeling something is more seriously wrong than that between you. Furthermore, were that not true, I don't believe you would have given your heart and your body to me."

"No, Ryan, I wouldn't have. Because doing so went against all of the principles I've built my life on and against all of the expectations of others that caused me to marry Daniel in the first place. I'm not sorry I gave myself to you. I can no more stop loving you than I could stop breathing and still live." Penny paused, not sure how to continue. "Maybe the first time, I thought about being with you was revenge and anger at my husband. I don't know. You see, Lucinda's child is his. I don't know if he forced her or if it was mutual. Either way I blame him. When that child was born with Daniel's eyes and the shape of his face, I could no longer deny the proof of my suspicions. Mammy, Lucinda, Moses all realize I know, but no one acknowledges the truth. This is the first time *I* have even openly acknowledged it. The child was born after Daniel left. I wrote him to tell him of the baby and I didn't mention any challenge to the child's paternity, just said that Lucinda had given birth to a male child. He's not written since he got the letter. Maybe he suspects I know and is ashamed. Too, he was injured when he wrote me from the hospital in Richmond. Perhaps he had a relapse from infection and has been too ill to write. The last letter I received was almost four months ago. He had not received mine when he wrote. Now, I find it hard to censure him for breaking vows that I too have broken. The difference is, I know that I love you like I have never loved anyone. Daniel and I never shared love between us and whether he loved or loves Lucinda, I don't know. It doesn't even matter."

"Penny, divorce him. I know it's a rare thing and may cause talk among your neighbors. But from what I'm told, they respect, admire, and treasure you. You have helped them all in one way or another. They will understand and forget in time. There are lawyers in Kinston who can arrange this. When I leave, and I must when the weather breaks, promise me you will go to Kinston and file for divorce. When it's complete, I want to marry you that very minute. This ring is my pledge to you that I am yours and want you for my wife.

"When the war is over, I will move to New Berne and make it our home. I'll open a law office and together we will create a life and in time, I hope, a family. We can keep your house here and we'll visit often. I can afford to sustain both a property there and this one. I'm a wealthy man, Penny. I inherited substantial property and resources when my grandfather died and more at my father's death. I don't need to work, but I want to. What I'm trying to tell you is that I can give you a good life. And Penny, I pledge to you on everything that I hold dear, I will be faithful to you until my dying day."

Taking his face in her hands, she kissed him softly on the lips. "I promise. I love you. I will marry you and together we will make a life with one another based on that love. I will never love another, only you."

They held each other, making plans for the future now open to them. Ryan described the land that he would buy and the kind of house he wanted. The more he described the land and the view of the river, the more excited he became. Penny added her own suggestions and suddenly they were planning the furnishings, including a nursery.

"This may be the happiest day of my life." Ryan laughed. "But if we don't get something to eat soon, it may be the last."

"Okay, let's get our lazy bones from bed and have breakfast. With the weather so nasty, it looks like a day for staying in. Maybe a nice bath by the fire would be pleasant after we've eaten?"

"Hmm. Sounds good to me and in that order." He laughed as she pulled him from the bed. "Bossy woman, maybe I should keep you here and tame you a little more."

"Now, just how tame do you want?" Penny asked with a purr.

Ryan merely lifted a brow and smiled.

They ate their breakfast and together stowed the things in the dining room they had used the night before. Afterwards with hot water, hauled up the stairs to her tub, they retreated there for the promised bath. Ryan climbed in after she had bathed promising that they would have a big tub in their new home, one big enough for two. It was a day of dreaming and planning for a future that now looked brighter than either of them had ever dared imagine or hope for. Penny knew that it was the happiest day of her life. The only one that could be happier, she thought, would be their wedding day. Whenever she looked at the ring he had given her, her heart welled with tenderness and joy. Ryan watched the changing emotions on her face and knew he would never tire of holding and loving this woman who had consented to marry him despite the difficulties. He swore he would make her happy and she would never regret her decision.

That night, they made love joyfully and tenderly but with an underlying sadness, for he had to leave in the morning. Neither of them would acknowledge that their time together was so brief, but neither could forget. When dawn came with a warming sun that splashed sunlight across their bed, he pulled her into his arms and kissed her as though he would never have another opportunity. Ryan realized that leaving her was the hardest thing he had ever done.

"I'll be back soon, dear one. I can't say when but I will be back the minute it's possible. I'll write you and would like you to write me as well if you can do so without compromising your situation in the community. When you write don't use my rank on the envelope and I'll leave an address for you to use that isn't associated with the Union army. That will make it easier."

"I promise to write. Just promise me you'll be safe and return when you can."

"I promise. I have had my allotment of bullets for this war. I promise I'll come every time I can get away, without fail. And I promise I love you with all of my heart and I will marry you the moment you are free."

"I'm here and I'm yours. Just come to me, because I love you more than life."

Reluctantly they arose and Ryan dressed and gathered his things. Mammy had a warm breakfast waiting with the good coffee Ryan had brought. Again Penny blessed him for his thoughtfulness as she inhaled the rich aroma. Too soon he arose from the table and pulled her in his arms for a goodbye kiss. Penny walked him to the door and handed him the package of food Mammy had prepared for his trip. Taking his hand she pressed her goodbye gift into his palm.

Looking down, Ryan was thrilled to see a beautiful framed miniature of her, which had been done in her late teens. The painting was a skillful rendering of her beauty and the artist had captured something of her personality as well.

"A present to remember me by. This way my face will always be with you wherever you are, and you'll know I love you and am here waiting for you."

For a moment, his emotion threatened to overwhelm him. Swallowing hard, he gathered her to him for a last fierce hug. "Remember your promise. Please do it soon."

He tore himself from her and was gone.

Chapter 10

That January was one of the hardest in memory. The cold was unrelenting. Sleet and then a heavy snow kept people trapped by their hearths. In the brief clear spells, Penny rode Polly to her parents to check on them. While her father had returned to his usual robust health with only a barely noticeable limp to allude to any injury, her mother continued to decline. Nancy and her father did their best to keep Sarah in positive spirits but Sarah knew her body well and realized her time was growing shorter. At times she despaired but not wanting John to suffer any more than he was going to when she was gone, she kept that despair hidden behind an unfaltering smile when he was with her. More and more he sat by her side and quietly read to her. The weather was not good for much else and it was the fallow season anyway. He was grateful for that, as it allowed him the luxury of days spent in the company of the woman he had loved for decades.

When he looked at her, it wasn't the emaciated woman before him he saw, but the young one who had captured his heart the moment he had seen her at the Woodington Church service one bright May morning. She had just walked from the church and the sun on her hair lit it like a halo. She looked up into the sky and laughed in sheer exuberance at the beauty of the soft spring day. He remembered sitting on his horse, struck dumb by this girl he'd known all of his life but never seen until that moment. He had decided before he rode from the churchyard that he was going to court her until she agreed to become his wife.

It had not been easy since Thomas Becton, son of a wealthy planter from Vine Swamp, was in determined pursuit long before he entered the field. Becton was good looking and charming, but John had been more persistent and in the end had won both her heart and her hand before the next season of dogwood blossoms. To console himself, Thomas began an earnest courtship of Nancy White at Sarah's defection. They had married shortly after John and Sarah and were the proud parents of eight children.

John and Sarah talked companionably about their early days together, the long-awaited arrival of a son and then their daughter. They shared their fears for Brett and both waited eagerly for his intermittent letters. He was such a bright, joyful young man and they feared that joy would be stripped from him by the horrors he lived through daily. Brett had been seeing Mary Nunn prior to joining the army. She was a soft-spoken, attractive woman who would bring a calming effect to the more volatile Brett. They had not heard if he was writing to her or she had found someone else. Both longed for the war to be over so he could return home, marry, and give them grandchildren. Sarah smiled at the thought but knew she would never see them.

And even bigger worry for them both was Penny. Although she was dutiful in visiting them and constantly bringing teas for Sarah to try in the hope that something would prove beneficial, she seemed distant and vague. It was apparent she was lonely. Often a wistful expression would cross her face when she looked at her mother and father holding hands by the fire, and she would quickly look away so they would not see the tears that sprang to her eyes. Sarah thought she was lonely for Daniel—at least she hoped that were the case. Her father didn't say it to his wife, but deep in his bones he knew it was not Daniel that made that soft vulnerable look on Penny's face when she thought no one was watching. He ached at the thought of the subtle pressure both they and the Kennedys had brought to bear on Penny and Daniel with their expectations of a marriage. When he himself would never have married for anything less than love, why would he have expected any less for his daughter? When he asked himself that question, the answer was troubling. He had watched them grow up together as fond playmates, and because both sets of parents were such good friends, they fell into the habit of anticipating that their children would marry, uniting their lands and their families in the future. Penny had seemed uncertain and unhappy after she had accepted Daniel's ring. They put it down to prenuptial jitters and assumed all would right itself after the marriage. Penny had tried, to give her fair credit, to be happy and all that a young bride should be, but somehow John had not believed her heart was in it. Sarah knew he had always been partial to his "Shiny Penny" and felt that it was just John struggling to let go of his little girl. Although she and Penny had always had a loving relationship, it was to her father she turned to share secret joys and sorrows. For John, the very fact that Penny confided nothing to him about her emotional state told a tale in itself.

Penny felt their worry and hated that soon they would not only be more worried but shocked at her course of action. She had written Ryan long letters at least once weekly since he left but had been unable to post them because of the weather. She had received nothing from him either and assumed it was for the same reason. She fretted constantly because the weather and treating people down with the flu had kept her from the post office and a visit to her father's lawyer. She promised in her letters that at the first opportunity she would post them and see the lawyer to begin the divorce process. She wrote of her dreams of their life together and how much she loved him. She wept when she penned her hope that he was well and would soon come to her.

Late in January after weeks of tending neighbors sick with the flu, Penny had fallen ill. By the second week of February it was a much weaker and paler woman who rose from her bed. Penny pulled on her warmest dress. A glance in the mirror told her that constant nausea had taken its toll. The dress literally hung on her. Despite Mammy's protest, Penny had Moses hitch Polly to the wagon. She was determined to go to Kinston. Bundling well to prevent getting chilled, Penny took her letters and drove into town. When she reached the town limits, she looked around, barely recognizing old landmarks with so many either gone or destroyed. But the town had pluck. It was already rebuilding.

The first stop was the post office, where she mailed the letters for Ryan addressed to Mrs. Lenora Ryan, general delivery, New Berne, as he had instructed. As she was putting her change in her reticule, Shadrack Loftin, the postmaster, stepped from his office and exclaimed in delight when he saw her.

"Penny, how glad I am to see you. I have a package for you I've been holding for the last two weeks and another came yesterday. If you'll wait just a moment, I'll get them for you."

While she waited for the package, she chatted idly with the Harveys and Marstons, who were posting packages to family members in other areas.

Shadrack returned with her bundles and presented them with a flourish. Knowing they had to be from Ryan, she was beside herself with excitement. Those letters were worth every dreary mile of the drive and more. A quick glance at the packages and the return address reassured her. She would save them for when she was at home and could read and reread them at leisure. Now the important thing was to find her father's attorney.

Walking to his office, she stopped at Walter Nunn's print shop to get a copy of his newspaper, *The American Advocate*, for her father. Mary Parker Miller, a good friend of her mother's, was buying a paper as well, along with R. W. King, a prominent and politically active member of the community. Penny paused to chat for a moment before hurrying on. Penny thought ruefully that of all the days to run into everyone she knew, this would not have been the one she would pick.

Arriving at John F. Wooten's shingle, she stopped in front of the door, took a deep breath, and walked in. Going up to his clerk, she asked if Mr. Wooten were in and if he would see her. The clerk disappeared briefly to reemerge followed by John Wooten. He had been her father's solicitor for years and knew Penny well.

"Well, my dear, to what do I owe the pleasure of this visit?" He took her hands in his and beamed with pleasure. "Do come in."

"Thank you, Mr. Wooten. Please forgive me for not making an appointment, but I've had no opportunity," she said, taking the chair he indicated beside his desk.

"Not to worry, Penny. I always have time for you. Now before we get down to business, you must tell me how John and Sarah are doing. The last thing Lewis Miller told me is that he's seeing your mother and she's ailing, and I heard John got shot up when he fancied himself a warrior."

"Mama's not well. We're all really worried for her because her heart seems to be growing weaker. As for Pa, he's right as rain again. You'd hardly know he'd ever been shot."

"That John's a tough one. Well, you tell them I asked after them and will look forward to seeing them when they're able." He smiled and leaned back in his chair. "So what brings you to see a crusty old man like me?"

Penny bit her lip, wondering how to begin. "Mr. Wooten, I don't know exactly how to go about this, but I want a divorce and I need you to help me."

He sat forward in the chair, his eyes drilling her. "Penny, do you realize the importance of what you're saying? This is no matter to take lightly and it would be a terrible embarrassment to your family and the Kennedys. Both your family and Daniel's have been clients of mine for years. I just wouldn't feel right about doing this, young lady, and I would advise you to give it a lot more thought before you go breaking so many people's hearts." Standing, he took her hand. "I'm sorry, Penny. I just cannot do it."

"Mr. Wooten, I would appreciate it if you said nothing about this." He nodded his head, reluctantly.. Embarrassed by his rejection, Penny hesitated before she too stood. Thanking him, she left wondering where to turn next.

On the way to her buggy, she saw the shingle for another attorney and on impulse stopped. This one was new to town and would not know her families; having nothing to lose, she went in. The clerk informed her that Mr. Allen was out for the rest of the day. Penny left her name and asked for an appointment for the following week.

"I'm sorry, Mrs. Kennedy. Mr. Allen will be in court all next week. The first date available will be February 26. Is that good for you?"

"Yes, thank you. I appreciate your help," Penny smiled with relief.

More than a little frustrated and sad that she had not been able to start divorce proceedings immediately, she wearily trudged to her buggy and drove home. She would write Ryan immediately to let him know that she had an appointment to start divorce proceedings.

Tired and dejected at the delay, Penny sat at the kitchen table trying to thaw out from the cold drive home. Mammy gave her a cup of coffee, the last from the Christmas bundle Ryan had brought, and Penny cupped it in her hands to warm them. She had unwrapped the packages from Ryan, thrilled that he had included more coffee and tea, just in the nick of time, too. The letters she slipped into her pocket to read in the privacy of her bedroom. She just wanted to feel them near her before opening them, extracting every ounce of pleasure that she could.

"Ain't you gwine open dem letters? Des from Mistah Ryan, ain' dey?"

"I'm saving them for later, Mammy."

Giving her a puzzled look, Mammy returned to the sizzling skillet to resume frying the pork she was preparing for dinner. Suddenly Penny bolted from the table and ran from the kitchen. Mammy could hear her retching in the yard.

When she returned, Mammy handed the ashen woman a glass of water. "Here, Miz Penny. Rench out yo' mouf. You feel bettah."

"I don't know what's wrong with me, Mammy. That flu has just ruined my appetite."

"Lamb, it ain' none my bi'ness, but you reckin you be habn a baby? Seem to me dis sick stuff you been habn ain' lack de flu."

Shocked, Penny sank into her chair. With all that had happened, that possibility had not occurred to her. Counting back she realized it had been two months since she had had her monthly courses. She knew her breasts had grown tender but somehow had not made the connection. Her faced suddenly drained. *Oh, my God, I'm going to have Ryan's baby*, she thought. "Mammy Rena, I think I'm in one heaping pile of trouble. I don't know what I'm going to do."

"You ain' gwine do nuthin' right now, ceptin' tryin' to git sump'n in yo' stomerk. I gwine fix you some dry toas' and some tea. Dat orta settle you down." Mammy shook her head. "My po', po' lamb. We gwine figer out sump'n."

To satisfy a determined Mammy, Penny pecked at dinner, avoiding the meat since the odor of it sickened her. She managed to keep down some peas; however, it was the toast that seemed to be the most soothing thing she had eaten in days. When she had finished it and the good cup of English tea, she bade Mammy goodnight and went to her room.

With a fire roaring in the fireplace, she pulled her chair near and extracted her letters. Caressing the first one, she gently opened the seal and unfolded the piece of paper within. The letter was full of love and longing and a reminder of their promises to one another. Ryan told her of his days but made little mention of his official duties, keeping the tone light to diminish his connection to an enemy occupation. He described the land he wanted and asked if she liked the name Fair Bluff. A promontory on the land, rising higher than any flood in local history, was the perfect place to build their home. He thought the local brick produced by the kiln near the railroad in New Berne would be a good choice for the house. She could see it taking form in her mind as he described all of his plans for their home. The other letter was much like the first, ending with the promise that at the earliest opportunity he would find a way to return to the woman who filled his heart and his dreams. Holding his letters to her heart, she knew that even if her body still belonged to another, it was Ryan that occupied her mind and her very being. Sadly she wondered if these pieces of paper were the last things that she would ever have or know of him, for how could she bring his child into the world when everyone knew her husband had been away for over a year? The baby would be branded a bastard for life and the scandal would devastate her family.

She wasn't worried about Daniel.

Her concern was for this life created by the man she loved and now lodged within her. Protectively she cupped her stomach and swore that she would love his child enough for the both of them. Ryan she would have to give up, for she could not have them both and there was no way she could destroy his child with the herbs that Granny had taught her. She sat by the fire where they had made their pledges and cried. Why, oh why, she asked herself, after nearly two years of being bedded by Daniel and no baby, was she so quickly pregnant now? She cried and she planned. She would write Ryan to tell him that she loved him and always would, but a divorce was something she could not bring herself to do with a baby seven months away. If only it were possible to get a divorce immediately so they could marry and he could claim the child he had fathered. She knew that was an impossible dream and she struck it from her mind. She had to in order to survive, for dwelling on all she was losing would surely kill her.

In the flickering light of the fire, she began the letter that was the hardest thing she had ever had to do. Words were so cold and impersonal, how could they begin to convey the heartbreak she felt at losing the only man she would ever love? She begged him to forgive her and make a new life for himself, for he deserved so much more than she could give him. She told him that she was reconciled to a life with Daniel, for he was a good man despite his faults. Reminding Ryan that he served in the army of the enemy, she told him that he would always be an outsider from the way of life and the people she loved. She could not tell him she carried his child. To do so, while allowing Daniel to believe he was the father, would have been a greater cruelty.

She had no choice but to find Daniel and give him cause to believe that the child she carried he had fathered. She only hoped that she could find him and he could spend at least one night with her. With that resolved, she went to bed. She didn't sleep, as she held Ryan's letters to her through the long bleak night, staining them with her tears.

She was up before dawn. Quickly, she packed a valise with the things she would need for a week or so away. Picking it up, she marched to the kitchen and got the fire going in the stove to make tea and a bite of breakfast. She also needed to pack something to eat on the journey. Mammy came in just as she pulled the crispy brown biscuits from the oven.

"Wha' cho doin' outta bed so early lack, Missy?" Mammy looked her over and frowned. "I fo' sho got a tell you, you look like de debil. I 'spect you ain' slep' none. And where you think you gwine to go wid dat sa'chel? I sho don' lack de looks o' dis."

"Mammy, I will not have our baby branded a bastard and his mother a whore. It would kill my parents and I cannot do that to Ryan's child. I'm catching the train to Richmond and somehow, I've got to see to it that Daniel has reason to think this is his baby. And if he can't sleep with me, there is no reason for anyone here to know that, they'll still know I was with him and assume the baby is his. I have no choice. It's killing me, because I truly love Ryan with every ounce of me, but I just can't have him now. You know that."

Mammy walked over and took her in her arms and wept. "I do, an' it break my ole heart. Not jus' fo' you but fo' Mistah Ryan, too. Dat man love you sump'n fierce. He love you mor'n Dan'l eber did. But you do what you gotta do. I take ker a things here til you git back."

"I know you will and thank you. If anyone from Pineview comes asking about me, say I'm out tending some neighbors who are sick or something...whatever you can think of that sounds reasonable. Or, maybe you should just tell them I went to Richmond to see Daniel. Of course, they're going to fuss about me going alone." Penny began packing food for the journey. "Mammy, please ask Moses to take me into town. I'm going to catch me a ride on the Old Mullet Line to Goldsboro and from there to Richmond. I'll check the train schedule when we get to Kinston so I can tell him when to return for me."

Moses was none to happy about the early drive, but at Mammy's hard look he set about his business and stopped the sotto voce grumbling. Penny arrived just as the train for Goldsborough pulled into the station. She had just enough time to persuade the soldier in charge to allow her on the train and check schedules so she could tell Moses she would be back on Friday at five in the afternoon. If she did not find Daniel in one day, she told Moses he would have to return for her on the Saturday train. That gave her two days for traveling and either one or two in Richmond to find Daniel.

The clacking, rocking, creaking railroad soon inspired a throbbing headache. She was freezing in the seat she initially chose and moved closer to the potbellied stove at the front of the car to try to warm up. That accomplished little more than baking one side with the other still freezing but at least her feet thawed enough she wasn't fearful of frostbite. A garrulous, bewhiskered old man seated on the bench across from her kept trying to start a conversation but Penny kept silent. Finally he seemed happy enough just to chatter away to himself. She was glad when he remained on the train, which was going on to Wilmington, while she had to change to the one headed north to Richmond. Taking advantage of the time between trains, she hurried to the nearby post office to mail the letter she had written Ryan. Back in the station, she found a warm spot to wait for her train and looked around with idle interest. The place was filled with soldiers. She couldn't tell if they were going to new postings or if they had been at home on leave. As a woman alone, she dared not approach to ask. The very fact that she was alone was enough to cause more than a few of the men to cast a speculative and appraising eye at her. Few decent women would make a journey unaccompanied. She was careful to catch no one's eye and to remain silently apart. It was a relief when the train arrived.

The trip from Goldsborough, with intermittent stops along the way, seemed interminable. The throbbing in her head became a relentless pounding that seemed to keep time with the *ca-clank, ca-clank, ca-clank* of the wheels. When she reached Richmond, it was late evening. Hasting to find a driver who would take her to the hospital, she nearly barreled into a soldier.

"Whoa there, Missy." He caught her before she could fall.

She looked up into eyes that were almost as blue as Ryan's. All she could do was stare and for a wild minute hope that it was.

"Are you okay, Miss?"

"Sorry. I'm fine, really," she stammered apologetically. "I'm just in a rush to catch a buggy to Kent Hospital. My husband's there. He's been injured."

"I'm sorry to hear that." Picking up her valise that had fallen when she bumped into him, he continued. "I'm going that way myself, if you'd care to ride with me."

Penny hesitated, not comfortable with accepting a ride with a strange man. He saw her hesitation and sought to reassure her. "Forgive me, I don't think I have introduced myself. I'm Lieutenant Perry Blizzard from Deep Run, North Carolina. My brother Hosea is in the hospital and I have permission to visit him."

"Mr. Blizzard, I'm pleased to meet you and I'd appreciate a ride with you. I'm Penelope Kennedy from near Woodington."

"Well, I declare, it is a small world. Woodington's not more than five miles from my home."

They talked on the way to the hospital and realized that they had lots of friends in common. Penny was comforted to no longer felt quite so alone. Perry was an affable man with a relaxed, easy manner and sensitive enough to know that as a woman, she felt uncomfortable in a strange city. For him, it was a joy to talk to a pretty lady who was from a neighboring community. He promised himself to give her letters to take to his parents, Fountain and Alcy Blizzard, once he had seen his brother.

At the front desk, they inquired for the men they sought and were directed to the same ward. As they walked down the long central corridor to the indicated door, Perry asked, "Mrs. Kennedy, do you have a hotel yet?"

"No. I left rather precipitously. I fear I made no plans beyond getting to the hospital."

"There's a very nice one across the street that you will find more than suitable, if you will forgive the forwardness of my suggestion. I would like to know where to reach you before you leave, if I may so presume upon you to take a letter to my parents. You can give it to someone in Woodington who is going over their way."

"Mr. Blizzard, I would be glad to do that for you. I'll take your suggestion of the hotel, as the location is ideal. Thank you for all of your help. You've been most kind."

"Not at all. I hope you find your husband much on the mend."

"And you, your brother."

Entering the ward, Perry spotted his brother immediately and left to join him. Penny started walking down the row of beds, looking at the wounded men. Some would obviously never leave the hospital alive, as their injuries were far too grave. Nearing the end of the beds, she looked past the last few to the bank of windows at the end. Daniel was standing looking out the window into the street below.

"Daniel?" she asked tentatively.

Turning he looked at her, saying nothing for several long seconds. "Is it really you, Penny?"

"It is. I was worried at having heard nothing for so long. It's so good to see you on your feet." She could see he had lost weight and his sandy brown hair seemed to have sprouted gray at the temples. Daniel was several inches shorter than Ryan with a heavier bone structure. He had never been overly muscular but now he looked soft and flabby from the months of inactivity. His features were regular and his eyes a dark brown. He wasn't an unattractive man, she decided, just an ordinary one.

"I'm sorry about the writing thing. I've just had a lot on my mind and this wound has been a problem. After I wrote you, I developed a major infection and thought at one point it would be my leg or my life. But thanks to a couple of excellent doctors, both are saved. In fact, I'm supposed to report back to camp day after tomorrow. So my time of leisure, so to speak, is nearing an end. I won't be sorry to go back, as these months have been tedious."

He had made no move to come near, nor had she. Hesitantly, she walked up to him and gently patted his arm. "I'm happy to see you well. Our parents will be so relieved when I tell them. They've been so worried."

"Let's sit and visit." He indicated two chairs by the far window. When they were seated, he asked, "Tell me, what's been going on at home? Tell me about you. Why are you so thin? How are your parents and my father?"

Penny told him about the bout of flu, the miserable winter, her mother's declining health, their father's adventure, and John's consequent injury. When she described the destruction in Kinston and Ann's death he was quietly furious. He laughed at her description of the invigorated Fitz and how he was flirting with Nancy Herring. When he seemed to have relaxed and was more like the man she knew, she ventured to ask the critical question. "Daniel, I'm taking a room at the hotel across the street. Do you think you could check out tomorrow rather than the day after and spend some time with me?"

She held her breath, waiting for his answer. She could see he looked troubled as he sat several long minutes, not looking at her and not answering. Nervously she fingered the fringe of her shawl and worried what she would do if he refused.

Finally he took a deep breath and looked up, meeting her eyes and holding them. Grimly, he answered, "I wasn't sure you would want anything to do with me again. I know I did you wrong and you know I did. I'm sorry, Penny. It's not something I'm proud of. I have no right to expect you to forget, nor to forgive, but if you can find it in you to forgive me, I would be grateful. We both know we married for the wrong reasons, but that doesn't excuse me. I'm afraid I'm a weak man. That's no excuse either, is it? At any rate, what I'm trying to say in my own bumbling way is that I'm happy you're here. I'll either be checked out tomorrow or I'll leave anyway."

"Good. Now I'm going to walk over to the hotel and check myself in and get something to eat before they shut up for the night. I'll come back for you in the morning." She smiled brightly as she rose. Pausing, she leaned over and lightly cupped his cheek in a gentle caress with the palm of her hand. "We won't talk anymore about the rest. We can begin again from here."

Penny left him then, nodding to Hosea and Perry on the way out. They were in deep conversation and did not see her. Daniel watched her leave and wondered if she knew the Blizzards, not surprised if she did because of the proximity of the communities. More than anything, he was shocked that she had come to him. He knew the implacable nature of her temper. Once she was wronged, she was slow to forget. After he had received the letter telling of Lucinda's birth of a boy, he had not had the nerve to write. Although she had never accused him outright, he knew her well enough to read between the cold clipped lines and know she was in a towering rage when she penned them.

A determined woman registered at the hotel and went to her room. Putting the valise on the bed, she walked to the full-length mirror on the armoire door and stood there staring. Feeling like Caesar crossing the Rubicon, she knew the die was cast. She had begun the course of action she was going to have to live with, despite the pain, despite the loss of the man she wanted with every fiber of her being, and she knew Daniel's infidelity didn't matter. In truth, she admitted to herself, it never had. Only her vanity had been wounded, not her heart. She had never given him her heart anymore than he had given Penny his. She didn't care how many children he had out of wedlock; he would never give her one. She might bed him once more, but never again. Ryan had promised her faithfulness that she had released him from with her letter; however, in her heart she was not free from her own pledge to him. If she could not have him, she would have no one. Her love would now turn to the child she carried and she vowed their son would come to no harm. She laughed to herself, a son? Now why do I think it's a boy and not a girl? She couldn't explain, she just knew. And she would name him Ryan.

Chapter 11

Ryan spent the weeks following Christmas trapped in New Berne. It was not a good time to be constantly near the general. Reading the proof in Ryan's report of the lack of any real accomplishment from the battles in Kinston, Whitehall, and Goldsborough had sent him into a towering rage. Ryan, bearing the brunt of the initial explosion, remembered well the fate of the bearers of bad tidings in ancient times. He laughed to himself and figured his life was safe as long as Foster was still trying to recover his poker losses from him.

He wondered if Foster were a little worried that he might be recalled from New Berne when the real facts reached Washington. He had lost two hundred men in the battle of Kinston alone, accomplishing little there except for substantial damage to the town. Foster still seethed when he remembered General Evans's response when he sent a courier asking him to surrender. The feisty Evans had sent word back to "tell your general to go to hell." When he realized that the Confederates had moved their lines to the west of Kinston near the Kennedy place, he had essentially left the town to the Confederates and gone on to Goldsborough. Kinston was a disappointment, as well as the Wilmington-Weldon Bridge, which was already open, and the ironclad with only minor damage was even now nearing completion of the wooden hull. Even so Ryan knew that Foster had graduated fourth in his class at West Point, served admirably in the Mexican War and at the battle for Fort Sumter, and was well enough liked and respected by both his troops and those in higher positions of authority that the occupation in both Virginia and North Carolina was under his command.

He kept Ryan and his other officers busy on patrols of the town and other adjacent villages. The vile weather only enhanced the grousing of the soldiers in Union quarters after returning from the discomforts of a day in the open. Regularly Ryan played poker with the general and some of the other officers to reduce the boredom of the long winter evenings.

Ryan spent as much time in the town as he could, generally running interference between overly rambunctious and bored troops and long-suffering citizens. Slowly the locals were beginning to treat him with greater civility and to seek him out to redress grievances. Carefully he nurtured their growing trust and began making discreet inquiries about the property he coveted. When he had an hour or so alone, he rode to what he now considered his land and future home. Sitting on the grassy knoll he named Fair Bluff, he wrote Penny long letters describing the site and the brick home he envisioned there. Those were the happiest moments in the weeks since Christmas when he had last seen her. In his vest pocket he carried the small miniature she had given him. While he wrote, he placed it on the weathered stump that stood just on the left of the one he used for a stool and from time to time, he would look at her painted image as he wrote trying to pretend that she was with him as he described his dreams to her. Along with the letters he posted the coffee and tea she so loved. He hoped that by wrapping them well, they would reach her safely. He knew such luxuries were well coveted.

Aware of the difficult of the mail service, he had not expected her letters to arrive with either ease or regularity; however, when he had heard nothing by the first of February he began to worry. He had gone to the post office daily for weeks to see if there was any mail for a Lenora Ryan only to leave disappointed. Finally in the third week of the month, the long-awaited letters arrived all at once. He hurried with them to his barracks, glad that Bobby wasn't there, and reclined on his bunk to read them. When he read the last one telling him that she had been ill but was finally on her way to Kinston to see the family attorney, his heart soared. He read and reread the passages telling him how much she treasured, adored, and missed him. She too dreamed of their home and was counting the days until it could all happen. After he had finished the letters, he was determined to see her. The two months since they had last been together seemed endless. He was glad that he had a card game with the general that night. He intended to lose and make sure Foster was in good spirits. To that end, he bought a bottle of good Kentucky Bourbon and walked to the William Horner Store, where Foster made his headquarters.

After a good dinner and cigars by the fire, Ryan produced the whiskey and they began the game. Ryan took the first one with two jacks and two queens. In the second game he kept three cards and drew two more to make a royal flush. When Foster raised the ante, the others all folded. The general looked at Ryan, waiting to see if he would meet the raise. Ryan shook his head and quietly laid his cards face down. Foster took the pot with three aces. From then on, Ryan made sure that Foster won more than he lost. At the end of the evening, the two of them were still by the fire after the others had gone. Foster was in an expansive mood and talked for some time about his service in the Mexican War and the campaign to retake Fort Sumter. Ryan was an attentive audience, encouraging the general to elaborate. When he rose to leave, Foster thanked him for a delightful evening and the addition of the whiskey. Ryan decided it was as good a time as any to ask for four days off to attend to a personal matter. Without hesitation it was granted. Ryan immediately returned to his quarters and packed. He would leave at first light. If he pushed and was lucky he would be at Pleasant Glade by dark.

In the early morning darkness, he made his way to the stables. Windfall whickered and stamped a foot in recognition when he heard the door open. Ryan soon had the horse saddled and was on his way. After thinking about it for some time, he had decided not to take his uniform, as it would save time not to have to change and it might even be safer not to have it with him were he to be challenged and searched by a group of Confederates. Ryan rode hard and Windfall, tired of the stables, was happy to stretch his legs into a gallop. As Ryan rode he worried that Penny had been ill, wondered what the attorney had told her and how long the divorce would take. But mostly he just longed to see her and hold her in his arms and tell her how very much he loved her and longed for the day when she would be his.

When he turned down the long winding lane leading to her home, both he and the horse were tired, but pushing Windfall one last time, he galloped to the house. Except for a light in the kitchen, the house was dark. He suspected he was going to surprise Penny at dinner and anticipated eating with her, as he was hungry after a long day in the saddle with only hardtack to sustain him. Leaving Windfall tied to the passageway loop, he entered the kitchen, excited that he was once again going to be with the woman he loved. He saw only Mammy alone at the table.

"Mammy, you're a sight for sore eyes, but I most particularly want to see Penny. Is she in the house?"

Mammy was shocked to see him standing there and sad to see the joy in his face. She thought it was for the best for both Penny and Ryan if she told him the truth, or at least a part of it. "Mistah Ryan, we ain' spectin' you, but it sho is good ta see you. You jes set down here and I git you some dinner."

Ryan took the chair she indicated and asked again. "Is Penny here, Mammy?"

"Naw suh. Afta you eats yo' dinnah and I tell you 'bout it." Mammy quickly got his dinner and put it on the table in front of him.

Ryan was puzzled by her manner but dutifully picked up the fork and began eating. "She's all right, isn't she, Mammy? I got her letter saying she had the flu. Are her parents not well?'

"Naw, naw. Eberbody fine. You jes eat some dinnah den we talk." Mammy watched him reluctantly resume eating.

Finally he stopped and laid his fork on the plate. "Thank you. That was delicious, Mammy. Now let's have it. What is it you're not telling me?"

"Mistah Ryan, Miz Penny gone ta Richmun ta see Mistah Daniel. She ain' gwine be gittin' no deevo'ce. I plum sorry 'bout dis, Mistah Ryan, sho nuff I is." Mammy said it softly but she might as well have shouted.

Ryan sat there in stunned disbelief, the words ringing in his ears. "Surely you cannot mean this. I just got her letters saying she was going to Kinston to see an attorney so she can divorce him and marry me. She doesn't love Daniel; she loves me."

"I don' knows 'bout all dat. I jes know she gone ta Richmun to be wid huh husband."

Ryan rose from the table and walked from the kitchen in a stupor. He might as well have been pole-axed.

Mammy stood looking at the closed door and wondering at the wisdom of what she had just done. Sorrowfully she shook her head and sat down at the table with her head in her hands. She prayed that somehow it would all work out. The problem was, she could not see how.

Ryan stood for a moment on the passageway, wishing with all his heart that he could walk through that back door one more time and find her waiting for him. With his heart breaking, he tore his eyes from the door and stepped down to the yard, where Windfall was patiently waiting.

"I'm sorry, old boy. There won't be much rest for the weary for a while. I'll go to the stable and get you some oats and then we're leaving. We'll find a spot somewhere to rest for the night."

With his horse fed, Ryan looked once more at the house, imagining every room and the things they had done and said there. With resignation he turned Windfall onto the lane to the road, riding away from all of the dreams he had so carefully nurtured and planned. As he slowly turned onto British Road and the long trek back to a bleak life of war and desolation, his heart felt as though it would break within him. He had so believed in her and her love, and against all odds he had dared hope that together they could make those dreams happen. He would have to learn how to live without her in his life. At the moment, he could not see how. When the moon was high and both he and the horse could go no further, he stopped in the edge of some woods, pulled his saddle from his horse, and made a crude pallet on the cold damp ground. At that point, he would have welcomed a bullet from a patriotic Rebel.

He spent the night letting his horse rest. For him there was little. His mood ranged between bleak despair and blind rage that someone who professed to love him could so delude him. That she could promise him a future with her in one moment and in the next flee to the arms of her husband made him furious with frustrated anger. At times he arose from the ground and paced about the small clearing, questioning what he could have done differently. He wondered if it was because she had been slow to get his letters but discounted that. Hers had been very late in arriving but it had not altered the course of his intentions.

Perhaps, he thought sadly, she really doesn't love me. Maybe she just wanted to revenge herself against her husband and merely used me to that end. After all, he reasoned, she had gone to Daniel. She was even now with him in Richmond. He tortured himself with visions of them together and cursed that he had not died at Southwest Creek. He should never have allowed her to hurt him so. By the weak dawn light of a winter day, he looked at the sky and resolved in his heart that he would pursue his dreams without her. He would buy the land and build the house that they had planned. And he would find another to share it with him or he would live there alone. It didn't matter. He felt his heart harden in resolve as he said to his waiting horse, "Never again will I allow another woman to hurt me." Hungry and tired, he rode into New Berne in a cold rain.

At the same time that he was making his way back to New Berne, Penny's train was bringing her ever nearer to the life she had chosen rather than the one she had wanted. Fighting waves of morning nausea as she road the Old Mullet Line to her destination, she thought back to the previous day in Richmond. She had gone to the hospital at ten in the morning and shortly after she and Daniel left together. He was still a little weak from the long period in bed so they took a carriage ride and ate a light lunch near the river. Afterwards he showed her some of the important buildings in the city. Her favorite was the classically beautiful capitol designed by Thomas Jefferson. She could tell he was tiring so they returned to the hotel. The desk clerk handed her a letter, dropped off earlier by Perry Blizzard, and a note thanking her for carrying it home with her. She explained to Daniel that they literally had run into one another when she arrived in Richmond. They ate their dinner in the hotel just as the sky darkened into black. He ordered a good wine to celebrate his release from hospital and her arrival. Then he ordered a second. She watched him drink it all and knew he was drunk.

When they entered her room she felt even more nervous and apprehensive than she had on their wedding day. All day he had made no move to touch her. They had neither hugged nor kissed since her arrival. She knew she would have to make the overture to intimacy and it sickened her. Rather than undressing behind the screen as he expected, she slowly removed her clothes and stood before him. He hid his surprised as he watched her disrobe, studying her as he did. Despite her thinness, her breasts seemed even fuller. He caught his breath when she was fully nude. She was a beautiful woman and he wondered how he could have spurned what she offered. And he asked himself why he didn't love her.

Penny saw his arousal and turned to pull back the covers while he disrobed. He was her husband but she felt soiled somehow. Shaking her head, she schooled herself to simply follow her plan without thinking or feeling. After all, she reminded herself, there was no other alternative. This child of her real love deserved a chance at a good life un-besmirched by the stain of bastardy.

She had never realized it before, but Daniel was a clumsy and selfish lover. But then prior to Ryan she had no one to whom she could compare him. He made no effort to arouse her, to caress her and make her feel cherished. She suspected he had no clue that as a properly reared woman she might want to feel arousal and fulfillment. After the long months of abstinence, it was over before it began. She felt his seed running down her thighs. He had climaxed and immediately softened without entering her. She hoped he was drunk enough not to remember the actual mechanics later. When he was snoring softly, she left the bed and washed herself, packed, and wrote him a letter wishing him luck and good health in the coming months. With the train departing at five, she intended to rise early and be at the railway station long before he awakened. She had no desire to face him in the morning. And if she had morning sickness, she wanted to be gone before he could know.

As she rode the Old Mullet Line into Kinston, the searing image of Ryan making love to her flashed across her closed eyelids, only reminding her of the sacrifice she was forcing herself to make. She smiled as she remembered his good nature, and the beautiful man he was, not just physically, but in every way she could have wished for. Penny doubted she could ever look into a clear blue sky again without seeing his eyes. The vision of long lonely days without him stretched in front of her, bringing tears of despair that silently rolled down her cheeks. She wiped them away with her sleeve and resolved to weep no more for what she could no longer have.

Moses was waiting in the station for her when the train rolled to a clanking, hissing halt. She stepped off the train, glad that he had remembered the time of her scheduled arrival. Riding in heavy rain back to Pleasant Grove that made her umbrella seem pointless, Moses told her that her father had ridden over to see her the day she left, looking for some herbs for her mother, who was daily growing weaker. Moses did not tell her about Ryan's visit because he didn't know. Mammy had kept that for herself. She felt it was best if no one ever knew.

Moses let Penny out beside the hidden lane to make her way to the house while he re-hid the wagon in the woods. She was drenched by the time she reached the back door. She went up to her room and changed into dry clothes and unpacked her valise. Despite the clock striking eleven, she went to the kitchen to prepare the herbs for her mother. She had worked quietly for twenty minutes or so when Mammy came in to see if she had eaten the dinner Mammy had left on the stove for her.

She looked up when Mammy stood waiting to take her supper. "I'm sorry, I was making the herbs for Mama and didn't think about dinner. I'll eat something now. Mammy, Moses told me Pa came over looking for me. What did you tell him?"

"I say to yo' Pa dat you gone to Richmun to see Dan'l since you be real worrit at not hearin' nuffin. He sho wuz mad you wen' traipsin' off on yo' own."

"I'm sure. I can hear him now. No doubt he would have insisted on going and then been miserable about leaving Mama. Besides, this was something I needed to do alone."

Mammy asked the silent question by raising her eyebrows and pursing her mouth. Penny nodded in answer; there was no need to elaborate. She had done what needed to be done.

"Did anything else happen while I was away?"

"Naw. It been real quiet lack 'round here dese las' few days." Mammy looked guileless as she said it, not wanting Penny to see what she was holding back. She knew it would only hurt Penny more to hear of Ryan's pain when she had told him that Penny had gone to Richmond to see Daniel. Mammy wondered what would have happened if Penny had waited to go to Richmond. Had she, she would have been there when he came. She wondered if Ryan would have found another solution to the problem than the one that Penny had devised. Not realizing she was voicing her thoughts, she mumbled, "Dat be watah ober de bridge now, sho nuff."

"Did you say something, Mammy?"

"I's jes grumpin' 'bout mah rheumetism. Dis rain sho make it hurt."

"Give me a minute and I'll find something that will help the pain," Penny promised on her way to the herbs in her pantry.

"Den you bettah git to bed. It aftah midnight."

Penny went to her parents the next day with the herbal decoction she prayed would offer her mother some relief. A stern John met her at the door when she stepped onto the porch. "Come back to the office, Penny."

At the uncharacteristically serious tone, Penny felt fear seize her. She thought wildly that somehow he had found that she had been seeing a Union officer on the sly, or maybe Mammy had told him she was pregnant. But how could he have found out about Ryan? She would never believe that Mammy, who was the soul of loyalty, would have told on her to her father. When she walked into the office, he closed the door behind her and motioned for her to sit beside him by the fireplace. She took the seat, searching his face for some clue for the grimness.

He looked her in the eyes and quietly said, "Before I get to what I need to say, I want to tell you that I'm sorry you went to Richmond alone. Even if I had known you were leaving, I couldn't have gone, but I might have at least had Fitz or Nancy go with you. It's just not right and it's not safe for a decent woman to go that distance on her own. I want you to promise me it won't happen again. I can't be worrying about you with all the rest I have to deal with. Now that is out of the way, I want you to tell me how you found Daniel. Poor Fitz has been beside himself with worry."

"Daniel's lost weight, Pa, but he's doing well enough. They discharged him while I was there and he's reported back for duty. He said he'd been really sick and just not up to writing." That wasn't a total prevarication, she thought, just not the whole story. "I'll be sure to tell Mr. Fitz all about Daniel when I see him. If you see him first, please tell him not to worry; Daniel's fine now."

"Fitz will be relieved. We're happy for you. I hope you and Daniel have found a way to make things right between you." He exhaled heavily and sat for a moment. "Penny, your mother doesn't have much more time. Dr. Miller came out day before yesterday to check on her and he told me that we need to prepare ourselves."

"Does Mama know?"

"What he said? No. But she's no fool either. She can tell she's getting worse. She tries to hide her worry with a brave front, but I've been with her too long and loved her too well not to know what she's keeping inside. I must say it about kills me."

"Me, too, Pa. I can't imagine life without her. I know how much this hurts you. I'm just so sorry. I would do anything to be able to help, but what I know how to do just isn't enough."

"She knows you love her and are doing everything you know how to do to make it better. By the way, she was actually tickled that you had the pluck to go all the way to Richmond to see Daniel. She's been worried about your marriage just as I have. Just be brave in the coming days. I may need you to be brave for me, too." He choked back a sob and looked at the ceiling until he was calm again. "So, did you hear anything of Brett while you were there?"

"I was only there one full day, Pa. I really didn't have time. He's so good about writing that as long as his letters keep coming, try not to worry. That reminds me, I have a letter for Fountain and Alcy Blizzard in Deep Run. I ran into their son Perry, who was visiting his brother in the same hospital ward as Daniel."

"I'll send Marcus with it. I need him to see the Cunninghams over that way about a new strain of corn they're planting that's supposed to be hardier than what we've been setting out. I'm sure Old Man Cunningham can get it to the Blizzards for you." John stood and pulled his daughter to her feet. "Right now, Missy, we're going in to see your mama and we're going to act cheerful for her sake. No long face now, and you've got to help me keep my own chin off the floor. Okay?"

"Okay, Pa. I'll surely try." Penny smiled reassuringly as she gave him a kiss on the cheek.

Together they walked to Sarah's sunroom. Sarah was lying on the chaise lounge, which had been moved closer to the fire. If possible, Penny thought she seemed even more pale and thin that she had just a few days past when she had lasted visited her mother.

"Penny, darling, I'm so glad you're back. How was dear Daniel? He must have been thrilled that you would go so far to see him."

"He's dancing jigs right now, I'm sure. He left yesterday to return to his own regiment. If I had not gone when I did, I would have missed him entirely. I didn't even think about that when I left to go to Richmond." Penny laughed.

"He said to tell you that he plans to visit the prettiest mama-in-law in the whole country just as soon as he gets a furlough."

"Oh, pish. I know you are just laying it on now," Sarah said with a laugh. "Did you hear any news of that boy of mine?"

"I'm sorry, Mama. Like I told Pa, I just wasn't there long enough. But don't you worry; Brett always was the lucky one." Penny looked around the room. "Mama, where is Nancy? I just realized that I haven't seen her today."

"She's with Fitz. I think they went for a buggy ride to visit the Wallers. That old reprobate is flirting something fierce, but it won't amount to a hill of beans. I'm just glad Nancy has her feet on the ground; otherwise, she might fall for his foolishness."

"I brought you some tea, Mama. I hope it does some good."

"Thank you, child." Sarah leaned back on the pillows and closed her eyes. "I stay so tired."

Leaning over, Penny kissed her forehead. "I love you, Mama."

Sarah had fallen asleep and did not answer. Her father led Penny from the room. "Can you stay?"

"I've got a lot to take care of, Pa. I'm going to try to organize things so I can move over here for a while. It will be easier if I'm here."

"That it will. I'd planned to ask you anyway."

"I'll try to move over in a day or so, soon as I see what all I need to do at home. Marcus may have to do some running back and forth to help me out. Once planting season starts, I'm going to have to get busy working at Pleasant Grove, but until then, it's mainly just getting the tools and things ready. Moses knows what to do; I just like to check in with him so he knows I'm still the one in charge." Penny bit her lip. "Pa, I'm not going to try to have a crop for sale. Exporting is too chancy and I don't have the workers anymore to justify the old kind of farming. I'm not going to pay for labor beyond those I'm already obligated to keep. I'm going to plant what I need to feed the livestock and the rest is going to be food, except maybe corn. I'm going to make everything I can and buy nothing I can live without. Most of what I want I can't get anymore anyway because of the blockade. If I'm careful, I can weather this war and come out of it, ready to go forward. But it's going to take some thinking and some cash. My money that Daniel converted to Confederate dollars is getting to be worth less and less. It's all I'm going to spend. I plan to stock up on some things that are going to get scarce like salt, flour, and sugar. When it's gone, I stop. Every gold coin and all the Yankee money I have from before the war, I'm saving. When this war is over, we're going to have to farm differently because we won't have the manpower to farm the way we have in the past. After the war I'm going to buy a reaper, one of those new two-horse cultivators, better-designed plows, and anything else they come up with that requires less labor. It'll be good for the land to lie fallow for a while. It was getting worn out from repeated growing of cotton. Moses told me that our cotton yield has been dropping every year. He says we need to let the earth rest up so it can get strong again. So that's what I'm going to do. If the Yankees will just leave me alone, we're going to just hunker down and survive. I also have thought of something to do to make some money. I'm not sure about it, though."

Her father stood looking at her, his face a study in amazement. Then he started laughing and just shook his head. "You do beat all. There has never been any telling what was going on in that pretty head of yours, but you have never ceased to amaze me. You've given your old pa some serious food for thought. What you're saying makes a lot of sense. My slaves are going to be gone when this war is over. Much as I don't like a new world order here, I'm not going to have any choice. Pineview is going to have to change, too. I've been hoarding gold and silver not knowing what we all might need. Maybe I need to have some more definite goals for it when this mess we're in comes to an end. Just pray when that happens the North doesn't decide to completely crush us."

Chapter 12

Later had anyone asked, Ryan could not have said how he got back to New Berne. He arrived wet, cold, and thoroughly miserable, happy to turn Windfall over to his orderly to feed and rub down. He himself stumbled into the tavern on Pollock Street that he and other officers frequented and proceeded to get thoroughly drunk. He knew he would hate himself in the morning; however, for that moment he just wanted oblivion, to forget the sense of frustration and betrayal that threatened to overcome him.

When Bobby found him the following morning, he was lying on his bed, still in boots and uniform. "Colonel Madison, sir? Are you all right?"

"What?" A bleary response was the best he could manage when he rolled over and opened reddened eyes, squinting at the morning light pouring in the window of the Slover house, where he had recently moved his quarters. Although the house was an elegant and well-appointed mansion, he was in no condition for the moment to appreciate his good fortune that Foster had given him better accommodations.

"Sir, the general is asking if you're back."

"Oh, dammit, I guess I'd better get a bath, shave, and into some clean clothes then. See to that and some breakfast. Send a runner to Headquarters in the meantime to say that I'll report in before noon." Ryan's mouth was set in an unaccustomed hard line and he was annoyed that he had to report in when he still had two days of leave remaining. He supposed that was the price for lodging in the same house as the general.

Bobby hastened from the room to ask the freed slave in the kitchen to hustle some hot water up the stairs to the colonel as fast as feet could get him there. He knew Ryan well enough to know that he was a grimly unhappy man that morning and would brook no delay in having his orders seen to. As he assembled a breakfast for him, Bobby mulled over what could have caused Ryan to become drunk. That event alone was a first, but the greater alarm for him was the loss of the ready geniality that he had come to expect from the man he served.

Cleanly attired and neatly shaved, Ryan knocked on General Foster's door.

"Come in," the general called. He looked up from his desk as the door swung open. "Colonel Madison, good morning. I need you to take a small detail across the river to inspect Fort Anderson and to Little Washington to assess the status of the fortifications there. I'm not real happy with some of the reports I'm getting on General D. H. Hill and what he's up to. I wouldn't put it past him to try to retake New Berne and Washington. I intend to be ready for him if he comes. Get your men organized and leave first thing in the morning. I'll have one of the Gunboats ferry you over to the Fort and then up the Pamlico to Washington. Don't waste any time, as I want this information as quickly as possible. Report to Lt. Colonel Hiram Anderson at the fort and see what he has to tell you about preparations there and send someone back with the report before you go on to Washington."

The expedition took the best part of a week and except for an occasional rifle crack, the nuisance of swamp mud, shallow water, and mosquitoes, the trip was uneventful. Ryan found the fort only moderately defensible if it were to come under attack by a determined enemy. Washington, despite good blockhouses and fortifications, looked to be an even greater challenge than Fort Anderson. He had only been back a week when New Berne was under threat of attack by General Junius Daniel.

On the morning of March 13, Daniel took Deep Gully to the west of town and was holding it. Union forces fell back to New Berne in total disarray. Organizing a three-pronged attack from his base in Kinston, General Hill set out for New Berne. Rather than the big celebration the Union army had planned to commemorate the one-year anniversary of the capture of New Berne, their focus shifted from parade and feast to holding on to their prize. A signal station was placed atop the Jones-Jarvis house for communication by flares, lanterns, and flags with the fortifications surrounding the town. Arms were cleaned and ammunition readied. Troops and hired contrabands worked to improve the battlements.

Ryan rushed to organize his men and ready for the coming attack against New Berne. He was relieved in a way to have something to occupy his mind so he did not have time to think of himself and his heartaches. At Foster's direction, he posted a lookout sentry in the belfry of the First Presbyterian Church on New Street and sent a runner to the New Bern Academy, which was serving as a hospital, to order any convalescing men who were able to report to duty post haste. On his way back to headquarters, on sudden impulse, he stopped by the post office in City Hall. The postal clerk recognized him immediately.

"Ah, Colonel Madison, I have a letter here for a Mrs. Lorena Ryan. You asked me to hold any such letters for you, I believe?"

"That's right. Thanks for remembering." Ryan waited while the clerk went for the letter, questioning whether he should even bother to open what Penny had written. He took the proffered letter and stuffed it in his pocket. He would deal with it later, he decided.

He had more pressing things to cope with at the moment. Skirting New Berne, Confederate General James Pettigrew had left Deep Gully on the morning of March 14 and crossed the causeway to Fort Anderson, where he attacked the fort. After a period of withering fire he sent Lt. Colonel Anderson an order to surrender. Keeping his troops tucked out of harm's way, Anderson asked for a cease-fire. When Pettigrew realized that the wily Anderson was merely buying time to allow the Federal gunboats to come into firing range of the Confederate position, he resumed the attack with a fusillade of armaments that rained a torrent of shell fragments over the area. Ryan participated in the battery assault from the opposite bank, ready if needed to mount Windfall and give chase should the call to horse be issued. With the fire from both the battery and the gunboats, the Rebels wanted nothing more to do with New Berne and withdrew from the scene.

With General D. H. Hill roaming the countryside, priming for another fight, and confiscating the foodstuffs that he himself depended on, General Foster took a number of his staff officers, including Ryan, and left for Washington. When he arrived there, Ryan received orders to immediately organize soldiers and contrabands, the name for escaped slaves, to begin felling the trees for a distance of a half-mile from all fortifications. General Foster wanted a clear line of fire with no cover for any approaching force. With twelve hundred troops and a small force of armed Negroes, they waited for the attack.

March 30, 1863, General Pettigrew, under orders to ultimately lay siege to New Berne, opened the campaign on Little Washington with a barrage of artillery fire. For the next two weeks, each morning brought a volley of shells keeping the Yankees penned down. Fearful of running short of ammunition, Pettigrew hesitated to make a greater demonstration. Each evening following dinner, a calliope on one of the gunboats in the Federal fleet would play a little music followed by a Union barrage of artillery on the Confederate lines. In order to reconnoiter, when dark fell the Confederate scouts tied cowbells to their horses as camouflage and set out to learn what they could of circumstances within the town. Catching on to the ruse, the Union broke the still of the night firing in the direction of the sound of tinkling bells and hooting at the Rebel "cowboys." Neither side was doing much damage to the other. Cut off from food supplies, however, the Union forces were in danger of being starved out. After two weeks the troops were down to a half of a dipper of coffee and a little pork and bread at supper.

The attempted reinforcement of troops from New Berne under Brigadier Generals Palmer, Prince, and Spinola had been a study in the art of bungling.

Despairing of any leadership from that quarter, on April 15th Foster, along with several of his staff, escaped to the gunboat *Escort*. The ship, despite all obstacles, had painfully made its way to the Washington wharf that night. Ryan was standing at the railing, wrapped in oilskin to ward off a pelting rain, when they slipped past the hot but relatively ineffectual barrage of fire from the Confederate battery the following morning. Even as the Union steamed away, mired knee deep in swampy muck and more than a little frustrated, the Confederates were preparing to leave their own dogwood-spangled trenches.

When he arrived back at his New Berne quarters, Ryan shoved the unopened letter he had carried with him for weeks into the top drawer of his bureau. He simply didn't have the strength left to deal with it. The following two weeks gave him little respite, as they seemed to be harassed from all sides as the determined Rebels peppered them at every vulnerable point. Again on the twenty-eighth of the month, Ryan found himself frustrated in a skirmish at Gum Branch. Once again he retreated with the Union forces to their stronghold in New Berne. Another excursion to Gum Branch, called by some Wyse Forks, resulted in the same scenario on the twenty-second of May. During the coming month, General Foster's troops licked their wounds, reestablished the customary routine, and readied for the next threat.

After two weeks of relative idleness, Ryan could ignore the letter no more. Taking a stiff drink of brandy for Dutch courage, he slit the envelope and slowly extracted the heavy embossed paper. Seating himself by the fading light of the window in his bedroom, Ryan slowly began to read Penny's letter. He could understand her fears that in a defeated South if would be difficult for him to be accepted. Difficult was one thing, impossible quite another, he told himself. The thing that stopped him and left him totally confused was her willingness to resume a marriage that she had formerly repudiated with gladness. Had she become so fearful that she could forget the love they shared and the promises they had made? Ryan stood up and tossed the letter onto the top of his bed and started pacing. He could not let it rest this way. He had to confront her and have her tell him to his face that she no longer wanted him and the life he offered.

Again he went to General Foster to request personal leave and again offered no explanation. Although he granted Ryan leave reluctantly, he still granted it and a determined Ryan left in the dusk of night to ride Windfall to Pleasant Glade. Early morning found him in the edge of the woods of her parents' property. Carefully he picked his way through the woods to the fields that belonged to her. Although he was tired from a night of riding and no sleep, he could not rest until he saw her. Leading Windfall, he carefully threaded his way through the swampy verge of the outlying fields to the field nearest the house. With the sun casting slanting shadows across the newly plowed field, Ryan peered from the covering brush. In the field, he could see Moses, Lucinda, and Penny walking slowly down the rows planting what he took to be kernels of corn.

Penny's back had been to him and he had watched for perhaps ten minutes, when she turned to begin a new row. He saw her straighten and, with her left hand in the small of her back, lean back in a stretch. There was no mistaking the fecund, silhouetted profile. She was pregnant. Ryan felt as though he had been punched in his stomach, knocking the wind from him as he fell to his knees. Ah, that trip to Richmond and now she was carrying Daniel's child. The thought beat like a rhythm through his brain until he felt he would go mad with the pain of it. Her visit to Richmond was a bitter pill. His focus on the betrayal represented by the visit so consumed his mind that he never considered the possibility that he might have impregnated her. One thing he knew. The child meant the end of any hope he might have that Penny would file for a divorce.

"Quiet, boy," he cautioned the patiently waiting horse. "I need to rest before we head back."

He watched them toiling in the fresh warmth of the spring day. As the sun climbed to its zenith, Mammy walked down the path leading from the house. Her grandchild was riding like a papoose on her back and in her hands she carried a jug of water and a pail. As he spied on the scene, the three toilers dropped their hoes and sank into the grass on the edge of the ditch bank that lined the field. He saw Penny shake her head in denial of the food Mammy handed her. And he saw Mammy insistently refuse to accept that rejection. She handed Penny what appeared to be a biscuit and then stood over her until Penny began to eat. Although he could hear the sound of their voices, they were too far away for him to understand the words. Even so, he knew Penny was arguing with Mammy.

"I swaney, Mammy. I can't stand the thought of one more piece of fried pork. Just the scent of it makes me sick as a dog."

"Miz Penny, you has got ta eat sump'um. It ain' jes you no mo'. It you and dat baby you got ta feed."

In resignation, Penny munched on the ham biscuit, masticating slowly and forcing herself to swallow each swollen lump. Mammy was right, she scolded herself; her baby deserved a chance even if she herself no longer particularly cared if she lived or died. Dully she finished the food and drank some water before lying on the soft spring grass that lined the ditch. Every muscle in her back seemed to be screaming in individual protest at the unaccustomed labor. Penny looked up into the lacy foliage of tender spring growth on the small sassafras tree that teased her with meager shade. Listening to the twitter of yellow tanagers, cardinals, and an occasional bobwhite, she closed her eyes against the light and found herself drifting into sleep. Her last thought was to wonder why she could sleep in mid-day when each night only brought the insomnia of painful memories.

From his cover in the dry broom sedge of last season's weeds, Ryan found his own eyes closing involuntarily. He didn't know how long he slept, but the shadows had again grown long and night was darkening what was now an empty field. He felt her absence like a pang of hunger in an empty stomach. When he awakened, Penny and the others already had left to return to their houses for the evening.

Slowly he stood and stretched. He was hungry and the horse was thirsty. There was no way he wanted to deal with the thirty-mile trip back to New Berne and another long night ride. He crept nearer the house and patiently waited for the candles to slowly die first in the kitchen, then in the darkies' quarters and finally her bedroom. Creeping to the well, he lowered the bucket, cursing each creaking crank of the handle. He drank his fill of the fresh clean water and then took care of his horse's own thirst. Sneaking into the barn, he found oats for the horse and tied him in one of the deserted stalls. In the dark back corner, he made a bed for himself on old straw that had begun to smell of rat urine. Chewing on hardtack, he pondered the circuitous and unlikely route that had brought him from being a New York attorney to wealthy clients, to a heartsick and weary Union soldier in a South who despised him as little more than a scourge upon the land. As the stars emerged to cast faint light on the troubled swamps and fields that stretched for miles around, Ryan could keep his eyes open no longer. His last thought was of her belly that held a child belonging to the man he had come to hate.

In her own bed not so many yards away, Penny tossed restlessly. The wind sighing in the trees sent soft puffs of fresh air through the lacy under-drapes that covered her open window. She thought she could hear the creaking of the windlass on the well but dismissed it as just one more of the night sounds common to the cooling timbers of a wooden house. Watching the shadows dancing a slow pattern on the ceiling above her head, she thought of the last time she had lain there secure in the arms of the man she loved. With a sigh of frustration, she punched the down pillow encased in lace-trimmed percale and struggled to find a place to rest that did not remind her of her swelling belly and aching muscles. Her weary eyes at last closed and she dreamed Ryan was near, missing her and aching for her just as she did for him. The vision was so real she awakened with a start. Refusing to believe it was anything but empty longing, she rolled over and tried to sleep.

A full moon rose over the swampy land as owls emerged for their nightly forage. Ryan awakened to the sound of a mournful *hoo, hoo*. Stiff from the uncomfortable pallet, he struggled to his feet and made his way in the dark to Windfall's stall. The horse perked his ears as Ryan approached and whickered. "Shh, boy. We're going to get you some more oats and some water and then we're going home. Don't make a bunch of racket, you hear?"

Swiftly he saddled the horse, working more from feel than any kind of visual clue. Once the horse was saddled and fed, Ryan again led him to the well and drew water for them both. The screech of the windlass sounded loud on the still-dawn air. Cursing the noise, Ryan hastily took care of their thirst and threw himself into the saddle. As roosters crowed the sun over the horizon,

Ryan quietly led Windfall into the woods to begin the trip back to New Berne. A noise that did not belong in the night awakened her from fitful sleep. For a moment she thought it had sounded like the windlass of the well. Perhaps the wind was swinging the bucket and making it creak. Slowly she stretched her still-tired muscles and watched the day lighten the shadows of her room. For the first time in months, she felt Ryan's presence like a physical ache that left her weak with longing. For a few long minutes she lay there, giving herself up to the agony. Then with a sigh, she struggled from the twisted sheets and walked to the window. Was it imagination and the soul-tearing loneliness of the last few months that made the shadows along the edge of the dogwood-dappled forest take on the image of Ryan riding his horse away from her? She knew there had been fighting between Kinston and New Berne and in the surrounding countryside and wondered if Ryan had been involved, if he had been injured or even killed. She sadly dropped the lacy sheer curtain and struggled to re-don the homespun dress, stiffened from the perspiration and the odor of previous labor. She absentmindedly tugged at the taunt fabric at her waist, trying to purchase a bit of ease for her expanding waistline. Stiff homemade shoes from a long-gone worker responsible for cobbling them taunted her with the anticipation of more blisters to join those that still wept painfully on her feet. For a fleeting moment she rued that she did not enjoy the luxury of the slave labor that worked the fields of her parents' and Fitz's plantations.

Walking to the table between the windows, Penny splashed some cold water into the basin and washed her face. That done, she struggled to pin her hair so it would stay up for a day spent in the field doing the work assigned to only the strongest men in prior times. She had only a few hair pins left and feared the loss of even one, as replacement would be impossible. For a moment she considered just tying her hair at the nape of her neck but the weight and heat of it would only become unbearable by day's end were she to do so. Bracing herself against the edge of the table, Penny prepared to begin another day of fighting the weeds that had invaded both the fields and garden. She had been determined to plant as many acres of corn as the seed they had hoarded would allow, then she would work with Moses to plow a garden and plant the food they would need not only for themselves but to supply ever more rapacious armies, both friend and foe. She was thankful that they still had mules to pull the plow, as some farms had only lone women to struggle at pulling a plow through resisting earth.

Were her little secluded haven plundered by either side, she planned a reserve of corn that she could reluctantly allow them to capture from her. The rest she would hide for her own purposes, for Penny had an idea of how to make the money she would need not only to survive, but also someday to prosper. She never wanted her son to be faced with the struggles and deprivations that each new day brought to her and her kindred, both those of her blood and those bound by the ties of geography. A wry smile crossed her face when she remembered the pampered girl she had been and the determined, hardened woman she was becoming. Feminine vapors and vanities were a luxury she could no longer afford. Suddenly, the mantle of a previously masculine domain now augmented her womanly household responsibilities. War was forcing a redefinition of gender identity and roles. Penny recognized that her previous *granny woman* status had given her a more community-focused, and thus masculine, role than that of most women. While she had never accepted payment in coin for her services, grateful families had repaid her kindness with gifts of food and other items. She had taken pride in a quasi-professional accomplishment that took her beyond the confines of her home. She had learned to deal with a world greater than that defined by her social connections and status and those who worked in her employ. Even so, she had never before toiled like a common field hand; hard labor had become not the exception in her day but the expectation if she were to achieve her goals.

Resolutely walking from her room, Penny descended to the kitchen and an increasingly meager breakfast. Finding it more closely resembled the flavor of the real thing than chicory coffee, she now used dried, parched, and ground okra seeds to substitute for the fine imported coffee Ryan had supplied for such a short time. Cold cornbread from supper the previous day and a little buttermilk to moisten it constituted the morning's breakfast. Lunch was increasingly restricted to what Mammy could serve in the field.

When she remembered the money she was hoarding so carefully, she was tempted to spend some of it to ease their daily lives. Until it became critical she would not. Even if she wanted to spend it, the importation of the things that the South had previously depended upon to augment what they grew or made was seriously curtailed by limited importation, army conscription, and poor transportation. Wanting to buy something had been the hardest to resist in April when a crop seemed so far away. The spring was always difficult, she had reminded herself. The former year's bounty was nearing its end and the current season's crops were but the promise of a sprouting and growing season away. She craved the day when tender young turnip and mustard greens could be harvested. Cooked and served with a dash of vinegar and hard-boiled eggs, some crispy thin cornbread, and maybe a newly caught fish or tender fried pullet sounded like the best meal from any fine restaurant she had ever visited in Wilmington or New Berne. She salivated at the thought.

That morning the others were already at work when she picked up her hoe and began to weed the corn that she hoped would insure her an edge against hunger and an avenue to wealth. Penny had planned and researched, stocked piled sugar, and purchased copper tubing, jugs, and kettles with the vanishing and depreciating Confederate notes. During the cold winter months, she sat by the evening fire carving corks from black gum roots, while Mammy patiently carded the wool and cotton they would need for thread and fabric.

During the previous winter, Penny had decided to go into business for herself. A cotton crop was too problematic because of the blockade. She needed something that was in demand and required little labor and complexity to produce. Even though she knew it would be anathema were she discovered, she was going to become a bootlegger of corn liquor for the duration of the war. She would not think about the five hundred-dollar fine and the risk of imprisonment imposed by North Carolina on convicted bootleggers.

Marcus knew what she planned and had coached her on what it would entail. It was to him she had entrusted the funds to procure the materials and supplies that had to be purchased. Between them they worked to devise the best way to distribute and sell the liquor they produced. He was not only her confidant, but in exchange for his expertise and labor, he would be equal partner. Swearing him to secrecy, they had plotted through that cold winter huddled by the kitchen fire. The corn crop was an essential springboard to the future. For that she would drive herself without mercy. By late summer, the labor she faced would not be in a field.

One day a week, Penny allowed herself the luxury of rest. That was the day she rode to her childhood home to sit quietly at the bedside of her dying mother. Her father's eyes had taken on a haunting sadness that she could not escape even when she left them. They all knew it was only a matter of time. They were so consumed by the agony of the ending days of her life that her parents did not notice her blistered hands and sunburned skin other than to make a passing comment that she should take better care of herself. Not caring to enlighten them as to the cause, she quietly agreed. The only thing that brought them joy was the sight of her swelling abdomen. Sarah had silently sworn to herself that she would not die before she could hold her first grandchild. She prayed it was a promise she could keep.

Often Penny walked back through the woods at the end of her visit so she could collect wild herbs to replenish the dwindling supply in her pantry. People in the community still called on her when they suffered various common maladies. At the end of a long day in the fields, it wasn't unusual for her to stand at the kitchen table working on herbal preparations when she was too tired to even feed herself. Occasionally a neighbor would work in her place in the field, in exchange for Penny tending to an ailing relative. Those days were like a vacation for her, as they relieved her from the increasingly difficult bending and hoeing that planting and weeding demanded.

When the planting season was done, she would walk out into the cool of the early evening to admire the fields covered in a pale green haze of tender corn leaves that had pushed a crack in the crust of the earth in order to unfurl into sunlight. She walked in her garden to admire the little plants emerging from the black soil, bearing promise of the fresh produce she so craved. The blossoms of the fruit trees fell like a benediction on her head as she ambled beneath them, smelling their delicate perfume. She laughed joyfully at the antics of newborn pigs, calves, and biddies that tottered drunkenly about on untested limbs. Watching them, she was again thankful that she had thought to procure a stockpile of salt while it was still easily available and relatively cheap. Without the salt, preserving meat would not be possible. As the fragile little plants grew stronger and reached ever higher, she felt a great pride in what they had accomplished. When gentle rain came, she looked up at the weeping sky and sent a prayer of gratitude heavenward. But when the clouds grew dark and stormy, she waited in anxious fear that heavy downpours would strip away her tender plants in runneling froths of muddy water or hail would shred them like tattered green ribbons. After the storms passed, she rushed into her fields to reassure herself that her crop still thrived.

The crop was going to be her avenue to survival as long as the war lasted. She would make the liquor and sell it. She would harvest the food and save it. And when the end of summer brought a new labor to her, she would bring her child into a world that did not carry the threat of starvation and poverty for him. This child she felt moving beneath her hand might never know his real father, but she would make it up to him by giving him every advantage in life of which she was capable. She apologized to him for the deception and asked him to forgive her, telling him that someday if he learned what she had done, she hoped he would understand. Talking to him and telling him of her plans brought her a peace with the compromise she had made with her life. She could no longer afford the luxury of dreams in a world gone mad. All she could do was find a way to mitigate the dangers inherent in her greatest fears. While storms were beyond her control, she could prepare for ways to deal with the peril of bummers and men who came skulking like the one Ryan had killed on her hall floor.

The struggle to harvest, preserve, dry, or store food occupied many hot days that summer. Penny found herself more and more tired as the weight of her belly increased. She knew soon, she would not be able to work the way she had done in the previous months. Then Lucinda, who had grown more and more helpful and considerate, Mammy, and Moses would be the ones to take up the reins where she left off. Marcus had promised to bring some of her father's slaves to harvest the fat ears of corn when they had dried and sagged on the withering stalks. The very best ears would be reserved to seed the next year's crop. Once the harvested corn was shelled, some would be reserved for the animals, some would be reserved for the sprouting corn needed for the liquor, and the rest ground into meal.

Walking in the woods on the verge of the swamp, Penny and Marcus had carefully plotted the best location for the still. By summer he had already built the still deep in the swamp where it was unlikely to be found but not too distant from the old mill that he had struggled to clean up and put in good working order. The creek would not only give them the water they needed for the operation, but it would also power the mill that would grind the mash. The old mill was the first one that her father had built on his land. Since then he had replaced it with a newer mill closer to his house. When he

divided off the land for Penny's farm, the old one lay on the creek bank within her boundary lines. With the equipment still in the mill, it had not been as monumental a task and an expense as it would have been otherwise. She was grateful they had forgotten it when they were donating metal for the Confederacy to melt into weapons. Of course she could always have taken the corn to her father's for milling; however, that would have meant answers to questions that she didn't want posed.

Chapter 13

Ryan hated the war and he despised his role in it. He would have resigned had it been allowed. The month of June was a quiet one and until the middle of July, when Foster was planning another incursion into the countryside, Ryan had time to ride out to the land he loved and sit on the knoll, looking out across the water. One day while he was sitting there, a still handsome though faded woman in her late seventies walked up to him. Furling her parasol, she demanded in the twang of a New Englander, "Well, sir. Just what do you think you're doing constantly trespassing on my land?"

"I earnestly beg your pardon, madam. I have no excuse except for a love of this place that brings peace in the middle of war. I assure you I mean no harm to either the site or anyone on it. I realize I represent the enemy that is occupying the town and the immediate surrounds, but I personally have no intention of robbing, damaging, or molesting anyone, as I find the entire process more than abhorrent." Ryan sprang to his feet and bowed as he said it.

"Oh, twaddle. Sit down and stop blathering. *I* invaded this town long before *you* were even born. Of course, Yankees weren't quite so vilified then." She laughed when she said it, putting Ryan at ease. "I think I'll pull up the neighboring stump and we can have a little visit."

Ryan extended his hand to help her as she lowered herself onto the stump. "Madam, allow me to present myself. I'm Colonel Ryan Madison, previously of New York, where I was a partner in my uncle's law firm. Prior to that I was born and lived in Baltimore. You might say there's a bit of a 'civil' war in my own family, as my mother and sister are southern sympathizers. My uncle is adamantly Union."

"And your father?"

"Regrettably he's deceased." Ryan smiled at her. "And you, Madam Yankee, tell me who you are and what brought you here."

"I'm Caroline Framingham. I came here nearly sixty years ago because I was swept off my feet by the charming speech and golden locks of a fine southern boy. I've never regretted it. I came to love the South almost as much as I loved my husband. Unfortunately for me he died in '61. I suppose it was fortunate for him, though, as he would have hated what has become of his hometown. With the contrabands running around looting and stealing, the Bushwhackers or 'Buffaloes' like the devil incarnate, and the soldiers on both sides grabbing anything that's not red hot and nailed down, and most of our friends fled inland a long time ago, this town is not what it was. I don't know if it ever can be again. It's a pity, too." She shook her head in resignation. "I suspect if I were not an irascible old Yankee from Massachusetts, I would have fared far worse than I have. Thanks to my Yankee birth, Ambrose Burnside and now Foster has managed to prevent my home from being robbed and my goods carried off by the various assortments of thieves. And when the threat is from Buffaloes and contrabands, my husband's old dueling pistols serve me and my butler in good stead. I can still shoot a squirrel out of a tree at thirty paces. But it has been touch and go at times, I can tell you."

"Mrs. Framingham, if you will permit me I can arrange for a little private assistance to insure a bit more security for you since you are on the outskirts of town. Some of my men would be glad for a place to visit in their off-duty hours. If you could arrange a spare room, I'll rotate schedules and put a proposal to the more dependable of them. I'm happy to offer my services as well."

She sat studying him with narrowed eyes and tongue tucked in cheek. "I don't know why I do, but I trust you, boy, and I like the looks of you, too. I may be old, but I still appreciate a handsome man to look at. If you want to pay me a visit from time to time, I'll pull out the brandy and we'll talk. As for the rotating guard dogs, I think I like the idea. I know poor old Rufus will sleep better for it. Besides, he is one lousy shot. He couldn't hit a whale turned sideways."

"I'll see to it."

"Now, tell me, what brings you to this little knoll?"

"Why, Mrs. Framingham, I'm planning on building my home right on top of that stump you're sitting on." Ryan grinned at her when he said it.

"You audacious whippersnapper. I do believe you mean it."

They both laughed until tears came. When the laughter stopped, Ryan added, "Indeed I am quite serious. I would be most happy to purchase this land, or at least enough of it for a home and some grounds around it. I'm willing to pay a more than fair price."

"I won't sell it for a fair price or any other. Riverside stays together. My husband would turn in his grave otherwise. We have no children to pass it to, but when I die I want it to belong to someone who will love it the way we have. In the meantime, it's mine and I'm keeping it."

"Were it mine, I would feel the same way. I fell in love with this the minute I saw it. I love the live oak trees draped with moss, the gentle knoll and the way it rolls down to the river; I love looking over the water and watching how it changes every hour of the day. I love the wind whispering through the branches, the dogwood flowering in the woods, and the cries of the seagulls. Whenever I'm sad or lonely or frustrated I come here and let the peace of this place soothe my heart."

"You sound more like a poet than a soldier, Colonel Madison."

"Would you consider calling me Ryan? At the moment, I confess to being somewhat less than happy with the military title."

"War's nasty. Did you think it wouldn't be? No war is noble when it gets into the trenches. I learned that in 1812." Remembering, she sat looking out across the sparkling blue of the water. She had been in Washington with her father, a senator in the young republic when it was attacked and torched by the British. She could still remember the devastation and terror.

For a long time they sat staring at the sparkling water. At last, Caroline said, "You come back, Ryan. You come any time you need to. I'll be in that big old lumber pile of a house over there in those oak trees if you need someone to talk to. By the way, my friends call me Caroline. Seeing as how we're in the South, maybe you should make that Miss Caroline."

"Miss Caroline it is." Ryan stood and extended his hand to help her to her feet. Using her parasol as a cane, she walked back down the hill in the direction of her home.

Ryan stood staring after her. Windfall turned his own head to watch the old woman walk away. Ryan saw his eyes following the woman and he walked up to the horse, patting him on the nose, and whispered to Windfall, "So she's the one who owns this land. Somehow I'm going to convince her to sell and in the meantime I'm going to enjoy the company of one delightfully feisty old lady. Do you have any objections to that, old boy?"

Windfall's ears pricked forward and he whinnied. Ryan laughed. "I'll take that as an encouraging comment."

Thinking of Caroline Framingham and the perils her outlying property faced, Ryan pondered the problems the Negroes were creating in the area. They were swarming in from the countryside, happy to escape their masters and gain freedom. Because the Union held New Berne, the town was becoming a Mecca for them. In the immediate aftermath of invasion they had looted the town unmolested; however, Burnside had shortly ordered a halt to both the depredations of the contrabands and of his own troops. It had been jubilee for the newly free Negroes. As more poured in, the alarmed Union command was increasingly hard pressed to deal with their swelling numbers. Their need for food, housing, sanitation, and healthcare placed demands on a system that was already groaning under an unaccustomed weight. Many of them had not thought to the future and the need to become self-sustaining. Loitering and bored, they created problems. The general created and staffed a school for the children and any interested adults. Eventually many would become peddlers, artisans, or casual laborers; however, others did nothing to provide for themselves.

Prior to the invasion, New Berne had been home to approximately five thousand citizens, making it the second-largest city in the State. Now the Union forces alone numbered nearly twenty thousand. Primarily they were housed in residences abandoned by panicked citizens who refugeed inland with the fall of the town. Only a few of the citizens had remained; even so the capacity of the town was at a limit. Stories of rape, murder, and pillage were rampant. The Bushwhackers, bands of deserters and outlaws, were a scourge on the land, detested by both the Union soldiers and locals, but they were more of a problem in the unprotected countryside than in the occupied town. He was pragmatic enough to realize that even with Federal protection, not all of the incursions against the citizenry could be prevented; however, he would see what he could arrange to protect Caroline Framingham.

He could understand her angst at the loss of the way of life she had enjoyed. New Berne was a felicitously situated town on the banks of converging rivers that supplied copious oysters, fish, and shrimp for local delectation and gave expansive views over the waters. While warm in the summer, breezes from the water brought some relief and winter was mild with little snow and ice. Flowered trellises, blooming gardens, and roses everywhere added both beauty and perfume to the mostly Georgian-style structures along the shady, tree-lined streets. Gaslights in the fine houses dotted the night with glowing windows. Artisans making furniture, bricks, and other products enjoyed comfortable homes purchased from a lively trade. Servants performed the daily work needed to run both homes and businesses. Vegetable gardens and surrounding farms supplied a bounty of food. The town boasted an excellent bookstore owned by F. W. Beers, where citizens and now soldiers bought newspapers from the North, the latest books, and various stationery products. The ice cream and soda shop on Middle Street was a popular destination that with the assurance of ice from the North continued to prosper. The newspaper, *The New Berne Progress*, taken over by the Union and renamed *The Yankee Printer,* continued churning out news both national and local. The Masonic Lodge, banks, and churches were well designed and prosperous looking. Theatrical productions and local musical talent had made for entertaining evenings. The Academy, now used as a hospital, was the first public school in the state. Doctors, lawyers, scholars, merchants, ship owners, and planters enjoyed a comfortable and enlightened life, causing some to call the town another Athens.

With the arrival of Burnside and the Union forces, the citizens who had created this little oasis had fled, leaving it to survive as best it could. Fortunately for them, as the Union base in North Carolina, it was safe from the sacking and burning that other towns experienced. When the war ended, they would still have a town and homes left standing.

Ryan, along with the soldiers stationed there, wrote letters extolling the town's virtues. But it also had drawbacks. In the hot and humid summers, yellow fever arose pervasive and deadly from surrounding swamps. To allay the disease somewhat, the troops took a daily dose of quinine mixed with whiskey. While it may have helped, it didn't prevent the annual scourge. Often-fatal typhoid stalked the community. With fire a constant threat in a town of mostly wooden structures, the Union forces built a second fire station to augment the original one.

Not only were the contrabands and the Bushwhackers a source of continuing worry for the remaining citizens, but for the Union as well. And the citizens who had stayed were mostly adamantly contemptuous of their invaders. The troops found pretty young women the most audacious of the rebels: often rude, verbally scathing, and willing to use their femininity to protect themselves from punishment for their offences. Women, able to move about with relative freedom, took advantage of the fact to carry information to the Rebels. Emmeline Pigott had been caught carrying papers in big pockets concealed under her skirts. She destroyed the evidence by eating the damaging letters before they could be seized. They discovered Mrs. Elizabeth Harland hiding messages in the small central bone of hams that she delivered to her allies. And Mrs. Meekins, who posed as a cotton seller with a bale of cotton as a prop, was really a spy. The Pollack Street jail did not suffer from a lack of occupants, including the rare female.

Enlisting Bobby's help, Ryan arranged protection for Riverside and the people there during the periods the army was idle. But when they were mounting attacks on military targets in the countryside, Miss Caroline would have to manage without them. In the meantime he used the few weeks of relative idleness to arrange an informal guard for her home.

It was not until mid-July that General Foster determined to attack Greenville, Tarboro, and Rocky Mount. Greenville fell on the nineteenth with almost no opposition, as the citizens had taken to their heels. After the staff enjoyed dinner and drinks in the local tavern and the troops looted and burned a good section of the town, they pulled out, burning the bridge over the Tar River as they left. On the twentieth Tarboro was attacked again with little opposition. The army destroyed an ironclad still sitting in stocks, railroad cars, and a hundred bales of cotton, food stocks, and munitions. In the meantime, troops under Major Jacobs marched on Rocky Mount. There he hit the jackpot: destroying railroad trains, the depot, the railroad bridge, cotton mills, a flour mill and a thousand barrels of flour, a huge supply of hardtack, a machine shop and store house, three trains of government wagons, and capturing Confederate officers. The destruction of country bridges reduced mobility for local troops and citizens alike. The seizing of additional wagons brought the total to twenty-eight, all loaded with supplies. A further eight hundred bales of cotton, a hundred Rebel soldiers, and three hundred horses and mules added to the procession that returned to New Berne. They were accompanied by an additional three hundred cavorting contrabands celebrating freedom.

On July 26th, Colonel Spear led a raid by Federal Calvary on the railroad bridge at Weldon but was defeated at Boone's Creek. For the next eleven months, the Union forces stationed in New Berne experienced relative quiet. It was during this period that Ryan conducted his own campaign, the capture of Caroline. He was determined to convince her to sell him the coveted knoll.

Many afternoons, following duty, he made it a point to drop by her house for a cup of coffee or tea. Each time he carried her some small luxury that he knew was increasingly expensive or more difficult for civilians to procure. He kept the chat casual and encouraged her to talk about her life in New Berne as well as her childhood in the North. He told about his own parents, childhood, school days, and law practice in New York and how he hoped to practice in New Berne after the war. He did not mention buying the land or his sad affair with Penny. Even so, Caroline was no fool and after listening to him for weeks, she wondered why he never mentioned a fiancée, wife, or love interest.

"So, Ryan," she began, "you've told me a lot about yourself, but there's one topic you never discuss. At the risk of sounding indelicate, I don't judge you to have abnormal interests; therefore, I'm surprised you've never mentioned a sweetheart at home waiting and pining for you. That leads me to think you've been mighty disappointed somewhere along the way."

"Miss Caroline, you're too shrewd for your own good sometimes." Ryan laughed but yielded nothing more to satisfy her curiosity.

"Well, I guess that's your way of telling me to mind my own business." She studied him for a moment and then demanded with a grin, "So you still want to live in New Berne but you don't want my knoll anymore?"

"I still intend to settle in New Berne and as soon as I can persuade you, I want to buy that land. I don't blame you for not wanting to sell it, but I surely hope some day you'll change your mind."

"You keep bringing me tea, coffee, and bonbons and I'll be some kind of grateful—maybe not that grateful, though."

"You can't blame me for dreaming, now?"

"No, we all dream, even old people like me." She stood up. "Join me for dinner. I've got oyster stew and some fine fried fish that Beulah is working on right now."

"I'd like that."

"Good. That'll give us time to figure out what to do about your empty social calendar that reduces you to courting an old woman like me." Caroline tossed over her shoulder as she walked through the double doors into her dining room.

Ryan had no intention of that discussion. He counted the days in his head from the date of Penny's trip to Richmond in February. Soon she would have

Daniel's child. The thought ate him like a cancer. The only way he could deal with it was to forget it whenever he could.

Some of the men had brought a wife to New Berne to share the essential exile. He'd thought of doing like many of the single ones and taking a willing widow or black woman as a mistress, courting one of the few single women left in town, or perhaps a clandestine trip to the area of Kinston, now called Sugar Hill, where Foster had left those camp followers. Digging in they had established a discreet and thriving red-light district that tempted more than one to enjoy their services. The obstacle to any of those choices was an aversion for settling for that kind of relationship after what he had shared with Penny.

Wryly he reminded himself that he had not been with any woman since Christmas, when he had given Penny his ring and his promise. He had no interest in any other, as for the first time in his adult life feminine charms held no attraction. He assumed that would eventually change, but it had not as of yet. That part of his dream for the future was a lost cause, the knoll was not. That eleven-month period free of military excursions gave him the time to continue wooing Caroline into selling her land. With patience and charm he hoped she would eventually relent.

Fall came bringing the relief of cooler and less humid weather. Ryan sailed the small boat he had purchased as far as he dared, enjoying the freedom of wind, water, and wide blue skies. He explored the broad flow of the joined rivers to where they poured into the Pamlico Sound, once going as far as Cedar Island to watch wild Outer Banks ponies frolicking on the dunes. He had camped for the night and awakened in the morning to find one of the sturdy ponies, descendants of horses shipwrecked on the island in years past, nosing at his knapsack. At other times, he saddled up Windfall, who was restless with confinement, and they would race around the Union's secured areas. The other officers and his men sensed that he was driven by some inner demon that gave him no rest. When November arrived, the pall of gloom that hovered around him became unbearable. He wondered whether Penny's baby was a boy or a girl and if she had come safely through labor. He doubted he would ever know and scolded himself for still caring. To escape from the thoughts that plagued him, he invited Caroline to go sailing with him while the weather was still mild.

Although she had initially refused, some sense of adventure urged her on and she relented. That Saturday dawned with soft blue skies and unseasonably warm temperatures. With a lively wind that would insure a good sail but not an overly risky one, Ryan sailed his boat to her landing. She was waiting for him with a big hamper basket of lunch. From the water he had not seen what she was wearing, but as he pulled to the wharf, his mouth dropped in astonishment.

"Close your mouth, Ryan Madison. Didn't you ever see an old lady in pants before? I'm not about to get in that boat in petticoats and hoops like some fool idiot. I sailed in New England as a girl and I know enough to think that wouldn't be so wise. If I have to, I can swim in my husband's old trousers but I couldn't in a passel of petticoats. Now give me a hand with this basket. I'm counting on you getting hungry."

"Yes, ma'am." Ryan took the basket she handed him and settled it in the boat. "If you'll give me your hand, I'll help you in."

"I may be crazy but I haven't been sailing since I was twelve years old. This is too good to miss because I used to love it so. Just don't scare me to death or turn this thing over. Just because I know how to swim, it doesn't mean I want to."

Ryan carefully pushed away and, catching the breeze in the sail, smoothly glided from shore into the water. With the wind and the current working together, soon they were skimming the shoreline east of town. Caroline lifted her face to the sun and wind, enjoying the speed of the racing boat. When the sun reached its zenith, Ryan spotted a small sandy beach with a clearing that was high enough to give them a good place to land and have their picnic. He helped her from the boat and carried the hamper to the dry spot of grass that she indicated. There they spread the blanket, dishes, utensils, and food.

"Beulah says you've been looking down in the mouth lately so she packed some happy food: fried chicken, biscuits, and her special red velvet cake. You're going to love it."

"I do love it," Ryan exclaimed. Before he realized he was saying it, he added, "I'd never had that kind of cake until Mammy made it for me when I was recovering from the bullet wound. Penny loves it, too."

For a moment, he regretted divulging so much and busied himself, shuffling food about and uncorking the wine. Caroline watched him for several minutes, realizing he had just told her a great deal about why he frequently seemed so sad and withdrawn.

"Penny must be a special woman for you to love her so much," she commented quietly. Cocking an eyebrow at him, she waited to see how he would react.

Ryan poured the wine and lifted his glass in a toast. "To another special woman. Thank you for your friendship and tolerance of my sometime melancholy moods. Yes, Penny was a special woman but unfortunately it's been many months now since I lost her."

Misunderstanding, Caroline replied, "I'm so sorry. Death comes to us all but it's so hard to accept when someone we love is taken from us. And for you it's harder; she was young and you had your lives ahead. My husband was old and I miss him sorely, but at least we had many good years together before he was taken. Did you have children?"

She saw Ryan's mouth tighten before he tersely replied, "No, we had no children together."

Caroline did not notice the wording of that *together*. "Maybe that's for the best. With you in the army, children without a mother and the father away in the war would have a difficult life."

"Well, enough of that, let's enjoy our lunch and this gorgeous day."

"It's a better day than you know, my boy. When we get back to Riverside, I've got a little surprise for you." Caroline looked at him with a teasing light in her eye.

"Now, you just wait a minute. I don't need you trying to fix me up with some woman like a couple of the officers' wives have been doing. I'm a big boy and I'll pick my own when I'm ready." Ryan was quietly annoyed at the constant attempts at meddling in his social life. He had dealt with a parade of daughters of his fellow officers, whose wives were determined to find husbands for their simpering offspring. The more he was forced to politely accommodate their stultifying company, the more recalcitrant he became and the more he missed Penny.

Caroline just laughed at his sputtering protests, divulging nothing more.

Chapter 14

The wind sighed in the tall pines around her house as Penny wearily finished the last of the day's pickling. The small pickled onions, carrots, and beans went on the shelf with the pickled cucumbers, peaches, watermelon rind, and beets. Her pantry was slowly filling with the food they would need until the following summer. The dried herbs, beans, peas, and tomatoes would be done in late September. But by then, she would leave all of that to Mammy, Moses, and Lucinda.

The still was finished, the logs to heat the mash had been cut and stacked, and all was ready for the first run, waiting only for the harvest of the corn. The growing season had been a good one despite the spotty rain and there had been no destructive storms. She could only pray that the autumn hurricanes would not destroy the corn crop that still hung in the fields as the cobs slowly dried and the shucks withered. When it was fully dried, it would be harvested and she and Marcus would begin their clandestine operation.

When the first of September arrived, Penny packed her valise and gave last-minute instructions to Mammy and Moses, knowing even as she did that they were unnecessary, as they knew what needed doing as well or better than she did. She was on her way to Pineview to stay with her parents until after the baby. They anticipated its birth in November, but she knew better. Had they known how close she was to giving birth, her unrelenting toil would not have been permitted. Mammy fretted about her, too, but knew she was driven and would not stop until she had accomplished what she intended.

"Pa!" she called as she walked into her parents' home. "I'm here."

A worried-looking Nancy emerged from the sunroom. "Oh, Penny. I'm so glad you're home. Your mama is having a really bad day and I don't know what to do to help her."

"Nancy, where's Pa?"

"He walked down to the pigpen. He should be back soon," Nancy said as the two women walked towards the sunroom.

Opening the door, Penny walked into the sauna-like heat. "Mama, Nancy tells me you're not feeling so well today. I'm going to go make you some tea from crushed bleeding heart roots that I brought with me. That ought to give you some relief. You just be quiet and rest, okay?"

"Penny, I'm so glad you're here. Are you going to be staying now?" Her mother's voice was almost a whisper.

"I'm here, Mama, and I'm staying until after my baby comes. Don't you fret. I'll be back in a minute with that tea. Okay?"

Nancy took her bag to Penny's old bedroom while Penny walked to the kitchen to make the tea for her mother. Just as she poured it into a cup to take to her, John walked into the kitchen. "I heard my girl had come," he exclaimed as he walked forward to give her a light peck on her forehead.

"I'm here now, Pa. I'll do what I can to help Mama. I'm just sorry I've been so busy that I've had little time for the two of you. I know you both need me right now."

"Don't fuss. We've managed, but no lie, I'm very glad you've come. Not just for us but for you, too. I know you've been working too darned hard for your condition. If I thought it would do any good, I'd have been over there trying to stop you."

"Thanks for understanding, Pa. You know it just had to be done."

"That I know, but I don't understand why you wouldn't let some of my slaves come over and do it for you. We still have enough here to take care of our needs and yours. Even if I didn't, Fitz has more than enough to help out. You don't need to be out there in the hot sun working like a field hand. What do you think Daniel would say if he knew what his wife was up to?"

"Let's not beat that dead horse again." Penny smiled. Love her he did, understand her he knew he did not. She had written Daniel that he was going to be a father. He had written back to assure her of his happiness that they were having a child and then proceeded to plan his child's future. Penny knew in her heart she wanted to circumvent his influence in the rearing of her son. If Ryan could not be there as the father, the substitute father would provide name but not control. She wanted her son to be a finer, stronger man than her husband.

She admitted to herself that Daniel was not a bad person, just not as fine a man as Ryan. Both she and Daniel had allowed themselves to be caught in a marriage that neither of them had really wanted. They were both to blame for the lack of compatibility and unhappiness between them. She acknowledged that she had been cold and distant and questioned if that was what had driven him to Lucinda for passion. Somehow for the sake of her child, she had to mend her marriage but she would not cede her growing independence and she would not allow Daniel to determine the rearing of her child.

"Fitz got a letter from Daniel the other day. He says Daniel is thrilled about the baby." He added as though he heard her thoughts, "So try not to worry about Daniel. When this war is over he'll come home and he's going to be a good father. He'll take over running the farm again so you have time to do women's things and take care of your baby. Until then Fitz and I are willing to take it on for you."

"Pa, don't worry about the farm. Marcus and Moses are helping me so it's not a problem. As for Daniel, it's not so much him I worry about. It's my baby."

"What do you mean?"

"I worry about what kind of world my child is coming into. Things are going to be so changed after the war and if it doesn't end soon, it's going to get pretty desperate for us all. I don't want my baby to starve or be ragged and poor. I want him to have a good and prosperous life."

"We all want that for your child and for you, too, darling." John smiled sadly.

"You know your mama is just hanging in there until she can hold her grandchild. Sometimes I think that's all that's keeping her alive. Even though I'll be happy to hold this coming child in my arms, I fear it, too. I'm so afraid she'll just give up then."

"Dr. Miller still comes to check, doesn't he?"

"Once a week and he promised me he'll come when you go into labor unless he gets tied up with the wounded. I'll have one of my men go for him when you need him. Fortunately, we've been pretty quiet here since the Wyse Forks skirmish in May. Let's hope it lasts."

"Yes, thank goodness for that. With all the rest there is to do, I just didn't have the time or energy to deal with soldiers or Bushwhackers." Bushwhackers, notorious gangs of deserters, thieves, and general good-for-nothings, while not as big a problem as in the western counties, still made life difficult elsewhere.

"It's for sure none of us want to deal with them anytime." He shook his head with disgust as he said it. "Some of the stories I hear are enough to stand your hair on end. The Bushwhackers are harder to deal with than the Yankees. They are rabble and scum with no discipline and no moral boundaries to inhibit their actions. So far we haven't had any Negro uprisings around here but there have been in other areas. That's a worry as well for all of us, whether we are with slaves or without. For sure the times are perilous, but we'll come through. You try not to worry—your Pa's going to take care of you now and that baby of yours, too."

"I know you will, Pa." She gave him a hug and then stood back with a grin. "So is Fitz still flirting with Nancy?"

Looking vaguely uncomfortable, John looked away and answered carefully. "I think he may have found a new interest. We don't see much of him anymore. I can't tell you any more than that."

Penny sensed he was not revealing all he knew but knowing him as she did, it would do her no good to pry for more.

Penny quickly settled into the routine of the house. It was comforting to be near her parents and to feel their love and protection surround her. At night it was reassuring to nestle into the bed she had slept in until her marriage and know that she was not alone in the house when so many dangers were abroad in the land. She found without the constant need for alert vigilance that marked her nights in her lonely bed at Pleasant Glade, she was beginning to sleep more soundly. She had left her pistol with Moses should her own house and people need it. Her father and the other men on his plantation would protect her now.

With Nancy's competent assistance, Penny kept her mother as comfortable as she could. Often the two women would take turns reading to the invalid woman. Sarah's favorite stories were those by Charles Dickens. Sometimes her father would join them for the reading but she knew he wasn't really listening; he just wanted to be near his wife. With a shock Penny saw that worry for her mother and the day to day running of a farm in the middle of a war were taking a toll on him. He looked ten years older than when the war had begun. She knew they both worried constantly about Brett, who had been involved in numerous battles in Virginia. His letters spoke little of his experiences, as he preferred to dwell on the humorous incidents of camp life. Penny knew it was his way of trying to spare them all from futile worry. At times she wished that he would have taken the exemption that he was entitled to since their father had more than twenty slaves, but he had given the exemption to Marcus instead. Brett had ignored the fact that overseers on large plantations were also exempt. He had laughed when he told them he was leaving, saying that Marcus was a better farmer but he was a better hunter. So he was off to bag some Yankees.

The second week of September began with a usually hot spell of weather. Penny had gone to bed but awakened almost immediately from a dream. In the vision she had sensed something sinister stalking the land around her. It was so vague she decided to ignore it and go back to sleep, but with her belly hugely distended she found herself miserably uncomfortable. Looking for a breath of fresh air, she left her bed in the small hours of the morning and walked onto the porch to sit in the rocker at the far end. There was only a faint breeze stirring but that was better than the hot mattress she had tossed on until she could stand it no more. She had sat there dozing for a couple of hours, she couldn't say exactly how long nor what jolted her into alertness. Grateful that the mass of the large camellia at the end of the porch kept her in shadow, Penny slowly arose from the chair to keep it from creaking and slid deeper into the shadow at the edge of the porch. From there she had a clear view across the yard to the hedge and the outbuildings beyond. Something or someone was moving stealthily across the space between hedge and outbuildings. She heard a cough and then a sibilant hiss of caution.

Silently, careful of every board, she made her way to the front door and slipped inside. Her heart was pounding like a drum. Suddenly she felt arms slide around her and a hand cover her mouth. Penny started to writhe and try to scream, but the quiet whisper of her father's reassuring voice made her slump with relief. "Pa, someone's out there. I don't know who or how many."

"I know. Something woke me as well. Take this pistol; it's loaded. You cover the front door and I'm going to go to the back. I just hope to God Marcus is aware something is going on."

Penny edged the sheer lace curtains that covered the side windows of the doorway and waited. She could hear her father creeping down the hallway to the back door. Carefully he eased it open enough to see out. At a creak on the stairs, she turned to see Nancy edging against the wall as she descended cautious step by cautious step. In her hand she held a bed-warming pan like a cudgel. Nancy saw Penny and quickly crossed over to her.

"I heard your Pa's door open and the cocking of his pistols. What's going on?"

"Somebody's out there. I can't tell what they want."

A loud shout and running feet behind the house renewed the heavy pounding of Penny's heart. Nancy gripped her weapon and moved to the opposite side of the door. As the two women waited, they heard the pop of pistol fire and her father's shout. There was an answering call from Marcus and more firing. Penny and Nancy were both turned toward the action in the rear of the house when the front door suddenly burst open. Whirling, Penny raised her weapon to fire, but Nancy had already swung the bed warmer, catching the intruder over the top of his head. The vile-smelling rankness of body odor assaulted her nostrils as she leveled the pistol at the man who had sunk to his knees with Nancy's blow from the bedpan.

"Move and I'll blow your damned sorry head off."

"Don't cha go shootin' that thar thang, ma'am. I jes want to git gone from here." The cracker twang of his groveling voice irritated her.

"Then what are you doing here in the first place, you sorry trash?"

"Me and mah frien's wuz jes lookin' fer a little grub. Tha's all."

"Did it occur to you to come in daylight and ask?" Penny inquired with sarcasm.

John entered the rear door and called out, "Penny, are you okay in here?"

"Over here, Pa. Nancy and I have collected some garbage for you."

After the three Bushwhackers had been tied up and stashed in the wagon, Marcus and one of the slaves drove them to the sheriff in Kinston along with the body of the one who had been killed. Penny, Nancy, and John retreated to the kitchen for a soothing drink of brandy once they had reassured Sarah that all was okay. Piecing the various versions together, it seems that the one Nancy bashed had been assigned to enter the house and take what he could while the others created a diversion out back. They had not been prepared for the alertness of the household, nor for Marcus, who was a notorious insomniac. He had left his cabin with a loaded rifle and drawn a bead on them almost by the time they had ridden into the edge of the yard. Counting four of them, he hesitated to take them on until he saw John emerging from the rear door of the house with pistol at the ready. John opened fire and then Marcus, catching three of them in a crossfire while the fourth slipped away. He was the one who had entered the front of the house.

"Nancy, I'm going to buy some more warming pans. Those things may be deadlier than a pistol." John laughed with admiration.

"I don't know but what I might prefer a pistol and some lessons on using it," she replied grimly.

"I'll see to it today. Penny can help you, too. She's as good a shot as any man I know. Heck, if you women had been drafted into this war y'all would have won it by now." John stood and yawned. "I don't know if I can sleep after the excitement but I'm going to bed and try to get an hour or two's rest. Why don't you ladies do the same?"

"In a minute, Pa. I'm so keyed up, I just need to sit here a little longer and calm down."

Nancy offered, "I'll keep you company, Penny. It's so darned hot, I can't sleep anyway."

Finishing her cup of tea laced with brandy, Penny stretched. "I think I'll go on up."

Just as she stood, a hard spasm rippled across her belly. Gasping she gripped the edge of the table, waiting for it to pass. Nancy jumped from her chair and ran around the table to hold her around the waist. "Oh, my goodness gracious. Do you think the baby's coming?"

"If that keeps happening, I would be sure of it. I'm going to go upstairs and lie down to see if it stops."

"I'll come with you just in case…."

As the sun rose, pinking the edge of clouds on the horizon, Penny knew that her child was on his way. The labor pains were becoming more regular but still far enough apart that she didn't think it would be anytime soon. Nancy left to summon Marcus, who had only just returned, to tell him he needed to ride into Kinston and get Dr. Miller. She then put water on to boil and gathered clean towels and sheets to take to Penny's room. She had never attended anyone in labor and other than the need for water and towels, she was at a loss as to what to do next except wait for the doctor. She hesitated to wake John or Sarah after the broken sleep they had experienced the night before. She was standing in the kitchen biting her lip indecisively when John entered.

"You're up early, Nancy."

"Actually I haven't been to sleep. Penny's in labor. I just sent Marcus into town to get the doctor. I was waiting to tell you and Miss Sarah because I hoped you were resting. I've boiled some water and have some towels and sheets to take up, but I really don't know how to help. I surely hope the doctor gets here soon."

"Don't worry. Delia has helped with enough birthings, she can take over here for you. I don't know what Penny has in the way of clothes and diapers for the baby. I've been too busy to ask about women's stuff. You might go to the attic and find the black trunk with brass bands on it. It's full of baby clothes and blankets, things Brett and Penny used when they were infants. I'm sure after all of this time they could use cleaning and pressing. I'll have one of the women come to the house and help you get things ready for the baby. Now you run along and don't worry." He paused. "I'm going to let Sarah sleep. I won't tell her until nearer time because I don't want her worrying needlessly if the baby is slow in coming."

Nancy was relieved that she had a chore that she knew how to deal with. She had been frightened that if the doctor didn't come, it might be left to her to deliver the baby. Breathing a sigh, she climbed the steps to the attic. When she reached the last riser the house vibrated from a peal of thunder. Maybe a storm will cool things off for the laboring woman, she thought. The house was already like an oven from the heat of the day before. Heavy raindrops began a drumbeat on the roof as Nancy reached into the trunk to extract the things that John had sent her for. Vivid lightning flashed through the small windows in the dormers on the front of the house followed by a loud crack. Hastily gathering the baby things, she scurried from the attic to the lower level. She had always feared electrical storms and this one promised to be a mean one.

Passing Penny's room, she paused before sticking her head in the door. "That's quite a storm but maybe it will cool things off so it's not so miserable. I'll just check to make sure the rain's not coming in your windows. If you'd like, I could close them anyway."

"Goodness sakes, no. That wind's the best thing I've felt in days." Penny lifted herself and adjusted the pillows behind her back. "What's that you've got there?"

"Your pa sent me to the attic to get the baby things you and Brett used. I'm taking them down to wash and iron. We didn't know if you've made things for the baby or not."

Penny's mouth dropped. "Oh, my God. With all I've been doing, I never even thought of it. What kind of mother am I going to be if I couldn't even remember to make some clothes for my child? At least Pa thought of it."

Nancy flinched as a rolling rumble of thunder followed another tremendous crack of lightning. Penny smiled at her fear. "I surely hope Marcus doesn't have trouble getting back with Dr. Miller. I don't relish the idea of Delia delivering my baby. She doesn't pay enough attention to cleanliness to suit me. Promise if he doesn't come, you'll help me instead of Delia. I'm not going to allow her to deliver my baby."

"Penny, I can't. I don't know what to do. Please, you can't make me. I would be so afraid, and what if I did something that hurt you or the baby? I just can't. I'm sorry."

"You may not have any choice. Now sit down and I'll tell you what you need to know and do just in case." An unhappy and worried Nancy sat as Penny explained. Penny didn't say it but Nancy could see that the contractions were getting closer and stronger. Even in the much cooler room, Penny's brow beaded with perspiration after each new spasm.

By eleven in the morning the storm had passed, leaving the air fresh with ozone and crisply cool. Sarah was awake and John had taken her breakfast and told her that the baby was about to have a birthday. As weak as she was she was still so excited that it was all he could do to prevent her from climbing the stairs to Penny's room. Nancy had the servant occupied washing and ironing baby clothes and she was busy pacing the kitchen, reluctant to go back to Penny.

"Lawsy, Miz Nancy. You making me nuvus as a cat 'round dogs. Why don' you git on outside an' cut sum ah dem fla'ers or sump'n? We kin han'le things in here." Delia shook her head with exasperation, muttering, "Babies cum all de time. It ain' no big thing. Lawsy! Fust babies always slo' cumin'."

Nancy fled the kitchen to gather the roses that bloomed in the garden on the south side of the house. She worried that she was not upstairs with Penny but didn't know how to face it. She knew she was excessively modest and reserved. Things of a physical and sexual nature made her more than a little uncomfortable. Having a baby was a symbol of all that made her uneasy. As she cut the roses and laid them in the basket, she heard the distant sound of hoof beats. Please, she prayed, please God, let that be the doctor. Please, just let that be the doctor.

Marcus galloped into the yard and swung down from the saddle. Running to him in alarm, Nancy demanded, "Where's the doctor?" She realized how shrill she sounded and added, "Sorry, I'm just so worried. The baby can't be much longer coming."

"It's all right. The doctor is following in his buggy. He should be here shortly. Why don't you go tell Penny he's on the way? That should be a relief to her."

"I'll do that and thank you, Marcus. It would have been just terrible if he hadn't come. Penny refuses to let Delia deliver her baby."

When Nancy reached Penny's room she could hear a low groan of pain followed by strenuous panting. "Hang on, Penny, the doctor's almost here."

"Oh, God. So is this baby!" Penny cried out in pain. She gripped Nancy's hands as she struggled against another hard pain. Just when Nancy thought her bones would be crushed, Penny eased her grip and lay back.

"He'd better hurry if he wants to deliver this baby."

"Oh, please hold on, Penny. It won't be long now."

"I'm afraid this baby has his own schedule. Oh, my God." Penny arched as another hard contraction distorted her belly.

Penny raised her knees and gripped her belly, pushing hard. The doctor came into the room just as the head began to crest. "Well, young lady. You seem to be in a bit of a hurry here."

Nancy slipped from the room but had not gone two paces when she fainted.

John heard her fall and came running. "Nancy, are you all right?"

She looked up into his face and replied, "I am now that the doctor's here."

Chapter 15

When Ryan tied the boat up to Caroline's wharf, he had every intention of assisting the elderly woman from the boat, handing her the empty basket, thanking her for her company and lunch, and then fleeing before she could haul him to the house to meet whatever woman she had waiting. Caroline knew him well enough she could have recited his planned course of action without error. To circumvent his protests, she took the offensive. "Would you mind helping me to the house, Ryan? For some reason I'm feeling a bit dizzy. Too much sun and excitement for a woman my age, I suppose."

He couldn't tell if she were acting or not but he had no choice. He could not leave this wily old woman to make her way alone when she had asked for his help. Simple decency forbade such rude action. Frustrated at not make his escape, he grudgingly offered his arm and assisted her to the house. Walking slowly and carefully, she leaned heavily on him. Perhaps, he reconsidered, she really is unwell. The thought left him decidedly shaken. He had come to treasure her irreverent wit and acerbic intelligence that kept his loneliness at bay during idle hours.

"Please help me to the parlor, Ryan. I want to sit there a few minutes and collect myself."

"Of course. May I have Rufus bring you something to drink? Perhaps some brandy?"

"No need to call him. The brandy and glasses are already on the side table in the parlor."

He had been in the house frequently and had never seen brandy and glasses sitting out in the parlor. They were always in the cabinet in the dining room. His suspicions were instantly aroused but he could not turn back now.

Sitting by the window in the parlor was a man who appeared near Caroline's age. Ryan looked but there was no calculating woman in the room he could see, excluding the one standing beside him. Caroline heard him sigh in relief and laughed.

"Ryan, I want you to meet an old and dear friend of mine who was kind enough to ride out here this evening. John Harvey, I would like to present to you my friend, Colonel Ryan Madison. Ryan, John has some papers I think you might enjoy reading."

Ryan shook the stately gentleman's hand and took the chair beside him that he indicated by a nod. He looked at Caroline and caught a look of absolute glee spreading across her face.

"Mr. Madison, one look at this woman in those ridiculous trousers and any idiot can see that she has an independent and willful mind. Against my emphatic advice to the contrary, she insists on pursuing a course of action that her husband would find ill advised in the extreme. I hope that you, despite any selfish interests of your own, will be decent enough to persuade her not to go through with this." He gave Ryan a stern looking, harrumphing as he did so.

"John, you're my attorney. I hire you to do what I need, not what you want." Caroline raised an eyebrow in admonition.

Ryan watched the interchange between the two with growing puzzlement. The attorney lifted papers from his pocket and handed them to him. Ryan turned in his chair so the fading light in the window illuminated the papers he held and began reading. When he finished he sat in stunned shock. "I frankly don't know what to say. This is an unanticipated but decidedly wonderful surprise. My dear, Miss Caroline, you cannot begin to realize the extent of my immense gratitude for the confidence and trust you place in me."

Mr. Harvey interrupted before Caroline could respond. "Surely you can appreciate the precipitous nature of this document and the constraints it places on your own future, Colonel Madison. I would advise both you and Caroline to think long and hard before signing this document."

"Mr. Harvey, I appreciate your concern. I'm a stranger here and an invader. No doubt that does not conform to the profile of someone you might wish to remain in your community. I find that deeply regrettable as I decided quite some time ago, that when the war is ended, I would move here and open my own law practice. I should have enjoyed the approbation of a collegial friendship and association with you and hope that at some future point, you will revise your opinion of me and extend that. As Caroline will tell you, repeatedly I have offered to purchase the tract of land in question at a price substantially above market value. I am still willing to do so if that will allay your apprehensions."

"No, Ryan. I don't want that," Caroline interrupted. "I think this is the ideal solution to both our dilemmas. I have no family here to leave this to when I'm gone. My husband's family is dead except for some distant cousins he never cared for. He wanted this land to be treasured and loved. I know already that you love it as much as he did. By giving you the knoll and the land around it for your own use, you have the land you want for that home you've already designed in your head. The remaining thousand acres I want to remain as a memorial park named for my husband and me. That's why I have appointed you as lifetime custodian of Riverside to see that it becomes a civic park that preserves the beauty of the site. The park area will be deeded to the city but you will retain the management rights and will appoint a successor. The five hundred acres that include the knoll, you will be deeded outright for accepting this responsibility. This house you may use as you wish since it is on the tract of land that I am deeding to you. I only stipulate that I have lifetime rights to live here and enjoy the fruits of the land. At my death, you will assume the custodian ship of Rufus and Beulah so that they are provided for in their old age. I have already signed the papers John drew up, giving them their freedom when I die. At my death, if they wish to leave they may and you must agree to support them until they die. If they wish to stay, they are to have their own house built on this land and you will continue to support them until their deaths."

Ryan went to Caroline and knelt before her, taking both of her hands in his. "I'm most honored to accept your generous offer. If you should ever need the money, I will happily pay you for the land or if you change your mind about this, I will accept that, too."

"Sit down here. Save those knees for the woman you propose to make your wife." Caroline patted the place beside her on the sofa for Ryan to sit. Arching her eyebrow at John Harvey, she teased. "Ryan needs to meet some nice young local ladies. Isn't that niece of yours—Hattie, isn't it—still unmarried?"

John shifted his weight uncomfortably on the chair. Ryan spared him the need to answer by laughing and saying, "Mr. Harvey, Miss Caroline is quite aware that I'm not looking to enjoy the state of matrimony any time soon. Please rest assured I have no immediate designs on your niece or anyone else. I assure you she is only teasing."

Ryan left her house that night the happiest he had been in nearly a year. He rode Windfall back into town with visions of his future rushing pell-mell though his head. He saw his home sitting on the crest of the knoll, looking out over the broad stretch of water to a distant shore. He saw dogwoods and cherry trees blooming on the lawn of a Georgian home with dark green shutters fastened by shutter dogs to the soft red brick of the walls. A broad tree shaded piazza wrapped around the front and one side with white wicker chairs for enjoying the view. Chimneys soared above a shingled roof and at the top a cupola with a view over the land he owned crowned his home. From it he imagined he could just glimpse the office he would build in town. And on the lawn, how he wished he could envision his children gamboling in innocent joy. But that vision only reminded him of what he could not have and so he stopped dreaming.

Had he but known, just over thirty miles away, his seven-week-old son slumbered in his cradle innocent of his parentage, content in his milk-sated sleep. And the woman he loved stood over the child, smiling in joy that her life had been blessed with this tangible reminder of the man whose loss she would always mourn. Had he but known, he would have gone for them and claimed them as his own. But he didn't know. All he knew was loss. And that loss took the luster of complete happiness from his dreams.

Ryan's son, also named Ryan, had arrived with relative ease for a firstborn, and Penny with determination and the resiliency of youth had quickly regained her strength and the chores she assigned herself in her parents' home. Sarah continued to decline but, with the birth of her first grandchild, radiated an inner contentment and peace when she held the child who represented the continuation of her bloodline, capturing a bit of eternity for her corporal life that was so rapidly slipping away.

John, while continuously worried with running the farm, supplying the army with the prerequisite supplies and, watching his wife's decline, grew more vigorous and energetic when he thought about this grandson whom he was going to launch on the road to manhood. At the end of every day, he raced to his home, where resided the people he most loved, except for the son who was in harm's way in Virginia. He walked through the door listening for the chatter of the women and the cooing of the baby and was reminded anew of the true verities of human life. Despite the war, they were almost halcyon days for him. As Christmas grew nearer, he ruminated on the changes since the previous year. Despite the deprivations brought by war, blockade, runaway slaves, and diminished crops, he looked forward to the holiday and the celebration around his hearth, content in those things he still had.

Penny too was content. When she looked into the eyes and features of this small son who so resembled his father, she felt that Ryan was still with her. For the hundredth time she said a prayer of thanks that the baby was small enough that no one remarked on the "premature" birth. Her life revolved around the child's needs: nursing, changing, rocking, and comforting. Most of all she loved the warm heart-beating nearness of his body to hers. In her childhood home with her family around her, she could momentarily forget the demands of those who depended on her as once again her father assumed the mantle of protection and support that she had relied on most of her life. Eventually she knew she must return to the lonely walls of her own home and to Mammy, who she knew missed her and loved her much the same way she loved Lucinda. Her only anxiety was her mother, for Marcus had taken care of the fledgling business and was producing the first run of liquor.

Sarah lived until December 26th. Christmas had been the happiest one she could remember. The only sad notes were the absence of her son and the knowledge that she would not see another Christmas in her home surrounded by those she loved. She drifted into sleep Christmas night with the arms of the man she had loved for most of her life tenderly holding her. Her last thought was of her gratitude to him for the life he had given her with his steady, true heart.

John found her the next morning, a smile on her still-beautiful face, and knew he had lost the only woman he had ever loved. He sat with her for a long time, remembering the days and nights they had shared. Finally he called Penny to him and told her that her mother was gone.

They buried her in the graveyard on the hill with the family that had preceded her. For the rest of his life, John walked to her grave at the end of every day and told her about everything that had happened during the day's course. When spring came he would plant flowers there, something that would bloom with every season of the year. His biggest consolation during the days that followed her death was having Penny and her baby under his roof even though he knew that Penny would soon return home. One of his favorite things was to hold the baby after he had been fed, rocking him while he fell asleep in his arms. He was glad it was winter when he had more time away from the many chores that demanded his attention during the growing season.

He found himself spending more time with Fitz, too. Since both men were now alone after years of marriage to women they had adored and missed sorely, and with a grandson in common, they felt a new bonding in their old friendship. The only thing that caused John to feel a slight unease was the feeling that Fitz was keeping some kind of secret. He respected his friend too much to pry and just hoped that whatever it was would not prove painful for Fitz.

As for Nancy, with Sarah now resting in the cemetery, there was less need for her. He felt uneasy about saying anything to her about leaving but worried that when Penny left, Nancy would feel uncomfortable about sharing the house with a man alone. She was an unobtrusive woman, comfortable to be with due to her quiet and peaceful ways, and she was an effective manager of his household. Even Delia respected her and listened to her quiet instructions. John decided just to leave the decision to Nancy whether to stay or go. If she said nothing, he wouldn't either. He knew that she was a little disappointed that Fitz had abandoned the incipient courtship, although she gave little outward indication. And he hoped that she had not been badly hurt. For himself, John knew that there would never be another woman in his life. Sarah had been his first and she would be his last.

Watching Penny holding her baby, he often caught a momentary look of sadness that she quickly hid. He suspected that she was missing her child's father. Little did he know that indeed she did continue to mourn the absence of the man who had given her the child she adored; it just wasn't the father he assumed. She smiled when she caught him looking and quickly began talking about the baby and what a sweet disposition he had. She talked about anything that would keep him from prying. Even Marcus seemed to be spending more time away from the farm and offered John no explanation as to why. John sighed and wondered why the people around him all seemed to be hiding secrets.

In late January a sleet storm wrapped the world around them in glistening ice that slowly dripped into frozen daggers hanging from the eaves. The weeklong storm kept them snug by the hearth. Cut off from the rest of the world and the vagaries of war, the household amused themselves watching the baby and all of his different moods. The novelty of trying to get a fist in his little rosebud mouth, hitting himself accidentally when his small hands flailed about, and the beginning smiles of recognition kept them all charmed. Among the three of them, there was a constant rivalry for a chance to hold and croon to the baby during his waking hours. Even so, by the end of the week they were all feeling restless from the imprisoned inactivity. Penny longed to be home in her own house and freer to consult with Marcus on the progress of their business venture. In her father's home, they had perforce talked briefly and carefully to avoid anyone learning what they were up to.

Fitz rode over as soon as the ice melted enough to make navigating the road safe. He too took his turn holding and cooing at his new grandson. Chiding Penny, he remarked, "I don't know how you came up with an Irish name like Ryan. Why couldn't you have named him 'Fitzhugh' for me, or 'Daniel'?"

Penny, refusing to be goaded, laughed. "You don't think Fitzhugh Kennedy sounds a bit Irish then? You know your own ancestors are Irish, so why object to an Irish-sounding name?"

John came to Penny's defense. "Personally I like the name, although I can maybe understand how you feel, Fitz. I know I was a little upset when Sarah insisted on naming our son Brett rather than John, Jr. We have no Bretts in our family so it was a puzzle where that came from. Later she confessed it was a favorite hero from some romance she had read. At any rate, Brett seems happy enough with his name. I'm sure Ryan will be too, so why worry? Besides, I call him Rye-Rye. Good as I love rye whiskey, I think it's a real compliment to the boy."

At that remark, they began laughing and smiling indulgently at the baby, who was happily blowing spit bubbles and ignoring them all. Penny was relieved that the subject was finished and they could move on to another discussion that left her without a feeling of unease.

When Fitz rose to leave, he turned to John and asked, "Would you mind walking me out? There's something I'd like to discuss with you."

Puzzled at the serious note in his friend's voice, John followed him into the back hall. Speaking in a lowered register, Fitz confided, "I've gotten myself in a bit of a ticklish situation over at Kinston. As a consequence, I find myself embarrassingly short of cash—temporarily, of course. I really hate to ask, but do you think you could see your way clear to loan me some money? I've drawn up a deed giving Belle Terre as a guarantee to you of repayment."

"Fitz, I've been your friend since we were boys crawling in the dirt. I don't need a deed to your house to help you if I can. I would like to know what kind of bind you're in. Mayhap I can help you figure out what's best to do."

Fitz looked at his toes, refusing to meet his friend's eyes; slowly he began to turn red. "John, after Cora died I got mighty lonesome for a woman. I decided to try a fancy woman over on Sugar Hill just to relieve a little pressure, if you know what I mean. I mean, I'm not so old that I don't miss being with a woman that way. Hell, I even thought of chasing Nancy."

"The last rumor I had didn't have whores costing so much that you have to mortgage your home and at your age, I don't fancy you can give them that much in the way of business. Now what exactly have you gotten yourself into?"

"Dammit, John. There's one of 'em I got to feeling right sorry for. Sally's only sixteen and she's from a good family. Trouble is her pa and brothers have all been killed in this damn war, so she's got no one else to support her ma and younger sisters except her. She wasn't exactly educated to practice law or anything else, and her family depended on her pa's trade as a blacksmith. She's a pretty little thing. One thing led to another and she found herself selling what she had to offer. Well, she sold it to me, and I was the first one. I just couldn't stand the thought of her doing it that way, so I set her up in her own little house over in Kinston and I've been supporting her. It took about all I had left in Confederate money to do it. And yes, I've been sleeping with her."

"Are you in love with her?"

"No. It's not like that. Hell, no. I just need a little company and I felt sorry for her. I don't want to marry her. I just want some loving from time to time."

"Then what you're telling me is that she's still working as a whore, but with an exclusive clientele of one. Maybe you ought to consider letting her expand her client base to ease some of the pressure on you. I'm not sure how you feel about owning a whorehouse, but you seem to have established one. Might as well run it for a profit, or give her the deed and be done. If she can sew, she and her mother and sisters could try that to make some money without selling rights to the space between their legs."

"I was afraid you'd feel that way. I suppose you're right, dammit." Fitz reached up to pat John on the back. "No hard feelings. I can't say I blame you."

"If you decide you still need the money, I'll give what help I can. No questions asked. Just go home and think about it."

John watched his friend ride away and wondered if his own loneliness would drive him to pursue the same path. He didn't condemn Fitz because he could well understand what had driven him to do what he was doing. He hoped that he himself would not as he felt it would dishonor both his dead wife and him. He knew himself well enough to know he never wanted another wife. No woman could begin to replace the one he had loved so long. Sighing he pulled on his coat and walked to Sarah's grave. He needed to talk to her.

After the men left, Penny sat quietly rocking her baby and thinking. Finally she began, "Nancy, I'm going back to Pleasant Glade in a day or two. I don't know how you feel about staying on here with just Pa now that my mother is gone. If you're planning to leave, I'd like to invite you to come stay with me. I confess to getting awfully lonely in that house with no one to talk to except my servants. I could use the help with my baby, too, as there are some things I need to see to. You don't have to answer me now."

"Actually, Penny, I planned to go back to my parents when you leave; however, if you need me and want me, I would love to go home with you. I adore taking care of Rye-Rye and I enjoy your company. And it's good to feel needed. Thank you so much for asking me."

"Good, that's settled. I'll tell Pa I'm going home tomorrow and you're going to come with me. He's going to be relieved. Since I'm not staying here he doesn't want me alone in that house. I'll tell him I'm giving you a new bed warmer and hiring you as a bodyguard."

Both women were laughing when John returned to them. "What's so funny, you two?'

"I just hired Nancy for a bodyguard, Pa. So you're going to have to swing your own bed warmer in the future."

Marcus drove the two women and baby to Penny's home the following afternoon. John stood watching them leave as lonely as he had ever felt in his life. Silently he swore that he was going to be a father to Rye-Rye until his own father could return. It gave him something to look forward to and helped stave off the loneliness that threatened to pull him under at every turn. Once spring planting began, he would be too busy working to dwell on the emptiness in his house. Or so he hoped.

Chapter 16

Taking advantage of the cessation of skirmishes during the months that followed the signing of the agreement that John Harvey had drawn up, Ryan researched building resources in the area. He needed an architect, a builder, as well as brick, lumber, windows, doors and other millwork, gaslights, laborers, landscaping, and furnishings. Some of what he needed was available locally but he knew he needed a woman to help with the furnishings and interior decor.

He sat at his desk looking out over the rooftops to the river, his pen in hand, and mulled how best to word the letter he wanted to write. To be sufficiently persuasive, he knew he had to word the inducements carefully. "Dear Isabel" he began, phrasing the letter in his head. *No, that won't do. It needs to be warmer.* "My dearest Isabel." Finding that had a better ring, he began to write. He described the town and all of its most charming attributes and studiously ignored anything that might seem a detriment. He assured her sea transportation from Baltimore directly to New Berne carried little danger to imperil the trip. Lastly he declared how much he had missed her and needed her to come share the home that he wanted to build. Signing, "With all my love, Ryan," he thrust it into the envelope and walked to the post office. With luck, his sister, Isabel, would be in New Berne by Christmas. Suddenly the idea of spending it with someone he had known all of his life sounded more than appealing. This was one Christmas that he knew he most particularly did not want to be alone, as it marked the anniversary of the last time that Penny and he had been together. He did not stop to consider how it would look to have a young, unmarried woman reside with him.

With the letter mailed he rode out to Caroline's to tell her of his plans and the invitation to Isabel to come to him. With her constant harping on the

149

theme, he knew she would be happy for him to have someone to share his time, although what he was planning might not be quite what she had in mind. Excitedly he told Caroline of the plans he had made and asked her for recommendations for an architect and builder. With so many of the townsmen decamped to inland towns for the duration of the occupation, she told him finding someone he could feel enthusiastic about might prove challenging.

Caroline offered, "See if Clarence Smith is still here. He's an excellent builder and he has some of the most skilled craftsmen around for moldings and detail work. I'll have to think about an architect, though. Maybe John Harvey knows someone. If you'd like I'll ask him."

"Please do. If I can't find the quality of people I want I'll have to wait. I refuse to compromise on any aspect of this project." Smiling mischievously, he added, "By the way, I've written a young lady to come live with me. I need some help with the furnishings and interior plans. I know you are more than capable of helping me yourself but I hate to impose. Besides, I think you're right. I need someone special to keep me company. Not that you aren't wonderful and a delight to be with." He was enjoying baiting her.

Taken by surprise, Caroline's mouth dropped. "Well, aren't you the sly fox. Keeping a little romantic secret from me, hmm?"

"Have some more wine, Miss Caroline?" Ryan changed the subject and began to talk about their plans for a park. She lifted that wicked eyebrow in the expression he had come to expect whenever she was thwarted, but he refused to be drawn into a discussion of Isabel. She was not so easily put off, however, when she walked him to the door at the end of the evening, and she bluntly asked, "I assume there's no *wedding* imminent since you failed to mention it?"

"Well, no. It's hardly appropriate. Besides, I have no home to take a wife or anyone else to until this one is built. I'm still trying to find somewhere for her to stay." Ryan had searched with increasing frustration to find a house or suite of rooms for Isabel. Unfortunately finding a suitable residence for a single woman in a town already bursting at the seams from the housing needs of the Union troops had proven a far more daunting task than he had envisioned.

"I see." It was a terse reply. Ryan knew she didn't see at all but perversely decided to provide no clarification. Again she raised that eyebrow at him. Caroline continued. "That being the case you must realize that you simply *cannot* cohabit with a single woman if you ever hope to reside as a respectable resident of this town. I *insist*, until you get your house built and decide what role this young woman is to fill, she reside with me, where she can be properly chaperoned."

"Miss Caroline, I accept your invitation most readily. I confess I was becoming quite perplexed with what to do to accommodate her suitably."

When Ryan stretched out on his bed that night, it was with relief that the dilemma with Isabel was resolved. He hoped it would be good for her to get away from Baltimore and their overbearing mother. He ruefully considered that it might even dampen the local enthusiasm to procure a wife for him. Now he had to find an architect and begin clearing the knoll in readiness for building. Casual labor was no problem with troops willing to do a little extra work in their spare time to earn money and the hoards of idle contrabands he would work for wages on occasion. In his mind he envisioned the general details of the building but knew he could not draw the kind of plans that a builder would need for the complexities of the house he had in mind. He wanted it to be a home he could love and live in with pride for the rest of his life. His childhood home in Baltimore, while imposing, had no beauty and was awkwardly arranged, built to the dictates of his domineering mother. Ryan wanted nothing to do with a home like that; he wanted one that was both beautiful and comfortable. The architect he hired would listen to him and design following his guidelines, just as Isabel would follow his tastes and plans for the furnishing and outfitting of the interior. He envisioned no problem, as their aesthetic sensibilities were similar. He realized before he fell asleep that when he thought of the interior of his new home, often the vision was overlaid by memories of Penny.

Ryan received a cable from Isabel that her boat would arrive on the morning of December 16th. He hired a buggy and was waiting at the dock when the boat rounded the bend in the river. Searching for her among those few lining the railing, he spotted her just as the boat pulled to the edge of the wharf. She had seen him as well and began waving excitedly. With her stylish dress and natural good looks, she was drawing admiring male attention from others waiting on the wharf. Turning, she reached back and drew an imposing older woman to stand at the rail beside her. The woman lifted a hand in regal salute. When Ryan recognized her, he groaned. He had not expected this turn of events but he knew he should not have been surprised. His mother, Martha, was willful, eternally presumptive of her welcome, and determined to control Isabel at every turn. He realized belatedly he had just complicated his life unnecessarily.

Ryan made his way to the gangplank to assist the women from the boat. The buggy driver stood at his elbow ready to take the luggage. As he waited Ryan wondered what he was going to say to Caroline when he presented her with an unexpected guest and a difficult one at that. He dreaded what the coming days would bring if Martha ran true to form. He thought ruefully that he would rather fight a regiment of Rebels single-handed that to get in the middle of any conflict between the equally stubborn Caroline and Martha. For Ryan the chief difference between the two women resided in the fact that Caroline was never malicious, arrogant, controlling, or bitchy. The same could not be said for Martha.

Planting a smile on his face, he extended his arms to hug first Isabel and then Martha. Martha's greeting immediately grated. "Ryan, how lovely it is to see you after so long. I can see the shaggy hair is quite suitable to this little backwater town; however, I should hope you find occasion to trim it suitably before too long. Oh, dear me, it really is quite a small town, isn't it?"

Isabel turned to their mother. "I think it's charming. I can quite see why Ryan is so enamored of it. As for your hair, my dear, it's most becoming a bit longer and I for one hope you keep it that way." Ryan gave her a smile as warm as the one he gave Martha was cold. It just so happened that he had planned an overdue trip to Barber John for the following morning. Unwilling for her to think that he'd cut his hair at her order, he knew he would not be going the next day.

"Let's get these trunks loaded and we'll drive to Riverside. A dear friend and charming lady has invited you to stay, as housing in town is not nearly so gracious for ladies at the moment."

On the ride to Riverside, Ryan kept the conversation away from himself. He was happy to ask questions of Isabel and have her fill him in on all of the events in Baltimore during his years away. He did not ask about Phillip, who had been killed at the battle of Bull Run early in the war. He looked up into the sunny blue sky, grateful that the Indian summer of the last few weeks still continued. The occasional flower still bloomed, not yet killed by a heavy frost. He wanted Isabel to like it here; as for Martha, he just wanted her to leave. Immediately he scolded himself not to be so suspicious and guarded. He hoped that perhaps he was being unfair to her and as unlikely as the prospect seemed, maybe she had changed.

Driving the curving lane to Caroline's house, he stole a glance in Martha's direction. Her nose was definitely quivering with interest and appreciation of the grand mansion before them. At lease she should have no complaints about their accommodations.

Caroline was waiting on the lower steps when they stopped just short of her.

She immediately walked forward with hands outstretched in welcome. "Do come in. I'm so happy to have you visit me."

"Miss Caroline, please do me the honor of allowing me to present my mother, Martha Culpepper Madison, and my sister, Isabel. At the time I accepted your invitation to bring Isabel here, I was unaware that my mother would be coming as well. I hope this will not discommode you."

Caroline lifted her eyebrow at him in acknowledgement of the ruse he had played on her before turning to smile at her guests. "Oh, don't be silly. This is a big house for just one old lady and I'm tired of rattling around in it on my own."

"Mother, Isabel, it's a pleasure to introduce you to Mrs. Caroline Framingham, the charming chatelaine of this beautiful home. She's been more than a friend to me, more like a mother, confidant, and companion all wrapped in one. My time here would have been not nearly so pleasant without her company. No doubt you will be as charmed with her as I am." Ryan had seen his mother stiffen with jealousy while he extolled Caroline's virtues and realized he probably should not have used quite that choice of words.

"Why, Ryan, you scamp, you know I'm no mother figure. Besides, you obviously have one already." Caroline had seen the hackles rise, too, and sought to circumvent what resentment she could. She had a feeling that she and Martha were going to have a little prayer meeting at some point. "Now both of you ladies come in and let's get you settled. I'll have Rufus help your man with the luggage, Ryan. Please, would you mind asking Beulah to prepare the bedroom beside Isabel's for your mother? Ladies, we'll go upstairs and I'll show you your rooms. I'm sure you would like to get settled and freshened up prior to lunch."

As they walked away, he could hear his mother asking, "So, Mrs. Framingham, is that a northern twang I hear in your voice?"

"Indeed and for good reason, I assure you. I'm quite the Yankee invader here myself. You see, I'm from Massachusetts. My husband was the southerner. I gather, unlike your son, your sympathies lie with the Confederacy. It's unfortunate that the two of you should be on opposite sides of the political fence; however, let's hope it's soon just a bad memory and we can all get on with our lives. Tell me, was your husband from the North?"

"Heavens, no. He was of one of the most prominent families in the country. His bloodlines like my own were impeccable. His brother, Andrew, is the misguided Yankee sympathizer. I absolutely blame him for Ryan enlisting in the Union army. If it had not been for his meddling and influence, Ryan would still be in Baltimore, where he belongs."

"I think you will find your son has his own opinions as to where he belongs," Caroline felt herself bristling.

"Oh, what a charming room," Isabel hastily remarked. "Goodness, Mrs. Framingham, Ryan should have asked you to help with his house. Your taste is exquisite." Isabel had calmed enough waters in Martha's wake to know when to pour on oil.

"Well, I can't imagine why he would ask either of you. After all, I'm his mother. Of course, I also quite fail to see why he would want a house in this God-forsaken place. I cannot imagine any civilized person wanting to live so far from the cultural advantages of a large city." Martha sniffed and walked to the door that Caroline indicated.

"Your room. Please settle in. I had no reason to anticipate an additional guest; however. I'll have linens brought shortly. Beulah's quite busy at the moment preparing additional lunch. It's unfortunate, Martha, but I'll have to ask you to make your own bed. as I currently have far fewer servants than formerly." Caroline smiled sweetly through gritted teeth. She had planned to have Teensy make the bed, but the imperious Martha had changed Caroline's mind. "I'll excuse myself now. I have some matters that need attending."

Ryan could tell when she entered the parlor Caroline had not been charmed by his mother. He didn't know what had transpired, but it was obvious that Caroline was seething.

Caroline caustically observed, "Your sister is a lovely, charming young woman. Not having had the pleasure of knowing your father, I can only surmise her personality is from the paternal side of your family."

Ryan began to laugh. Despite herself, Caroline laughed, too. "I think I appreciate the inspiration for the move to your Uncle Andrew in New York."

"Miss Caroline, had I only know that Mother would be coming, too, I would never have accepted your hospitality. I will renew my efforts to find them somewhere in town if you could keep them for a few days."

"Fiddlesticks. I think I'm up to the challenge. They'll stay right here and I don't want you to stew about it."

There went that eyebrow again, making Ryan decide that Caroline seemed to be relishing the prospects of an invigorating face-off. He knew her well enough to know that if Martha wanted a catfight, Caroline wouldn't be one to back down. Poor Isabel, somehow he would have to keep her from being caught in the middle. She had enough to deal with trying to get over the loss of her fiancé, Phillip Wharton. He had hoped a change of scene and something new to do would be good for her. Now he wondered what he had gotten them all into.

Seated at the table, Ryan and Isabel made a concerted effort to keep the conversational ball in their court and away from the two older women. Isabel unwittingly provided the spark that lit the first conflagration, when she complimented Caroline on the succulent seafood stew.

Martha immediately commented, "Certainly it's tasty, but I've found to get the best food from your cook you need to first understand fine cuisine. I make it a point to go over my recipes with our cook personally and provide detailed instructions. Of course, not everyone is as comfortable as I with an active participation in the running of a home."

"Why, Mrs. Madison, what a lovely idea. I've been wondering what to do tomorrow with the kitchen. Unfortunately Beulah has to be away to attend a funeral. With your knowledge of the kitchen, we shall eat quite well after all." Caroline refused to catch Ryan's eye.

Not expecting that rejoinder, Martha sputtered before she recovered enough to say, "Regretfully, I did not bring my recipe books with me."

"Nonsense. That's no problem. With your sense of what constitutes good food, I'm sure you will do just fine." Caroline was not going to let her off so easily.

"Well, Mother, this gives you the opportunity to earn your keep, so to speak. I must say I'm sorry I can't be here to appreciate your culinary efforts; however, when I'm back day after tomorrow, I'll look forward to hearing all about it." Ryan decided he might as well stoke the flames.

Normally Isabel was quiet and conciliatory. It was quite unlike her to abet Ryan in a struggle against her mother. But now she said, "Mother, anyone with your knowledge and years of experience in running things should have no problem. I'm sure you will do yourself proud. It's so opportune that you can help Mrs. Framingham in her hour of need."

Caroline gave Isabel a genuinely warm smile. "Isabel, why don't you call me 'Miss Caroline' like your brother?"
Martha's mouth twitched but she made no more protest. Caroline's eyebrow was cocked dangerously high for Ryan's taste. He truly was glad he would miss what he labeled the First Skirmish at Riverside.

With lunch finished, Ryan rose from the table. "Isabel, I have to report back for duty this afternoon. Would you walk me out to the buggy? Miss Caroline, Mother, I apologize but I have to leave you now."

Standing by the buggy, Ryan quietly asked, "What happened? I thought you would come alone."

"You know Mother as well as I. Once she learned that I was determined to come, she refused to allow it unless she came as well. For goodness sakes, Ryan, I'm a grown woman of twenty-four years of age and she treats me like a child. I so hate confrontations that I know it's partly my fault because I let her get away with it. I just miss Papa so. He was quiet, too, but he always managed to get around her and soften her abrasiveness. I wish I had his knack, but I don't. I feel so sorry for Miss Caroline. Mother is really going to be difficult, I fear."

"You know, Isabel, I think Mother may have met her nemesis. Miss Caroline is one shrewd, tough old lady. Watch her eyebrow. When it climbs, she's got those claws out. Don't let the kid gloves that hide them fool you." Ryan laughed and shook his head ruefully. "I'm sorry to leave you in the middle of a battle zone, but it can't be helped. I really do have to get back."

Ryan was kept busy for the remainder of that day and the following one. In November, General B. F. Butler had assume command of the Federal troops in New Berne. Ryan was under orders to convert the old Bishop's Mill into a coffin factory. Recruiting Robert Keho, an Irishman from New York, as his assistant, he rode to the factory to begin the process. He couldn't think of a gloomier duty even while accepting the necessity. Not many of his duties recently had been pleasant, he ruminated. Butler was cut from a different cloth from Foster. Ryan, like many of the other Union soldiers in New Berne, felt no great liking for him. He missed his card games with Foster as well.

Leaving Keho to oversee the workers after he had assigned them their duties, Ryan took the opportunity to ride over to Rhem's sawmill to negotiate a tentative agreement for building timbers. He wanted to reserve a reasonable amount at the current price, as the cost of things was soaring daily. He didn't know it, but he was doing the same thing that Penny had done, stockpiling against the future when things would be either more expensive or unattainable. Next he went to the kiln and negotiated a similar agreement to buy the needed brick at current prices and have it held for him. He had already had an interview with Clarence Smith, who had begun the process of clearing the knoll of stumps and leveling the land for building. He needed only to get an architect to help him and he was ready to begin. Not knowing how long his regiment would remain in New Berne or what the future might bring in the way of increased military obligations, he did not want to waste any of this time of relative ease.

Riding back to the Slover house to bathe before going to dinner at Caroline's, he saw John Harvey waiting to cross Middle Street. "Mr. Harvey."

"Colonel Madison," John Harvey acknowledged him with a nod. "What may I do for you?"

"Miss Caroline suggested that you might know the name of a good architect. I would like to employ one immediately to begin drawing up plans for my house."

"You're still determined to go through with it, I take it?"

"Absolutely."

"In that case, you might want to talk with Jonathan Hawkes, the grandson of the man who designed the old Tryon Palace. You may have seen the fine brick stables. They're the only part of the structure not destroyed by fire. At any rate, it was one of the finest houses in the colonies. His son Francis and now his grandson have continued the tradition of designing buildings. I think he's the best for what you want. I'm not sure if he is here or on his plantation, but I'll find out and let you know if you're interested."

"Thank you very much. It sounds as though he will suit admirably." Ryan smiled his gratitude and rode off whistling "Poor old Ned." He felt he was beginning to make progress and far sooner than he would have dreamed when he first found the knoll. He had a committed price on materials, a builder, the lot was being cleared, and now he had the lead on an architect of apparent merit. Even the staunchly Confederate John Harvey seemed to have thawed ever so slightly. At least Caroline's old friend no longer looked at him as though he had a cloven hoof and horns. He could understand the protectiveness of client and friend that caused John to be upset when he saw Caroline carving off a third of her property to give it to a much younger man—and a Yankee at that.

When he approached Caroline's house, the lights were already glowing to dispel the coming gloom of evening. He hoped the atmosphere within was as warmly welcoming. Isabel met him at the door, grinning like a cat in cream.

"Round one to Miss Caroline," she whispered. "Mother made such a mess of things that poor Beulah came and ran her out of the kitchen. She burned or broke about half of everything in there. I don't think she's going to be bragging about her domestic skills anytime soon. Right now she's upstairs lying down, nursing a headache, she says. It looks as though something finally got her goat. Over an inedible lunch she actually apologized to Miss Caroline for any 'less than gracious comments' and thanked her for her hospitality. Miss Caroline just smiled through it all, never batting an eye at anything. Mother may not be cured but she sure got a heck of a comeuppance today. And thank goodness, Beulah's back in the kitchen. I'm about starved."

"Ah, somehow I knew Mother was going to be the worse for wear if she took Miss Caroline on. Let's just hope she's on good behavior until I can either get you both into my house or her back to Baltimore. The problem, of course, is it's months before my house can be built. There isn't really much that we can do until spring and I still don't have plans drawn up. As gracious as Caroline is, that's still a long time. I suppose I could have you take the boat to New York to shop for the furniture. Maybe she would be happy to go home to Baltimore and check on the house there."

"I wouldn't count on it. She's determined that your house is going to be 'suitably' decorated. It's going to be a battle for me to have any say."

"Then I'm going to have to devise a way to get around her. I certainly don't want my house to look like our home in Baltimore."

Ryan didn't know it then but before too many months passed, Martha would have been happy to be back in Baltimore and as far from New Berne as possible.

Chapter 17

January was miserable. The cold that began right after Christmas seemed to have the earth in a death grip. Stories came to them of soldiers in the mountains of Virginia who had frozen at their posts like statues. While it wasn't as cold around Kinston as in the mountains, the cold drizzly weather was uncomfortable enough to keep most people inside. Not so for Marcus; he and a couple of trusted hired hands were ready to jar their first run of doubled, twisted, and proofed malt whiskey. He figured he would end up with twelve gallons for every bushel of corn.

He had made the still from sheets of copper and then partly buried it in the earth to make a hog still. Ash logs, which burn slowly and produce little smoke, had to be found and hauled to the site. Even using ash, Marcus had started the first fire in the night to prevent the danger of smoke from the still being detected by neighbors. The leafed-over branch roof also helped reduce the risk by dispersing the smoke. The worm that he had formed by wrapping copper piping around a small tree became the coil used for condensation. It was placed in a flake-stand or barrel filled with cold running water from the creek. Mash stick, relay arm, relay barrel, thump barrel, cap arm, bail, headache stick, heater box, and mash stick all had to be made and properly installed. He had scoured Kinston to find the jugs and bottles he would need for the finished product.

The still required constant vigilance during the cooking to prevent scorching. The sprouted corn for the malt had to be turned to keep it from becoming slick and overheating during the sprouting process. Both corn for the mash and the sprouted corn had to be milled. Once the alcohol consumed the cap and dog heads were forming, no time could be lost before the running. The mash or "slop" was fed to the delighted swine in Penny's pigpen. Afterwards they might totter about a bit unsteady but were more than ready for some more. He laughed every time he fed them the slop, thinking about the old saying, "as happy as a hog in slops," for that they were. And then everything had to be scrubbed spotless prior to making another run. Marcus conserved as much sugar as he could because of the difficulty of finding reasonably priced sugar once his current stock was consumed. When he had no more sugar, he could still make good shine but the yield per bushel would go down.

After a careful surveying trip, he had lined up tavern keepers happy to get his liquor now that the war had interrupted their normal supply sources. By prudent marketing of his product he planned to avoid calling undue attention to their little business. He had made a path that roughly followed the creek through the swamp utilizing any areas of high ground available to route the path. Neither he nor Penny wanted the path to and from the still to be accessible through Pleasant Glade or Pine View.

The whiskey was hauled and delivered on Monday night of February 1st. Dividing the profits from the first run, he carefully hid his share in a hidey-hole he dug under a corner floorboard in his cabin. One day he hoped to have enough saved to buy his own farm. He paid two happy workers theirs along with a bottle of the shine, and the rest he took to Penny on Tuesday morning after first grabbing a few hours of sleep. He found her sitting in a rocker by the fire in her office. Rye-Rye, the name everyone now called Ryan, was blowing little milky bubbles as he slept in her arms.

"That's a mighty contented looking boy you've got there, Penny."

She smiled fondly at her baby. "Yes, he is. I'm so glad he has such a happy little disposition."

"I 'spect everybody else in the house is, too." Marcus laughed.

"Have a seat, Marcus. Let me give the baby to Nancy to put to bed and we can have a good talk."

When she returned Marcus was sitting by the fire snoring softly. The firelight picked out golden highlights in his hair and along those of his muscular arms. He was a nice-looking man in a rugged kind of way and not more than thirty-two or -three years old. Penny had asked once why he'd never married but he had shrugged her off without answering. She leaned over and gently touched his shoulder.

"So, Marcus. How did it go?"

"Excuse me for nodding off but I didn't get much sleep last night because of delivering the shine. It's all sold and we're beginning another run. The quality and taste are good enough that everybody who bought it was happy to get it and didn't quibble at the price. They placed orders for a continuing supply so it looks like our business is up and running. I got paid in gold and silver, like you asked, but they didn't particularly like having to pay that way. If things get tougher we may have to take Confederacy notes."

"If we are forced to do that we'll have to adjust the price, I guess."

"Absolutely. The way it is now, specie is dropping all the time. Every time I go into Kinston to buy something it will buy less. I don't see it turning around either." Marcus stood to fumble in his britches' pocket. "That reminds me. I got this letter for you while I was in town. Looks like this package might be from Daniel and there's a letter from Brett. I have one for your Pa, too."

"Thanks, Marcus." Penny took the package, laying Brett's beside her on the desk. "Let's see what Daniel's up to now that he's back with his regiment."

Marcus used his pocketknife to cut the string around the parcel she held up for him. When she folded back the heavy paper of the package, she found a single piece of paper on top and underneath a smaller piece of paper, Daniel's wedding ring and the pocket watch that Fitz had given his son when he turned eighteen. Puzzled she laid the watch and ring to one side and picked up the larger paper. The letter was from Perry Blizzard, whom she remembered meeting in Richmond. She could not imagine why he would be writing her. She unfolded the paper and began to read.

"Oh, my God." Penny looked up at Marcus and shook her head in dazed disbelief. "It can't be, surely? It says Daniel's dead, killed two weeks ago by a sniper while on picket duty. Perry Blizzard, who was in his unit, sent me his things and says that Daniel's body is buried in Hollywood Cemetery in Richmond. I have to go to Fitz. This is going to kill him after losing Cora."

"Stay, Penny. Let me tell your, Pa. He's the one who had best do it. They've been friends a long time and it might be easier for Fitz to hear it from your Pa. I'll take Perry's letter if you don't mind, as I'm sure Fitz will want to see it. You take some time for yourself first and deal with your own pain and shock. You can go over to Belle Terre later. I'm just real sorry, Penny. Daniel was always a fair man with me, decent and a gentleman. I'm sad he never got to see his fine little boy."

Penny nodded as the tears began to spill down her cheeks.

"I'll send Nancy in to sit with you."

She looked up and smiled sadly, nodding her head.

When Marcus had gone to tell her father about Daniel's death, she picked up the smaller paper and began to read. Daniel had written:

Dearest Penny,

If you are reading this then you know that I am dead. They say that sometimes a soldier knows that his time is up. I have a premonition that my time is near. I almost died once before, next time I don't think I will be so lucky. I am so sorry that we never had the opportunity to see whether or not we could make a good marriage between us. I am forever grateful for the son you have given me. Your letter came today telling me of his birth and I knew that I had to write this. You are a woman any man would count himself

*lucky to call wife. I regret that I spent the time with you resentful
that I allowed our parents to push us into wedlock. If we had been
left to our own devices we might well have arrive at the gates of
matrimony without their help and had a far better marriage for it.
I blamed them for that for a long time. I don't any longer, as I realize that they acted out of love and good intentions. Please know
that in my own way, I do love you and I pray that you will teach
my son to know me and hopefully think well of his Pa. Forgive me
for leaving you alone with a child in the middle of a war. Thank-
fully my father and your own are with you and will help you. Please
tell Pa that I love him and I am sorry for this hurt he must bear.
At least he has you and our son so he is not entirely without family. From beyond the grave that will hold me, know that my love is
only yours.*

With love forever,
Your husband and friend, Daniel.

Penny thought the pain of her loss and remorse would kill her. Clutching the
letter to her breast, she repeated a litany of "I'm so sorry." Of course he would
never know that now. Like Daniel, she regretted that they had not had a chance
to make things right between them. She was so lost in her thoughts she did not
even realize it when Nancy came in and calmly sat with her through the storm
of tears.

It was a thoughtful Marcus who rode to her father's house with the grim
news. He had been in love with Penny for years and, without prospects of his
own, knew it was hopeless even before she married. Once Daniel had claimed
her for his wife, he had resigned himself to never having her. Someday he intended to be a man to be reckoned with and a planter, not a mere overseer.
Since he was twenty, he had carefully hoarded his money, denying himself the
little luxuries he would have liked but could not afford if he wanted to reach
his goal. Now with a growing pile of money and the prospects of more, he
could become a landowner and make a living for a family. If he were patient a
little longer, he could slowly get her to see him as a man, not just a business
partner and her father's overseer. She already trusted him and seemed to like
him. Maybe if he made himself even more indispensable she would come to
love him as well.

Marcus and John rode together to Belle Terre, both dreading the pain
they had to bring to a man already suffering from the loss of his wife. One
look at their solemn faces, and Fitz wheeled on his heel.

"Y'all come on back to my office. Damned if y'all don't look as grim as a
hell-fire preacher sermonizing unrepentant sinners. I think I'm going to pour
me some whiskey and branch water. Can I fix y'all one, too?"

"Suits me," John said.

"I could use one myself," echoed Marcus.

"Pull up some chairs then and I'll pour." Fitz handed them each a drink before sitting in the leather chair behind his desk. "So what brings y'all over here this morning?"

"Fitz, Marcus picked up a letter in town that Perry Blizzard from over in Deep Run wrote to Penny. I think you ought to read it." Slowly John extracted the letter Marcus had given him and handed it to Fitz.

"Dammit to hell. Why on God's earth did my only child have to die in this Godforsaken war? Those pusillanimous son-of-a-bitch Yankees, I'd like to kill every last one of them with my bare hands. Dammit to hell. Why did Daniel have to go? They would have exempted him under the twenty darkies rule if Penny hadn't so damned stubborn about giving the ones on Pleasant Glade their freedom. Dammit." Fitz swallowed hard to keep the tears back that threatened to choke him.

"Now, now, Fitz. You don't want to go blaming Penny. You know yourself Daniel was determined to go regardless. He felt like it was the honorable thing to do. He gave his life doing something he believed in, a way of life we all believe in, so try to remember he died with the honor due a patriot. He hated the way the darky rule made so many soldiers feel as thought it's 'a rich man's war'."

"Patriotism and noble motives be damned. I want a living son, not a dead patriot."

John stood and put his hand on his friend's shoulder. Quietly he said, "I'm thankful he left a son to carry on his name. You still have a grandson, Fitz. He's going to need you to be the father he will never know. And Penny's going to need us both."

"John, Penny is stronger than the two of us together for all that she's a woman. But my grandson is another matter. He's all I have left now." Fitz took a gulp of the liquor, grateful for the burn of it when he swallowed. Clearing his throat, he continued. "I'm going to Richmond and I'm bringing his body home. I want it in the cemetery with Cora's, and with me when I die."

"I can understand that because I would feel the same way if something were to happen to Brett. When you go, try to see him if possible and let us know how he really is. I don't think he's honest in his letters. They're always so positive and cheerful. It's like he is just trying to keep us from worrying about him." John knew enough from what he and Fitz had seen during the Battle of Kinston to know that it was not all peaches and cream where he was. "Let me know when you're going and I'll drive you to the train depot. Don't worry about things here; Marcus and I will help if need be while you're gone. Of course your own overseer is very capable, but just in case let him know we're available if needed."

Marcus, who had sat quietly, spoke up. "Mr. Fitz, I don't 'spect you're going to be able to get out just now. I think the Rebs are up to something big around here because they've got men stationed at every intersection around and on the railroad crossings. George Taylor, owner of King's Tavern on King Street, told me that they had fourteen navy boats and thirteen thousand men in Kinston January 30th. He says Jeff Davis put the navy under the command of his own aide, Commander John Wood, and gave the army to Major General George Pickett. George told me Pickett divided the troops into three forces and they all set out heading east by different routes. The rumor is they're planning to try to retake New Berne by going at it from three different directions. Kinston was a beehive of goings-on yesterday. I ran into Shadrack Loftin in the tavern. He says he thinks they attacked somewhere around New Berne on Monday. Looks to me like the only one using the train at the moment is the army. I don't believe they are going to be issuing any civilian passes for a while."

"Damned if I don't hope they can get New Berne out of the hands of the Yanks. It would sure make it easier to get things in and out, and with one less army scavenging the countryside, things ought to ease up for everybody in this part of the State," John remarked.

"Well, I guess I won't be going anywhere until we find out what's going on around here." Fitz sighed in resignation.

"Come on with me, Fitz. I'm going over to Pleasant Glade and see Penny and Rye-Rye. You don't need to be here alone right now brooding. Marcus, you coming, too?"

"Maybe later, Mr. John. Right now I've got some things I need to tend to."

"I swear, Marcus, you've been busier than bees in a honey tree lately. Have you gone and found yourself a woman to court?"

"No time for that."

"Well, if you decide you need a woman, I can recommend one," Fitz remarked with a wry grin.

"If it's all the same to you, I'll find my own eventually." Marcus laughed when he said it but was thinking to himself that he already knew the one he wanted.

When John and Fitz arrived at Penny's they found her in the parlor by the fire. Nancy was with her and Rye-Rye in his cradle between them. She looked up when they entered, dried her eyes, and went to them. Hugging Fitz, she said, "I am so sorry. I know Daniel meant the world to you and I cannot even begin to imagine the pain you're feeling. I have the pocket watch you gave him if you would like to have it as a remembrance. Perry sent it in his letter."

"You keep it and give it to our boy someday when he's old enough for it. I don't need it back." Fitz walked over to the cradle. "Do you think I could hold the baby?"

"Please do." Penny knew that at that moment it was the best comfort she could offer the bereaved man. He never needed to know that the child he held was Ryan's baby and not Daniel's. The tragedy of it all brought new tears welling in her eyes. What a tangled mess I have made of my life and my baby's, she thought.

"Penny, if you have no objections, I'm going to go to Richmond and bring Daniel's body home. I can't stand the thought of him all alone way up there. Seems to me he belongs here in the Kennedy graveyard with the rest of his family."

"Of course, I don't mind. I think he would have liked that. Will you go soon?"

"I'd planned to but it looks like I'll have to wait. Marcus says the army's tied up the railroad at the moment. He thinks they're planning a heck of a big shebang over New Berne way to try to retake the town. I just hope they kill every damned Yankee there. Beg your pardon for the cussing, ladies."

John had been looking at Penny while Fitz was talking and noticed her visibly startle. He wondered what seemed to agitate her about the news that New Berne was being attacked.

Penny knew she had reacted and hastened to hide it by getting up and poking the fire. "Y'all excuse me a minute, I need to go see if Mammy has dinner underway. I'm going to tell her to make enough for us all. So y'all plan on staying, you hear?"

"That'll be fine, darling. Fitz and I don't much relish our lonely dinners now that we're bachelors."

After she told Mammy that the two men would be staying for dinner and maybe Marcus, she slipped out and walked down to the stable. Quickly sliding the door back she crept inside and went to the old hay in the back corner. There she sat and said a silent prayer that God would watch over Ryan and keep him safe. Idly she began plucking at the musty straw, flicking stray pieces to one side. Reaching for another she felt something small and metallic under her fingers. Pushing the straw aside, she could see the pale glint of brass in the dim light of the stable. She picked up the object and carried it to the door to better see what she held. There in the slant of afternoon sunlight, she looked down at the object in her palm. It was a Union military button. Since no other Union soldier had been on the farm, she knew it had to be Ryan's.

Curious as to why it would have been buried in the straw in the back of the barn, she stood for a moment considering. Going back to the corner she knelt in the straw and searched to see if there were anything else hidden there. Again she felt something and took it to the light. It was a partially eaten piece of hardtack. Ryan must have been here when she didn't know it, for he would never have eaten hardtack if either Mammy or she knew he was at Pleasant Glade. She had heard nothing from him since she had written the letter telling him that she would not divorce Daniel. He must have come after then to see her, but if so, why had he not? She considered that maybe another Union soldier had spent the night in the barn, but were that the case he would have taken food and she knew nothing was missing. So it had to have been Ryan.

Standing by the door she tried to imagine what might have made him go away without saying anything. Suddenly it hit her: He saw me and knew I was pregnant. He must not have wanted a child and when he saw me that way he turned around and left. I never told him I was going to Richmond to see Daniel, so he had to know that I was carrying his own child. So that's the kind of man I loved and still love: one who would not only reject me but his own child as well. The pain of that thought on top of the guilt she felt over deceiving Daniel was almost more than she could bear. She could not go back in the house. She did not want the others to see her until she had calmed down. Slowly she walked into the woods and wandered along the creek to the mill until she found herself at the whiskey operation. She saw Marcus stirring the mash he was cooking in the bottom of the still. She could smell the smoke coming through the woods. Marcus stood with his back to her when she walked up. She stepped on a twig at the edge of the clearing; in the quiet woods it was as loud as a gunshot. Immediately Marcus whirled around, pistol already cocked.

"Good God, Penny, don't ever come up on anyone here like that. You're liable to get shot. Moonshiners are a jumpy bunch."

"Sorry, Marcus. I didn't think."

"You coming to check on the operation or did you just need some fresh air?"

"I needed to get away from the house. I really hadn't intended to come here, as I just set out walking."

"Are you holding up all right? I know Daniel's death is a hard thing to deal with."

"It is." Cryptically, she added, "In a lot of different ways."

"Well, if you need someone to talk to, I'm always here."

"I know that. Thank you, Marcus. You're a good friend."

He wanted to take her in his arms and tell her that she was far more than a friend to him but he didn't dare. All he could do was watch as she turned and walked back the way she had come. At the edge of the woods, she turned around and called out, "Pa and Fitz are at the house and are staying for dinner. You come, too."

"Thanks, I'll do that."

Frustrated he picked up the mash stick and began to stir with a vengeance. He knew he had to be patient as it was much too soon to tell her how he felt, but patience did not come easily at the moment.

Chapter 18

On February 1, 1864, Union pickets were posted eight miles from New Berne to protect the bridge at Batchelder's Creek. Spotting the Confederate camp two miles away, the strongly entrenched pickets opened fire on General Robert Hoke's troops. Hearing the gunfire at Steven's Fork, troops rushed out from New Bern to reinforce the picket outpost but were overcome by Hoke and pushed back to within a mile of town. While Hoke awaited the expected gunfire from General Seth Barton's force on the opposite side of the Trent River, two trainloads of Union troops from Morehead City arrived into New Berne. Barton, who had met with initial success, had quickly halted when he caught a good look at the Union fortifications on the Brice Creek side of the Trent River. He sent word to Pickett to advise of the obstacles about the same time that Colonel Dearing, whose orders were to take Fort Anderson, reported that he too faced overwhelming defensive works. Pickett frustrated at the inability of his forces to take Fort Anderson, cut the railroad and join for an assault on New Berne as planned, withdrew forces from New Berne on February 3. It had rained overnight and the mud from the rain and the heavy artillery traffic had reduced the road to a quagmire. It was a muddy Confederate army that marched away from New Berne, leaving it still securely in the hands of the Union. The assault had managed to kill or wound about a hundred Union soldiers, take thirteen officers and two hundred eighty-four privates, arms, ambulances, wagons, equipment, and over a hundred animals. The Confederates had lost about forty-five, either killed or wounded. Twenty-two of the men captured by Confederates were former Rebels who had deserted and joined the Union ranks. These men were marched back to Kinston and hanged.

For Pickett the biggest potential success of the whole endeavor was the capture of the Union ship the *Underwriter.* Had the South succeeded in seizing it to patrol the sounds and rivers of the coastal plain it would have been a triumph indeed. Upon seeing Commander John Wood and his forces had taken the ship, however, the Union opened fire sinking it. The ship thus became a serious loss for both sides.

General James Martin, coming up from Wilmington, had attacked the Union garrison at Newport Barracks, a railroad depot about twenty miles south of New Berne. There he managed to overrun the defenses and sent the Union soldiers scampering for New Berne. Pretty much destroying it, he had accomplished his goal and was awaiting orders from Pickett to join him in attacking New Berne. Finally on February 3rd General Barton relayed word for him to fall back. The invasion of New Berne had been a failure.

Pickett went back to Virginia and Hoke took command of the Confederate forces in North Carolina and proceeded to attack and capture Plymouth on April 20th, a strategic victory, as it provided a port for the newly built ironclad *Albemarle* to stalk and destroy Union gunboats in the sound. From there he obtained the surrender of the town of Little Washington, which was half burned during the evacuation of the Union forces. The senseless destruction so incensed Hoke's men when they entered the town that it fired them up to snatch New Berne from the occupation forces, now under Brigadier General I. N. Palmer, who had taken command of New Berne on April 19th.

That plan was to be undone, however, when the *Albemarle* sailing towards the town came under attack from Union gunboats. Rammed by the intrepid Captain Roe of the Union ship *Sassacus*, she was forced to limp back to Plymouth on a fuel of butter, lard, and bacon. The assaults on New Berne were over with the recall of a disappointed Hoke to Virginia in early May.

It had been a harrowing time for Ryan and for his family at Caroline's. Martha had been terrified when the distant gunfire sounded. The thought of being in the middle of a war zone and a contested turf dawned on her in its full reality. Unfortunately Caroline and Isabel caught the impact of her case of nerves and did the best they could to allay it, putting their own fears aside to deal with her. Ryan was too busy leading his men and responding to the different threats to do more than warn them at the first rumor of an impeding attack. He wanted them to be ready to come into town behind the demarcated lines should it appear that the area around Riverside were in danger of being in the middle of any action. Isabel and Caroline immediately packed evacuation bags with the items that they would need were that to happen. Martha just marched around in circles, furious that she should be in such jeopardy. She took turns blaming either Ryan or Isabel for bringing her to New Berne. That she had deliberately placed herself in the path of peril she conveniently ignored.

For the first time since coming to New Berne, Ryan was seriously concerned by the size of the opposition force. The routed soldiers rushing into town added to the turmoil of alarmed citizens, excited slaves, and the frequently drunk soldiers already there. He was sick of dealing with so many constant petty nuisances that at times swamped the more overarching ones inherent to maintaining the security of the occupied city.

He soon had bigger problems than those in the town. He was ordered to reinforce the troops at Brice's Creek. Leading his cavalry to the skirmish, Ryan unsheathed his sword and, holding it in his right hand, his pistol in his left and the reins in his teeth, plunged into the action. It was a mad melee of whistling bullets, screaming Minié balls, and booming cannons with the relatively sotto voce screams of the wounded and dying. Feeling the hackles rising on his neck, he twisted in the saddle just enough to dodge the bayonet of a determined Rebel coming up behind him. A quick backhanded downward slash of his sword severed the boy's arm. He looked to be no more than fifteen. Ryan felt sickened by the carnage and knew the boy's face would haunt him. Before he could turn his horse, Windfall stumbled and he lurched to one side. Both he and the horse regained their balance and he plunged back into the action. As the fighting grew heavier, he slid from Windfall's back and slapped him on the rump, sending the horse bounding from the battlefield. Ryan knew the animal was intelligent enough to find his way home. He was more worried for the horse's safety than his own; otherwise, he would have stayed on the horse's back, as it gave him increased maneuverability should he need to decamp.

A resounding Rebel rang out on his flank and he realized that an avalanche of screaming enemy was overrunning his troops. He signaled the trumpeter to sound retreat and started back toward the relative safety of a revetment. The gray tide kept coming. Swamped by the overwhelming enemy force, he ordered their white flag unfurled. He, along with a number of his men, found himself a prisoner. Resigned they lowered their weapons and stacked them on the back of a wagon as ordered. Weary and blood-splashed, he fell in behind the column of Confederate troops and began the withdrawal from the ramparts. Tired and cold from the damp wind that blew from the water, Ryan struggled in the sucking mud as he and his men were forced onto the road leading to Kinston. It was early evening before the exhausted troops and their prisoners stopped to spend the night about midway between New Berne and Kinston.

Exhausted, the hungry men stretched out as best they could on the cold damp grass on the edge of the road if they were lucky; otherwise, they slept in mud. Ryan's brain was working feverishly. He had no intention of docilely marching to the notorious Confederate prison at Andersonville or the closer Salisbury Prison in the western piedmont of the state. He stretched out and feigned sleep as near the woods as he could get, looking for a chance to escape. Watching the guard, he waited for the moment he turned and Ryan slowly crawled nearer to the woods. When the guard was again looking in his direction, he lay still and pretended to sleep. Each time the guard looked away he moved a little nearer to the dark tree-lined verge. After perhaps two hours, he was finally able to slip into the woods and make his way deep enough to avoid being seen. He waited there for daylight, dozing off and on, counting on the laxity of the guards and the uncomfortable night they had spent to protect him from any strenuous search efforts if and when they realized he was missing.

Unfortunately he was an officer and thus a bigger prize than a mere private. He knew they were on his trail when he heard thrashing in the woods just after first light. Quickly he moved deeper, looking for better concealment. They were gaining on him and he would have to hurry. Stumbling in his rush to escape, he tripped over a log and fell into a small stream swollen from the recent rain. They were too close now for him to move. Burrowing furiously he buried himself in the muddy bank, leaving only his nose protruding alongside the log. The rushing guards stepped on the log and leaped the stream going deeper into the woods. When he realized they were circling away from him, he eased out of the muck and stood. With disgust he realized he was covered in mud. A little water splashed on his face at least got the mud from his eyes and mouth but did nothing for his hair and clothing. It was cold, too, and he knew he had no way of getting warm except moving and that he had to do if he wanted to make good his escape. The good news, he supposed, was the mud rendered his clothing unidentifiable as either Union or Rebel.

He began the long walk back the way he had come, avoiding the road and staying in the woods. It was slow going and he was soon exhausted and more than a little hungry, as he had been given nothing to eat the night before. The Rebels themselves had only a handful of parched corn for their own supper. They might looked scrawny and malnourished, but Ryan knew firsthand it had not stopped them fighting with determined ferocity. The Union had suffered a close call and Ryan suspected that had the Rebels continued to attack, they might well have taken the city. He was a little surprised that Pickett had ordered them to fall back. When he thought of his mother, sister, and good friend, he was relieved that he would soon be back to assure their safety. He hated passionately this war he had gotten himself into. The now armless fifteen-year-old boy's face distorted by a scream of anguish flashed before his face and he wondered if he still lived. He had seen boys as young as thirteen and fourteen and men in their late fifties and sixties augmenting the forces of the dwindling Confederacy. Even knowing they could not win, they continued doggedly on. He admired them for their courage and perseverance even while his ire rose at their persistence in the face of certain defeat, diminished forces, scant supplies, and suffering families waiting at home.

With the constant need to hide, it was a weary bedraggled man who approached the sentry when he neared New Berne. Looking more like an apparition of mud than a Union soldier, it had taken some minutes to persuade the reluctant private of his identity and to let him pass. When he reached the stable he stopped to see if his horse had made it back. Stepping inside he saw Windfall in his usual stall contentedly munching on some oats. Windfall turned his head and watched the approaching man, suspicion evident in the dilation of his nostrils.

"Whoa, boy. Don't you recognize me under all of this mud?" Ryan gave him an affection pat and recognizing the voice, his horse whinnied in greeting. "I'm glad you made it back and in a lot better shape than I've managed."

When Ryan reached the Slover house, he went straight to his room, calling for Bobby as he walked. He was shortly stripped and in a welcome bath. Realizing the first bathwater was full of mud, he was forced to call for another bath in order to clean himself. He hoped Bobby could salvage his uniform but it looked doubtful. Once he had bathed, shaved, and eaten, he reported back to headquarters. That done, he knew despite the hour, he had to go to Caroline's and make sure everyone there was okay.

He went back for his horse and was soon cantering down the road to Riverside. Ryan could see the reassuring sight of chimneys silhouetted against the sky before he reached the yard and saw the house was untouched. A glowing light in the parlor indicated that someone was still up. Caroline met him at the door, both relief at seeing him and weariness in her face.

"Thank God, Ryan. We have been so worried; when all of the firing stopped and you didn't come we feared something had happened to you."

"Unfortunately, it did. I was taken prisoner but finally managed to get away and back here tonight. Other than sore feet and considerable annoyance at being taken, losing some dignity, my sword and pistol, and a good night's sleep, I'm not too much the worse for wear. Unfortunately nearly a three hundred others are in prison in Kinston by now, not to count the killed and wounded."

"At least y'all held onto to New Berne and the town itself was untouched except for an influx of wounded and dead. It's a good thing the coffin factory is making boxes to put them in. I hate to think of all those poor men on both sides just being dumped into the ground in mass graves."

"I try not to think about it," Ryan responded grimly. Looking beyond her to the parlor, he remarked, "I see my mother and sister have gone to bed."

"Yes, poor Isabel is exhausted. It has been difficult for her the last few days, as Martha has been furious at being caught in the middle of the war. I'm afraid she didn't consider that possibility when she made the precipitous decision to come with Isabel. I confess she's a difficult guest. I'm happy to have her because she's your mother, but it would be nicer if she were a bit calmer person."

"That would be nice but this side of the grave, I'm not sure it's possible." Ryan laughed. "I'm so sorry to put this problem on you. Please forgive me. I won't keep you tonight because I can see how tired you are. Just let my sister and mother know I'm back and unharmed when you see them in the morning. I'll try to come back tomorrow."

"They'll be relieved, to say the least. Do stay for dinner tomorrow night if you can get away."

Leaving, Riverside Ryan turned his horse and rode to the knoll. Despite the cold night air, he got down and sat on the grass looking over the moonlit river. Around him was evidence of the work on the site: Stumps were removed and the land was being leveled of small trees and bushes. He hoped he would have some time to interview Mr. Hawkes before the next call to battle.

His duties in New Berne kept him in the town, where news trickled in about the continuing Confederate action around Plymouth and Little Washington. It was not until May that the town could breathe a sigh of relief and get back to normal occupation routine. By early August the newspapers that came in from the North had begun to report how low morale had become on the Union side. Grant's campaign to push Lee from the wilderness near Fredericksburg to his defenses in Petersburg had cost the North fifty-five thousand men. By summer of 1864, it was apparent that Grant was no nearer taking Richmond than McClellan had been. The staggering losses and lack of progress increased calls for some kind of truce. Heartened at the hope of triumph, the weary Confederacy struggled on.

The only bright spots for Ryan were the growing rapport between his sister and Caroline, the lessening of tension created by his mother, and progress on the building site. Hiring Hawkes had been a wise decision as they had quickly agreed on a building plan, thus giving Smith the go-ahead. The foundation was in and the framing finished by late July. Ryan hoped the following summer would find him in his home. Neither he nor anyone else realized the calamity that they would soon face. By late August the town had come to a stop.

It was a miasmic hot summer, humid as only the South could be. The daily dose of quinine and whiskey had been doubled but it did not stop the virulent epidemic of yellow fever that soon threatened the entire town. The first to die, John Taylor, was the well-respected owner of the town's principal drugstore as well as a business dealing in naval stores. Lieutenants Johnson of the ambulance corps and Vanderbeck of the 158 N.Y. Volunteers died next. They were followed in death by Captains William Holding, Charles and A. Q. Hoskins, and the detail clerks in the Post Commissaries office. Medical Director D. W. Hand ordered the Commissary buildings on the Craven Street wharf destroyed because of the putrid water that filled the basements. Major H. T. Lawson and his men removed the stored goods and armaments and torched the buildings. The well-loved and gentlemanly Lawson himself soon died of the fever he had tried to contain. Prior to his death, Charles Weigand, Joseph Beetzkes, J. Breen, Mr. Cipher on Pollock Street, and Lucien and Charles Perkins, all leading merchants of the city, died. James Bryan, an attorney only recently returned to the city, and his wife died shortly afterwards.

Only a handful of businesses stayed open, the rest were all shuttered and dark, as their owners had fled the confines of the town. Through it all the Gaston House Hotel stayed open. Of those who stayed, William Poalk, auctioneer and commission merchant; Henry Mandeville; Curtis Pecford; William

Moore, Jr.; James Allen; W. P. Ketcham; C. H. Alexander; G. G. Manning; and S. Kahn, leading citizens all, joined the ranks of the dead. Mournful eulogies kept Reverend Rouse constantly busy. Along with the merchants and other citizens, soldiers, soldiers' wives, doctors, and contrabands all died without respect to position.

Far more soldiers would be killed by the disease than by the battles for New Berne. Soon twenty to twenty-five people were dying daily. By late October the city was abandoned to the moaning wind as it blew fallen leaves down the deserted streets and to the sound of wagons creaking as they hauled away the dead. It was not until the autumn chill of November that the pestilence released its grip on the city.

Through it all Ryan had remained healthy but those at Riverside had not been so lucky. In October Martha fell ill and remained deathly sick until early November. Thanks to the devoted nursing of the other women, it was a weakened and greatly subdued woman who finally left her bed, grateful that her life had been spared.

The only news to cheer the decimated Union troops in New Berne were reports of Sherman's conquest of Atlanta on September 2nd. For the North, the electrifying news restored morale and assured the reelection of President Abraham Lincoln in November. General Jubal Early's defeat in the Shenandoah Valley shortly after was one more bonus for the year. In eastern North Carolina, Southerners pinned their hopes on the *Albemarle*. They were dashed on September 27th when the daringly courageous Lieutenant William Cushing, against all odds, successfully torpedoed the ironclad ram. With the *Albemarle* sunk, the vulnerable town of Plymouth was retaken by the Union on October 31st and Little Washington shortly after. By mid-December the Union army once again turned its attention to Kinston, sending four hundred men on a raid on entrenchments near Jackson's Mill Pond on Southwest Creek that lasted for nearly five days.

Chapter 19

For Penny, the year of 1864 had been one of mixed blessings. She watched Rye-Rye growing daily, celebrating the milestones in his march from infancy: rolling over, sitting alone, pulling himself up, and then learning to walk. He continued to be an unusually sunny child, cooing and babbling in delight with the world around. She laughed aloud when she caught him watching the dust motes dancing in a sunbeam and trying to catch them. He would grab, close his fist tightly, and then open it to see what he had caught, only to be disappointed when he saw nothing there.

Nancy had been worth her weight in gold, not only for the company she provided, but also for her assistance in tending to Rye-Rye. She also helped with the routine of growing and preserving food and weaving cloth for everyday clothing. With her artistic flair, the cloth she wove was far handsomer than what Penny and Mammy had managed. Despite never having children or a home of her own, she was an accomplished homemaker.

Penny sat watching Nancy at the loom. "You know, Nancy. That cloth you are making almost seems like a parable of life. The warp threads are like our basic personalities and principles, while the weft are the people and events that give our lives pattern and color."

"Some people sure have a lot more pattern and color in their lives than others. I'm just thankful that you and Rye have added so much more to the fabric of my own life. I confess I was feeling kind of sorry for the drabness of it before I met y'all."

"You've added to my life, too. I'm grateful for all you have taught me and for your steadying influence when I've needed that. Rye adores you and I would have been so lonely here without you. I'm glad you came here after Mama died,Penny said.

When not tending his own farm, John spent his spare moments at Penny's playing with his grandson. It was soon apparent that he dotted on him. No matter what Rye-Rye did, her Pa thought it was wonderful. An even more indulgent Fitz visited frequently once he had brought Daniel's body home. He had left for Richmond in early April and, after some bureaucratic red tape in Richmond, had succeeded in recovering Daniel's coffin and shipping it back to Kinston. His overseer had met him with a buggy and they had taken it to the Kennedy cemetery at Belle Terre.

The pastor from Woodington Church had conducted a small ceremony for family, friends, and neighbors. Afterwards Fitz had seemed more at peace than John or Penny had seen him in a long time. Once again he was flirting with Nancy in a lackadaisical kind of way and he no longer spent his money in Kinston, or at least not enough of it that he would again need to ask John for a loan. John didn't ask, but he suspected the young woman at Sugar Hill had found economic reasons to expand her trade.

It had been a good year for crops, despite the fact the yield was down from previous years due to a shortage of labor that affected not only slave owners but those like Penny as well. Both Fitz and her father had watched their slaves slowly vanish in the night until only a devoted few remained by the end of summer. They heard that some had gone to James City, a town of contrabands just outside of New Berne, others had fled to a thriving Negro settlement on Roanoke Island and a few younger men were working for, or serving, in one or the other armies. At one time, there were slave catchers who would hunt for them and return them to their owners. Recognizing the new order of their world, wisely John and Fitz refused to try to reclaim them.

Marcus effectively managed Pineview and all of the complexities of a large plantation, and he had succeeded beyond their expectations with the moonshining business. Not only was he supplying the taverns in the area, he was also supplying the daily ration of whiskey used by the Confederate troops around Kinston, despite laws that made the private production of alcohol unlawful. Thanks to the inefficient distribution system of the Confederacy, their moonshine was the best and often the only source available for local troops. Recognizing the need, the sheriff quietly looked the other way. Slowly Marcus's hoard of coins was growing. When gold and silver had tightened up, he had been forced to accept specie, but he had quickly used that to buy things that he could either sell later or use immediately. Barter was quickly becoming a necessity as the South's economy spiraled ever lower. He traded when he could and accepted Confederate specie only when he must.

Penny was pleased with her own growing wealth and anticipated the day when she could use it to modernize her farm with the new machinery that would lessen the need for the large numbers of cheap or enslaved laborers on whom the South could no longer rely. Her corn crop was adequate for the needs of the business, the animals, and her people. Other than that they had grown only food and enough cotton for their own needs.

She noticed with concern that the hard work that once had been shared among many fell increasingly on the shoulders of Mammy and her aging husband. Soon she would be forced to hire someone to do their chores for them as they became increasingly frail. Lucinda was a problem she had not yet solved. The woman had become more and more hostile and bitter during the course of the year. Penny wondered if Lucinda was mourning Daniel in her own way. After all, she reflected, the only true son he had was the one Lucinda had given him. She questioned whether or not Lucinda suspected that Jeremiah was the only one he had left behind and not Rye-Rye as well. She debated with herself about approaching Mammy with her concerns but decided against it.

Finally after a particularly contentious week, she asked Fitz if he could use a housekeeper since his own had quietly decamped in the night. It was a relieved man who agreed to let Lucinda, and the child he did not know was his grandson, come live with him. Penny's relief was even greater. Mammy and Moses also seemed glad that their daughter had moved as her unhappiness had spilled over on them, too.

That left Penny with two unresolved problems: She could not forgive Ryan the pain she felt when she thought of his clandestine visit and she was uneasy at the increasingly amorous overtures from Marcus. Although she liked him and even felt a small attraction to him as a man, she knew she was unready for anything beyond the friendship that they already had. It was not until summer that she had begun to suspect his feelings exceeded her own. She had looked at the work they had accomplished together and the money he had made for her and spontaneously hugged him. He had quickly encircled her in his arms and she could tell by the look in his eyes that he wanted to kiss her. Gently pulling back she had talked of something inconsequential until he left. Now she studiously avoided any opportunity for intimacy. For his part, she felt that he had moved to a waiting game. Penny decided she was like a piece of cheese in a trap that the mouse was eyeing from different angles until he could safely figure out how to pounce on it and claim it for his own. During frustrating nights of mourning Ryan's rejection of her and his child, she considered the possibility of allowing Marcus to court her, but when morning came she knew she wasn't over her love for Ryan.

When news leaked in from the outside of the battles around New Berne, her fear for him drove her nearly mad. Again Penny found her sleep broken by nightmares that gave her no rest. One night she had envisioned Ryan slashing with his sword in a mad melee, only to be taken prisoner. She prayed that the vision was just a dream of anxiety and nothing more.

Those who fled inland from New Berne that Fall brought news to Kinston of the terrible sickness that was killing so many in the occupied town, adding anew to her fear for him. Fortunately the Kinston area had not suffered unduly from the fever and she had treated only four with her remedy: a tartar emetic divided into four doses of one ounce each and followed by large doses of quinine afterward.

When they heard of the failure to capture New Berne, the loss of the *Albemarle*, the reoccupation of Plymouth and Little Washington, and the fall of Atlanta, it was if they waited only for the final demise of their dream of an independent and separate Southland. Marcus, Fitz, and John spent hours debating the merits of the different generals and their successes and failures, the shortages of materiel and food, and the tighter Union noose that was slowly squeezing the pipeline of supplies and the chances for victory to a close. They questioned what the loss of the war would mean to them and their families and how best to prepare for the eventuality. Listening to them, Penny had her own questions of what the future would bring to her son and her. She prayed that her decisions had been wise ones. When she looked at the frustrations and guilt she felt, she wasn't so sure; however, she argued to herself, what could I have done differently? Even if I'm alone and miserable, Ryan rejected me when he saw I carried his child and I would not have my son born a bastard.

They had celebrated Rye-Rye's first birthday, September 16, 1864, with a cake, the first they had eaten in months, as the price of flour had become prohibitive at nine dollars a barrel. The Kinston paper had carried an article describing a group of women in Salisbury who, frustrated at merchants who were holding on to their flour supply, marched on them with hatchets and managed to get three barrels of flour. In Greensborough women had been jailed for trying to get food. Hungry women tired of watching their children starve had written a barrage of letters to Governor Zebulon Vance, demanding he do something, anything, to help them. Across the South starvation was making the weakening population gaunt and angry. The soldiers were faring no better. Despite the reports in the North that the South was deliberately starving Union soldiers held in Confederate prisons, the prisoners received the same rations as the Rebel soldiers. There was simply not enough food for the South to feed its civilians or army. Fallow fields grew lush with weeds where men, both black and white, once toiled. Women, some who had previously done no physical labor, were now hoeing fields, struggling to pull plows and harvesting barely enough to survive. When tools wore out there were none to be had for replacements. Cotton carders, a necessity for processing cotton for spinning, were notoriously fragile and now hard to obtain.

By her baby's birthday, salt was selling for eight dollars a bushel, a pound of sugar cost seven, a dozen eggs went for three, sweet potatoes for seventy-five cents a pound, and molasses commanded twenty-four dollars a gill. Those prices were only the going rate when and if the goods were actually available. To add insult to injury the state instituted a one-percent property tax in addition to the ten-percent tariff on all goods produced. For North Carolina and the South the situation was fast going from grim to desperate. With its block-ade-runners still bringing in a trickle of goods, Wilmington was arguably be-coming the most important city in the Confederacy second to Richmond. Unfortunately the runners could not bring in enough goods and more and more the destitute population could not afford the prices if they had.

Despite the rigors of life that increased daily, Rye-Rye's birthday had been a happy one. Penny's father, Fitz, Marcus, Nancy, Mammy Rena, and Moses were all gathered with her to sing Happy Birthday. They had used the last of their sugar for the celebration. Rye-Rye's first tooth must have been a sweet one, as he wasted no time in cramming a fist of the red velvet cake into his mouth. Penny caught Mammy's eye and knew they were both remembering the baby's father, who also loved that cake.

Marcus was ebullient, pleased with the continuing success of the moon-shining operation. Although they were producing less without the addition of sugar, the quality was actually better. They did not have enough corn or jars to continue forever, but a few more months would be enough to enable him to buy a farm when one came available. Penny was more and more comfort-able with him as he had made no more attempts to be intimate. John was beam-ing, too, as he had received a letter from an elated Brett, who had been made an aide to General Lee, his idol. He no longer suffered the rigors of life in the field nor the immediate dangers of battle. Penny rejoiced as well, as she could-n't bear the thought of losing him.

Fitz seemed happier than he had been in months. Penny did not know it, but Fitz told John that he had abandoned his "fallen flower" to other customers and made peace with his widower status. He spent more and more time with the baby, for which Penny was grateful, as it freed her to attend to the many chores that the summer and fall brought to a farm. She was thankful that de-spite shortages of sugar, flour, and various items she would have liked, they still had adequate food and were thus far luckier than many. Nancy had been a blessing in her household, providing Penny with the company she craved during the long lonely evenings. She was often the one who picked up Rye-Rye to soothe him when he fretted. Nancy loved it there and felt as though she had become one of the family. She knew that it would not be forever, as her parents were aging to the point they would soon need her, but until then she intended to enjoy every day at Pleasant Glade.

Fortunately Penny's stockpile of salt was ample for the meat preserving on all three farms. Fitz and John both thanked Penny for the foresight that they themselves had lacked. Without the salt there would have been no pre-served meat to tide them through the winter. They waited only for the first hard freeze and colder weather when they would all work together to kill, process, and then begin the curing on each of their plantations. With labor in-creasingly short, there was no other choice than to help one another with the labor-intensive work that had to be done quickly.

In mid-December, just when the community thought it could relax and enjoy a holiday season safely gathered around the family hearth, about four hundred Union troops from New Berne raided the area over a period of five days. The skirmishes accomplished nothing militarily for the Union unless it was to give the soldiers a chance to blow off some steam. For the community, however, it meant dealing with the danger inherent in their presence: livestock taken or slaughtered, houses pillaged, a couple of homes burned, and terrorized women and children.

On December 10th, when her father learned of the first of the skirmishes around the Southwest Creek area east of Kinston, he sent Marcus to Penny's with instructions to stay with her until the Yankees left the area. He did not want two women, a baby, and the two elderly servants without the protection of a man should a band of the enemy invade her land. Marcus was more than delighted to comply, as he anticipated the opportunity it would give him to gently pursue the reticent woman. Penny was decidedly not happy about it but knew her father was adamant and Fitz was backing him up. Marcus slept for five nights in the bed that had last held Ryan.

For the entire time he was there, Penny managed to frustrate his intentions by constantly keeping Nancy with her. On December 16th, Marcus packed his things and walked downstairs to the kitchen. Penny and Nancy were there feeding Rye-Rye breakfast. When he entered, Nancy made a mumbled excuse and hastily left just as he had privately asked her to do the previous evening.

"I've packed my things, Penny, and I'll be going on back to your Pa's. He told me yesterday that the word was the Yankees were leaving to go back to New Berne. He asked me to stay one more night just until everything is back to normal."

"Yes, he told me too when he was here. I really do appreciate you staying with us. It was reassuring to have someone besides just us in the house."

"Penny, Daniel has been dead a year. Maybe that's not so long, but it's time that I say something to you. I don't want you to answer me, please. Just think about what I'm going to say."

Fishing for an excuse to delay the words she knew were coming, she said, "Really, Marcus. Can't it wait? I really need to change Rye-Rye's diaper. He gets a rash so easily if he stays wet long."

"His diaper is dry, Penny." Marcus was determined. "Now, sit back down and stop fidgeting. I'm not going to take all that long to say what I need to say."

Not knowing what else to do, Penny sat.

"You know I admire and respect you for all of the things you are and for the things you do for so many people. You're a good woman and a beautiful one. I think I fell in love with you the first time I laid eyes on you when you were maybe fourteen years old. It was the first day that I came to work for your pa and from that day to this one, I've never stopped. I knew with no prospects and without the education and background to match yours, I didn't stand a chance. When you married Daniel, I tried to stop my feelings and find someone else. It was no use." Marcus smiled. "I'm a lot older now and I know what I want, just as I did then. The difference is that I'm no longer without prospects. I've saved every dime I could all of these years. I have enough to buy a decent farm, build and furnish a house, and outfit the farm. I can finally support a family and provide a good living. It can't be that big a secret how I feel about you. I've watched you get nervous when I'm near for fear I'll try to kiss you again. I'll not do that until you tell me you're ready, so you can stop worrying about it. Just now I'm probably the most patient and doggedly stubborn man you'll ever meet. I'm waiting for you. Just know that when you're ready, I'll be here. I want you for my wife and I want to be a daddy for your boy and the children we'll have together."

"Marcus, you're a good—"

Interrupting, he reminded her, "I said don't answer me now. Just chew it over a spell." With that, he stood and, smiling at her, put on his hat. He turned and looked back at her and winked just before he walked through the door. He acted downright jaunty, she thought.

Penny stared at the closed door, surprised that he had so clearly stated his intentions after so long and yet not surprised at the feelings he had expressed. She and Nancy had talked just the day before about Marcus. Penny knew he had an ardent ally in Nancy. She had carefully listed for Penny all of the positive attributes that Marcus possessed.

Quietly she had added, "He's so in love with you, Penny. At least give him a chance. He would make you a good husband and a good father for your baby."

"I know all of that Nancy, and I do like Marcus a lot. I'm just not in love with him. I want to love the man I'm married to, not just *like* him. I don't know, maybe in time...just not *now*."

Marcus was a good man and an attractive one. He didn't excite her like Ryan had. With Ryan it had just felt so right. Yet could she really trust that feeling? He obviously wasn't the man she thought he was to turn away when he saw her pregnant. Maybe she should try to be a little more open emotionally to Marcus and see if her feelings would grow deeper. Penny stood. "Rye-Rye, baby boy, I'm going to bundle you up and we're going to get ourselves ready for your second Christmas. I think we need a tree."

"Da-da."

"Not Da-da, sugar. Say Ma-ma." She tickled his little tummy to make him giggle. "Ma-ma."

"Wha' cho doin' to my boy? I kin hear'im gigglin' from out de do'." Mammy laughed. "He be de spittin' image a 'is daddy, sho nuff. Ain' no mistakin' dem eyes. It sho ain'."

"Mammy, please be careful. Only you and I know about all that. It's our secret."

"What's the secret?" Nancy asked, coming into the kitchen. "Don't tell me you agreed to marry Marcus after all."

"Wha' cho mean? Is dat boy tryin' ta marry you?" Mammy Rena looked shocked. She knew Penny well enough to know she was still in love with her baby's father.

"Oh, don't be blooming idiots, you two." Penny forced herself to laugh. "I have no intention of marrying anyone. Right now I'm planning on bundling the baby and me in some warm clothes. We're going to cut us a Christmas tree. Come on, Nancy. You can help me select a tree and choose some branches for the mantles. Mammy, do we have enough molasses to make gingerbread men for Rye-Rye?"

"I 'specs I does, an' iffn we ain' I kin git some from Delia."

"Good. We're going to have ourselves a festive, fun holiday, aren't we, Rye-Rye?"

Kicking his feet, he cooed, "Da-da."

"Well, *you* seem to like Marcus. Don't you, little man?" Nancy grabbed one of his little feet, grinning at Penny when she said it.

Penny and Nancy took the baby and walked into the woods to find a tree. Rye-Rye continued cooing and babbling with delight at being outdoors. Rain the last few days had kept them all inside, making the excursion even more welcome. They were nearing the creek when the two darkies Marcus had hired came through the woods with eyes the size of saucers. In their rush they nearly knocked the two women down.

"Hey, watch it!" Penny struggled to keep from dropping the baby while she regained her balance. "What in the world is going on?"

"Dey's hants down der. I ain' workin' no mo' in des woods. Naw, suh. Sho ain'." Leroy shook his head emphatically.

"Ain' workin' neider, ain' workin' 'round no dayd mens," the other one, Josey, added.

"What are you two babbling about?"

"Deys a dayd man in de crick." Leroy pointed the way they had just come.

Penny had a strong suspicion she knew who that dead man might be. "Is Marcus down there now?"

"Yas'am."

"Nancy, would you take the baby back to the house. I'm going to find Marcus and see what's going on." When they had left, she continued down the path leading to the creek and then downstream to the still and the gristmill.

She found Marcus sitting on a stump, fuming to himself. "Dammit to hell. This is a fine time for this to happen. I'm going to have to finish this run alone now. Damn."

"Marcus, what's going on? Josey and Leroy nearly knocked me down trying to get away from here."

"It looks like the rain we've had washed loose a pretty much rotted-away body and it lodged at the mill. They were grinding the corn sprouts when they saw it. They're so damned spooked they'll never come back and once they tell the other darkies, there won't be anyone willing to work here. I'm going to have to finish this run alone. I don't know how I'll cover being here night and day for the next couple of days. I have to come up with something to tell your pa."

"What can I do to help?"

"Figure out a reason I can give your pa that he'll believe." Marcus shook his head with disgust. "I'm glad I've about made all I can this season because we're going out of business."

"It's okay. We've done well enough and the longer we continue the greater the chance of running into a problem with the law. I'll think of something to tell my father and I'll bring you a blanket and some food." Penny smiled at the dejected man. "Don't look so sad. At least you won't be stuck down here with a dead man once this is finished."

"I suppose I should get a shovel and bury him. Best I can figure, he must be from the fighting a couple of years ago. The only thing that doesn't fit with that is his clothes don't look like a uniform."

"Maybe he was a Bushwhacker?" Penny offered.

"Could be, but I doubt we'll ever know who he is or how he died."

That was just fine with Penny. "I'll think of something that I can tell Pa you had to go to Kinston to get and if it's not there, to Goldsborough. Any ideas?"

"We don't need anything at Pineview at the moment, so it'll have to be something for you. Do you need something for Rye-Rye, the farm, or some medicine, maybe?"

"I know. Fitz has been wanting a monument for Daniel's grave. I can say I sent you over to Goldsborough to get one and you're going to stay until it's finished. I'll tell Fitz you're going and ask him what he'd like on it. I just have to be sure to keep him from wanting to go with you."

"Penny, think again. That won't work. I don't have time to leave here to get a tombstone and if I show up without one, what will they think?"

"Hmm. You're right. It'll have to be something else. Let's think on it while I get some food and other stuff for you."

Chapter 20

When Colonel C. C. Dodge of the First New York Mounted Rifles rode back into town following the mid-December raids on the Southwest Creek entrenchments near Kinston, Ryan's trigger finger itched. Dodge had become notorious in the area for pillaging the homes of hapless southerners. He and his men had looted Edenton in August of 1863 and stolen so voraciously that the people of Edenton called his men "Dodge's Mounted Thieves." Judging by the jewelry that Dodge was flashing, Ryan knew he'd done some liberal stealing around Kinston as well. He swore to himself that if he saw the ring he had given Penny, or any of the other jewelry he had seen her wear, in the possession of Dodge or any of his men, that man would answer to him. Disgusted at the excesses that some of the soldiers were bragging about, he asked for an audience with General Palmer.

General Palmer listened quietly while Ryan vented his frustration at the lack of restraint of some of the Union troops and their commanders. Explaining how his life had been saved after the December 1862 battle at Southwest Creek, he ask Palmer to honor the previous pledge that General Foster had given him not to allow any attack or incursion on either Penny's property or her father's.

"Colonel Ryan, I personally don't condone the kinds of behavior that you have detailed for me. While I'm aware that unfortunate incidents have occurred, they haven't been with my sanction. When soldiers have their blood up during battle and the aftermath, it isn't always possible to control them. It is a sad commentary on war that women and children must often pay a heavy price for the politics of their men. I will instruct my officers to pass on to their men the names and locations of the property you mentioned and ask that they allow no trespassing. That's the best I can do."

"Thank you, sir. I appreciate that very much." Ryan left. He didn't know what more he could do to protect the woman he still loved despite her treachery. On days when he was more forgiving, he fantasized that Daniel would not return to Penny and she would be free at last. Rarely a day went by that he did not think about how much he had loved her and believed in her promises of a life together. And every time he did he remembered seeing her in the field with a belly swollen with her husband's child. He found himself wishing it were his child she carried and wondering what she would have done if that had been the case. Then he remembered her letter and became angry again. It never occurred to him that he had fathered the child and she had done the only thing she could do in the world in which she lived.

With the arrival of the Christmas holiday, Ryan carefully collected what foods he could obtain for the people at Riverview and drove out to the plantation. On the way, he stopped at the building site. With the end of the fever, work was again progressing. The framework was going up on the house so that he could begin to visualize it as a finished building. He realized that it was going to have much the same feel as the Slover house in New Berne, where he now resided. The red-brick, dark green shutters on either side of long casement windows fronted by wrought-iron balcony railings and white trim were features he would include in his own house. He had added a fanlight over the front door and a long side gallery facing the river, where one could catch the evening breeze. Because it stood on a bluff, the water table wasn't so high as to prohibit a cellar. He envisioned it stocked with wines like the cellar at Pleasant Glade. Remembering Penny's annoyance with her separated kitchen, he had worked with Hawkes to design a brick-walled kitchen separated from the house but yet attached by a short passageway lined with paired French doors. With the French doors opened in nice weather, a breeze could circulate and in winter, the sun shining through glass onto the brick floor would hold radiant heat. A slate roof would be a further deterrent to fire.

Martha, who had always loved plants, had talked with Caroline to see what grew best in the area and the two women were now spending happy hours planning his garden. With something to do that she both enjoyed and was good at, Martha became invigorated and happier. Caroline was not only helping Martha to select plants but also laying out a format for the flower-filled park she envisioned for Riverview. The women employed a workman to begin digging some of the overabundant bulbs and shrubs that Caroline could spare and transplanting them to the outer garden areas, where they would not interfere with the workers building Ryan's house.

Isabel used a copy of the house plans to draw up a list of the items Ryan would need to furnish the necessary portion of the house. When she suggested he might want to furnish it all, he hesitated but offered no reason for his objection. She persuaded her mother to part with heirloom items in their own house in Baltimore that she knew Ryan loved, unlike the new pieces his mother had added when decorating their home. While the list was insufficient, the pieces would form a core around which she could design each room. Staying busy with the house plans kept her from dwelling on her fiancé's death and like Martha, she found that she too was happier. Isabel had come to love Caroline just as Ryan had done and even Martha seemed to like her a great deal.

Isabel wondered if one of the reasons her mother seemed happier had to do with the increasingly admiring attentions of the widower, John Harvey. Ryan could have done without his mother's suitor as John's niece, Hattie, often came with him. He could tell by her simpering manner that she had set her cap for him. Isabel knew that Ryan was keeping a wary distance from Hattie's tentacles. She found Hattie vaporous, anti-intellectual, and flighty and could not imagine that Ryan would ever fall for such a vacuous, self-centered woman.

Ryan leaned against one of the bare studs of the room that would be his favorite in the new house. The sun parlor surrounded by French casement windows on three sides would command a sweeping view of the river. He longed for the day it would be finished and he could live in his home free of the worries of war. Carefully he had nurtured the growing respect of the townsmen and had sought out the company of fellow soldiers who had fallen in love either with the town or local women and were planning to stay after the war just as he did. He had written his uncle to begin liquidating properties and assets in New York and Baltimore and banking the proceeds. After the war, he planned to transfer his funds to the local bank. With his mother and sister increasingly happy in New Berne, he wondered if they too might settle in the town.

A number of officers had begun to look longingly at his attractive sister whenever he escorted her into New Berne. At the moment she could have her pick of suitors in a town where the odds were so overwhelming. Even without the odds in her favor, Isabel would make any man a fine wife and a sweetly gentle companion. With the return of the soldiers to their northern homes, the odds would swing very much the other way. North Carolina had endured the highest mortality rate of any of the Confederate States. Far fewer men would be returning and among those would be many who were severely maimed. The ranks of spinsterhood would explode.

Ryan shrugged his shoulders as he watched the sun set and walked to where Windfall was munching grass. "Old boy, I've decided I'm not going to have a dirt yard around my house. I'll have some nice green grass so you have lots to eat."

The lights blazing in the windows of Riverside cast a warm glow into the night. Riding up to the house, he realized that Caroline's home had become home to him far more so than the family house in Baltimore. He suddenly hoped that not only Isabel but his mother as well would decide to stay. He would have more than enough room for them and he did not relish the idea of living alone in the house he had begun to call Fair Bluff. Isabel and Martha had both begun to make friends in the community and to enjoy the milder climate.

Martha had made the biggest change since her sickness, becoming far more tractable. He decided that she was a woman who needed a mission and that the garden provided. But more than that, he suspected she had been lonely for male admiration and attention. She was still a handsome woman for all her years and possessed a fine intellect. Martha could be a witty and charming conversationalist when she chose. Remembering his father's adoration of his mother, he began to see what had enamored his father of her. She was a demanding and even exciting woman. Ryan decided that his more docile and retiring father had needed and relished the stimulation she brought to what would have been a too quiet life.

When he looped Windfall's reins over the iron hitching post, he noted that John's horse and buggy were already there. He said a silent prayer that Hattie had not come as well. He walked into foyer and hung his hat on the hat tree just inside the door. He could hear inane laughter in the parlor and instantly recognized the voice. His prayer had gone unanswered, he noted. Deciding to delay going into the parlor as long as possible, he walked to the back of the house and left the coffee, tea, and other difficult-to-find food he had brought on the table, where Beulah would find it and take it to the kitchen. He stood there for a moment, looking out the window to the back lawn.

"Ryan, stop hiding. I heard you come in." Caroline laughed as she held her cheek for his kiss of greeting. She whispered, "If I didn't know better I'd think you're afraid to go into the parlor. Don't tell me a mere woman is more intimidating than a Rebel soldier?"

"Intimidating is hardly the word I'd use; however, as a guest in your home, I'll bite my tongue and be nice."

"Just stay quick on your feet, my boy. This 'Diana the Huntress' has you in her sights." Caroline winked at him. With resignation he led her into the parlor.

"Mother, you look lovely this evening," he said as he kissed her cheek.

Indeed she looked the best he'd seen her in years. The outdoor air had brought color to her complexion and the dark red dress, with snowy white lace draped at the shoulders and hem, enhanced her dark hair with the streak of gray down the center.

"I told her she's the epitome of the Southern Belle, sassy and gorgeous." John looked fondly at her as he said it. "And how are you this evening, Ryan? I trust you stopped by your property on the way here. Hattie and I did as well and were pleased to see the progress you're making. That's going to be a fine-looking house when you're finished."

Hattie spoke up before Ryan could thank him. "Oh, Ryan, I just love it. You can have such gorgeous parties there and everyone is going to be so jealous of you for having such a nice house. I wish it were finished so we could be in it right now."

"Thank you, John, Hattie." Ryan turned to his sister. "Hello, sweet sis, don't you look beautiful in that dress. Isn't that the one you wore for your engagement party?"

The minute he said it he regretted the reminder of the fiancé she had lost, but Isabel seemed serene when she replied. "Yes, it is. I think it's my favorite. Phillip loved this dress on me. He said the powder blue is good with my eyes."

Caroline offered, "Ryan, we're having sherry. I know you don't care for it, so I have some wine as well. Would you care for a glass before dinner?"

"Thank you, I would." He sat on the chair she vacated, leaving the seat beside Hattie on the sofa empty.

Masking her annoyance that he had not joined her, Hattie asked cloyingly, "Ryan, Uncle John tells me you're an attorney like he is. Is that true?"

"Yes. As a matter of fact, I believe we discussed that on your last visit. Perhaps I misled you with my conversation. I beg your pardon if I caused confusion."

"My goodness, you must forgive me. I can't imagine why I didn't remember that."

"Hattie, would you like to play a song for us on the spinet? I confess I cannot play at all and I do so enjoy music." Isabel invited to spare Ryan further conversation.

"Why, I'd just love to. Miss Hatcher insisted all of her students learn to play and sing. She says it is an absolute necessity for ladies of any refinement," Hattie simpered.

Ryan wondered if she were so stupid that she did not realize the implied insult to his sister. With a decidedly cool tone, he remarked, "Fortunately, Isabel is an educated and interesting conversationalist and an accomplished artist. I applaud her for her excellence in areas that I find most enjoyable in a companion."

Ignoring the implication if she even understood it, Hattie minced her way to the spinet and flipped thought the music, finally deciding on "Somebody's Darling." She played woodenly if accurately. Unfortunately, her voice was nasal and the song was a mournful one of the loss of a beloved man on the field of battle.

After the first two stanzas, Isabel's eyes had begun to shine with tears waiting to spill down her cheeks. Knowing she was thinking of Phillip, her mother interrupted Hattie. "Heavens, child, let's have something more festive. Play something cheerful. Perhaps 'The Yellow Rose of Texas' or a Christmas tune. I particularly like 'See Amid the Winter Snow' or 'We Three Kings of Orient Are.'"

"Forgive me interrupting, but Beulah has dinner ready in the dining room. She will never forgive me if I allow it to grow cold before you can enjoy her efforts. Let's save the music for afterwards," Caroline smoothly interrupted.

Ryan decided with the completion of dinner he would find an excuse to flee any further attempt on Hattie's part to add musical refinement to the evening. Martha and Caroline kept the conversation going at dinner. With their witty repartee, soon all were enjoying the evening, including Ryan, who was relieved not be seated next to Hattie. Judging from the two women's rapport, they were fast becoming good friends despite the rough beginning. When they arose from the table to adjourn to the parlor, Ryan made his excuses. He didn't have duty as he claimed. He fully intended to stop by the hotel and have a glass of wine with some of his fellow soldiers.

"Ryan, would you mind terribly giving me a ride into town? I seem to have developed a frightful headache." Hattie batted her eyes at him.

"Unfortunately I didn't use a buggy this evening. Your hoops are hardly suited for riding behind me on horseback. I'm sorry I'm unable to oblige."

"Oh." Hattie looked crestfallen.

"Hattie, go upstairs and lie down. I'm sure you'll be fine shortly. I can have Beulah take you a soothing drink and a cloth for your head." Caroline took her firmly by the elbow and led her to the stairs as Ryan made his goodbyes to the others.

The last thing he ever intended was to be alone with Hattie in a potentially compromising situation. Without a chaperone she could well claim an intimacy that had never occurred, and it did not stretch his imagination to picture her doing just that. Of course the horse was impossible for her, and he would make it a point to ride the horse in future whenever there was a chance she would be at Riverview as well. Riding back to town he decided against the hotel, took Windfall to his stable, and then walked to the Stover house. A good book seemed more appropriate to his mood.

Ryan was happy when John and Hattie made plans to spend Christmas with relatives in Dover, a small farming community between Kinston and New Berne. Over Christmas dinner at Caroline's he remarked that he found Hattie's company increasingly uncomfortable. As the woman was unpopular with the three women at the table, he had allies in his efforts to squelch her fixation on him.

Martha laughed in amusement at her son. "I'll make it a point to subtly let her know that you have a fiancée in Baltimore with whom you are deeply in love. What shall we name her? I think Lorena sounds good."

"That's fine, Mother. Lorena suddenly has won my heart." Ryan laughed while Isabel softly hummed the popular song "Lorena." Suddenly it dawned on him that Lorena was the name he had chosen when he asked Penny to write to him. He could not help the flicker of pain that crossed his face.

Remembering the conversation of many months before about the woman he had lost, Caroline gave him a hard look and that eyebrow went up. "I don't think a fictional woman is the one who still has your heart."

Isabel and Martha gave her a puzzled look, but neither Caroline nor Ryan provided any edification. Ryan forced himself to grin at them. "I want to see my Christmas gifts. Let's go to the parlor and open presents."

He could not help remembering the Christmas two years previous when he had been with Penny. Although he told himself to forget, his heart would not let him. He wondered if he would ever have a Christmas that would be more than the marking of another year without her.

Caroline saw his thoughtfulness and knew he was thinking of the woman he had lost. Walking with him she whispered so the others could not hear, "Ryan, some day you'll find someone else. You're still young and the time is wrong anyway. When the war is over and you no longer have so many things demanding your time, perhaps a good woman will come along."

"I'm not ready one way or the other. I don't know that I ever will be again."

"What are you two whispering about?" his mother teased.

Ryan turned to his mother and sister. "I was just telling Caroline that you're going to love your gifts from me."

"Well, then let's have them," Martha said.

Isabel knew that there was some unhappiness Ryan was hiding from them and she suspected that Caroline was privy to the secret. She too felt sad at another year without the man she had planned to marry and now never could. Planning for the future seemed to her as a futile thing with the uncertainties of life in a nation torn asunder by war. When she thought back to the period before the war, she knew that none of them could ever have visualized what changes they would face in their lives. None of the three of them could ever have envisioned living in New Berne, North Carolina, that Phillip would be killed, that Ryan would be a soldier and Martha would have an admirer. Secretly she was happy for her mother but knew the woman well enough to avoid saying anything one way or the other for fear she might become contrary.

News began to come into New Berne of Sherman's march to the sea and the fall of Savannah. Nashville had fallen as well. The pincer was clamping down on the South from every direction. Locals walked about with somber faces and soldiers placed bets on the month it would all end. Even the most diehard of them realized that the end of the Confederacy could not be that far away. The newspapers reported that Fort Fisher, the main protection for the South's vital port in Wilmington, was arming for eminent attack. After a terrible firestorm of shells and cannonade from Admiral David Porter's warships, General Alfred Terry's troops swept through the fort on January 15th. Wilmington fell shortly after. The South no longer had access to the outside world by sea. The vital access to food and weapons was at an end.

Across the South soldiers who had fought with nothing but scraps of carpet cut from Turkish rugs to keep them warm at night could not go on in the face of starvation. Quietly they began to desert the army and wend their way homeward to families who were equally hungry. Despite Davis's earlier aversion to arming Negro soldiers to fight for the Confederacy, he was forced to approve a measure to do so. It would never be put into effect. It was too late.

And Sherman kept coming like a scourge from the maws of Hell. He swept like a hurricane through South Carolina and then, in February of 1865, into North Carolina, destroying everything in his path. Colonel Palmer convened a meeting with his officers in late February. The troops in New Berne had been given a new mission: rebuild the torn-up sections of railroad between New Berne and Kinston and capture Kinston and the Ram Neuse that lay at anchor there.

General John Schofield had been instructed to capture the New Berne to Goldsboro railroad. He ordered General Cox to march from Wilmington to Goldsboro and to open the railroad to support Sherman's advance with access to needed supplies. New Berne's troops came under General Cox's immediate command and Ryan with his fellow officers began to ready their men for battle.

The Confederates, desperate to protect the vital rail link, sent twelve thousand men under the command of General Braxton Bragg to intercept the advancing Union troops. Bragg decided to utilize the existing defensive works running south from the Neuse River along the banks of Southwest Creek to Jackson's Mill Pond, which lay about three miles east of Kinston. On the way to their position many of the Rebel troops left their units and visited family in the area, not knowing when or if they would see them again. After a brief reunion they reported for duty, determined to hold the railroad. Boys as young as twelve years old and men with the gray whiskers of old age marched to war with them.

The Union forces left New Berne on March 7th to bivouac at Gum Swamp, about ten miles from Kinston. It had been difficult, as the troops had often been knee deep in water and mud. Felled trees blocked the road that was pocked with deep mud holes. These trees had to be moved from the road. To make the road navigable, saplings were felled to corduroy the roughest stretches.

General Cox ordered Ryan to ride with the 12th New York Calvary southward on British Road to guard critical road crossings. Ryan was glad that he was the one assigned the duty rather than the notorious Colonel Dodge. Taking the Dover Road, Ryan discovered heavily manned fortifications and fell back to Wyse Forks and from there moved to the intersection of British Road and Upper Trent Road well south of Jackson's Mill Pond. His post was near enough to Penny's farm to easily have walked there. He made it a point to ride by the road in front of her home to see if the fence that belied the road behind was still in place. Relieved he noted that since the fence had been built, the road had become less discernable than ever due to the growth of shrubs, tall grasses, and saplings. He worried for her safety but other than stationing one of his troopers at the entry to her father's farm and in the woods near hers with orders that no one was to trespass per orders of General Palmer, there was nothing more he could do.

Soon Cox, worried about the security of the light defenses that the 12th Calvary could provide, sent infantry reinforcements. Ryan and his men had already begun digging trenches and felling trees when the infantry arrived.

They too pitched in and soon had an earthen embankment completed. A local Negro, observing the feverish activity, came into camp and reported a force of two thousand Rebels was moving down Trent Road. A dispatch was sent with the news to General Cox. Furious his Union forces were in danger of being split, he sent a note of warning to Colonel Upham that the colonel never received. Soon Upham was under attack and scrambling to avert disaster.

On March 8 the Confederacy had drawn the noose around a segment of the Union forces in the vicinity of Dr. John Cobb's house by taking the troops there prisoner. After a terrific fight that now was occurring on several fronts, thousands lay dead or injured. General Bragg ordered General Daniel Hill to retrace his route along the Neuse Road to join the main Confederate line near Southwest Creek. Ryan's troops attacked but did not succeed in stopping Hill's force. All in all it had been a very bad day for the Union.

When the sun dawned on Wednesday morning, Bragg was determined that the day would be decisive in crushing the enemy so Cox could not join with Sherman in the drive to Goldsboro and the critical supplies. General Hoke made a bad decision when he found the Yankees had heavily entrenched overnight and withdrew his troops, effectively splitting the Confederate front. Additionally, the swampy terrain was making it difficult for both sides to effectively maneuver. Wednesday ended with no decisive action for either Union or Confederacy.

The morning of the ninth was so quiet that some of the Union soldiers began to hope that the Confederates had retreated; however, a barrage of artillery and the wildly piercing Rebel yell shortly after noon disabused them of that hope. Cox succeeded in pulling his troops together and using bayonets, cups, and bare hands, they desperately dug in. The arrival of General John Schofield forced the Confederates to assault Cox's heavily entrenched position before General Couch, marching from Wilmington with two divisions, could further strengthen the Union position. Firing continued all that night, as Bragg readied his troops to attack from the rear, weakening the center where he hoped to penetrate. Quietly moving through the woods in the cover of dark, they burst forth in a wave of gray and butternut uniforms, yelling and shooting. Withering gunfire forced them to retreat, but they regrouped and came again, and then again. Unable to adequately coordinate the various Confederate attacks, Bragg began to watch his efforts fall apart. Frustrated in stopping the Union forces, he left to join General Johnston at Goldsboro.

The four-day battle of Wyse Forks had ended and a tired Union army began the doleful duty of burying the dead.

Chapter 21

Penny lay in her bed, listening to the boom of cannon, and remembered the last time the sounds of nearby battle had interrupted her sleep. Just as before in the first battle of Kinston, Fitz had left his home and gone to war. He father had been determined to go as well, but Marcus had insisted that he should be the one, as he was the younger and more able man. Her father had not liked it but had accepted the responsibility of watching over both his plantation and his friend's. He begged Penny to come to Pineview but feeling safer at Pleasant Glade, she had refused and instead pleaded with him to come to her. He promised that if it appeared that the Yankees would be invading their land, he would come to offer what protection he could. She wondered what hope any of them would have of safety if the Yankees actually came onto their land.

Rye-Rye, sensing the fear of the adults, was restless in his crib. Listening to him thrash about, Penny got up and walked with him to the rocker. Poking up the fire with one hand, she sat down in the rocker and began to croon to her fretful baby. Although she tried to control her reactions, a loud barrage of gunfire made her flinch. Instantly the baby, attuned to her alarm, began to cry. "Shh, darling. Mama's going to take care of her sweet boy."

"Mama," he said plaintively.

"It just a big old noise, precious. Noise can't hurt us," Penny tried to reassure him, but this sounded so much worse than the first battle of Kinston.

"Penny, are you awake? I heard the baby crying." Nancy stood in her doorway with her own eyes opened wide with alarm.

"Come on in, Nancy. I don't think any of us will sleep much more tonight. I just wish Pa would come here. I would feel so much better about him."

"I know. His farm is much more open than yours and now he's trying to protect Belle Terre for Fitz. What one man can do in the face of an army, I'm

191

sure I don't know," Nancy said as she paced the room. "I swaney, I'm as nervous as a turkey at Christmas. That blasted racket just messes me up something fierce."

"Well, the sun will be up soon. Maybe Pa will come then so it's not just us women." Penny sighed. "Let's get dressed and go down and make some breakfast. I'll think I'll cook something for later on, just in case."

"Good idea. I'll be right there soon as I throw on some clothes."

When Penny walked in the kitchen, she found both Mammy and Moses there already. The fire was going in both fireplace and stove and breakfast was well underway.

"Thank you, Mammy. I was going to get that going myself, but you have beaten me to it, I see." Penny smiled at them, hoping to offer reassurance.

"We be sum kina nurbus, Miz Penny. Lucinda and Je'miah be all alone ober der at dat Belle Terre. It mighty close to de road an' de fightin' ta suit me," Mammy fretted.

"Moses, if you'd like, go over this morning and bring them back. I know you'd feel better if all of you were together. Besides, I also feel like it's a little safer here."

"Thank you, Miz Penny. I do dat soon as I git sum breakfas'."

"Moses, if Pa is there or at his house, tell him I need to see him here this morning. If he asks why, just say you don't know. I want him here, too, but he's so stubborn I'm afraid he won't come if he thinks I'm worried about him."

"Dat's fo' sho. I do it iffn I kin fin' him."

Another volley of artillery fire made them all startle. "Mama." Ryan cried to be picked up from his high chair and held.

"Come here, sweet boy." Penny picked him up. "Nancy, will you hold Rye-Rye? He's really nervous from all of this loud noise. I want to check to make sure that everything in the house that might be too tempting is put away. Moses, the animals are all well hidden down in the swamp, I hope?"

"Yas'am. I dun been down der dis mawnin' gittin' 'em hid real good."

"Mammy, I want the smokehouse emptied so I'm going to get started on that as soon as we've finished breakfast and I get the house checked. After I check the house, I'll get Nancy to help me with the smokehouse if you'll watch Rye-Rye."

"Yas'am. I do dat fer you."

At Pineview, John quickly ate the breakfast that Delia had prepared and saddled his horse to ride over to Belle Terre. When he neared the end of his lane that turned off British Road, he was startled to find a Yankee soldier partially hidden in the tall grass.

"Hey, there. What are you doing on my land, sir?" John had his pistol drawn and cocked.

"I've been assigned here to make sure none of our troops bother your farm, sir. Colonel's orders."

John lowered his pistol. "Why is your colonel protecting my farm?"

"I can't tell you that, sir. All I know is that Colonel Madison stationed me here and another man in front of your daughter's farm."

"Is that a fact?"

John rode on to Fitz's farm, puzzling over the reason for some Yankee trying to protect them. When he arrived at Belle Terre, Moses was already there. Lucinda and Jeremiah were standing beside him with a basket holding a few clothes.

Lucinda explained, "We're going to Miss Penny's to stay until things settle down. It's safer there than here."

Moses added, "Miz Penny say fo' you to cum ta huh house. She say it real pawtant she see you dis mawnin', Mistah John."

"Did she say what she needs?"

"Naw, Suh. She ain' tell me nuffin'."

"Tell her I'll come as soon as I can." John paused. "Did you see a Yankee soldier on Penny's land?"

Moses eyes widened with fright. "Lawsy, you mean deys sum Yankees on our lan' a'ready?"

"Don't worry about it. I was just asking." John saw no point in alarming the man needlessly.

When Moses left with his family, John checked with the overseer to assure that all was as protected as it could be on Fitz's land. Going to the house, he let himself in and went to the study, where Fitz had asked him remove the safe box that held his money and Cora's jewelry if it looked like the armies were in the vicinity. Looking around the house, he regretted that he could not do more to secure the valuable things in the house. Finding a pillowcase, he stuffed in the small portrait of Cora and Fitz painted shortly after their wedding. He stuffed in the silverware and sterling candlesticks. Grabbing another case, he carefully wrapped the gilded ormolu clock from the mantle and shoved it in. Back in the study, he grabbed Fitz's favorite pipe. He closed and latched all of the shutters and doors and locked the last one behind himself as he left. In the face of an army, he knew it was all futile, but it made him feel better to at least try to do something.

When he reached Penny's farm, he dismounted his horse and, leading it quietly, he walked onto the hidden lane. Off to his right, he saw the movement of a thick bush and a brief glimpse of a dark blue uniform. Again he wondered why their farms were being watched and not Fitz's plantation.

He reached the house to find everyone gathered in the kitchen for a late dinner. Penny rose when he entered and gave him a warm hug.

"I'm so glad you're here, Pa."

"So am I." John handed her the pillowcases. "These are some things from Belle Terre. After dinner, would you mind finding a safe place for them?"

"Of course. Now sit down and have some food. With all the gunfire and racket from the battle, there's no telling what's going to be happening. We figured we'd better cook and eat while we can."

"Penny, is there some reason why the Yankees would be protecting your farm and mine?"

Penny looked up from her plate, the fork in her hand dropped with a clang. "What do you mean?"

"There's a Union soldier hidden in the bushes on both our farms. I saw the one on mine when I came up behind him unexpectedly. He says his colonel...hmm, Madison I think he said...told him to protect my farm and that he stationed another soldier on your land. There's no one protecting Belle Terre that I could see. I just find it real curious." He caught Mammy stealing a glance at Penny and realized he was missing something. "Mammy, Penny, can either of you tell me what's going on?"

"Naw, suh. I don' know nuffin 'bout it." Mammy turned to Penny and waited for her to speak.

"I'm sure I don't either, Pa. But I can't say that I'm sorry to hear it." Her father had always taught her to be honest and she could see in his eyes that he recognized her words for the lie it was. A small ray of sunshine lit her heart that Ryan would try to protect her. It was at least proof that he had not completely forgotten.

Rising from the table, Penny picked Rye-Rye up and announced he needed changing. She needed to escape the room and the danger of further questions. It was the only excuse she could think of. In her room she laid her baby on the bed and sat beside him. "Rye-Rye, your daddy is close by and he still thinks about me. He sent some soldiers to protect us. I do so wish he could see his beautiful little boy."

"Daddy?" He reached up and touched her arm. His face was tense with concentration. "Daddy?"

"That's right, honey. But it's our secret, okay?"

" 'Kay, Mama." Rye-Rye smiled.

Penny picked him up and swung him around and around as she danced with the lightest heart she had had in months. He was squealing with delight when she stopped and took him back to the kitchen.

When she entered, the others except for Mammy had all left. "Any more questions from Pa, Mammy Rena?"

"No'am. An' I ain' sayd nuffin." Mammy shook her head. "Sho do beat all. It sho do. Dat Mistah Ryan be one good man, Miz Penny. 'Spite eberthin' he still ker 'bout you."

"I know, Mammy." Penny beamed with joy. "Let's just pray he'll be okay in the coming fight."

"I do." Mammy pointed to the pillowcases. "Yo' pa say put dat stuff in dos cases away safe lack. He gon' wid Moses to check on de animals in de woods. He say he be back."

"Where is Nancy?"

"She and Lucinda be gittin' de las' o' de stuff in de smoke house an' puttin' it in de attik."

Penny looked at the calendar and noted the date, March 9th. It was the third straight day of cannons shaking the earth until windows rattled. Each time she felt as though her heart would stop with fright. She thought not only of Ryan, but Fitz, Marcus, and her neighbors out there in the middle of a man-made hell. Dear God, she prayed, how long must this go on? The constant noise and fear made them all jumpy and tense. She was glad that when night fell, her father made no attempt to go home.

Once again they all gathered in the kitchen to eat leftovers for supper. The guns continued fired into the night. In the morning, there was a temporary lull before once more the cannonading rattled windows and jangled nerves. At the breakfast table, they all sat around yawning. Penny knew no one had really been able to sleep.

"I'm going to ride back over to Pineview and Belle Terre to see if everything is still okay. I'll come back afterwards, if the racket continues, and spend the night with y'all. Frankly, it's amazing to me with all of the cannons and gunfire we've heard that there's anyone left alive to fight." John shook his head sadly. "Penny, I think you folks ought to all stay inside until this is over. You've done everything you can do out there."

"I'll keep everyone inside, so don't worry. You just take care of yourself."

"I'll do my best."

Penny did not promise that she would stay inside, only that the others would. She was determined to talk with the soldier Ryan had posted to protect her. When her father was well gone, the others all given chores to distract them, Rye-Rye fed and napping under Nancy's care, Penny quietly let herself out the front door and began skirting the yard to the woods. Softly she walked to the edge of the road, where her father had reported seeing the soldier. "Hello?" she called softly. "Please, could you come out so I can talk with you?"

A young soldier in his late teens emerged from behind a low longleaf pine tree. "Yes, ma'am. What is it you need to know?"

"Your colonel, he told you to watch my farm and protect me?"

"That's right, ma'am."

"Did he say why?"

"No, ma'am."

"He's all right and everything?"

"Yes, ma'am. He's fine."

"Is he in the battle over towards Wyse Forks?"

"No, ma'am. He's stationed down near the bridge over southwest Creek where we were fighting in '62. We're guarding it."

"I see. Please tell him that I wish him well and thank him for trying to help us." Penny couldn't think what else to say or ask. Longingly she looked at the road hoping to see him riding her way. It was empty.

"Is there any thing else, ma'am?"

"Do you know when you're leaving?"

"I suspect it will be today. From the runner I stopped about an hour ago, it's looking pretty grim for your boys." He smiled apologetically.

"I see. Thank you."

Penny walked away and hid herself in the woods. If Ryan rode by she wanted to at least see him and know that he was unharmed. Crouching in the woods, she remembered the last time that she had waited in the woods and the man she had found. She wished she could turn back the clock and have him in her home once more. The sun was sinking low and she knew she had to return before the others came looking for her. The cannons and gunfire had stopped so there was little likelihood that her father would return for the night so she wasn't worried about him finding her. She stood and brushed the weeds and leaves from her skirt, pausing to push a stray strand of hair into her chignon. The sound of distant hooves caught her attention. She could not judge how many horses but knew it was a lot. Looking from her hiding place, she could see a column of cavalry coming down the road towards her. Leading it on a prancing Windfall, she saw Ryan. He pulled to one side and waved the others on while he stopped by the road to call for the hidden sentry. The boy she had talked with walked up to Ryan and swung up onto the horse behind him. She watched until they rode from sight. She would have given her last dollar to be sitting where that boy was with her arms around Ryan and her check pressed into his back. Slowly she walked back to the house, happy to have seen him but sad that she could not go to him.

With the cessation of fighting, silence returned to the countryside around Penny. Only the chattering of the squirrels in the branches above her head or the twitter of birds interrupted the quiet. She was so weary of war, deprivations, and constant fear. She longed for the day when the world could be normal again and she could have such simple pleasures as a good cup of coffee or tea, milled soap, hairpins, needles, good leather shoes imported from Europe, fresh citrus fruit and pineapple, and all of the flour and sugar she could want. She didn't care if she never heard another gunshot. Let the hunters use bow and arrows or traps, but please no more gunfire, she prayed. She never wanted to watch the young men leave for war, nor the old and very young. She never again wanted to see another newspaper listing the roll call of those who would never return. The pinched and desperate faces of widows and orphans all weighed on her mind.

In the kitchen, they had all gathered. Although the supper was a simple one of leftovers, no one cared. Once again they had been spared the wrath or deprivations caused by either army. With the many tales of carnage, destruction, and hardship that they had all heard from so many, they counted their blessings and rejoiced that they could return to their beds and a good night's sleep. Lucinda and Jeremy left after supper to walk back to Belle Terre. She wanted to be there in case Mr. Fitz came home that night. Penny said goodnight when she left and, picking up Rye-Rye, went to her room to prepare them for bed. Nancy, Moses, and Mammy, after nights without sleep, shortly went to their own beds.

Penny and Rye-Rye were both sleeping the next morning when the sound of a horse making its way down the lane awoke her. Looking out the window, she saw her father emerging from the canopy of tender green leaves that was just beginning to mist the trees. Checking to see if Rye-Rye still slept, she hastily donned her gown and went to the kitchen to meet him. Mammy was there already and breakfast was on the table. Due to the scarcity of flour, corn-bread and bacon served with okra-seed coffee awaited. Penny had been so nervous the day before she had eaten little, now her stomach growled with anticipation when she entered and smelled the aromas.

"Sho be good ta git a night's sleep, ain' it, Miz Penny?"

"That is for sure. By the way, Pa should be in any minute. I just saw him riding up."

The kitchen door swung open and John walked in just as she finished saying it. "Ah, Penny, I'm glad you're up. I need you to come with me to Pineview. Marcus just brought Fitz home. He's been bad shot. I don't know if you can help him but we have to try."

"Mammy, have Nancy take care of the baby. Let's go, Pa." Penny turned to grab her shawl as they hurried from the kitchen.

When they reached her father's house, Marcus was waiting for them on the back porch. "Better hurry; he's having a tough go of it."

"Where is he, Marcus?"

"On the kitchen table. I figured that was best if you're going to have to go for the bullet."

"Where was he shot?"

"The gut." Marcus knew how unlikely it was that the man could be saved. They all did.

Penny patted her father's shoulder comfortingly and said, "Pa, I'll do what I can for your old friend. Why don't you come help me? He would want you there."

"Don't worry. I intend to do just that." John almost choked with emotion and quickly turned his head to wipe the tears that spilled from the corner of his eyes.

Penny paused to give Marcus a fierce hug and tell him she was glad he had returned unharmed. He was surprised and thrilled at the intimacy and prayed that it meant she had begun to consider his proposal. "Marcus, I may need you to help hold him. I'm sure you're tired from the fighting but if you could help just a little while, you can soon get some rest."

"Of course I can. It'll take more than a passel of Yankees to keep me from doing what I can for the people here."

Fitz was conscious and obviously in tremendous pain and although he tried not to, he kept groaning with agony. Gasping, he turned his head to Penny.

"Girl, I don't know if you can work enough magic to save me but you'd better get on it. I don't know how much more of this I can take."

"Don't worry, Mr. Fitz. Pa will never forgive us if you'd don't pull through this. I'm going to do my mightiest." Penny was checking his pulse and noting his color as she said it.

His pulse was rapid due to loss of blood and he was pale and sweating. Cutting away his shirt, she could see where the bullet had entered his abdomen on the outside of his left side just below the ribcage. She suspected it had hit in the area near his spleen but prayed it had missed the organ itself. Since he had not already died of internal bleeding, she felt the chances were good. "Delia, I need some boiling water, a sharp knife, needle and thread, clean cloth, and some whiskey."

"I already gots 'em 'ceptin' de whiskey. I knowed you'd be needin' 'em."

"I'll get the whiskey." John immediately ran to his study for the needed liquor.

While she waited on her father's return, she readied the things that Delia had prepared.

"Mr. Fitz, this is going to hurt something fierce. I'm sorry but I have to try to get that bullet out and stop the bleeding and infection. I want you to drink some of this whiskey to kill the pain." She took the liquor her father handed her and with the two men lifting the injured man, she held it to his lips.

"Damn, that's your good stuff, John." Fitz managed a weak grin. "I guess I'm really bad off if you haul that out."

"Hush, you old fool. I pour the same stuff every time you come over here." John smiled at his friend. "Next drink, you buy."

"I sure as hell hope so." Fitz heaved a sigh. "Let's do it."

Quickly Penny washed her hands with the whiskey and then poured it over the wound. She wiped the area around it and sliced it open. Using her finger she gently inserted it into the opening and probed for the bullet. Her father and Marcus struggled to hold Fitz, who writhed in pain. "Try to hold still, Mr. Fitz. I know it hurts but moving around when I'm doing this can cause more damage."

"Damnation." Fitz gritted his teeth and nodded.

Again Penny probed. This time she felt the end of the bullet. Using the knife to help, she slowly lifted it from the wound. Immediately a gush of blood poured from his side. Grabbing the clean cloth her father handed her, she pressed it against the incision, hoping to staunch the flow of blood. He could not afford to lose much more, she surmised. Checking his pulse, she noted that it had become even more rapid. Seeing that the pressure she was applying was slowing the bleeding, she prayed that a few more minutes would stop it enough that she could close the incision.

She held the cloth for a few more minutes and then eased the pressure. The bleeding had slowed.

"He's passed out, Penny," Marcus quietly remarked.

"Good. It's easier on him that way."

She bent to the task of stitching up the wound. Other than her herbs and some beef broth to build him up, she didn't know what else to do for him. Now nature and luck were in control. As long as the internal bleeding did not resume and there was no major infection, he stood a chance of living. With John and Marcus holding the limp man, Penny quickly wrapped a pressure bandage around his middle.

"Well, it's the best I know to do. Let's just all pray it's enough."

Marcus smiled. "You're the best doctor I know and the prettiest."

"Penny, do you want us to carry him to bed?"

"I don't think so, Pa. I'm afraid to move him right now. Let's just get a pillow to put under his head and cover him with blankets for now. Later, if he seems to be doing better we'll move him."

Chapter 22

"Oh, yes, you do. I saw an entire shelf of it yesterday so I know you have it. I also know how much you were charging for it. I insist you sell me a bottle or I'll report you for profiteering. You know the Union has forbidden speculation here." She glared at the man who stood before her, his hair on end where he had repeatedly run his hands through it in exasperation.

Peering down his pince nez, he glared at the irate young woman. "I told you I have no vanilla flavoring."

"And I know you're lying, sir. So sell me a bottle now." She stamped her foot with emphasis.

Ryan had come into the shop unnoticed by either of the two and now stood watching. He couldn't help admiring the lovely and determined woman before him. Her long blonde hair was caught in a cascade of curls, and while her dress appeared a trifle faded it was obvious that she had reworked it to make it more fashionable. She was a small curvaceous woman of about twenty-two, with a pert nose, brown eyes, and a full mouth. For the first time in over two years, Ryan felt the stirring of desire.

"Excuse me, Miss. May I be of some assistance?"

"Drat it. This man has vanilla flavoring and he won't sell it to me. He thinks if he waits until tomorrow he can mark it up again. Every time I come in here he's marked prices up and I'm sick of it. I demand he sell it to me *and* at the same price it was yesterday."

"So why didn't you buy some yesterday if you want it so badly?" The merchant was furious but, wary of the uniformed officer, was trying to mask it.

"I didn't bring enough money to get it yesterday, so I came back today. I saw you put it under the counter when I passed the window. You knew I was coming back for it because I told you yesterday I would. Now, sell it to me."

200

Ryan walked around the counter to where the older man stood. He could see the vanilla underneath. "Did you tell the lady that you have no vanilla?"

"It's spoken for, sir. I have none to sell."

"And who, may I ask, has reserved it?"

"It's for the general."

"An entire case? Even if he drinks it for a toddy, that's a bit excessive." Ryan sized the man up for a bully who needed backing down. "I'll take it to the general for you and make sure you charge the established price. If he has not reserved it, he's going to be very upset when I tell him this little story."

"Please, I don't want any trouble. Perhaps I was mistaken. Let me check my ledger again." He turned away to busy himself at his desk.

While he went through the pretense of checking, Ryan stood smiling at the young woman before him. "May I ask your name, Miss?"

"Mama and Papa don't want me giving out my name to strangers and particularly soldiers, sir." She batted her lashes prettily.

Ryan knew she was flirting and enjoying baiting him. "I promise not to tell if you won't," he whispered.

"Oh, well, if you insist. I'm Elizabeth Berkely, Lizzy to my friends. And just who may you be?"

"Colonel Ryan Madison at your service, Miss. It is Miss?"

"Yes, at the moment. But I am sort of engaged." She arched her brows, cocking her head saucily to one side.

"So how is it that one can be 'sort of engaged'? I confess I don't know the term." Ryan smiled.

The merchant interrupted before she could answer, "It appears I've made a small mistake. It's not the general who reserved the flavoring but someone else."

Ryan gave him a hard look. "All of it?"

Stammering, he replied, "Well, no. I'm happy to say I can sell the young lady a bottle."

"You could have all along, you old liar. So let's have it." She reached into her reticule for the money and put it on the counter in front of him.

The transaction completed, Ryan escorted Elizabeth from the shop. "Okay, Miss Lizzy, I'll walk you home now to make sure you get into no more arguments."

"I don't believe you should do that, sir. My parents would be most upset."

"Then we'll stop short of your house." Taking her by the elbow, he looked quizzically to his right.

"No, it's the other way, near the water on Pasteur." She couldn't help a small smile of triumph that the handsome officer was obviously attracted to her.

They talked of various topics in the age-old process of getting to know one another. By the end of the walk, Ryan had her promise to meet him for a buggy ride the following day. He walked away whistling. The tedium of the days would be relieved by the flirtation with an attractive woman.

Since Kinston, he had done nothing but routine duties in the town of New Berne. In the newspapers he followed Sherman's ruthless march across the State, quelling the Confederates at every turn. Fayetteville had fallen even before Kinston, from there Sherman had sent troops towards the Faison Depot, planning a feint on Raleigh. The remainder of his army he ordered on a more direct route to the main objective, Goldsborough. In the meantime, unsure whether Sherman meant to take Goldsborough or Raleigh, the State Capital, General Johnston concentrated his forces at Smithfield, approximately midway between the two. After heavy losses on both sides, Smithfield fell to the invaders. In the aftermath, with Sherman's forces divided, Johnston prepared for another battle. Learning that Federal troops were on the road to Goldsborough, Johnston swung twenty miles west to the small village of Bentonville, where he prepared for battle.

The Sunday morning of March 19th was a sunny beautiful one. The Federals under the command of General Slocum anticipated a quiet march through the sleepy little town of Bentonville with much-needed rest awaiting them in Goldsborough. The unsuspecting troops were completely unaware that Johnston's entire army was dug in and lying in wait. The battle raged until the twenty-first, when Johnston ordered his men to retreat to Smithfield. Despite a force nearly double in size, Sherman's army had gained little. Only nominal Union possession of the battlefield at the end of three days allowed him to proclaim victory. He marched on to Goldsborough to be met with bad news. The railroad that he had anticipated would bring him needed supplies had not been repaired. To remedy the situation, Sherman ordered the army scavengers or bummers to fall in with the regular army, thus gaining their horses, mules, and supplies garnered by a merciless ravaging of the countryside from Fayetteville to Goldsboro of everything they could carry off. In their cruel and ferocious wake they left a starving and abused populace, burned buildings, destroyed fence rails and wholesale destruction. It was not until the twenty-fifth that the railroad from New Berne could be repaired and supplies transported by rail to a waiting Sherman. Later that same day he boarded a train for Virginia, where he hoped to join Grant in the final push to victory. Sherman wanted the glory of defeating the Confederates in Virginia and taking Richmond.

From Tennessee, Union forces under General Stoneman were moving east to destroy the Tennessee-Virginia railroad and other important supply and manufacturing resources along the North Carolina border with Virginia. On April 13th, with the mission a success, they turned back to Tennessee, wreaking havoc as they went.

In the meantime, Sherman returned to his army in Goldsboro to prepare them to unite with the Army of the Potomac under Grant by swinging in from western Virginia. Learning on April 6th of the fall of Richmond, he abandoned the plan and instead focused on Raleigh. On the night of the eighth, Sherman learned that Lee had surrendered to Grant at Appomattox.

Hearing the news as well, Johnston met with Jefferson Davis in Greensboro on April 17th and was instructed to offer surrender to Sherman. Hillsboro was the acceptable meeting places for both sides, but Sherman was delayed in his departure on the eighteenth when a clerk handed him a coded message forwarded from the Union headquarters in Morehead informing him of Lincoln's assassination. Satisfied with the terms negotiated for the surrender of Johnston's army, Sherman returned to Raleigh, where he announced the tragic news from Washington. It was a surprised Sherman that greeted Grant in Raleigh on April 24th. Grant had come to tell him that the lenient terms agreed to at the Bennett farmhouse in Hillsboro were unacceptable to the government in Washington. Once more Sherman met Johnston at the Bennett farmhouse for the final signing of terms that were the same as those offered in Virginia. For the South, the road to repatriation would have been far less onerous had the initial Hillsboro terms been honored. He had been an implacable enemy in his march of destruction, but his heart had not been as cold as the intellectual impetus to destroy his enemy's resources. Criticized by Northern papers and politicians, a bitter Sherman left for Wilmington, his heart filled with sympathy for the South.

In New Berne, the Federal forces were readying for the arrival of Grant by train from Raleigh. A jubilant garrison met the train at the depot. Along the streets newly shaded by fresh green leaves and made colorful by blooming azaleas, citizens and freed Negroes mingled with the troops, trying to catch a glimpse of the great general.

Ryan breathed a sigh of relief. The war was over and he could begin building a life for himself along the banks of the Neuse. He had already received permission to leave the military and it was with no regret that he resigned his rank of office and entered into the civilian world. The general asked him to assist as needed in the transition of the town from military garrison to free city and Ryan, eager to secure his position as an intermediary in the city, hastened to agree.

Martha and Isabel made plans to return to Baltimore where Martha would stay until she could close her house and put it on the market to sell. She had come to enjoy the small town she once scorned and with Ryan and Isabel both determined to stay, she did not relish the thought of living there alone. Isabel was traveling on to New York to shop for the things that she and Ryan had worked together to list. Uncle Andrew had already wired that he would meet her and assist with the liquidation and transfer of Ryan's funds as soon as Ryan notified him of the bank he would be using in New Berne. He also had begun the preliminaries of assisting Isabel and Martha with transferring their own assets.

Although Martha said nothing to him, Ryan suspected that the flirtation with John Harvey had become serious. He surmised that, as much as anything, lay behind her decision to make her home in New Berne. Although Isabel had enjoyed the company of a number of the officers to whom Ryan introduced her, none seemed to receive any long-term interest from her. As for his own casual courtship of the feisty Lizzy, Ryan wasn't sure. Some days he could foresee asking her to marry him. He knew that she had begun to fall in love with him and while he didn't encourage it, he did nothing to squelch it either. Her parents had at first been reluctant, but he had eventually won their acceptance. The other women in his life liked her and quietly encouraged the courtship by including her in various functions. But there were days when the ache of longing for Penny drove all thoughts of another woman from his mind. It had been all he could do not to turn into the path to her farm when he had ridden away that last day of the battle of Wyse Forks.

With the war ended, even though materials for rebuilding and expanding the town were growing scarce, he had enough for his house due to the foresight to purchase early and stockpile. Craftsmen were putting the finishing touches on the moldings and other decorative features of the house and Hawkes had procured a talented man to carve the mantle pieces that Ryan wanted. Many of them were based on the designs that Hawkes' ancestor had created for Tryon Palace. Ryan found a house on Pollock Street that he purchased to use as a law office. The upstairs would serve as adequate living quarters until his house was finished. Although there was a bedroom that Martha and Isabel could share, Caroline insisted that they remain with her.

It was a comparatively happy and industrious time for Ryan, following the relative inactivity of the war years in New Berne. Dividing his hours between the renovation of an office and the rapid completion of his house, often he found that he was ignoring Lizzy. It worried him that he did not miss her when he was away from her presence. But then he reminded himself that while he liked her well enough, he had no intention of falling in love with her as he had with Penny. He swore he would never face that kind of pain again.

His revived sexual need for a woman kept the flirtation alive even when his heart wasn't in it. As for Lizzy, she seemed not to notice his reserve. She reminded him of a playful, headstrong puppy intent on her own goals and not distracted by anything that did not fit her immediate agenda. He enjoyed her simple straightforward personality and her fresh beauty. She made him laugh and she made him hungry for physical gratification. Therein lay his dilemma. With her gentile southern upbringing, she was not a prospect for a casual dalliance and he was unready for a greater commitment.

Spring was a season of tremendous gardening activity for Caroline, who had dictated her wishes for the park while Ryan drew the plans. Martha leaned over their shoulders, offering surprisingly insightful and helpful suggestions. Often the two women could be found either at Riverside or at Ryan's house, Fair Bluff, digging in the soil and planting and moving various shrubs, bulbs, and small trees to conform to the designs for both properties. He was proud of the garden that they had created and decided to show it off.

Ryan picked up Lizzy in a rented buggy and drove out to Fair Bluff the first Sunday in May. They had first attended the Presbyterian Church, where she was a member, her beaming parents sitting beside them in the pew. With lunch packed in a hamper, they took advantage of the pleasantly sunny day to picnic at his house. The grass seed he had imported from Florida had already created a lush green carpet around the house that extended down to a small pier where he kept his sailboat. Ryan carried the hamper down to the pier and spread the blanket.

"Oh, Ryan, what a glorious spot this is. I can see why you wanted it so much. After we have our dinner, you must give me a tour inside. I've just been dying to see it."

"Then you shall. I confess I'm well pleased with the house both inside and out. Isabel is leaving with Mother to go to Baltimore and close down the house there. Mother is giving me a few pieces that are Madison family heirlooms and the rest Isabel will get in New York with Uncle Andrew's help." He seated himself on the blanket with his feet hanging over the edge of the pier.

"I'm surprised you don't wait for a wife to decorate the house. Surely you don't plan to live here all alone?"

Ryan chose not to answer. "This lunch looks good. I think you're trying to spoil me."

"That is certainly my intention or had you not guessed?" Lizzy smiled coquettishly and fluttered her lashes. "I'd like to be spoiled, too."

"And what may I do to spoil you, Lizzy?" Ryan studied her to see her reaction to the deliberately provocative question.

Hiding her face from his scrutiny, she looked down to rummage for a piece of fried chicken to hand him. "Why, Ryan, I'm sure you know how to spoil a woman."

"I suppose that depends on how you interpret the word *spoil*. It does have some rather interesting connotations."

"Are you referring to something nasty?" Her eyes hardened. Lizzy was no longer smiling.

"Please, don't be offended. I'm merely making idle chatter."

"Yes, you're very good at that. Perhaps you think I'm just an empty-headed silly woman, but I can have a serious conversation." Lizzy sniffed. She knew her education had been sadly lacking and her provincial upbringing left her decidedly short of more worldly social skills.

"I don't think that at all. I think you are a lovely, desirable woman."

"Are you saying you desire me?"

"Absolutely."

"I suppose that leaves me rather confused as to your intentions." She stared directly into his eyes, challenging him to declare himself.

"Let's not push things, Lizzy. I like you quite well. We'll see where things go from there." He would not be pushed into either proposing or ending the relationship.

Changing the subject, he pointed over the water. "Look at those seagulls. They're waiting for a chance to snatch our crumbs."

"Well, they can have my lunch. I don't feel terribly hungry anymore." Lizzie was in a pout.

Looking at her pursed lips, he leaned forward and kissed her.

"Don't be impertinent, sir." The snapped words were followed by a slap.

"I beg your pardon. Perhaps we should call it a day." He stood up, repressing the fury he refused to vent.

The ride into town was frosty. When they reached her house she jumped from the buggy without waiting for assistance. Snatching the basket from the back, she stormed inside. Ryan sat a moment looking at the door that had banged shut resoundingly before slapping the reins on the horse's back and driving off. Ah, well, she wasn't quite so oblivious of his aloofness as he had presumed. It was apparent that she was provoked that he made no declaration of love or proposal of marriage, despite the many weeks they had spent in close company. He didn't want to lose her, but he most particularly didn't want to drive back to her house and ask her to be his wife as she so patently expected.

He toyed with the idea of just driving to Sugar Hill in Kinston to relieve his immediate need for a woman. But that would only bring him to close to Pleasant Glade and the woman he really wanted and knew he could not have. The thought that even now the man who claimed her had returned to their home and their child tortured him.

Every day brought more and more former Rebel soldiers and families who had abandoned the town back to the houses they had left. The exodus from the Confederate army of local boys had begun with the defeat at Wyse Forks and accelerated after Bentonville. With the war ended, those stationed with Lee in Virginia were also making their way home or to what remained of one. Since Penny's husband was stationed in Virginia, Ryan surmised that any day would see him back at Pleasant Glade. He wondered what it would feel like to be returning from war to a beloved wife and child. For a moment jealous despair threatened to swamp him.

"Ah, hell. I don't have time for this," he told himself as he walked into the Pollock Street house. The new shingle on the door announcing "Ryan C. Madison, Attorney at Law" clattered after him. He walked into his office and began unpacking the shipment of law books that Uncle Andrew had sent from the New York office. Ryan fretted about how to find a set of books on North Carolina law. After four years of war with few books of any kind printed in the paper-starved South, it was a daunting prospect. Perhaps he could buy them from the widow of an attorney who had died of the yellow fever or in the war. He made a mental note to begin the search the following day. He wondered if John Harvey might be able to help him and thought of riding to his house, but the idea of dealing with Hattie after the afternoon debacle with Lizzy was enough to scotch that idea. Thinking of Hattie, he realized it had been months since he had last seen her. After several hours of work sorting things out and placing them on the newly built shelves or in filing drawers, he supposed it was time for supper even though he wasn't as hungry as he should be after the curtailed picnic. He thought of riding out to Caroline's, where he was always welcome, but feminine company had lost some charm for the day. It would have to be the iffy cuisine of the hotel.

Ryan walked in and took his usual seat at the bar and ordered a whiskey. He sat sipping it and trying to regain some semblance of inner peace.

A cheerful voice called out, "Colonel Ryan, they told me you had stayed. I'm sure glad you did, as I can use a familiar face."

Ryan turned. "Bobby, don't tell me some pretty little Rebel gal has conquered that roving eye."

"As a matter of fact, one has. I'm getting married next Saturday. I'd be pleased to have you as best man."

"After the devoted service you have given me for four long years, that's the very least I can do. Just say when and where." Ryan was pleased for him and more than a little surprised. Bobby had been one of the most devoted womanizers in his entire company. He looked forward to meeting the woman who had tamed him.

"It's at three o'clock at the First Baptist Church. You may want to show up a few minutes early, though, to share a drink with me."

"I'll do it." Ryan grinned. "So tell me, what do you plan to do with yourself here. Do you have a job prospect lined up? If not, I could use an assistant."

"I thank you, but her uncle is loaning me the capital to start a small furniture store. I ran one before coming down here with the army, so I feel pretty comfortable with that. So many people around here had their furniture destroyed by bummers or the army, I figure I can do a pretty good business."

"No doubt. In fact, I can throw some business your way myself. Do you have a location yet?"

"Her uncle has a building on Middle Street that I've got a mortgage on. It's a little big for now, but it gives room to expand later."

"And just who is this nice uncle?"

"John Harvey. He's an attorney here, too. Perhaps you know him?"

"As a matter of fact, I do. And the woman who has made you a lucky man, would her name be Hattie, perchance?"

"Oh, you know her?" Bobbie looked up in surprise.

"Not well, just in passing, so to speak." Ryan wanted to laugh. "Do join me for supper, my treat. I've suddenly developed quite an appetite."

Chapter 23

At that moment Penny would have given all of her hard-earned money for a bucket of ice. She touched Fitz's forehead for the hundredth time, praying that the fever had receded; however, it continued to burn. She knew he was badly infected and there was little she could do except keep him sponged with cold water from the well and the little bit of distilled alcohol she had left. Marcus had ridden into town to find a doctor willing to come out but had not returned yet.

"Penny, where are you?" her father called from downstairs.

Penny walked out into the hall and leaned over the banister to call softly, "Shh. I'm up here, Pa. Fitz is sleeping but he's terribly sick. If the doctor doesn't get here soon...." She didn't finish the sentence because he knew as well as she, the wound would probably be a fatal one even if the doctor came.

John shook his head sadly. "If there is anything I can do let me know. I thought if you don't mind, I'd ride over and get Rye. It might do him good to see the boy."

"Do that, Pa. And ask Nancy to come, too, and bring overnight things for them both. I think it would be good to have the baby here but I'm too busy right now to pay him enough attention."

"I'll be back soon. Hopefully the doctor will be here by then."

Fitz's death would hurt her father terribly, especially after the loss of her mother. They were the two people who had been dear to him for most of his life. Penny felt saddened for the sick man. The only remaining blood kin was a grandson he would not have acknowledged even if he knew of his existence. The grandson he thought was his, and loved deeply, carried none of his blood. Again she felt that ever-present pang of guilt.

Her father had been gone for only a few minutes when Marcus rode into the backyard and tied his horse. The doctor was with him. Hurrying down the steps, Penny met them at the back door. "Dr. Miller, I am so glad you're here. My father-in-law is seriously ill and there is nothing more I know to do. He's infected where the bullet pierced his abdomen and though I removed it, I had nothing for the infection."

"Don't fret, Penny. I know you well enough to know that you did the best you could do and probably as well as any doctor, me included. Is he upstairs?"

"Come in. I'll show you where he is." Penny stepped back as the doctor entered. "Thank you so much, Marcus. I don't know what I would do without you."

Marcus grinned. "And I don't intend for you to find out."

Dr. Miller chortled softly at the exchange as he followed Penny to Fitz's room. He pulled back the sheet that covered him, exposing his body to the waist. "Penny, let's get this nightshirt off. He'll be cooler without it and I need to see that wound."

Penny helped him with the shirt and then watched as he slowly and methodically began his exam. Fitz groaned into consciousness with the removal of the shirt and the ensuing palpations. "Mr. Kennedy, I know you feel like the devil but I've got to get this bandage off and see what's going on under there." He turned to Penny. "Give me your scissors. I'm going to cut this off. I don't want to lift him to unwind it all."

Fitz closed eyes dulled by fever and pain and resigned himself to more hurt as the doctor probed.

"It's possible there's a pocket of puss in there. I'm going to have to think about what to do. You hang in there, Fitz. I'm going to do what I can to try and get you fixed up."

"You've got your work cut out for you, then," Fitz said quietly.

"Penny, could you come with me?" The doctor walked to the door and waited for her to follow.

Sitting at the kitchen table sipping the sassafras tea she had brewed earlier, they debated what to do. Penny wanted to reopen the incision and try to drain out the infection. The doctor was more cautious and worried about the patient's ability to sustain more trauma from a treatment that could well prove terminal.

"Doctor, I think you have to try. If you don't do something the infection is going to kill him anyway. You know it," Penny pleaded.

"All right. I'll do it. I need Marcus and your Pa to make a stretcher and bring him down to the table. We'll do it here. Get me some hot water and some clean rags. I have a little morphine I can give him for the pain."

"Thank you. As soon as Pa returns, we'll get started. He shouldn't be more than a few more minutes."

"Good. There's no time to waste if we're going to do this thing."

Standing up the doctor began removing his instruments and preparing for the surgery. Penny heated water and scrubbed the table. That done she quietly stacked rolls of clean bandages on a platter and sat it on a chair near the table. Her father walked in with the baby just as she finished. Nancy entered with a bundle of clothes.

"Pa, would you take Rye up to see his granddaddy? Thanks for coming, Nancy. I can use your help. After Rye sees Mr. Fitz, I need you to keep him occupied until we're finished in here." Penny turned to the doctor and continued. "I'll have Marcus rig up a stretcher."

She found Marcus in the overseer's house. She had never been in it before and noted as she entered the front door at his bidding that it was neatly and comfortably furnished. Suddenly she was exhausted.

Marcus looked at the tired face he loved so well and. holding out his arms, encircled her and rested her head on his shoulder. "Poor girl. You are so strong but even the strong get tired."

"I think I'm beyond tired." Penny sighed. It felt so good to have a man's protective arms around her, holding her near. The soft caressing circular motions of his hands on her back felt heavenly where her muscles had knotted from hours of leaning over the bed to nurse Fitz.

Reluctantly she stepped from the comforting embrace. "We need a stretcher of some kind so you and Pa can bring Fitz to the kitchen table. The doctor's going to open up the incision to see if he can drain some of the infection."

"Where are the quilt stretchers? I can use them to rig up something."

"They're in Mama's work room next to Pa's office. Shall we go? The doctor says we need to do something fast."

"Come on then. Time's a wasting."

They walked back to the house. Penny noted that Marcus kept his hand comfortably nestled at her waist. She couldn't decide if she minded the familiarity of such a possessive gesture.

Fitz lay on the kitchen table a short time later. Rye was standing on a chair beside him, chattering in his own particular language. Penny reached to pick him up.

"No." Rye shook his head adamantly. "Kith, Gwampa." Leaning over, he stretched until he could kiss Fitz's forehead.

"I love you, boy. You be good now. Make us all proud of you, you hear?"

"Yeth, Gwampa. Wye-Wye good." With that he climbed down from the chair and took Nancy's extended hand.

"Thanks, Nancy." Penny smiled as her son tottered from the room. "I think we're ready, Dr. Miller."

Quickly he gave Fitz morphine to help against the pain and waited for it to begin to take effect. As soon as Fitz closed his eyes and began to breathe deeply, he laid the wound open with a few strokes of the scalpel. Bloody yellow pus welled in the opening and began to run down the side. Opening even more, the doctor waited for the draining to stop.

"Hmm, it looks like a bit of his clothing was pushed in by the bullet. No doubt that was the source of some of the problem. Give me some of that boiled water if it's cooled off." The doctor looked up at Penny. "I'll debride the wound as best I can and then get it stitched back up. That's the best I can do. The rest is going to be up to him and whether or not his body can beat the infection. He's weakened to the point it's going to be problematic."

"At least you've tried. That's better than just waiting for him to die." Penny smiled at the troubled doctor.

When the surgery was finished and Fitz had been bandaged and taken back to his bed, Penny and the others sat at the kitchen table for supper. They were all exhausted from the tension of the past hours and looked forward to an early bedtime.

John leaned back when he had finished eating and asked, "Marcus, when you were in town, did you get a chance to find out what's happening? I've not seen a paper in months so it looks like word of mouth will have to do."

"It appears to be just a matter of time. Sherman is on his way to Goldsboro, according to what I could pick up in town. I don't see how our boys are going to be able to stop him. I watched little twelve-year-old boys crying for their mamas when the Yankees charged them at Wyse Forks. Men old enough to be my grandfather were dying alongside the children. The veteran soldiers are so damned underfed and worn out the only thing keeping them going is just pure grit and cussedness. There's too little ammunition and too few people to fire it. From what I hear we're mighty lucky our farms weren't hurt. There are miles of burned-out towns and farms all across the South."

"Funny thing about that. Seems my farm and Penny's had a guard posted. I guess Fitz just got lucky. I still can't figure that out."

"No kidding?" Marcus looked surprised at the news. "How did you find out about that?"

"I spotted a Yankee trooper hidden in the bushes near the road. He told me his commanding officer had assigned him and another guard at Penny's to make sure we were unmolested. He didn't seem to know why either."

"The Nobles weren't so lucky. As you know, their farm backs up onto Jackson's Pond. There was a sight of fighting around there and I didn't get it straight whether it was soldiers or bummers, but a bunch of the bastards went to the Nobles' place. They demanded their silver and when Old Man Nobles wouldn't talk, they raped Mrs. Nobles and then hung him. Their three children saw it all from where they were hiding in the woods. Some of their neighbors have taken them in until some family can come for them. It's pitiful how so many people have suffered. I count my blessings we've been so lucky. Having to do without things seems just a minor inconvenience when you look at what so many others have endured."

"How awful. They were the nicest couple. I can't believe people can be so mean to other people," Nancy said. Tears began to roll down her cheeks.

"No, cwy, Nanthy. Wye-Wye make it all bettew."

"Yes, you do, precious." Nancy gave him a kiss on top of his dark curls.

Penny picked him up and cuddled him to her as she thought of what Marcus had said. "Let's just pray this is all over soon. I'm sick to death of war."

It was a common feeling expressed all over the South and in the North as well. Too many people had suffered in too many ways. In the South the very fabric of life had been destroyed, deprivations were widespread, and the loss of life was enormous. In the North, many sons, husbands, or brothers would never return home. Even though the deprivations of the South were not a factor there, the psychological costs of war were a major issue. Too many families had been ripped asunder by the divide. It wasn't unusual to find a family like Ryan's, where part of the family supported one side and part another. Brothers sometime fought brothers. A quasi-fraternal divide fractured even generals. Many who had gone to school at West Point together, fought in the Mexican War together, and served the Union together now found themselves facing one another across a battlefield. Friends killed friends. Never in the history of the nation had it suffered the carnage of internal strife on this scale. Too many young men would never return home to grow old, never marry, and never father children. Too many women would die spinsters never knowing the joy of a lover, a husband, and father, or dreamed of children who now would never be born. For four long years the wealth, energy, and resources of the nation had been blown up, burned, fired, or killed on blooded fields that ranged over hundreds upon hundreds of miles. Burned-out chimneys stood like lonely sentinels over once-verdant fields now growing shrub pines and weeds. The seas from America to England to the West Indies rang with the cannons of warring American ships. And the very Ship of State had foundered on the shoals of political divide gone mad. Yes, people were weary of this war that had seemed to go on and on with no apparent end in sight. Now, despite the ongoing struggle, a small glimmer of the end seemed just on the horizon. Around the table at Pineview, each face reflected the anguish of shared losses and hard memories as they sat there pondering their private anguishes. Only the fresh, innocent face of the child was unscarred by years of war.

"I'm going to go sit with Fitz and see if there's anything I can do for him." Penny stood up and stretched.

"I'll come with you, darling." Her father took her elbow as they left.

The room was dimly lit with one small lamp and the glow of a low fire in the grate. Fitz's face was turned to the wall and his eyes were closed. John smiled at his daughter. "It looks like he's sleeping."

Penny felt her father-in-law's head and then took his pulse. "I don't think so, Pa. I'm sorry, but your dear friend is gone."

"Oh, dammit to hell. I despise this war and what it has done to us all. He didn't deserve to die this way, dammit." John sat in the chair by the fire as fat tears sparkled on his cheeks and slowly dropped to his chest. Penny pulled the sheet over Fitz's face and then sat on the floor by her father, her head resting on his knee.

"I'm so sorry, Pa. He's the oldest friend you had and you're going to miss him something terrible."

"More than you know, much more. I think I'll walk down to the cemetery. I need to talk to your mother for awhile."

"Don't be too late, Pa. You've had a hard day and you're tired." Penny stood and hugged him before he walked from the room.

Wearily she followed him down the stairs. Nancy and Marcus still sat at the kitchen table. When she entered the room, Marcus took one look at her face and knew what had happened. Standing, he walked to her and gathered her into his arms for the second time that day. Gently he picked her up and sat down with her in his lap as Nancy quietly slipped from the room with the sleeping child.

Penny cried as he held and rocked her. Marcus kissed her hair and murmured softly to her, trying to comfort with words that he knew were inadequate. Not only was she dealing with the loss of her father-in-law, but also he sensed that a small part of her questioned her inability to save him.

The next morning, Marcus went to Hines' sawmill in Woodington to have a casket made. At the mill, the workers told him that the preacher had just ridden over to the Meeting House. Leaving the mill, he stopped by to ask the preacher, who had ministered to the family for years, to come to Belle Terre and lay Fitz Kennedy to rest beside the wife and son he had never stopped mourning.

The tender leaves of spring cast dappled shadows on the three graves in the Kennedy cemetery. The white marble of the newest stone glistened in the sunlight. Penny had ordered a tombstone from Kinston and with her father rode in to pick it up when it was finished. The streets in town were a turmoil of people huddled in groups and talking. Many appeared to be holding a newspaper. Some wept openly, others stood in mute sorrow. John reined in the horse and called out to Shadrack Loftin to inquire what was going on.

Walking up to them, Shadrack smiled wryly. "Looks like we are all damned Yankees again. Lee surrendered at Appomattox courthouse in Virginia yesterday. It's just a matter of time before old Joe Johnston has to follow suit. My friend, the South has lost. The Confederacy is dead."

"Well, at least the boys we have left will be coming home soon. I sure will be a happy man when my son, Brett, gets back from this Godforsaken war." John shook his head. "The cost was too high, much too high."

"It was that." Shadrack walked off, shaking his head in sorrow.

One week later, Sarah Johnson, Nalphus' wife, rode over to tell them that Lincoln had been assassinated. Sitting on the front porch in the creaking old rockers, Penny and her father were joined by Nancy, Rye, and Marcus to listen to Sarah tell them about the news. Marcus and John looked at one another with alarm. They had long argued that Lincoln would not deal harshly with the South. With Lincoln dead, all bets were off the table. Both of them speculated on the possible consequences for the South while the alarmed women listened in silence.

"John, I'll ride into town and see what else I can learn. Would you like to come with me?"

"It's okay, I'll stay. If you could find a newspaper, I'd dearly love to have one."

Penny spoke up. "If you don't mind, I'll come with you."

Marcus beamed with ill-concealed delight. "Please do. Would you like to bring the baby?"

"Why not? Give me a minute to get him ready and we'll go."

"No rush. I need a little time to hitch the horse to the buggy anyway." Marcus could not believe his good fortune that she would ride into town with him. More and more he sensed a thawing of her reserve with him. He could only pray that it was the harbinger of something deeper between them.

Penny was elated to be on an outing, as she had been sequestered in the country for months. The chance to get away was too good to be missed. She happily held the bouncing baby, who repeatedly tried to grab the reins from Marcus. "Precious boy, you'll get to drive a buggy soon enough. For now you'll have to wait. You're just not big enough yet."

"Am so. Wye want to dwive hoosey."

"Give him to me, Penny. This boy's going to drive a horse."

Marcus held him in his lap and with Rye's hands inside his own, the two of them drove the buggy across the bridge and down the street to the corner of King and Queen. Just as they turned the corner, a man on horseback reined in his horse and watched them pass. Seeing him out of the corner of her eye, Penny noted the familiarity and turned to speak. The words froze on her tongue as she found herself looking into the eyes of the man she loved. Doffing his hat to her, he spurred his horse and galloped away. Watching the dust well in his wake, she wondered what Ryan was doing in Kinston. Staring after him, she longed to call out but dared not.

Marcus, busy with the child, remained oblivious to Penny's reaction to the man. He only knew that the sunny open expression she had worn all morning had been replaced by one of brooding melancholy. He mulled over what he might have said or done to cause the sudden chill but could think of nothing. Shrugging, he handed Rye over to her as he stepped down at the newspaper office to try to procure a paper for her father. She didn't appear to hear him when he said he'd be back shortly.

Ryan was also lost in thought. The image of Penny and the man he assumed to be her husband laughing as he held their child who was pretending to drive the buggy was seared on his brain. He wished with all his heart he had not once again weakened to the impulse to visit Sugar Hill. Even that had been less than satisfying. Sally was young, pretty, more than willing, ran her own house, and was selective in her clientele. While she had relieved his immediate sexual frustration, she couldn't fill the lonely place in his heart that still ached for only one woman. And now he had the added reminder of the life Penny led with another man. He could not get back to New Berne quickly enough. As Windfall pounded the miles beneath his hooves, Ryan relived the magic moments he had shared with this woman he could not excise from his heart.

Penny sat in the buggy as frozen as a statue. She thought her heart would break with longing. Questions without answers reeled drunkenly through her head. If Ryan knew that she was now a widow, would he still want her? Would he remain in New Berne now that he thought she was gone from his life? If he knew what she had done, could he forgive her for keeping his son a secret from him? Did she have the courage or the moral right to face him after the pain she had willfully inflicted? Suddenly she knew, she had to at least try. But how could she a lone woman drive over thirty miles in a country still at war and into an occupied town? Biting her lip with worry, she struggled for an answer. She knew she could not ask Marcus to take her or her father. Both would insist on answers that she did not want to give and there was no one else she could ask.

"Penny, Penny? Did you hear me? I asked if you'd like to see the paper. Fortunately I managed to buy the last copy." Marcus looked at her with concern.

"Sorry, I was lost in thought, I'm afraid." Penny tried to smile but it was a weak effort.

"Is there something wrong? Have I said or done something to offend you in some way? I really thought everything was fine up until we rode into town. Now it's like a curtain dropped between us."

"It's nothing, really. I was just thinking about all of the people I've lost from my life since this war began." Penny realized as she said it that it was not a lie. She had lost Ryan, the question was: Could she find him again?

"We all have, darling. The only thing we can do is remember them with joy and not let it take the pleasure of what remains from us." Marcus longed to take her in his arms and kiss away the lines of worry from her face. Helpless to know what to do, he slapped the reins on Polly's back and began the drive home.

"Dwive buggy?" Rye again tried to capture the reins.

Marcus laughed. "You are quite the determined one, aren't you, little man?"

"Take him before I drop him. He's squirming like an eel." Penny handed Rye over, grateful for the change of subject.

"Penny, I know I said I wouldn't plague you for an answer, but can you at least tell me there's some hope? You know I love you and I love your son. I'll be the best husband and father I know how to be, if you will give me the chance."

"Marcus, I can't explain it, so please don't ask. There's something I have to resolve in my own mind and heart before I can be free to answer you. I care for you and I know you are a good man. Please give me time."

"I've waited nearly twelve years. I guess a little longer won't matter, now will it?"

Chapter 24

By the end of April, the farm was once again a concern. Fields had to be tilled, seeds planted, baby piglets and calves delivered and tended. Now Penny found herself faced not only with her own acres but those of Belle Terre that Fitz had left to her. Lucinda remained in his house but the workers who had once tilled his fertile acres were either sitting idle or gone. She knew she did not have the energy or resources to manage both that farm and her own. She drove to Pineview to talk with her father and ask his advice.

"Penny, I'm not sure what to do. I would hate to see the farm sold to a stranger, but I don't have the energy or resources to take it on and neither do you. It will be years before Rye will be old enough to run it. Besides, unless you have more children, he will already have your portion of Pineview and Pleasant Glade." John was deeply saddened at the thought of his friend's plantation being sold and equally frustrated by visions of fields laying fallow slowly to be reclaimed by the forests and the house falling into disrepair.

"Pa, I've thought about it. I want to give Lucinda and Jeremy the overseer's house and the fifty-acre field around it. I know Marcus has been looking to buy a farm. Would you object to him buying it? The money from the sale, I'll put into trust for Rye."

"Lord, for selfish reasons I would purely hate to lose Marcus but with Brett returning, I can manage. If he can afford it, that's a mighty nice thing to do and he would make a good neighbor. I confess, however, that I'm more than a little surprised by your generosity to Lucinda. I didn't think you much cared for the woman."

"I guess with Fitz and Daniel gone, it's okay for you to know my reason." Penny sucked in her upper lip in thought, wondering how to continue. "Pa, I don't know how to pretty this up, so I'll tell you straight out. Daniel is Jeremiah's father. I think it is only right that he have something."

"Jesus H. Christ," John exclaimed. Standing up he walked to his office window and looked out at the shady yard. Turning back to her, he said, "Dammit, Penny. I knew something was wrong between you. I just never guessed that Jeremiah was the reason. I am so sorry, so very sorry. Your mother and I never meant for this marriage to be anything but good for you. Please forgive us."

"Pa, it's not your fault. I don't even know that it's Daniel's fault. We were never in love. I was upset and hurt but it didn't break my heart when I learned the truth about Jeremiah. You and Mama only encouraged; you didn't force us. We were the ones who decided to get married. We could have said no."

"Do you think Marcus will object to carving off that piece of the farm? The rest of the land wraps around it on three sides, you know."

"We can ask him. If he does, I can slice off another piece and pay for building a house on it."

"I'll call him in here and we'll see what he's got to say about the offer."

Penny waited for her father to return with Marcus. She hoped it would make him happy and soften the pain she would cause if she declined his offer of marriage. As for that, she decided if Ryan rejected her, she would marry Marcus and try to be a good and loving wife. She didn't want to live the rest of her life alone and she didn't want Rye to grow up without a father. If she could not have Ryan, Marcus was as good a man as she could hope to find. But first she was going to pay a visit to Ryan, some way, some how.

"Penny, your Pa says y'all have something to discuss with me. What's up?"

"Marcus, I'm going to let Pa tell you." Penny smiled at her father as he seated himself at his desk.

"Well, it's this way. I purely don't want to lose you, but there's a farm for sale you might be interested in. We have all we can deal with without taking on Belle Terre. Penny's willing to sell it to you, if you're interested."

"Are you sure, Penny?" Marcus wanted to dance around the room for sheer joy. Belle Terre and the spacious and pleasant old house were more than he had ever envisioned owning. Now he could be a landowner and a peer, not just an overseer.

"I'm sure. There's just one more thing you should know. I want to give the overseer's house and the fifty-acre field behind it to Jeremiah, Lucinda's son. If you have an objection to that, perhaps there is another field you would prefer to deed to her."

"I'm afraid I don't understand why you're doing that. It's not that I object, I'm just puzzled, to say the least."

"Marcus, Penny told me that Daniel is the boy's father. She feels like Daniel owes the boy something."

"Jesus H. Christ."

"You sound like an echo of Pa." Penny laughed. "So do you have an objection to separating that piece from the part you buy?"

"First of all, I'm sorry for the pain that must have caused you. It's not uncommon for that to happen, but it's still inexcusable and difficult for everyone involved. I confess I wondered at times who Jeremiah's father was. I knew it had to be a white man. He's just too light not to have white blood."

"Well, now you know. So, do you object to Penny's decision to deed that portion over to him?"

"I don't see where that's any problem. I guess the thing now is to work out a price so I can see if I can buy it outright or if I need to mortgage part of it."

Penny, John, and Marcus shook hands on a price that Marcus knew was more than fair. He would buy the plantation with the buildings, the livestock, most of the household furnishings, and all equipment for a price that would still leave him the money he would need for seeds, fertilizer, and start-up funds. There were a few heirloom pieces that Penny wanted. That resolved, she asked her father to meet with John Wooten and have him draw up the papers. She did not want to meet with the man any longer than necessary after the embarrassing interview when he had declined to file for a divorce from Daniel. If her father was surprised that she asked him to meet with his old friend, he didn't show it.

Marcus and Penny left together, he to go back to the barn, where he was dealing with a cow in labor, and Penny back to Pleasant Glade. He helped her onto Polly and, sliding her foot into the stirrup, held it gently in his hand.
He looked up at her with his heart in his eyes. "I love you, darling. Thank you so much for selling me Belle Terre. It's the answer to my prayers and years of hard work."

"There's no one who deserves it more, Marcus." Penny smiled with genuine warmth. She was glad that she could do this for him. She had deliberately sold the farm for far less than it was worth because of her desire to give him what she could. It hurt her that she could not give him the love he wanted.

Penny trotted old Polly down the lane towards British Road. It felt good to be in the sunshine and crisp spring air. It felt good to have done this for Marcus and for Jeremiah. She knew Mammy and Moses would be thrilled for the boy, and for that matter Lucinda as well. She would not go to Lucinda. Her father would handle that for her.

"Penny!" A tall man on horseback was riding toward her, shouting her name.

"Oh, my God, Brett! Pa's going to be beside himself with joy. He's done nothing but talk about you coming home since he heard the Confederacy had fallen." Penny slid from the saddle just as Brett swung down from his own, sweeping her into an embrace.

"Stop spinning me, fool. You're making me dizzy." Penny laughed at her exuberant brother. The war had not squelched his joyful nature, but there was now the hint of crow's feet around his eyes and lines at his mouth and forehead that had not been there before. His auburn brown hair, darker than her copper-colored curls, sparkled in the sun. He was still a good-looking man.

"It's good to see you, little sister. I have purely missed home. I can't believe it's been four years."

"It been much too long. A lot has changed here since you left, with both Ma and Fitz gone."

"And you're a mother. I can hardly wait to see my nephew. Pa says he's a real pistol jack."

"I'll go get him right now and come back to Pa's for supper. If I keep you here any longer, Pa will never forgive me."

"Don't worry, I'll race up the lane to make up for lost time."

"Go slow. I wouldn't want you to break that neck of yours now." Penny laughed with pleasure at her adored brother. "Give me a boost up, will you?"

Penny rode back to Pleasant Glade with her heart singing. She would have Brett take her to New Berne. They had always told each other everything. If she had to, she could tell him the truth, but she would avoid that if possible.

It was a happy group that sat around the dining room table at Pineview that night. Delia had cooked a feast and joyfully brought it to the table. Brett had always been her favorite and she was determined to put some meat back on him. Brett had laughed when she told him he was too skinny.

From the same highchair that both Brett and Penny had used as children, Rye sat studying the stranger. "Unka Bwett, awe you my daddy?"

"No, my boy, I'm your old *uncle*. But I'll *pretend* I'm your daddy if you want me to." Brett tickled him in the side, sending Rye into gales of laughter.

"All wight, Unka Bwett." Rye beamed at his uncle, deciding this new man in the family was a good one.

"With Pa and you and Marcus, he's not going to suffer too much for lack of male attention." Penny laughed.

"That reminds me. Pa told me you're selling Belle Terre to Marcus. I think that's mighty decent of you, but something tells me that the farm is not all Marcus wants. How about that, Marcus? Is there anything else that's caught your eye?" Brett grinned at Penny and then winked at Marcus. He knew that Marcus had been in love with Penny from the beginning. Now that she was a widow, she was available again.

"Maybe?" Marcus did not want to upset Penny by revealing to the others that he had asked her to marry him, but he refused to out right deny it, either.

"Now that's a noncommittal answer if I ever heard one."

"Stop teasing and eat your dinner, Brett. Delia thinks you're as scrawny as scarecrow. Obviously Marse Robert didn't feed you boys too well." Penny sought to steer the conversation in a new direction.

"There wasn't much to feed us. He didn't eat any better than we did either. With the railroad problem, there might be too much food in one place and none in another. I saw food that was badly needed go to rot because there was no way to move it to where it was needed. It was a real shame when so many of ours boys were so hungry. The sheer inefficiency of the whole system was as big a reason for our defeat as any. We jumped into this thing too fast to build the structures and organization that we needed to pull it off."

They finished the meal with casual chatter, filling Brett in on what had occurred in the neighborhood in his absence. Leaning back in their chairs after finishing the apple pie Delia had knowing it was Brett's favorite, the talk turned back to the war.

"Son, with Lincoln dead, is there any talk about what the South can expect now?"

"Pa, I'm sorry to say, but this new bunch is not too kindly disposed to deal with us in a way we would like. I think they're going to do their damnedest to punish us any way they can. I think the war may have ended but our struggle is going to go on. At this point it's a waiting game to see what they end up doing here."

"I heard New Berne is going to be the district office for the military government they're putting into place. Have you heard anything to that effect, Brett?" Marcus asked.

"No, but that makes sense. Since they have been there for years now, it shouldn't be too difficult to shift priorities from occupation to administration."

Nancy looked at the men. "Y'all don't sound like this next period is going to be any more fun than the last few years."

"All these idle darkies roaming around the countryside are going to be a problem they're going to have to deal with mighty soon if we are to avoid some major trouble around here. When people get hungry, trouble doesn't follow too far behind. Some of mine have come back because they had no place to go and nothing to eat, but I can't take them all back because I can't afford to pay them and I don't have the food to feed them all with the resources we have now." John was worried as were his neighbors. Rumors of problems with the darkies had already cropped up.

"They've all been promised forty acres and a mule. The Yankees are going to play hell trying to deliver on that one." Brett snorted. "Especially since most of the mules and horses in the South got killed off in the war just like our boys."

"We for sure have barely enough left to plow the few acres we've been cultivating. No telling how long before you can buy more stock." Marcus shook his head with annoyance. With his new farm to till, the two sorry old nags that Fitz had left were not going to suffice.

"You men are going to have to discuss this without us. Nancy and I need to get Rye home and to bed." Penny stood to leave.

"I don't want you women out there alone at night. Marcus, would you mind taking them home?"

"I'd be pleased to, Mr. Bartlett."

"I'll ride in to town tomorrow to get John Wooten to do the paperwork for you."

"Thanks, Pa. Again Brett, welcome home." Penny hugged her brother and father goodnight.

"Wye want to kith Unka Bwett and Gwampa." Rye held up his arms to be taken from the chair.

"Okay, Master Rye. You give me a big old kiss and then Pa's going to collect his." Brett decided he could get to like being an uncle.

A week later, Brett, her father, and Marcus rode with Penny to Wooten's office to sign the papers making Marcus the official owner of Belle Terre. When they left the office, Penny asked if they would drive her by the druggist to buy some quinine. With summer coming she did not want to be without a supply for the needs of her family and her neighbors should yellow fever attack the community.

Whenshe climbed back into her father's buggy with empty hands, her brother asked, "Where's the quinine, Penny?"

"Oh, Brett, they don't have any in the whole town at the moment." Penny was genuinely worried, as it was the best medicine available to deal with miasmic summer fevers.

"Why don't I drive you to New Berne tomorrow and we'll see if we can get some there? If we leave really early we should be able to go and come back by the following day, especially with the roads good and dry. Since the Yankees have been able to get things in, it shouldn't be a problem to find some," Brett offered. "Besides, there's a mighty pretty gal there I met before the war and I want to see if she's still as pretty as she used to be."

"Thank you, that would be great." Penny silently thanked her lucky stars that the solution for a trip to New Berne had presented itself so neatly. On the ride home she debated what to wear. She wanted to be pretty, but all of her day dresses were faded and worn. Maybe Nancy could help her freshen one of them up, she decided.

The minute they left her at Pleasant Glade, she ran in the door, calling for Nancy.

"Dey be down at de pasture looking at de new ca'f. What gots you all work up?"

"I'm going to New Berne tomorrow and I want Nancy to help me freshen up one of my dresses."

"Uhuh. I been 'spectin' you be makin' a trip down der now de wah done. You gwine tell Mistah Ryan 'bout dis baby now you a widow womern?"

"I am, Mammy. It's time he knew. And it's time I figured out how to get on with my life."

"Time you tol' Mistah Marcus sumpn, too. He gwine be one hurt man iffn Mistah Ryan marry you."

"I know."

Penny left the muttering woman in the kitchen and called down to the pasture. Nancy came with Rye running behind. "Hello, Penny. I guess you finished all that paperwork and Marcus is the owner of Belle Terre."

"He is that and happy about it." Penny smiled at her son strutting along. A long flowering weed was draped over one ear and dirt smudged both cheeks. "Looks like Rye's been having a good time."

"That's for sure. He's getting to be one busy little boy." Nancy smiled fondly at the child she sometimes pretended was her own. She didn't know what she would do when it was time to return home. Leaving them all would just about kill her, she suspected, as she had grown to love them as much as she did her own family.

"Nancy, I need your help. You're a much better seamstress than I am. Do you think we could remake one of my old dresses so it doesn't look so dowdy? With no new clothes for quite a while now things are beginning to look pretty dated. The only nice dresses I have left are fancy ones, too fancy for daytime or else they're winter. I'd really like to look nice when I go to New Berne tomorrow."

"Of course, let's go see what we've got to work with." Nancy loved to sew and the prospect of designing a new dress for Penny delighted her. It also was a way she could show her gratitude for the joy that Penny and her family had brought into her life.

They sat in the floor with her dresses and those that she had saved of her mother's and Cora's piled around them. Picking up first one then another, Penny sat helpless as to which to choose and what to do.

"Nancy, what do you think about this pink one?"

"The color's all wrong for you. I like the pale blue or green and white striped one better, or even that yellow." Nancy studied the pile a moment longer. "I know. Let's see how this yellow one fits. I can take the gold trim from the blue one and some strips of fabric from the green and remake it so it looks like new. We can put a band of the striped fabric just above the hem and band the sleeves between the elbow and wrist. If we changed the buttons to green ones that will help tie it together. I can use the cording around the neckline and cuffs. I think the neckline would be nice square shaped and not so high necked."

"It can't be too low, either." Penny looked doubtful.

"Oh, no. Just enough to show off your emerald necklace." Nancy stood up. "Okay, let's fit the yellow one that belonged to your mother and then I'll get started."

"Don't you want me to help you?"

"You take care of the baby and do something about washing and curling your hair. I'll do this."

"Drat it. With so many hairpins gone now, I'll have to use corn shucks to curl it."

"I think they work better than pins anyway. They don't make the curls so tight."

Both women excitedly set about their tasks. Nancy was still sewing when night fell. Penny lit candles and sat, reading to her as she worked. With her hair screwed up in corn shucks, she had caused the amused child to break into gales of laugher. Now Rye cooed drowsily in his crib. Lulled by the sound of his mother's voice, he was soon sleeping. It was nearing eleven when Nancy finished sewing the dress. Going to the kitchen, the two women put irons on the stove and waited for them to heat so they could press the dress free of wrinkles.

"I think I want a glass of wine and some of those biscuits. What about you, Nancy? You could use a treat after all of this work."

"Wonderful. You get the wine and I'll start the pressing."
Penny returned from the cellar with a bottle of wine, opened it, and poured two glasses. Nancy was humming happily as she worked. Looking up, she said, "I'm pleased with your dress. It's going to be gorgeous on you."

"I love it. I don't know how to thank you. I could never in a million years have made anything half so pretty. You should go into business. With your talent you could make a fortune."

"Lord, Penny. You do get strange ideas. I wouldn't know how to even begin to run a business."

"I could help you. I helped run a bootlegging business."

"You didn't!" Nancy's eyes were round with shock as she held the iron in the air.

"Yeah, I did. I had to do something to make some money around here and it wasn't going to be cotton with no one to tend it." Penny was enjoying the woman's surprise. "That's how Marcus could afford to buy the farm. He was my partner."

"Good Lord! Do you still do it? Aren't you afraid you'll be caught?" she asked with genuine dismay.

"No more. We had to go out of business when Marcus's helpers decided the woods are haunted."

"I heard. The darkies say there's a dead man in the swamp dressed in rags that howls at night when the moon is full."

"The only thing howling at night in that swamp is some old polecat or some other four-legged critter." Penny laughed. The dead man did not haunt her dreams.

Chapter 25

As Ryan watched Caroline's eyebrow climb higher and higher, he knew he was in for a dressing down of some kind. They had just waved goodbye to Isabel and Martha, who were on their way to Baltimore. He had known from the moment he had picked the three women up in his newly purchased carriage that Caroline was in a major snit with him.

"So, Ryan, are you off to Sugar Hill or can you spare a few minutes for an old woman?"

Ryan would not have been more shocked if she had confessed to murdering the local bishop. "I beg your pardon?"

"And well you might, boy. I will not have you ruining your reputation with some sordid dalliance with a whore in Kinston. You've been seen whether you know it or not. It was all I could do to keep your mother and sister from knowing where you've been going on these little out of town jaunts of yours. After all, eastern North Carolina is not New York City. So, what have you got to say for yourself?"

Ryan groaned inwardly. "I fear I'm at a loss for words."

"Well, I'm not," Caroline snapped. "Furthermore, I had a visit from a very irate young lady who implied that you had made improper advances."

"Lizzy?"

"Ah, hah! So you admit it." Caroline was bristling with righteous indignation.

"I admit nothing. I have no clue what she told you. I only know I kissed her one time and got slapped for the effort. She seems to be laboring under the notion that I plan to marry her and is highly incensed that I'm taking so long to get around to it. I never did anything to alter her virginal status, I assure you."

"That still leaves these trips to Sugar Hill unaccounted for." Caroline raised the eyebrow so high, Ryan momentarily imagined it floating off of her forehead.

"Nor shall I."

"What did you just say?"

"Miss Caroline, I love you, I respect you, and I admire you, but I do not answer to you. You are old enough and wise enough to know that a man of my years finds it most difficult to live a celibate life. I have been as discreet as possible. Were that not the case, there are establishments here that a number of gentlemen of both your acquaintance and mine avail themselves. At least I went thirty some miles away."

"Humph. You know in this town as a damned Yankee, you've got to be better than good if you plan to make a life here." Caroline was quivering with rage. "It's about time you made an honest man of yourself with a decent woman."

"I couldn't agree with you more; however, at the moment I have no candidates."

Ryan was becoming agitated as well and cautioned himself to cool off. Breathing deeply, he continued in a lower register. "Miss Caroline, my heart was sorely wounded a number of years ago. I still love her. It's not so easy to find someone new but as a man, I do grow lonely. I cannot deflower a lady, for Christ's sake. Ergo, with great discretion and undue inconvenience to myself, I go to another town."

"Men! You're all dumber than dirt."

"On that, my dear, I'll agree."

Ryan delivered her back to her door and declined a rather offhanded invitation to dinner. He needed to escape any more complications for the day. Riding from her house the short distance to his own, he had a sudden urge to walk through the rooms that sat completed but empty, awaiting the day he moved in and made it his home. He tied Windfall to the hitching post and quietly walked through the rooms, imagining where he would put the furniture that he had sent Isabel to find for him. In the master bedroom he stood looking out over the river and the distant shore. The afternoon sun sparkled on dancing white caps. It was going to be a joy to wake up to the view each morning. He envisioned the bed on the wall opposite the windows and knew that he wanted to share it with a woman he could love the way he had Penny. Frustrated at himself for wishful thinking, he quietly locked the door and rode back to his rooms above his office.

He stopped first in his law library on the first floor to put away the books he had purchased on North Carolina law. He suspected the widow he bought them from had cheated him, but he didn't care. At least he had the books he would need to study in order to truly establish himself in the legal profession in New Berne. Picking up the last one, he sat by the window to read in the afternoon light. He had read only a few minutes when he heard footsteps in the hall and Lizzy calling his name. Resigned to a potential scene with her, he walked out to greet her before she could invade his space any further.

"Lizzy, what an unexpected pleasure."

"Ryan, I just had to come. I have thought about it and thought about it, and I think I was too hard on you. I want to apologize and ask if we can be friends again."

"As far as I'm concerned, we never stopped being friends, now don't you worry yourself about it anymore."

"You're sure you forgive little ole silly me?" She was so obviously flirting he felt sorry for her.

"You shouldn't be here where I live unchaperoned. Let me see you to the door." Not waiting for a response, he took her elbow and walked her to the sidewalk in front of his office.

The rattle of a buggy coming down the bricked street caused him to turn his head. With shock he realized it was Penny, looking as fresh as a daffodil in a pretty yellow dress. He looked at the man beside her and was puzzled, as it was not the man he had assumed to be her husband. Wanting to make her as jealous and as unhappy as he had been when he had seen her in Kinston, he suddenly pulled a surprised Lizzy to him and kissed her warmly on the cheek.

"I just knew you would forgive me. Thank you, Ryan. You've made me so relieved."

He noted that the buggy, which had been slowing to a stop, suddenly sped away with Penny's face averted. Wildly he wondered what he had just done. Was it possible that after all of this time, she was coming to see him? Did he even dare to hope that was the case? Cursing himself for his stupidity, he walked down the street in the direction her carriage had taken. He could find it nowhere along Pollock Street, so he turned at the water and walked back down Broad Street, looking down each cross street along the way. He did not see her buggy anywhere. Heaving a sigh, he walked to the nearest tavern and ordered a double whiskey. He drank until he knew he would be drunk unless he stopped and then he walked home and went to bed.

Penny had spent an uncomfortable night in the small hotel in New Berne and then cried most of the way back to Kinston. Upset that he did not know what was wrong, Brett finally demanded, "Sis, I've known you all of my life and we've never had secrets. I want to know what in the hell upset you so much when we passed that lawyer's office in New Berne. Pa told me the officer who posted guards around our farms was named Ryan Madison. That's the same name on the attorney's office. You know that man, unless I'm a lot dumber than I think I am."

"Yes. I did know him." Penny wiped her eyes and with relief told Brett of the secret she had kept hidden for so many months, that Ryan was her son's father. "You see, I really wanted to see him and let him know that I'm free now if he still loves me. I really do need the quinine but that wasn't the main reason for this trip. When I saw him holding that woman, I realized how stupid I've been. He's moved on with his life and I need to do the same. I'm going to tell Marcus I'll marry him. There's no point in chasing after foolish romantic dreams any longer."

"Lord, when you complicate things you surely do it right." Brett shook his head. "Sis, I damned well don't blame you, okay? Any fool could see you and Daniel were all wrong for each other. Our parents and Daniel's just didn't want to see it. You and Daniel were foolish to allow expectations to force you into a marriage, but it certainly isn't the first time something like that has happened. I want you to promise me not to say anything to Marcus for a few days. It's not fair to him to marry him if you don't love him. Both of you deserve better than that and there's no point in making the same mistake again that you made last time. Don't let your head control your life when your heart isn't in it. Just wait. You lose nothing by waiting a little longer."

Penny looked up dully. "Okay, I won't say anything, but I don't see how waiting will make any difference."

"Right now, I don't either. Just wait."

The remainder of the trip home, they rode without talking. Slowly a plan began to materialize in Brett's mind. When he drove her into her yard, he pulled to a stop at the back door and helped her down. "I'm going back to New Berne tomorrow to buy that quinine. I'll take Rye with me. It'll do him good to get out, you good to have some time to yourself, and me good to get to know my little nephew."

"Are you sure he won't be too much trouble?"

"I fought a whole damned Union army and survived unharmed. I do believe I can take on a two-year-old boy. Have him ready first thing in the morning, okay?"

"Fine. He'll be ready. And Brett, thanks for listening. I have held it in so long, it felt good to tell someone."

"Hey, what's a brother for? You may have to do the same for me someday."

As promised, he was at Penny's before six the next morning and a thoroughly excited Rye was hopping on both feet as he stood on the passageway between house and kitchen looking for him. By late afternoon, they were on Pollock Street. Brett stopped the buggy in front of Ryan's office and prayed the man was in. Taking a deep breath, Brett picked up Rye and walked to the stoop. "Okay, Mister, you be a really good little boy because you're about to meet your daddy."

"Daddy?" Rye wrinkled his nose in confusion.

"Yeah, your daddy. Now be good, okay?"

"Okay."

Brett rapped on the door with his free hand and without waiting turned the knob. It was unlocked, so he walked in. "Anybody here?" he called.

"Just a moment. I'll be right out."

Brett studied the man who walked from the inner office into the vestibule. He would have known him for Rye's father the minute he looked into those eyes, even if Penny had not told him.

"Good morning, sir. May I be of some assistance? My office is still in a bit of turmoil but you're welcome to come in. My name, as you no doubt surmised from the shingle, is Ryan Madison."

"Thank you. I'm Brett Bartlett."

Ryan startled visibly as he studied the man, noting his resemblance to Penny. "You're from near Kinston?"

"That I am. You know my sister, Penny, and I do mean that in the Biblical sense."

Ryan said nothing, just stood in open-mouthed confusion. Finally shaking his head, he gestured towards a chair. "Please, be seated."

"Thank you, I will."

"Well, Mr. Bartlett. How may I help you?"

"I think first thing you could do is take a long hard look at Penny's boy here."

Ryan looked into eyes as blue as his own and features that were identical to those in his baby portrait in the house in Baltimore. The truth dawned on him. "My God."

"Your son, if you'll excuse my correction."

Rye looked up at Ryan and gave him a sudden sunny smile that crinkled his eyes at the corners. "Daddy?"

"Yes, son. Daddy." Tears threatened to spill from his eyes as he studied the little boy.

Unexpectedly, Rye slid from his uncle's lap and walked up to Ryan, resting his hands on his knees. "Don't cwy, Daddy. Wye's being good," he announced with emphasis.

Gently Ryan reached down and gathered his son to him. "Why didn't she tell me?"

"You're not a stupid man. Could she announce that she had borne a child to another man when her husband was away at war? I don't know about the North, but we're a trifle more conventional here."

"Her husband?"

"Dead, over a year now." Brett looked in Ryan's eyes. "She still loves you. She was coming here day before yesterday to tell you when she saw you with that lady. She thinks you've moved on with your life and she's lost you. If that's not the case, you need to do something damned fast or you're going to lose her for good this time. That would be the dumbest thing either one of you could do."

"I've never stopped loving her, but are you sure she still wants me?"

"Christ, get your sorry butt off that chair and come with me. There's one way to find out, now isn't there?"

"Right. Let's go." Carrying his son, he followed Brett to the buggy. He could not believe the turn of events in his life. They made arrangements to meet the following morning to begin the journey back to Penny.

All the way to Kinston, he held the warm body of his son to him and listened as Brett talked of Penny and the changes the war had brought to their family and home. He dared to believe that the woman he loved was finally going to be his. When they turned into the lane to Penny's house, Brett stopped the buggy, "It's all up to you now, buddy. Take your son and go claim that woman if you love her.",

"Thanks, brother. I'm going to do just that."

Ryan and his son walked hand in hand to the door of Penny's house. "Mama!" Rye called. "Daddy came home."

"What, honey? I'll be there in a minute. I can't hear what you're saying from here." Penny walked from the study into the hall.

As in a dream she walked forward and stopped about three feet from Ryan, looking into his eyes.

Slowly Ryan smiled at her. "Our son brought me home. Would it be all right if I stay?"

"I think forever sounds like a good start." And with that she ran into the outstretched arms of the man she loved.

Bibliography

Books

Barrett, John G. *The Civil War in North Carolina*. Chapel Hill, NC: The University of North Carolina Press, 1963.

Barrett, John G., and Yearns, W. Buck, eds. *North Carolina Civil War Documentary*. Chapel Hill, NC: The University of North Carolina Press, 1980.

Campbell, R. Thomas. *Storm Over Carolina*. Nashville, Tennessee: Cumberland House Publishing, 2005.

Cooper, Edwin B.; Fuller, Dorothy B.; Mathis, Mildred M.; Landauer, Elizabeth A.; eds; and Lenoir County Historical Society. *The Heritage of Lenoir County*. Winston-Salem, NC: Hunter Publishing Co., 1981.

Edwards, Tom J., and Rowland, William H. *Through the Eyes of Soldiers: The Battle of Wyse Fork*. Kinston, NC: Lenoir County Historical Association, 2006.

Faust, Drew G. *Mothers of Invention*. New York, NY: Random House, Inc., 1996.

Massey, Mary E. *Ersatz in the Confederacy, Shortages and Substitutions on the Southern Home Front*. Columbia, SC: University of South Carolina Press, 1952.

Mussey, Barrows, and Needham, Walter. *A Book of Country Things*. Brattleboro, Vermont: The Stephen Green Press, 1965.

Thomas, Mai. *Grannies' Remedies*. New York, NY: Gramercy Publishing Co. Date not given.

Watkins, Sam R. *Co. Aytch*. New York, NY: Simon and Schuster, 1962.

Wiggington, Eliot. *The Foxfire Book*. Garden City, NY: Doubleday and Co., 1972.

Articles
Blizzard, Dr. Lonnie H. "First Battle of Kinston." Kinston, NC: Kinston Free Press, 2004.

Lave, Dr. Lathan. "Papers of Dr. Latham Have, Story of Yellow Fever Here." New Bern, NC: *Sun Journal*, March 13, 1962.

Rouse, F. L. "Woodington and Vicinity, Lenoir Co. NC—"Families and History." Kinston, NC, 1991.

Rouse, F. L. "The Rouses of Southern Lenoir County and Related Families." Kinston, NC. No date given.

Sloatman, Fred. "General Foster's Big Celebration—1863." New Bern, NC: *Journal of the New Bern Historical Society*, Vol. VI, No. 2, November 1993.

Thornton, Mary Lindsay. "A Southern Town Under Federal Occupation." Thesis, University of North Carolina, Chapel Hill, NC.

Online Articles
"Time Line of the Civil War." Accessed April 2009. *http://memory.loc.gov/ammem/cwphtml?tl1864.html*.

"Aspects of the Antebellum Christmas." Accessed April 2009.*http://www.connerprairie.org/HistoryOnline?xmas.html*.